REVIEWS

A page-turning thriller, as a father seeks vengeance for his son's death.
—Steve Wilson, West Point Graduate

A touching tale, with an underlying streak of violence.
—Dick and Char Burrill, avid fiction readers

DEADLY OPTICS

A DEL SANDERSON ADVENTURE

DON JASPERS

ACKNOWLEDGEMENTS

Coleen and Bryan, my version of perfect children and
My most special friend, wife, and lifetime companion, Patsy.
She keeps me together.

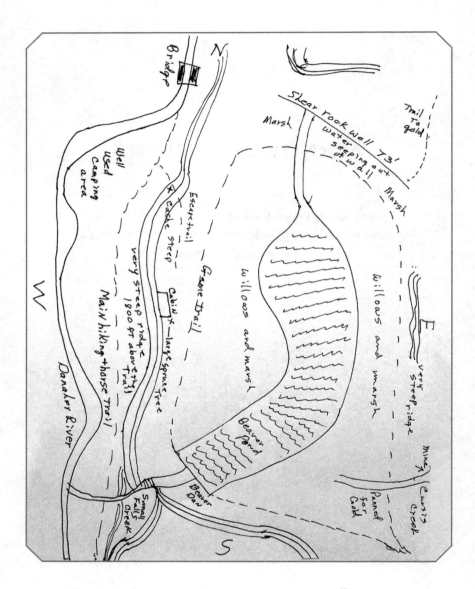

Del's Map
The Bob Marshall
Wilderness

CHAPTER 1

"If anyone had asked if I was going to be a competitive
long-range shooter, I would have said, 'No way.'
If anyone had asked if I would plan and execute events to
assist criminal justice, I would have said, 'No money.'
If anyone had told me I would have all the money I would
ever need, I would have said, 'Slim chance.'
Things change." —Del Sanderson

Sliding his quad to a stop, Rick jumped off and handed me the 650-yard target.

"Six for six, Del! That's very good. You're a natural. Two days of classes and one day of shooting, and you are hitting targets at a range of 650 yards, six of six. Easily, you are the best student I have seen come through my range." Rick lowered his binoculars, told the shooter next to me his scores, then turned to look at me and said, "Come with me."

We walked out of listening range, and he added, "Long-range shooting isn't easy. Some contestants at long-range shooting contests can't do what you just did. Six for six at 600 plus yards is more than good enough to get into a competition. You can try 800 yards tomorrow. You have two days left of classes and practice, and I'll have you shoot at 800 and 1000 yards. I'm excited to see how you do."

Rick Sherman's Shooting Range was near Manhattan, Montana, close enough to Great Falls, where I lived and worked. This allowed me a chance to practice at least once or twice each year. Rick's setup was very professional. Most of the shooting was done on the section of land he owned. A natural old erosion gully provided the safety needed, and it had been modified to provide targets up to 700 yards. He has written permission to set up portable shooting stations on bordering State land. A gravel county road marked his eastern boundary and provided the only access to the range office and parking lot. A small ranch-style building served as the office and retail space. Rick added a sixteen-by-sixteen-foot concrete vault and customer rifle storage facility. He said it was 'dynamite proof.'

His house and garage were located at the far western edge of the property in a similar gully hidden by huge cottonwood trees and a hedge of choke-cherry bushes. Well water and solar power provided the necessary comforts.

I worked the bolt action and ejected the empty shell casing, not allowing it to fall. If you know your rifle, you expect the shell to eject exactly the same each time. I have always tried to catch mine. It is nice to show off once in a while. I like catching it before it falls to the ground. Rick smiled but didn't say anything.

"That will be a fun challenge, Rick. I am hoping to become good enough to shoot a trophy elk and deer. Weather says some wind tomorrow." I tossed Rick the empty shell casing.

"Yes, and you will learn how to adjust for that." Putting the shell casing into the box and lowering his voice, Rick added, "Two questions, Del. Do you want your own gun? I could find you one. We shooters have a loose network and usually know if a certain type of gun is for sale. So, finding one would be easy. The other question, are you available in October to go to a competition is Las Vegas?"

"How many days?" I asked.

"Minimum of three, maximum of five."

I scraped my toe in the dirt, erasing some tread marks. "I would love that, but must check with my wife Amy, and my work schedule. We only have five days of family vacation days left this year. I promised Amy and my children we could do family visits."

"Okay," said Rick. "I'll send you the details as soon as the schedule comes out. The dates are October eleventh through the sixteenth."

"I cannot afford a gun of my own now, Rick. In addition to my regular job as a personal financial planner, I work one night a week at Home Depot and am still saving for some camera equipment I wish to buy. That will take about a year, so I cannot add the price of an expensive gun. How much are we looking at?"

"Anywhere from $1200 to $4000, depending upon the condition and the optics. I'll start looking and contact you if I find something worth pursuing."

"That works, Rick. Like I said, I hope to shoot a nice bull elk and a trophy deer. Being able to shoot long distance will make that easier. I will not have to walk so far and get extra tired before preparing for the shot. I will start planning how to purchase my own gun, after I have my camera equipment purchased."

Gathering our gear, we walked back to the range office. The small glass-topped counter had space for ammunition for rifle and pistol shooting but little else. Five black recliners circled a bear picture rug in front of a small fireplace. Often the shooters used those chairs to read shooting magazines and catalogs. Rick said he made more income from orders out of the catalogs than from shooting fees.

The vault door was never ajar, open, yes, but others could not see the inside contents. Rick put the guns away when shooters were done with their sessions and retrieved them when a shooter arrived, signed in, and asked for their gun. The range was generally closed Mondays and Tuesdays.

Rick used a small, all-glass, sparsely furnished office. He could see everyone arriving or leaving the range from his vantage point. I never saw anyone but Rick inside. Two Terry Redlin prints hung on a side wall. They showed sunrises over a small lake, and a cabin with the duck hunters up and getting ready.

Three shooters came in, and Rick stowed their rifles. They were going for pizza and invited us to join them.

"Sounds good," said Rick.

"I am in," I added. "I will give Rick a ride, and we will meet you at the Pizza Barn."

The three shooters left.

Rick put all the guns in the security vault, then said, "I added this room right after I bought this place. I wanted to advertise my extra value security and let the shooters have a place to safely store their guns."

Before leaving the range, Rick said. "Just a sec, Del, for your eyes and ears only. This range is my hobby. It doesn't make money. It's not important how and why, but I will never want for money. I can have the range and shoot whenever I want. Lucky for me, but I earned it."

He went into his vault, and about two minutes later, returned with a camouflaged sniper rifle with very sophisticated optics.

Handing it to me, he said, "One-thousand-yard shots are easy with this. I know you have questions, but I won't answer them. We have become friends, and I don't have many. But I won't answer any questions."

I studied him for a few seconds. I knew he had special skills. I also sensed he was better trained than he let us shooters notice. I was also positive he would not tell me how he received his money.

"I agree we have a lot in common and have become friends. I will not ask. We all have secrets. I hope to be here often and polish my new-found skill. I will be hunting this fall and will scope the distances to visualize the look of longer shots. Are you interested in hunting with me?"

"Not now, Del. Maybe after you retire."

"Only six years to go, then freedom to hunt as often and as hard as I wish. We can plan something."

"No promises, Del. Let's go eat some pizza."

Nine months later, Rick called me to say, "I bought your gun. A Browning .308 with Bushnell Elite tactical optics. It's here at the range, and you can shoot it the next time you come."

I wanted that rifle. If Rick said it was a good buy, I had to agree to buy the gun. I can visualize every long-distance shot I take. I can feel it in every way, and I am excited to see the results. I imagine those feelings will be more intense when hunting big game...a different kind of rush.

"I do not have the money yet, Rick. How much is it?"

"Not a problem. I know the seller. His eyesight is going bad, so he asked me if I could find a buyer. I made a deal on the spot. It's a very good gun with better-than-average optics. You pay when you can if you decide to buy it. I'll have no problems selling it if you don't buy."

He did not tell me the cost. But his offer to allow me to pay when I could piqued my interest. Small monthly payments—that I could afford.

I went to shoot two or three times a year to practice, and I started paying for the gun, but left it at the range. I did not want the gun affected by the extra handling and the jostling of the vehicle. Amy supports my new passion and will be happy for me. She will tell me to just pay for it, but I felt

I needed to earn the extra money. I did not go to the shooting competition in Vegas. But I went to practice at Rick's as often as I could.

Rick watched me prepare a shot the next time I visited his range. "That's your first shot out of the ten-inch circle in five years," Rick told me after I fired and before he retrieved the target, "That last shot may have missed the target completely. Del, you didn't follow the breathing process." He was right. The bullet nicked the target on the top left edge, over a foot from the center. My last time down to the range before I retired, Rick said with a big smile, "I have another gun for you. It's a Win-Mag Browning X-bolt Pro-Long 6.5 Creedmoor with Bushnell Elite tactical optics, like the other gun. Same deal as before. You pay when you can."

"Why would I ever need two guns?"

"Del, I intend to get you to do at least one competition shoot! If you say that is enough, I'll take the gun back."

"Okay, Rick, you win. Deal. I will be back to shoot after I retire in eleven months, and we will plan it. I only hope to use long-range to hunt, so I will not need two guns."

CHAPTER 2

The Bob Marshall Wilderness is a huge, wild, beautiful place. Located in West Central Montana, its backbone is the Continental Divide. Accessible from many trailheads, either on foot or horseback, it is a camper and hiker's dream. Some campsites are well-used, but most of the rugged wilderness is unexplored. There was evidence of long-ago searches for minerals. Locals call it just *the Bob*.

In the summer of 1979, my eleven-year-old son, Curt and I spent a week in the Bob. Most of that trip we walked along the Danaher River. We entered using the trailhead at Benchmark—a two-day hike each way. The fishing was great, and the exploring even better.

Early on the third day, after making it reasonably bear-proof, we left our camp and decided to hike up one of the nearby feeder streams. Soon, we came to a five-foot waterfall. We could see nice cutthroat trout in the pool below the falls.

"We will catch a couple for dinner on our way back," I said. "Let me help you up to the top of the waterfall, and you can tell me what you find."

After about twenty minutes, his head peeked over the ledge, "There is a meadow and a beaver pond up here. Let's go check it out."

"I will get some rope, the fishing gear, lunch, and we will do just that." Returning from our camp, I handed up the fishing gear and the lunch, made three stirrup steps in the rope, and tossed Curt the rope to secure. After climbing up and leaving the rope for our return, we set off to explore.

We followed the game trail along the west side of the meadow and the pond. It was an active beaver pond; we could see two swimming in the clear water. With a slap of his tail, one beaver warned the other about the intruders, and they were gone. The pond looked to be about three-quarters of an acre and mostly lined with willows. We found two places where we could fish from shore. It looked like a trail crossed the stream above the shallow end of the pond.

The meadow and pond created a beautiful setting. The forest, with its many shades of green and the blue shimmering water, lifted our spirits even higher. Pine forests have a unique smell all their own—nothing like those air fresheners hanging from a rearview mirror.

"We should move our camp up here, Dad."

"Good idea. We have found our secret place, Son. It would take many written pages to describe this." (see map)

The pond and the trail turned sharply to the north. Just a few steps later, we saw the small cabin. It was tucked under a huge Douglas fir and built tightly up against a sheer rock wall that rose forty or fifty feet above the roof. The cabin could be seen from the front, but not from the air. The ground was covered with pine cones and needles we could use as fuel for our fire.

The cabin appeared empty and abandoned, as if it had not been used in many years. Some essentials and remnants of the owner's clothes shared the space with a small barrel stove and a one-person bunk bed framed against the back wall. The entire structure enclosed about one hundred-fifty square feet and was about seven feet high. The roof slanted slightly down from the rock wall to the front eave over the door. Pack rats had made it their home. Evidence of two nest sites and a gathering of everything belonging to the past occupant littered the top of the bunk bed.

A carefully crafted structure, the cabin had stood the test of time and Mother Nature's wrath, yet it would not need much work to be livable.

"I will call my friend Dave and learn the rules that apply to wildernesses. He works for the US Forest Service."

"Our secret?" offered Curt.

"Sure is. We do not have to share with anyone. We will keep this hideaway to our-selves. No one has visited this spot in many years. We will make it ours."

We were not prepared to spend the night, so we returned to our camp. We caught three nice 'cuts' for dinner from the waterfall pond with their favorite bait, yellow salmon eggs. Our secret place monopolized conversation over trout and rice dinner.

After an early breakfast of toast and homemade chokecherry jelly, we made our Danaher River campsite look unused. We hurried back to our meadow. With all our gear, we eagerly hiked to our new camp. Carefully, we erased all evidence of leaving the main trail by walking past the creek and turning often toward the river. We hoped anyone coming by would think we were fishing. When we left the main trail, we each took three steps in the water, before continuing up Small Falls Creek. Curt named the small stream, as the map did not have a name for it.

Entering the cabin, we started a fire in the stove. It burned nicely until the fire was almost out, filling the cabin with smoke.

We pitched our tent outside and made a fire pit.

"Need a damper for the stove."

Curt chimed in, "Need a broom."

"Need a list," we said together and laughed.

"We should try another small fire in the stove and watch where the smoke goes." While starting the fire, I noticed the first match flickered wildly and went out. I tried a second match, and it too, flared up and died. I gave Curt a match. We moved to opposite sides of the cabin, and each struck our matches. Both flashed and snuffed out. I strolled outside and lit a match. It continued to burn nicely. Odd.

We pulled our plastic ground sheet from under the tent, and using three old nails and the old rusty ax, hung the sheet over the back wall. The next match burned steadily down to my fingertips, until I blew it out.

"Now what, Dad?"

"A complete inside and outside inspection of this cabin," pausing, I added, "It was built touching the rock wall. Why?" We looked at every board, every crack, inside and out, and after two hours, found that the bunk had a splash board that hid how the bed frame could slide back and forth to reveal a small cave. The well-constructed bunk fit tightly.

Now we knew why the cabin was against the rock wall. The builder wanted to make the cave both hidden and usable.

The cave extended to about twenty feet deep, ten feet wide, and nearly fifteen feet high at its back wall. There were many cracks in the ceiling less than a foot wide, yet one larger crack seemed to be blocked by many smaller rocks. The floor consisted of sand. We could feel the air currents that extinguished our matches. There must be a hole up on the mountainside that would be hard to find. We would save that exploring trip for another day.

"Whoever built this cabin wanted it to be his secret place. Now it's ours," Curt whispered.

We fished together and caught some brook trout for dinner. Side by side, we explored the meadow until dark. We carried some stones to make an almost dry path across the creek.

The next morning, while waiting for the coffee to boil, Curt asked, "Why don't you use can't, shouldn't or don't when you talk? Most people do, my teacher does."

"Good question, son. I took a speech class in college, and my professor told us to be precise in our use of our language. She deducted from our grades if we used contractions in our speeches. Also, I am a personal financial planner and feel it is important to be exact when I visit with clients. I guess that method of speaking has become a part of me. I can hear myself using the full words."

Curt turned back to watch over his cooking duties and continued to make the coffee, the pancakes, and the lunches. He boiled the canteen water, while I checked over the old tools to see if any were usable. I put a keen edge on the old ax. The maple handle looked like it was still okay.

Changing the subject, I said, "We need a good ax and a decent shovel, and thanks for breakfast."

"No problem. Add them to the list, Dad."

We crossed the creek at the head of the beaver pond, taking off our shoes and freezing our feet.

"We need a bridge, Dad. We can find some more stones after dinner, add them to the bunch from last night and fix our path, no more ice-cold feet."

After crossing, we started up the narrow trail. We had not gone far before we came to a small side stream seeping out of a brushed-choked break in the hillside. Curt crawled through the thick alders and soon yelled, "There's a mine up here, Dad. Come on!"

I struggled to get through; the brush blocking my path only lasted about twenty feet. As soon as I could stand, I saw the diggings. "Well, what do you know, a mine and a spring-fed creek. I bet this water is clean enough to drink without the purification tablets."

The cabin owner, whom we decided to call 'the prospector,' had worked both sides of a small alluvial fan. The slide blocked the creek when it first came down. But Mother Nature had all but erased the dam. The diggings were not deep and showed no quartz or pyrite-looking rocks, often indicators for the presence of gold. The prospector seemed to have given up on this site. We took turns using his old pan, sifting sand in the small creek, but we did not find any gold. With no experience in mining, maybe we just did not do it right.

Curt caught six brook trout for dinner, using small Mepps Spinners that usually worked.

"Mosquitoes are bad, Dad. We need more *Off*."

"Add it to the list," we chimed in together.

The next morning, we returned to the mine with some of the old tools. Curt could not carry a tune if he had a ten-ton truck to help. But he sang his favorite KISS song as we walked along.

We dug around some, panned places we thought were good spots, but were just guessing. We did not know what we were doing; just being together was enough. We climbed up to the small spring that fed the stream. We had a great day but did not find any gold. I knew Curt felt disappointed.

"I wonder what happened to the prospector."

"Lots of things, I suppose," I answered. "He could have just left, predator problems, illness, weather, accident—who knows?"

"He never left, Dad. This was his place. He is still here in some way. Maybe there is another mine somewhere close."

"Maybe. We could look next year when we come back."

"This is fun, Dad. Fishing in remote spots and pretending to be miners is really neat. I will remember this trip forever."

"Yes, Son, a lifetime memory. We can learn more about prospecting, geology, and minerals by finding some books to help. More fun."

"Dad, I think the person who built that cabin liked it here, and this was his dream."

"I think you are right, Son. He knew a little about rocks and panning or he would not have been digging by that fan. Also, the cabin was built to last."

"We have to leave tomorrow, right Dad?"

"Yes, we do. Otherwise, we would be late, and we do not want people worrying."

Before we left the next morning, Curt whittled a peg to secure the door. His initials were added to one side.

Driving home, we chatted about our special trip and place.

"Will we go back to our secret place?"

"I hope so, Son. There is so much to explore and some climbing to try. We should call our little valley Curtis Castle."

"I would like that, Dad. I felt at home there. Really special."

We were never able to return together due to a tragedy I still cannot talk about.

I knew I would return as often as life would allow. I would take his spirit with me. I know I will never totally recover, not having him physically with me, but he walks with me where ever I go.

CHAPTER 3

Seven years after Curt and I found the cabin in the Bob, I made a return trip. Solo hikes are not recommended, but I needed to go alone. I have always been very comfortable in the woods. The cabin was to be a personal place. Mine. Curt would want me to return and find some gold.

I wanted to leave some items in the cabin. These items would be stored in two aluminum lockable containers. Dutch, a good friend for over fifty years, owns a metal fabrication business in Great Falls. He created two canisters for me that could be attached to my backpack frame. The sleeping bag would be tied on top. My daughter, Molly, crafted the ten-inch-wide denim band. It circled the container with pockets for special items, like a compass, fire starters, and lunches. These canisters were critter-proof. When fully loaded, they weighed seventy-eight pounds each. With shorter distances and lots of rest stops, I felt I could pack both in on one trip. I tried new fishing places I always walked by during my other hikes. Fishing was a great way to rest.

After four days of hiking, instead of the usual two, I arrived at the waterfall with my heavy load. I pulled down the rope Curt and I left in place so many years ago. Somewhat anxiously, I tested it by jumping up and down with my foot in the bottom stirrup step. Luck was on my side. Safely at the top, the old rope became a spare as part of my supplies and replaced with a better-camouflaged one.

After hauling up the containers, I set off for the cabin, carrying both at once, it was not far, and I was excited. Curt's peg was still in its place. Removing it, I felt a deep sense of loss. Tears are okay. I remembered watching him carve that peg and the satisfaction written on his face when he closed the door and inserted it. After the gear was stowed in the cabin, I walked to a tree stump chair by the pond, sat down, and softly cried. I would be alone, but not lonely.

Most of day one was consumed with cleaning the cabin, so I could stay inside. My stay would be ten days to two weeks (if my rations held out). It was time to explore every nook and cranny of the entire meadow. Testing the panning knowledge I learned from a local miner's club was another item on my list. Then try to climb the ridge behind the cabin to see if there was a better way into the meadow from the main trail. Maybe I would not have to climb the falls. And for my son, I would try to find some gold. Curt always worked beside me. He could keep track of the things to add to our lists.

Sunday, I meandered to the origin of the stream that fed the pond. Water oozed from a mostly sheer rock wall, at least forty feet high. I could not see the top nor see a way up. Three small waterfalls of cool, pure water trickled from small cracks in the rocks. The gurgling sound made its own soft, soothing music. I risked drinking it without boiling, since it was at least as safe as the spring we found earlier, and much closer.

The wall looked climbable, but I would need the proper gear. I could hear Curt say, "Put it on the list, Dad."

I took a canvas bucket of water back to the cabin and set about gathering enough wood for a week or so. I ranged far and wide but left the meadow untouched.

My backpack containers were filled with items from 'our' list, including a damper for the stove and my rations, so no fire until the damper was repaired. A sandwich, a fruit bar, and cool water filled my needs for now.

The next morning, I installed the damper. An easier job than I expected. It fit perfectly. The smoke went where it was supposed to, and the fire heated the room nicely. Outside, I watched the smoke dissipate into the big fir that hid the cabin. The smoke would become too visible, so I studied how to run pipes into the cave and wrote the needed items on the list. Maybe that smoke would lead me to the outlet for the cracks from the cave, if Mother Nature made one of those cracks as an updraft.

I filled the solar shower bag first thing yesterday and hung it in the sun. The water was warm enough after finishing with the stove, so I took a 'solar shower'. Tomorrow I would explore the ridge behind the cabin.

The sun awakened me at five a.m. Wonderful, beautiful day. The sun had no company when it peeked over the continental divide. The blue sky surrounding it showed why Montana was called the 'Big Sky Country'. Watching the sunrise, I marveled at the color change, as the mountain shadows slowly disappeared. The sound of the birds and bees filled the meadow. Constant small breezes carried a scent that told me an elk or two must have crossed the valley last night.

There was no better environment to me than the mountains in summer.

While making breakfast, I serenaded some chickadees, and two gray jays, sometimes called camp robbers, with my rendition of "Oh What a Beautiful Morning" from Rogers and Hammerstein's musical, *Oklahoma*. Fried eggs, bacon, and pancakes with homemade chokecherry syrup is the best way to start any day. But at a camp, it is a king's feast. I had two more of these good meals in my provisions, the rest of the mornings of my stay would start with oatmeal.

With a pocket lunch, a canteen of water, and a day pack, I started up the game trail behind the cabin and along the meadow that appeared to climb and cross over the ridge. The trail steeply climbed more than I expected.

Small Falls Creek emptied into the Danaher River. The pond, then had to be parallel to the Danaher. The game trail stayed on the west side of the meadow but climbed quickly. Nearing noon, after numerous stops to look back at the meadow to keep my bearings, I reached the top. Curt would have loved this view. I missed my hiking partner. I started to softly cry. Then before I could control my emotions, I was sobbing.

A deep anger surfaced. The tears returned. I relived most of that fateful night when a Police Captain knocked on our door to tell Amy and me our son had been killed in front of the school gymnasium.

The policeman briefly described the circumstances. The junior varsity wrestling tournament ended around nine-thirty. Curt and his two closest friends, who wrestled with him, were waiting outside the gym for three girls from their class to go to the local pizza shop. They were still standing together in front of the gym when a speeding car skidded to a halt next to the curb. Three teens exited the vehicle and started a yelling match with another group of teenagers. The fracas soon escalated into a fist fight. Curt and his friends stood back and watched. One of the teens from the car produced a handgun and began shooting. A second and a third gun materialized. Witnesses said up to twenty shots were fired. When the police arrived and settled everything, four people were dead: Curt and his friend, Nick, and two of the combatants. One girl was also injured but recovered. The word was that those two boys bravely shielded the girls.

Telling our daughter, Molly, was heart wrenching. That was the longest night of our lives.

We were close friends with Nick's parents, Sandy and Jim, and grieved together for a time. During the long wait for the trial, we all became bitter as we gradually learned the whole story. We felt the system failed us. One young man was tried as an adult, the rest were processed under juvenile procedures. We never learned where the money came from to hire a law firm for the defense. No one admitted shooting. No bullets were found. It was believed by law enforcement that during the chaos, one of the teens ran away with two of the guns.

We sat through five days of the trial process. Our sons were dead. The young man tried as an adult received a twelve-year sentence. The four processed under juvenile rules served time at a juvenile detention facility. The rest were hardly punished. Throughout the process, none of us detected any remorse.

We were able to arrange a session with the presiding judge. Essentially, he said, "My hands were tied." Collectively we all said our own version of "bullshit," and stormed out.

Our families drifted apart. Life became too painful. Amy, Molly and I continued to go on. We talked a long time once and agreed to try outside help. Over time, life became a little better and we could laugh as we relived some special times. But it was a lifetime burden we carried.

The senseless killing of a child shreds the family's hearts and leaves them less whole. Coping, at best, is difficult.

I stared into space, looking at the valley scene below me. A pine squirrel interrupted my thoughts. I welcomed the intrusion. His scolding brought me back to the tranquility of the valley.

Beautiful. The beaver pond was visible to the right of my vantage point, but smaller than I had imagined. Below and west of me, the Danaher wound its way in the meadow, just as I had expected. I visualized a path from the trail along the Danaher River, but it would be a much longer hike and a steeper climb—an emergency option only.

I resolved to mark the trail on the way back to my truck and select a place for an emergency cache; a preparation I hoped I would never need. But I had an escape route, part of the big plan.

After an early trout dinner, I wormed my way across the beaver dam to see if there were any game trails on that side. Nothing promising, but I hoped to make that tomorrow's hike. The rest of my stay would be consumed trying to release the deepness of my anger. I knew when I embarked on this return to the Bob, being alone here in the wilderness would stir things up. I did not realize those feelings were still so strong.

I compiled my own list of persons involved in the shooting, while sitting through the trial, and it is now in the safe deposit box in Great Falls. I can still see all the faces. I was not liking some of the thoughts spinning around in my head.

I sat on the stump chair, and sang some Eddie Arnold songs to myself. Singing will calm me down.

I worked on my list of items I would need to bring on my next trip, adding a pack fly-rod. I made a rough map of the valley. (see map near the front of the book) I planned to research every solar option, so roughing it up here would not be so—roughing it. I sang a couple of John Denver favorites to no one but myself. No critics here.

I tried panning for gold every day, testing five other small creeks and the Danaher River. Either there is none to be found, or I did not have the skill to find it. I decided to do more research and talk to others that have more experience.

I was going to leave early, after only eight days. I made the cabin and my possessions winter ready, storing almost everything in the canisters in the cave. The cabin still appeared vacant. Only the stove pipe did not look old.

At sun up on day nine, with a very light pack and a fast, keep-the-feet-moving hike, I made it to the Meadow Creek trailhead in two days. During the entire hike, I worked overtime to release my brooding feelings. By the time I reached my truck, I was close to feeling okay. The drive to Evergreen, a small town near Hungry Horse Reservoir helped tone me down more. I changed clothes in the restroom at Charlie's, ate one of his famous hamburgers, then drove to Great Falls. I wanted to return to the Bob in a week or so. Plans change.

CHAPTER 4

My wife, Amy, began her first bout with breast cancer in 1982. A battle we fought together for more than twenty years. Life is rarely easy. Then after many years of remission, her doctors diagnosed pancreatic cancer. She was admitted to Benefis Hospital in Great Falls, Montana. Together, we decided she would try whatever options they offered, and do everything we could to make things as easy as possible, including selling our home and two rental properties to make life flexible, while pursuing every chance to improve her quality of life.

The first day in Amy's hospital room, we were greeted by Toni. "Good morning Mr. Sanderson, good morning, Amy. I am Nurse Toni O'Keeffe and monitor of the day shift on this wing. The young lady with me is Jenny Anderson. She will be your primary care nurse. If you need anything, just ask." She turned to Jenny, gave some instructions, and left.

Blue-eyed Nurse Jenny wore a blonde ponytail, and a perfect smile on her young face. She seemed a little afraid of Nurse O'Keeffe. Amy liked Jenny immediately, and so did I. Amy was like that. She made Jenny feel important when it was supposed to be the other way around. "I'm so glad to meet both of you," Jenny said as she started to fix the bed for a trip to somewhere for something. "You have two tests this morning, so we better get you ready." They left, and I wandered.

I found a newspaper in the lobby. Most newspapers are a wealth of information; some is even true. Too much is slanted to a particular bias, or negative in tone, or just plain crap! I read them regularly, buying when I must. I often visited libraries and read from their daily supply.

I read the local paper provided by the hospital as I waited alone in the lounge, while Amy received her treatment. Those days were long days.

Day thirty-two. I knew the hospital by heart. I did not like being here. I did not like the smell, and I did not like the intercom.

"Have you finished the crossword yet?" Amy asked, tucked in hospital blankets on her bed. Her pale face seemed somber and sad, as if she knew her time was near. "What will you do?" she asked. I sifted through many thoughts about being alone.

"I do not feel I can stay in Great Falls. Beyond that, I just do not know," I finally answered.

Before I could answer further, Nurse O'Keeffe entered and started her daily check-up, so she could make the entries in the bedside chart. Nurse Toni O'Keeffe was a petite woman. She wore minimum makeup. She looked all business, acted all business, and wasted little time.

Finishing her tasks, she said to Amy, "Jenny will be here in twenty minutes to take you to your treatment." Looking at me she said, "Good morning, Del," and walked out the door. "Good morning, Toni." I answered trying to smile. A poor effort, I was sure. "There are two crossword answers I do not know. So, I guess I will leave it with you, Amy, and go get some coffee."

"Good plan. Then I can finish it for you and solve the Sudoku." Amy attempted to be cheerful, even with this shadow hanging over her. It was hard to watch.

"I will be right back." I shuffled toward the door trying not to looked dejected.

As I walked down the hallway for what seemed like the millionth time, I reflected on how lucky I was to have shared my life with her for over forty years. She always let me read the papers first and do the crossword. She never asked to hunt or fish. "Those are your pursuits," she always said when I asked her to go along.

She did not have many days left, and I was already lost.

I passed by Patrolman Wyatt and said, "Good Morning."

"Back at you," was his only answer. "How's the wife today?"

"She is the same. Thanks for asking." We say the same thing every day. Today was his day ten of guard duty.

I never learned Wyatt's first name. When he introduced himself his first day, he said Patrolman Wyatt. He covered the eight a.m. to two p.m. guard duty shift in front of the intensive care room that housed one Jonny Stigman, a Native American Blackfoot Tribe member from Browning.

Wyatt only called him Stigman. Jonny shot two policemen, killing one during a drug bust gone wrong. According to the newspaper, the police hoped he would live so he could provide information about others in the drug business.

Wyatt did not say much, but I wondered if he was tempted to go into the room and pull the plug.

I did not think Jonny was worth saving; Amy was.

In today's paper, several letters to the editor suggested that it wasted taxpayer's money to keep him alive and then pay for a trial. I smiled to myself at those comments thinking, *I feel the same way.* Life is precious, but it is a serious crime when a life is taken.

I rode the elevator down with a young couple and their new baby. They were so happy, and their good mornings were radiant. The newborn baby helped bring back memories of my children and softened my dreary day.

Leaving the elevator, I turned toward the cafeteria following a short, petite nurse, Toni O Keefe.

"A sunny day, Nurse Ratched," I greeted her.

"And good morning to you Mr. Grump," she said sternly, but the twinkle in her eyes showed her true meaning.

"Join me today?" I asked.

"Thank you for asking. I would like that."

We talked about many things: the movie, *One Flew Over the Cuckoo's Nest*, and the source of 'Nurse Ratched'. She knew the others used the name, but also knew I liked and respected her. That was important to her. We did not talk about Amy.

We visited many times over the course of Amy's fifty-three-day stay and always tried to make each other's day better.

Knowing Amy would be having a tough time, I was slow returning to her room. I couldn't bear to see her suffer. I was surprised to see Patrolman Wyatt's station empty. I opened the door slightly and peeked into Stigman's room. Wyatt stood next to the bed with his hand on a drip line. I suspected he heard me come up behind him. I touched him softly on his shoulder. Trance-like he hardly moved. I do not know why, but I just stood next to him and watched his fingers squeeze the line. Soon, Johnny Stigman left us.

Patrolman Wyatt could have earned an Oscar for his cool performance. I was not sure how I felt, certainly, no remorse. I was surprised I did not care. I had witnessed a killing and felt zero sympathy, a remote strangeness.

Wyatt and I stared at each other, I nodded silently. We hurriedly walked out the door, Wyatt sat in his chair.

I entered Amy's room holding the door slightly ajar. Almost immediately, an orderly and a nurse came running down the corridor and into Stigman's room. Across the hall from my vantage point, I watched, through my barely open door, as I could see into Stigman's room. The hospital staff followed protocol to a tee.

Closing the door, I took my usual place next to Amy's bed. She slept quietly as I slumped in the chair, closed my eyes and processed some special memories. I heard her call my name.

"You haven't answered my question, sweetheart."

"Amy, I have a hundred thoughts to sort out. I will have a bunch of stuff to take care of. Then, will go see Molly and our handsome grandson Trevor. I will make it a camping and fishing trip. A realtor guy in Lincoln is looking for a place for me to rent and maybe find a cabin to buy. I am sure I will go to Arizona for the winter."

I paused from my ramblings. I sorted through my callous feelings about what Wyatt had done. I had changed. I realized, yes, I could, without guilt or remorse, kill a hardened criminal. Wyatt and I shared a secret that would die with us. I never saw Wyatt again.

"I have two different reservations at Lion's Head Campground located at the north end of Lower Priest Lake, in Northern Idaho: One is for July 12-16, and the other for July 18-24. Huckleberry season was coming soon. So, I will go to my favorite spot by Upper Priest Lake, when the Forest Service Rangers say the berries are at their peak to pick. I will camp three days, and pick each day. Lots of time to exercise the mind, and I can sort through what I need to do. I will spend the fall hunting near Lincoln and the winter in Arizona. I will keep my promise to you, Amy.

"I plan to visit our old friend Dutch before I go the Priest Lake. Lots of other things have been running through my mind. I think maybe update my pilot's license and see if I can fly Dutch's plane a time or two. Semtec Trucking would let me drive some long hauls for them, but that is only if I need to. I know Dutch has been by to see you, Amy.

"I may start writing a book. It would be neat to say I have a book published. I am just rambling, right?" I turned from looking out the window. "Molly will be arriving tomorrow. I already miss you."

"I'll miss you, but watch over you. I know my Del will be fine." Shifting herself, showing a small touch of pain, she added, "That will be wonderful to have our beautiful daughter, Molly, come back again. Trevor took a few days off from his college teaching job to come by. I know Molly has pulled every string, and that you have helped. Dave came by one day and said, 'I was in the area.' He is a poor liar. Did you know Cliff was here three times? Jack came twice and Dutch often."

"I only knew about Dutch."

"You have nice friends."

"Yes, Dave, Dutch, Cliff and Jack have been our good friends for as long as I can remember. I am lucky. I hope to bring our old friendships and closeness back. I know I will need each of them."

Amy reached out to hold my hand. "Promise me," she whispered. "Promise me you won't do things that make you lonely, sweetheart. Have a purpose for each day for the rest of your life...."

I sat with my head in my hands, then dried some tears. "That is an easy promise. I will live that way always thinking of you."

Her last day was two weeks later. I stood by her side holding her hand. We shed some tears and a last 'I love you.'

I pushed the call button and Nurse O Keefe soon opened the door "I will take care of things." I just hugged Nurse O Keefe and turned away.

Walking quietly down the corridor, I softly sang our favorite song to myself. I had no idea how hard leaving that hospital would be. My mind was full of stuff. Sorting that stuff was difficult. "I will live the rest of my life keeping that promise," I said aloud as I passed through the exit.

I drove to Bozeman, Montana and stayed in a kitchenette. It was the only room I could get, due to some kind of convention at the ski resort nearby. The house I arranged to rent in Bozeman will be ready tomorrow.

I sat at the kitchen table with a cup of coffee and enjoyed my own special omelet. I read the morning *Tribune* article that told those who cared: *Jonny Stigman, who had been involved in a shootout with local Police, succumbed to his injuries.*

CHAPTER 5

I decided to leave from Bozeman for a trip to Oregon to see Molly. I wanted to make sure she was all right. My whole life I have worried about others. I am a sentimental person. I am not ready to worry about myself. I will want things I cannot have. It is going to take some time to come to grips with my new life. I finished my drive to Corvallis, Oregon to visit my daughter at her job.

She has a happy life here. We talk often. Molly is a case worker for a non-profit organization that tries to help the homeless find their way. She is passionate and very capable. One of our favorite sayings is, 'Love what you do and do what you love.' I am proud and happy that she is so dedicated to helping others.

"Hello Dad! So great to see you. Come in."

The smile and the hug were worth the trip. "Are you open for dinner?"

"That would be great, Dad. I'll close up a couple of things, and we can go now."

"Okay. Pick a place."

She chose a place called Sellers. Not my kind of food, but the pasta salad and the fresh bread were quite good. No Rubens. We talked for three hours. She loves to talk about her job, and I enjoy listening. We shared tears as we talked about her mother, but avoided the really painful stuff. But I wanted to personally fill her in on my plans.

"Molly, I have a long bucket list, and most items involve traveling. I plan to see you as often as I can. We will need each other.

"I plan to see you and Trevor every chance I can arrange. Since Trevor started teaching at the Community College in Oregon, I do not see him very often.

"I will keep a safe deposit box in the West Central Branch of US Bank in Great Falls, Montana. But I will relocate to Bozeman. I do not wish to stay in Great Falls. I know I must start over. Please sign this signature card and take your key. I will explain.

"I am going to work hard to set up a new life, and especially do some flying. So, if you do not hear from me in any three-month period, ever, you are to drive, not fly, to Great Falls and open the box. Take Trevor with you. Everything you need is there, including where the money is, any property papers, my will, and where I may go if the world is closing in."

"*The world closing in?* What does that mean?" she asked, giving me her 'tell-me-now' frown.

I just held up my hand. She knew what that meant. "I have perfect health as far as I know. I am just going to travel a bunch. I never expect the world to close in. We should call each other more often. We cannot let time go by and not share everything. I will call you when I can, but some places like the Bob are not phone assessable."

"We will make sure to be close, Dad. I'll need those close feelings," nodded Molly.

"I intend to sign a year lease on a three-bedroom older house in Bozeman, and since I often fly out of Great Falls, I will keep the information at the U.S. Bank there current. You remember Dutch, I am sure. I will fly his plane whenever I can. You can ask him for help anytime."

I paused while she signed the card and took the key. "Can you get away for a day or two?"

"Yes, I can get Thursday and Friday off. I'll call my supervisor, Nadine, and make sure."

After getting Nadine's approval, Molly smiled. "Let's go to Newport and enjoy the beach."

I rented a very nice suite on the beach. Molly and I dug for clams, hiked the dunes, waded in the ocean and enjoyed fine dining. Wonderful time. Four days passed too quickly.

Back in Corvallis on Monday, we shared breakfast at the Whole House Cafe.

"Just nice and special you could come to see me. Dad, being in Great Falls and watching Mom die was awful. I want to visit about that one day, but am not up to it now. We should do a backpack trip sometime."

I looked at her a long time then said, "Bob Marshall Wilderness, next August around the fifth. We would be in the woods six to eight days. Let me know what day you can start your vacation. I will buy your airline ticket." Handing her three hundred dollars, I suggested she get a top-quality backpack and a good pair of hiking boots. "Break them in. I'll send you a list of stuff you need to bring."

Before she could ask questions, I said, "You mentioned something dear to my heart. You know backpacking is special to me. Be ready. All you will need to do is pick up the ticket. Deal?" I gave her the palms up, eyebrows-up look and grinned.

"Deal. Dad, let's go now. Everyone's workload is light, and so is mine. Action will pick up in the fall when the cool weather starts. I already have a very good pair of hiking boots. They are soft, light, and comfortable. Let me call about a ticket. What days should I ask for?"

"I will need to drive to Great Falls and arrange things and then drive to Kalispell. I need three days, so Monday is for you to land in Kalispell, and then fly back to Portland the following Wednesday. I will get my forest service friend, Dave, to give us a ride to the trail head. He lives in Evergreen."

Twenty minutes later, she had her tickets. While she was on the phone, I wrote a list of things she would need to have in her backpack.

"I wouldn't miss this for the world. Love you."

"Love you too, Molly."

Then I drove away, straight through to Great Falls. I picked up one parachute at a pawn shop and ordered a better one from Great Falls Tent and Awning. I went to the storage unit and picked up one of Dutch's canisters. I called Dutch to see if I could fly his plane. He did not ask if my pilot's license was current. He just said *yes*.

I packed the canister to overflowing, drove straight to the airport, loaded the canister, and placed it for an easy exit out of the passenger door. I hoped my drop system worked.

The flight into the Bob was exciting, something new to try. I pushed the canister out and the twenty-foot lanyard opened the chute nicely. On my circle back to watch and retrieve the rope lanyard, I saw the chute in the willows at the north edge of the pond. Perfect, our packs could be lighter.

Our backpack adventure started today. I was in Kalispell waiting for Molly's plane to arrive.

We greeted with a long hug. "Your flight, okay?"

"The Portland airport is easier than most," she answered as we walked to the baggage claim. "I am so excited. I haven't camped in years. There will be no mosquitoes, right? You promised."

"I am excited as well, Molly." *A special memory,* I thought. "I doubt the mosquitoes got the word, though."

We gathered her gear, loaded it in the truck and drove to Evergreen, Montana. It is near Glacier National Park. We were going to Curtis Castle. We talked about the cabin often after that long-ago discovery. I think she suspects where we were going, but has not asked.

Her new Sherpa backpack did not look full. She noticed me lifting it. "It has only the things you listed, Dad."

"I have a few other items for you. Your own emergency kit, a ground sheet, a top of the line sleeping bag, some energy bars you like, and a nine-millimeter Smith & Wesson pistol." Handing her the gun and two clips, I asked. "You remember how to use it, slide and shoot. If we need more than twenty-six shots each, we are in deep trouble. I have never had to be concerned in the wilderness, but my forest service friend, Dave, suggested I carry one. So, I do. Wolves, bears, and idiots, he says."

"We will stay in a cabin in Evergreen tonight. Dave will pick us up and give us a ride."

She looked at me and smiled, "O-dark thirty?"

"Yup."

An hour or so after sun-up, Dave dropped us at the Meadow Creek Trail Head. We walked in silence mostly.

"I have missed this quiet beauty, Dad." We stopped for a light lunch, resting on some rocks by a small stream. "I feel more alive when in the mountains. How many times have you been in the Bob?"

"Eleven or twelve, but save the questions for tomorrow night. How are the boots holding up?"

"Fine, I have used them a lot."

We made the Danaher River Camp late the next afternoon. Sitting by our fire, we ate our *Hobo Burgers.*

"It's been years since I ate the last one of these. What's in this one?"

"One beef patty, special sauce, cheese, lettuce, pickle, on a sourdough bun." Laughing I added, "We will have a new camp tomorrow, so do not unpack too much."

Up with the sunrise. Toast, huckleberry jelly and coffee for breakfast.

"Is this your own homemade huckleberry-jelly?" She asked as we packed up our gear, cleaned the camp, and made sure the fire was out.

"Yup." I answered after chewing my last mouthful.

We walked side by side to Small Falls Creek. We cleared all evidence, leaving the main trail. When I pulled down the rope ladder, Molly said, "Curtis Castle up ahead?"

"Almost. You remember the stories."

"Yup."

We negotiated the falls and took our time moseying along the path to the cabin. She took the latch peg out and saw the initials. Then, sighed and wiped a tear away.

"You have lots of stuff here. Does anyone know you are making the place livable?" Molly asked.

"No. No one. Not even Dave. I have to make some more air-drops. I will show you my containers and the 'chutes. We have one to find and recover. I have so much to show you." I gave her a can of 'OFF', "You will need this or the mosquitoes will drain you by nightfall."

In the cabin, I showed her how to move the bunk, enter the cave, how to use the solar power and the solar shower. I demonstrated how to operate the damper on the stove.

We hiked to the rock wall and filled our bucket with fresh water. Then, we found the canister. After hauling everything back to the cabin, we fixed the steaks, potatoes and carrots. It was a super meal, and we did not have to carry it. All of our meals were in the canister.

I knew Molly watched me as I sat on the stump chair with my head in my hands, but she left me with my thoughts. I'm sure she had her own thoughts about being here.

The next morning, I showed her the abandoned mine on Curtis Creek, and the trail with the alternate way out to the Danaher River. The emergency cache was as I had left it.

"Is this creek the same as small falls creek that empties into the Danaher River?" Molly asked, as we stood next to the alluvial fan.

"Curtis Creek runs a short way from the spring above us to the pond. Small falls creek begins where the water seeps out of the rock wall, then passes through the beaver pond, the falls and over the trail to the river. The person who built the cabin, must have found this hideaway just like Curt and I did.

I let her catch dinner.

While we ate our pan-fried brook trout dinner with a noodle side, I related the story of when Curtis and I found this place. Enough was said to Molly about why I intended to make the cabin into a hideaway from the world, but not the real details. I planned this wilderness setting to be my last refuge, if I should feel compromised. I do not know much about the criminal world, but I do know there are many efficient and effective police men and women. If someone finds out about me, they will have to come to me in my environment. I intend to create an escape route from the cabin, cross country, marked for night-time travel to the Bench-Mark Trail Head. That will be fun.

"You could find this place now, if you needed to. If I do not get to bring Trevor here, you will need to bring him sometime. My spirit will be here just like Curtis' is."

Gathering my thoughts, I turned to her, "Tomorrow we have a big hike. But first, I must tell you about the money. I am financially comfortable, but not rich. Your mother and I sold every piece of property, except one eight-unit apartment building. We wanted financial options during her cancer fight.

"I have created two corporations. Those corporations own the property I have title to now, and will own any others I may buy. The safe deposit box in Great Falls will have everything you need for the rest of your and Trevor's lives. You have a key. I have one, and there are two spares. When you visit me in Bozeman over Thanksgiving, I will show you where the others are. I have a storage unit in Evergreen now, but am working on a transfer to Lincoln. "You met Dave. He and I have been friends for a long time. He will help you, no questions asked. I am also working on an out-of-country residence. More research, and then maybe we will go there together."

"WOW!"

"Yes, wow. Enough for now, we should enjoy the beauty and each other."

Day three. We had fun hiking, fishing, and trying to make the most of our four days. We repaired the rock foot bridge crossing the pond's inlet stream, making it look as natural as possible. Doing everything together made our closeness feel extra close. Very special moments.

On the way to the airport, I showed Molly where the storage unit was, but we did not stop there. I asked her to think about all this, and when I visit her in a month or so, we will cover more details.

In the airport parking lot, I gave her ten thousand dollars in cash. "This is a part of your inheritance. Your Mother and I decided it was important to give you some now. You can use it any way you wish."

"Do I have to declare this money?" she asked.

"No, it qualifies as a gift. Just tell the truth. Your Mom recently passed away. Your Mom and Dad sold almost everything to have money to fight cancer. Your Dad wanted you to have some money now.

If anyone ever asks, it is just part of your inheritance. Deposit some in various places and use the 'eggs-in-one-basket' answer."

A long hug and she was off through security. Watching her walk away, I wondered about her thoughts. We have always talked about everything. I will wait until she decides she is ready to talk about her mom.

Back at Evergreen, I used the rest of the day getting things ready to move. After spending the night, I left for Bozeman at "0-dark thirty".

CHAPTER 6

I wanted to see Dutch before I went huckleberry picking. We flew together in the USAF. We have been the best of friends. He knows Cliff, Jack, and Dave. The five of us played basketball together, backpacked together, fished and hunted together, and shared family time. Life took us in different directions, but we always managed to spend a little quality time. Dutch lived in Great Falls, but after his wife left him and his son, we saw less and less of each other. He visited Amy many times during her hospital stay. I saw him in the corridor as he was leaving after one of his visits. He just said. "You take care of her, then come by." I was determined to bring our closeness back.

Dutch owned a Cessna 182. I needed to fly a check ride and renew my pilot's license. Since, I could not afford my own plane, maybe Dutch and I could make a deal where I pay my way and fly.

I stopped by Dutch's shop and opened the door. His smile was worth the trip.

"Del, you, old varmint, so happy you came by. They don't need me here—let's get a beer." During our ritualistic bear hug he added, "So damn sorry about Amy, she was one of the best." Changing the subject quickly, he smiled." You are still in shape, man. I like my beer. Got old and fat."

"Thanks Dutch. She loved you too. We should go to the Club Cigar." We sat in a booth reliving the past. Sipping on the third beer, I asked about the plane.

"Just had the hundred-hour done. She's ready to go. You can go any time you want."

"Only if I can pay my way. All gas I use, and the hundred-hour costs are mine and half the hangar rent."

"Too much, Del." He thought for a while. "Gas, the hundred-hour, but no hangar money. I use it for much more than just the airplane. I don't fly much anymore. Neither does my son, Eddie. He thinks I should sell it, so it will be great to have someone keep the cobwebs at bay."

"Deal. Is Sparky still flying so I can get current?"

"Sure. His hangar is the one on the north end of the row."

"I plan to fly as often as I can afford. I have the time, and there are lots of places I wish to go . . . South Dakota and Arizona are only two on top of a long list.

♣ ♣ ♣

The next morning, Sparky took me up, acted important, laughed a lot, and patted me on the shoulder. "You don't need me, so do what you like to do, and I'll sign you off. Fun to fly with you again."

I went back to see Dutch after the flight. On the way, I developed a better way to drop supplies to Curtis Castle. "Thanks to you, I found that old-time flying feeling again. Could you make me a few critter-proof, yet light enough to carry, containers? I need lots of external handles for straps to tie them down in the truck. I want to find a small cabin near Lincoln, and would like to leave some things locked up. They need to be smaller than the two backpack ones you made."

"How big?"

"I have a drawing for you. Sort of rough, but you can tell what they should look like."

"Piece of cake. Four enough?"

"How much for each?"

Dutch turned and yelled, "Kenny, come over here." Kenny walked slowly up to Dutch. "How much time and materials to make one of these?"

Kenny, a big smooth, florid-faced man about forty, studied the crude drawing, then handed it back to Dutch. "Forty to fifty depending on if we use bolts or weld on the handles. Fifty-five if we put all eight handles on."

"Thanks Kenny. Fifty each, Del. Kenny knew you get the friends-rate. He is way smarter than he acts. He can figure all that stuff in his head."

"Let's make six."

"Six it is. Takes about a week. When you come back to pick them up, we can go shoot some pool."

I drove to Great Falls Tent and Awning, and ordered four camouflaged parachutes, that would be almost-impossible to spot if they caught in a tree. Just big enough to handle the canisters when loaded. The clerk promised them in a week to ten days at ninety dollars each. They would be much better that the one I found at the Army surplus store. It tore badly on the first drop I completed before Molly and I hiked to Curtis Castle.

I am excited to try them out with a drop at Small Falls creek. Much easier way of getting everything I need to make my hide away in the Bob. And, I get to fly.

CHAPTER 7

After my visit with Dutch, I completed most of the necessary, but unpleasant tasks remaining after Amy left us, including a visit to the attorney, paying all the bills, and the laundry chore. Then packed my twelve-year old pickup and ten-year old camper, tied the canoe on top, and headed for Huckleberry season at Priest Lake.

As a young single man, I worked for the U.S. Forest Service on a fire crew. I always had lots of spare time waiting for a fire-assignment, so I hiked many mountain trails and logging roads. We were usually assigned to a work camp to earn our keep while we waited for fires. My favorite camp was near Upper Priest Lake. On one of my wanderings, I found a superior patch of huckleberries. The spot was remote and off the beaten path. I went there every year, and never noticed anyone else around.

I used the scenic route to Lions Head campground at the north end of lower Priest Lake. The Regional Forest Service Ranger Station said there were lots of berries and they were ready to be picked. I arrived at the campground near dinner time, found a spot close to the beach, and set up my camp. A meal consisting of pasta, fruit, and a wonderful New York steak, medium rare, followed by chocolate ice cream for desert was perfect. Sitting on a log near the beach, I thought about many beautiful memories Amy and I shared. Made me feel better, not much, but better. I planned to launch the canoe at sunup, paddle through the channel connecting the two lakes, and go to my favorite huckleberry spot.

The sun was aglow on the eastern horizon, changing the sky from starry night to big sky blue, when I paddled into the connecting stream between the two lakes. The channel was not long, but had a decent current. By six a.m. I hid my canoe on the eastern shore in a clump of willows. Singing a John Denver favorite, I climbed the hillside and crossed the well-used hiking trail that paralleled the lake. I have never hiked the trail, but knew it crossed into Canada. My special huckleberry patch was loaded with berries. I was within sight of the hiking trail, but about sixty or seventy feet above it. Lots of brush allowed me to pick in the shade most of the time. I could smell the unique odor of gooseberry bushes. A knowing soul could smell them before they became visible.

I picked berries for about three hours, took my treasures down to the canoe, and put the berries in the small cooler on ice. I quickly hiked back to my spot hoping to reach my goal of two gallons. Time for a break in the shade under a manzanita bush. I took a sip from my water bottle, removed the wrapper from my snack bar, and sat quietly enjoying the serenity; I heard voices. I had not expected to have company. Picking on this hillside has always been a solitary event.

Two young men carrying large backpacks topped with sleeping bags appeared on the trail coming from the north. I heard them argue over whether to hurry to the rendezvous or set up camp and finish the remaining three hours in the morning.

I heard the lead hiker say, "This is my last trip, Zach, and I want to be done! Pepe Jiminez gets out of prison next month. Vinny got this job when Pepe went to jail, and Pepe will want it back. That's war Zach, that's war! I have shown you all the markers and camping spots. You can lead these trips yourself. So, let's finish the hike today."

"Yeah Bo, but that means at least two hours after dark, and I prefer to be in a camp when its dark. We could get hurt carrying this load in the dark. We have been on the trail four days, so let's just make the logging road and set up camp and rest. Only three hours left tomorrow."

"You're a wimp, Zach! Just a wimp. Take a break and have some water and a snack, and we will decide after we get down to the road. We do have the steep narrow trail along the cliff to go down now. Let's get at least that part over with."

As I watched using my binoculars from my vantage point hidden in a manzanita bush, they took off their packs, drank some water, and ate a couple of handfuls of trail mix. They had their break without saying a word to each other.

Bo was a lean man about 170 pounds, black curly hair, long arms, and a slight stoop in his posture. His face reflected a smiler or a brooder. He could be both. He had a narrow face with dark eyes and full eye brows.

Stronger than he looks, I thought. He stood up, easily shouldered his pack and said, "Let's get going".

Zach was a fullback type. Maybe five foot ten, 225 pounds, he was a block of muscle. A ruddy complexion showed signs of acne trouble on his round face. His scruffy whiskers would make a poor beard.

He wildly jerked up and swung his pack over his shoulder, lost his balance, slipped off the trail and slid a rough and tumble twenty feet down the mountain. He screamed, "Bo, I hurt my leg really bad, I can't get up!"

Bo returned and yelled, "Get up here, you stupid shit. Get up here."

Zach cried and whimpered, "I can't get up. I don't think I can walk."

Bo put his pack on the trail and carefully skidded down to Zach, picked up his pack and hauled it up to the trail. He stood there and swore a blue streak. "Get your ass up here, we gotta go. We gotta go."

"I can't man, my leg is broke, I think. Hurts bad." He made a real honest attempt to get up. "You gotta help me."

"Don't be a pussy. Don't be a pussy," Bo yelled, as he climbed down to help Zach. It took them thirty minutes to get Zach back up to the trail.

I know I could have helped, but my intuition told me not to. I stayed hidden in my manzanita bush, watching. I have often helped people I did not know, just because it was the right thing to do. This time my instinct told me to stay hidden. Those two could be armed and violent. So, I just watched. They did not know I was there.

Pacing back and forth Bo finally decided what to do. "We'll stash the packs behind this big log. I'll help you down the cliff to the road, and come back to get the packs.

Then we will make camp at the road and fix you up as best as we can. We'll plan what to do. Maybe in the morning you could guard the money, while I go find some help. I don't like leaving those packs out of my sight for a second, but it's better to leave them up here now, than down on the road, while I get you down safe."

Bo put both big pack bags behind a huge Douglas fir log in a cluster of alders just off the trail, then helped Zach. It was slow going as Zach dragged his leg, wailing the whole way. Zach whined," We deliver all that cocaine to Sophie in Creston, and then haul all this money back. Vinny doesn't take any of the risk, so he's gotta help us."

"Boss don't see it that way. He can get others to do this. He don't need us. He don't need us." They soon disappeared, starting down the steep section of the trail.

I could tell it would be a long, tough descent for the boys.

They packed drug money back to a major dealer. There must be a lot of money in those packs, and I doubted *they were carrying one-dollar bills.*

Wow! I thought. *Do I dare?* A million thoughts whistled through my head. All of the bad and all of the good. I started to sweat as my pulse quickened.

Bo and Zach were out of sight, but making a lot of noise. I put my huckleberries in a zip-lock bag, and hid the picking bucket under the bush, knowing I would retrieve it next summer during picking season.

Hurrying to the trail, I snagged both packs, one on my back and carrying the other in front of me. I reached the canoe in record time. I unstrapped the sleeping bags and left them under the willows. Then, I loaded the packs and my berries in the canoe and paddled away as fast as I could. Making little noise, I reached the connecting stream in twenty minutes, never looking back.

Arriving at the campground, I put the packs in the camper, tied the canoe on top, and drove away. I did not stop until I entered the campground at Farragut State Park on Pend Oreille Lake about fifteen miles north of Coeur d' Alene. This state park is roughly a safe sixty miles from the Priest Lake campground. I washed and bagged my treasured huckleberries, making room in the small freezer. I ate slowly thinking about my impulsive behavior. "Dumb and Dangerous. What have I done?" I mumbled aloud to no one.

I cannot go back and say I am sorry. I knew I might have cost Bo and Zach their lives.

I opened the packs by cutting a slit in the bottom. Without counting the money, and there was a lot of it, I transferred it into two canvass duffel bags. I removed my canoe from the top of the camper and attached the little two-wheel cart, which was stored in a compartment of my camper. I would load the hikers' packs in the morning and haul them easily in the canoe to the lake shore. I filled the torn money packs with a few rocks from the fire pit, and carefully sealed the openings with duct tape. After a restless night, sunup found me paddling across the lake to the opposite side from the campground and boat launch. Being alone at the launch eased some tension. My reflection followed me as I crossed the perfectly calm lake. The south shore does not have dwellings or campgrounds.

Pretending to be fishing, I slipped both packs into Lake Pend Oreille. It was around six hundred feet deep at that location. I watched them sink out of sight, trying to feel relieved.

I had not seen any booby traps in the money packs, but would look more thoroughly to make sure when I counted the contents. I sang to myself and smiled. But my neck became sore from looking at everything around me twice, at least.

The sunshine glistening over the water promised a beautiful day. There were three or four mountain goats about a hundred feet above the lake. Their white coats gave their presence away. I paddled back, my head raced with what-ifs. A good breakfast will calm me down.

I headed to a fishing spot I knew near Lincoln, Montana. It was reasonably remote, and a safe place to count my 'newly found drug money'. I was working hard to not feel guilty.

Bo and Zach were in big trouble and they were afraid of Vinny. My guess, Bo would look out for himself and abandon Zach. They said they had three more hours of hiking left, but now that would take at least twice as long. And, Bo had to go for help because Zach could not keep up. I believed they would camp and wait until morning.

From Farragut Park to Lincoln, I imagined every car to be Vinny and friends coming after me. I knew it was stupid, but felt scared the whole five hours. I was much better after making camp by the small beaver pond a mile or so off Montana Highway 200.

The next morning, I decided to count the money after fishing the Blackfoot River awhile, and eating breakfast. I caught and released two nice Browns to grow bigger. Fishing was a peaceful exercise. I returned to my camper by seven thirty, took my time brewing another pot of coffee. I revisited what I had done, then told myself I could live with it.

I was 99.99% sure I was home safe, but I had not slept a wink.

"Was I a criminal now?" I mused aloud. "It was drug money." I hoped Bo and Zach would find a way out of their predicament, but they chose to be mules. They knew the risks. There was no going back for me. I needed a plan. First, count the money.

I made a sandwich, poured a cup of coffee, and started counting. Three hours later, the coffee and sandwich were gone, and I was in possession of just under three million dollars, all in one-hundred-dollar bills. I did not find any hints of traps, just a coded note, which undoubtedly told Vinny how much money the boys carried.

I know Montana well, so I decided to make Bozeman my new home city. I had arranged a lease option on a house after Amy and I had sold almost everything to fight the cancer battle. Time to put my plan in motion. I called the landlord asked to have the house ready and when I expected to arrive. I knew I could not live in Great Falls anymore. I would get a library card in Bozeman.

Along with the money left over from my own property sales, I was in possession of over three and a half million dollars.

Whew, was all I could say. My heart raced, and not from the coffee. I was scared, excited, happy, and nervous, all at the same time. I realized that if I had decided to take the second huckleberry reservation after visiting Dutch, I would not have this money. I also believed if the drug guys knew about me, I would have already met them.

I drove to Bozeman and checked into a motel. I slept like a baby with my two duffel bags. I did not dwell on the fate of Bo and Zach. It is time to move to Bozeman, I called the landlord. He said my house would be ready tomorrow. Wonderful.

Most of being alone is downright crap. The financial windfall changes things. I can actually afford to implement my plan. I promised to make a difference. The criminal world has a new player.

CHAPTER 8

Bo and Zach took almost an hour to navigate the steep trail to the road. Zach collapsed. Bo turned around immediately and climbed back up the treacherous trail to get the packs of money.

Looking behind the log where he'd left them, he gasped, "Oh shit, shit, shit. They're gone!" Bo panicked and ran to every log he could see, hoping he had remembered wrong. They were gone, and he didn't see any other person. Expanding his search, he reached the shore of the lake. He found the sleeping bags confirming his worst nightmare. Some rotten bastard stole the packs! He hadn't heard a boat. There were no boats on the lake. Swearing and running to every big log he could find, he was near exhaustion with panic. Bo's head filled with scary thoughts. He knew Vinny would be royally pissed and blame him. He lost the money. Zach wouldn't be held responsible.

He climbed back to the trail with the sleeping bags, sat on the log. He was terrified first, then hated the thief. He was nearly insane with fear. The money was gone, and Zach would be no help. He didn't need Zach, and his partner wasn't anyone to risk his life for!

He decided to run as soon as the sun came up.

Reaching the bottom of the steep trail where he had left Zach he yelled, "Guess what? The packs are gone! The packs are gone! Only the sleeping bags were left by the damn bastard who stole them. We're dead, dead, dead!" Frantic, he paced and swore, staying away from Zach, who was strong and could be radically violent.

Zach started to ask Bo if he took them, but changed his mind because he needed Bo to help him.

"What do we do? Vinny is going to go nuts. And stop saying everything twice. It just pisses me off!"

"I told you this was my last trip. I have money stashed I can get to. I'll help you get to the pick-up point, then I'll hike to the campground and see about some wheels and come back and get you. Zach, we are in deep trouble! Vinny will kill us, no question about it. Worm fodder. That's what we are. Worm fodder, worm fodder, worm fodder, worm fodder! I'll say what I want. I'm nervous, and I don't give a shit if you like it or not. See, I just don't give a shit."

"I'll go find something and make you a crutch," he said walking away and trying to calm down.

Bo Returned with a piece of Douglas Fir that was long enough and strong enough to work. He used his Buck knife to shape the crutch and some rope from his fanny pack to tie one of Zach's tee shirts to the arm rest, and they started off.

Still keeping a safe distance, he turned to Zach, "We'll go as far as we can now." Zach had a tough time and sat on the first stump he came to. "I can't keep up man, my leg hurts bad."

Bo stopped and turned around. "You are a damn wuss. You are a big damn shithead wuss. I'll go get help. You know your way to the pick-up point. Keep trying to get your ass down there." Turning his back on Zach, he started walking down the old logging road. When out of sight, he picked up his pace. He thought he heard Zach yell, "Don't you leave me, Bo!"

He just hurried faster all the way at the north end of Priest Lake and the State Park campground. He had walked most of the night. Zach had both sleeping bags, so Bo was sure he would stop and wait. Bo was tired. He sat on a log by an empty camping spot. He noticed a set of narrow wheel tracks showing a trail through the sandy soil. He owned a kayak so he was positive this set of tracks fit a canoe carrier. He smiled. He suspected this camper contained his money.

By early morning, Bo sat next to a trail head sign hoping for a ride. It was over twenty miles to anywhere, and he did not want to be walking when Vinny rolled up the road.

He looked like a hiker, so when an elderly couple in a small motor home stopped, he explained he often hiked the trails here and bummed rides. He told them his car was by the school in Priest River. They gave him a ride, a sandwich, and a diet Coke.

He got out near the school and offered to pay them.

"No chance. We were coming this way, and you were no trouble." Wishing him good luck, they drove away. He caught a ride to Sandpoint with a teenager in a rattletrap red Ford pickup.

"Where's your ride man?" the kid asked.

"My girlfriend took it. She is pissed at me. Probably in Sandpoint by now."

"That's where I'm going. Be nice to have someone to talk to, 'cuz my radio is busted and the truck would quit runnin' if I started to sing."

Arriving in Sandpoint, Bo gave the kid a twenty, and ten minutes later, he found a white Dodge truck in the Staghorn bar parking lot with the keys dangling in it. Without hesitation, he climbed into the cab and drove away—all the way to Alamogordo, New Mexico. He stopped only for gas, food, and one short nap at a rest stop. Using the interstates and following all the rules, he was sure he had made his getaway.

He was down to thirteen hundred dollars of his traveling money. He went to a local bank and opened an account and started the wire process to get all his 'stash'. He knew he could get his money quickly, but needed to be extra careful not to alarm his bosses. They had people in lots of banks. Bo was sure his four money stashes were safe, but he took no chances.

During his idle time while waiting for his money, he visited the White Sands National Monument. A beautifully unique place with drifting Gypsum, making dunes high enough to ride snow boards down.

He washed the truck and had the entire interior detailed, wiped it down with a disinfectant, then parked it in a McDonald's parking lot. He visited the library and typed a 'clean' note to leave in the truck, so the police would know how to get it back to it's owner. He left the keys in the glove box, and would call the police from a pay phone on his way out of town.

Three days later, he converted his money into four cashier's-checks of forty thousand each; three cashier's-checks of nine thousand each; and nine thousand in cash. He went shopping for a car good enough to get him to Fort Lauderdale. First, he went to a bank he had not been to and cashed one of the checks. He bought a white 2008 Honda Civic for ninety-three hundred dollars.

Bo knew that crooks got caught because they stupidly went to places where they were known, or had friends and relatives. "Vinny would try everything he could to find me," Bo said to himself. "I'll go to Fort Lauderdale, sell the car, find a no-brains job, and be a bum for a while. I've never been to Florida."

Arriving safely in Fort Lauderdale, he decided to keep the car. He rented a clean apartment in a used-to-be old motel and found a job in a Taco stand on the beach. Next, he bought a nice bicycle and started over.

He visited the library daily, making sure to leave the impression he was just a nice guy. He read two articles in the *Spokesman Review,* a Spokane, Washington daily paper. One article covered the details about a body being found by a hiker at Priest Lake, and the other unidentified body in a house in Spokane. He knew the unidentified body found by Priest Lake was Zach, but the cops didn't.

He said in a whisper to himself. *I'm through with crime. I'll change how I look, get a haircut, stop slouching, learn to speak Southern, and find a girl Yeah, a new man."*

CHAPTER 9

Z ach tried valiantly, but did not have the mental or physical strength to overcome his injury. His leg was so swollen it would not bend. He was over a mile from the pick-up point when he quit, sat on a rock and just cried. Then he labored to untie and unzip the two sleeping bags. Finally, he placed one on the ground on a bed of pine needles near a large stump just off the logging road. He shivered as he covered himself with the second sleeping bag. The night was long for him with little real sleep. Every noise scared him and caused him to frantically look everywhere for real or imagined dangers. His fear consumed him.

Near dawn he heard familiar voices. Vinny and his body guard were coming and would soon see him. He thought he should try to hide, but it was no use. In plain sight, they found him instantly.

It didn't take Vinny long to realize he didn't see any money packs and only Zach. He walked up to Zach and yelled, "Where have you *been* and where is *my money?!*"

Zach started to cry. Vinny slapped him. "Answer me, you stupid shit!"

Whining in a high-pitched tone and showing how scared he was, Zach answered," I broke my leg, and Bo went to get help." Tears streamed down his face. He tried to get up but the pain made him lay back on the ground. "He said he would get wheels and come back to get me. I couldn't walk."

"You think he's coming back? You are a dumb shit," Vinny screamed. "Where's the damn money?"

Zach told the story of how he broke his leg and how they stashed the money, "Bo helped me down the steep part of the trail, and went back for the money. He said someone stole it."

"Bullshit," Vinny yelled, shaking Zach. "Bo stole the money, and he ain't coming back. You're dead."

"He walked down the road. I saw him. He didn't have the money, and he was scared, real scared."

Vinny turned to his bodyguard and nodded. Little Zap was a tank. Five foot eight and two-hundred-fifty pounds, he was a powerfully built, no-neck dark skinned man. He walked with that, feet-wide-apart gait, and the I-am-damn-tough swagger. Zach felt Jesus "Little Zap" Zappata wrench his face around, and sputtered as dust from the trail filled his nostrils. He heard the pop, then everything went black.

"We going to look for the money boss?" Little Zap asked.

Vinny was a short, strong, fat man. His reputation painted him as a guy who would fight and not stop, until he or his enemy could not continue. He had a mean, swarthy face, crooked nose, fleshy jowls, and two thin scars on his chin.

"No, we are going to look for Bo. We better find the son of a bitch, or we are as dead as the kid over there. Bo has more than eight hour's head start, so he could be anywhere. He would have to steal a vehicle, so we'll listen to the scanner, and go back to our rental house in Spokane." He scuffed the ground violently two or three times and strode briskly to the car.

"Sure thing, Boss," Little Zap got in the car and drove to Spokane. Neither said a word for many miles. Vinny continued to sweat.

"Zap," he said, "we will secure the Spokane house, take the money stash, and drive to Marana, Arizona. We'll go get our money there and leave the country." He was sweating and slobbering, and swaying in the back seat. "We tell no one, no one, you hear?" he shook Zap's shoulder and wiped spittle off his chin.

Zap knew about Vinny when he was like this. He would watch his back. He was sure he could win any fight with Vinny, but he knew not to trust him.

"Okay, Boss."

They arrived at the house, a two-bedroom bungalow on Spokane's South Hill. It looked like a vacant dump. The only valuable furnishings were the fifty-two-inch TV, and two new recliners. Vinny sent Zap to fill up the car, go to the credit union, and take the money out of the safety deposit box.

Zap took everything out of the box, then told the clerk he wouldn't need it any longer. Back in the car, he made a call. He worked for the real boss, but his only loyalty was to himself.

He told the story to the real boss, and where they would park in Marana, north of Tucson, when they arrived in Arizona. He returned to the house and parked in the garage.

Zap walked into the house and Vinny shot him in the right knee—the pain was fierce, and he fell. Vinny also shot him in the left knee and in both shoulders. The suppressor muffled most of the sound.

"You rat bastard," a slobbering Vinny whispered. "I took you out of the slums and gave you everything. I have a listener in the car. You sold me out. Is Rocco with you, too? Is he a rat bastard, too?" Vinny was wild. He kicked Zap in both knees.

Zap just lay on the floor, not saying a word. He knew he was dead, but he knew, so was Vinny. He was almost numb from the intensity of the pain.

Vinny loaded the car with only the minimum he would need. He had only been in three rooms, so he cleaned every surface. He loaded the sheets and everything he could think of into a plastic bag and put them in the car. He closed all the windows and blinds and turned on the TV. Walking past Zap, he kicked a knee and a shoulder.

Zap could move his left hand just enough to get his hide-out gun, so when Vinny took some things to the car, he hid the gun under his hip.

After dropping his bag of personal items, Vinny came back to grab the last load. He looked down at this turncoat with disgust and cocked his leg back to kick him again. Suddenly, he saw Zap aim a gun at him. He dodged as Zap unloaded the revolver's six-round magazine. One of the bullets grazed Vinny's shoulder. Anger flashed inside like wildfire. He shot Zap in the head. "Done. You traitor bastard."

Vinny searched the dead man's pockets, took his money, ID, and gun, then left. He drove straight through to Marana, only stopping for gas and food. Vinny liked to eat, anywhere anytime. In Marana, he made four stops, got his money, and drove the nine miles to Motel Six in Oro Valley, fifteen minutes northeast of Tucson.

He slept a couple of hours, but worry was his only friend. He decided to leave for Odessa, Texas. He had a brother there and could make his way out of the country.

He went out to his car, opened the door and fell like a sack of potatoes to the pavement. He never heard a thing.

🌲🌲🌲

A black van quickly arrived and parked next to Vinny's car. Two men exited the van, and threw Vinny into his own car. They each drove a car away into the darkness.

From deep in the shadows, a limousine slowly crept forward in the gravel. The man in the back settled deep into the luxurious leather seat. "Vinny took too many chances and was skimming more than his share. Call Rocco," he said to his driver. The phone rang on speaker.

"Rocco," a bored deep voice answered.

"You take over Vinny's business."

For a moment, there was silence. "Okay." It was a well-known fact; everyone in the organization was expendable. "What about Pepe?"

"Not your business. You tell Zap's brother." The boss hung up before Rocco could answer.

CHAPTER 10

Denny's was across the street from my motel, so a good choice for breakfast. I parked my three-million-dollar truck right in front, visible from my window booth.

The waitress found me the local paper and a copy of the local self-sell weekly.

Starting with the *Bozeman Chronicle,* I scanned both papers for trucks and a good boat.

I paid for my meal with one of Vinny's hundred-dollar bills and smiled. Then I remembered it was dirty money from drug addicts trapped in a life of misery. I wasn't going to have a second of remorse, ridding the world of a few of these drug dealers.

The house I had a lease option on looked nice enough. The owner could be at the house in ten minutes, so I walked both sides of the street on my block while waiting. Two curtains moved, one next door and one directly across the street. Guess the neighbors like to keep track of things. A ten-minute tour of the house and yard was enough for me. The house also had a twenty-by- twenty covered rear patio, and was on a one-traffic-light route to the interstate. A one-year lease with open options completed the deal. John Vesty, my new landlord, gave me the keys and the garage door opener, adding a card for a yard service. "They do all my rentals. I'll be back with all the papers at two o'clock, if that works for you?"

"Perfect. I will go find some of the things I need and be here at two."

I furnished the place mostly from thrift stores. All the selections were real wood items that I could refurbish to look new. The bed, TV, and recliner, were new.

John met me at two. We signed the paperwork and amended the lease to include year-round yard service. So, in one day my new place was livable.

I wanted a new boat, with at least a one hundred twenty horse outboard motor, and a zip on and off cover. I must have a new truck to pull it in style. I have lots of free time and lots of money to spend, Vinny's money. Fun times.

I found the truck first. A young single man lost his job and could not make the payments on a plain white, year-old Ram 1500 Classic Big Horn crew cab. The bank let me assume the note, which surprised me, and I gave the kid fifteen hundred dollars. He was happy, so was I. Three weeks until the new title arrived.

On day two in Bozeman, I looked at a dozen boats. Most were abused. Only one had all the items I wanted, but it was way over-priced. Helena, Montana's capital city, may be a better market for used boats, as there were a couple of big lakes nearby. I did an internet search and found exactly what I wanted. Cash spoke loudly. Counting one-hundred-dollar bills was a great feeling.

The Ram included a heavy-duty towing package, so the trip to Helena to get my seventeen-foot Lund will be a joyride. I arrived back on Friday and pulled into my new house's driveway with a new beautiful toy.

All of these trips and acquired items were opportunities to launder the stolen cash. I safely cleaned up $550,000 so far. I will be able to do a better job faster, once I get a legal alternate identity or two. I hope my old friend Cliff will help. Cliff is a supervisor with the FBI.

I talked a good cover story. "Getting myself set up for hunting and fishing trips," was the conversation with neighbors and the licensing offices. I took a joyride on Ennis Lake, a small mountain lake south of Bozeman. I showed off the boat, and it was a success. Many people noticed and stopped to look. I parked the truck and boat at the library and later at Home Depot, chatting and answering questions, mostly to feel I belonged.

I traded my old pickup camper for a barely used one with a lowering and roller system that allowed the camper to be stored in my garage. After I launder another hundred thousand dollars, I plan to buy a storage garage that will hold all the toys. There are some new ones that are not rentals, but set up to own, on the way to Manhattan fifteen miles west of Bozeman. I had paid my deposit and was on their list. It was a perfect location, not far from Jack's big rig repair business.

Mostly, I am set up for my 'adventures'. Every time I thought about them, I felt a pulsating excitement. It was not an obsession yet, I told myself, but I could feel an excitement.

Libraries are important to me; I have cards for Bozeman, Helena, and Great Falls. Using them will be my primary search venue for my 'adventures'. At a library, I can search the world and not leave a telling signature. If the authorities start to figure out things about me, I will quit and start over. I know it is not completely true regarding online papers, but there are many businesses that provide free internet for customers. I have learned it is possible to establish coded identities, which allow searches.

I watch enough news on television to become alerted to stories about bad guys. I will add two or three libraries in Arizona, when I go there to spend the winter months. Searching the Nation's newspapers for criminals and bad guys will make it easier to identify potential 'adventures'. It is critical to my safety for all my inquiries to be untraceable. Another question for Cliff, if he will help me; I will have to think of a way to ask him how the FBI traces those inquiries.

CHAPTER 11

My new residence is taking shape, so decided to go drop in on my old friend, Jack Letcher. He knew I was in the market for a used eighteen-wheeler that could be modified to haul a car. He did not know I now could afford to actually buy one.

Five years before I retired, I acquired a Commercial Driver's License (CDL). Because of the constant medical bills, I always needed money, and the CDL opened doors to a much better-paying part-time job than a one-night-a-week shift at Home Depot. I ended up keeping that job as well. I could still buy my camera equipment and not affect the budget. I hoped I could find an occasional driving job. I imagined that a big rig would become an essential part of my restructured life. I spent two weeks of my vacation and $3,100 of my hard-earned money to obtain a Commercial Driver's License.

Twelve licensee prospects were in the small classroom on day one at "Over the Road Driving School" in Spokane, Washington.

"Delbert Sanderson."

"Here."

After roll ended, the instructor continued, "Today, we cover the class-room requirements, the driving process, the testing process, and introduce you to the hands-on driving instructors. We will include everything needed to be successful here. I am George Templeton. I am responsible for the class-room portion and the practice CDL test portion. If anyone is not making the grade, they will meet privately with the instructors. Let's go through your materials.

Eleven days into the process, I felt good about my chances. Nearing the end of class, George stopped at my table, and while pretending to write on my tablet, he dropped a small note on my lap.

Please come to the office before you leave.

It surprised me. I thought I was doing at least as well as anyone. He made no comments, and neither did I.

When I knocked on the door, I heard, "Come in Del and have a seat,"

He stood to greet me and, smiling said, "Thanks for coming."

I sat on a small folding chair and projected a lame 'I do not want to smile' face.

"I'll get right to the point. Your application indicated you were interested in part-time driving, only in the Western U.S."

"Yes, I love being a financial planner and have a lot of flexibility in my schedule. I pull a once-a- week night shift at Home Depot and will keep that, as it is my source of fun money. I have no intention of applying for a full-time driving position."

"You know you are doing well. More than okay. You have great test scores, and the feedback from the driving instructors is you drive quite well. You should only need the minimum time to complete the course and earn your CDL.

"Semtec Trucking, based in Missoula, Montana, likes to use drivers with your kind of availability. They are in the market for two new drivers. I took the liberty of calling my friend, J.J. Berdelle, and he would like to talk to you. Interested?"

"Yes, I am."

"J.J. said he could meet with you before class for breakfast at the Denny's just up the road from the school any day you chose next week."

"Any day except Tuesday."

"Wednesday it is—at six a.m."

"I know where Denny's is. Thanks."

"You'll like J.J., and you're welcome. I like to see people reach their goals."

I met with J.J. the owner of Semtec Trucking and agreed to start as soon as I received my license. Lucky me.

I cannot wait to tell Amy. I hope she will ride along on some trips.

Tonight's entry in the travel book (I started the day class began), would be an extra special one.

Amy rode along on a few shorter trips, but did not want to ride endlessly on the longer ones. She rode with me on the first long one to New Mexico, because we were to stop in Taos. We both had a visit to Taos on our bucket list. We vowed to return after I was retired. Some things are not meant to be. She declined all other long hauls.

CHAPTER 12

Never in my wildest dreams did I think I would have a 'rig' of my own. On some of my hauls, I would imagine owning a rig to travel the whole of the USA. Not a motor home, but a custom job that would haul a car and Amy and me. A pipe-dream. I entertained fun thoughts about the design while the wheels were turning. Driving an eighteen-wheeler, gave me an 'I own the road' feeling.

There were lots of reasons for choosing to live in Bozeman. Top of the list, it was the home town of one of my four best friends, Jack Letcher. He and his twin sons, Jacob and Jason, operate a five-bay big rig repair and maintenance facility just off I-90 in Manhattan. It borders a giant Love's truck stop.

Since I moved to Bozeman, Jack had been helping me look for a complete rig that I could modify, allowing me to drive a compact car into the rear half and set up the rest as a hideaway. The back panel will look like any other, but be hydraulic and act as a ramp for entry. This truck may be another way to make myself hard to find if ever the world closed in on me.

I was on my way to see Jack. He said he found one.

He finished some routine maintenance for a longtime client, then called the man to tell him it was ready. The client asked if he could just leave it there, while he looked for a buyer. Jack agreed and called me.

"I found you a good one, Del. I know it is in great shape. I have kept it up since it was new. The owner said after forty years, the miles have caught up with him. He has enough money, so he is quitting. We can meet at Perkins tomorrow, then drive out and look the rig over. You get to buy."

"Great idea. Do you know how much he wants?" I hoped cash would do my talking. I have $150,000 in hundred-dollar bills in a safe deposit box, waiting for a good deal.

"He will be here tomorrow and you two can work it out."

The next morning, we both drove to his shop to meet the truck owner.

"Jack, tell me it is not the all lilac one," I laughed.

"Yup, that *is* the one. His wife picked it out a while back. It's four years old and in top condition."

The owner and I agreed on the price, and he walked away with the cash. I had the keys, the title, and the bill of sale.

Yes, it took three weeks for the new title to arrive.

I briefly explained to Jack the modifications I hoped to do.

Jack estimated it would take three or four weeks to complete the changes I wanted. They will exchange the rear doors to look like double doors with locks' but design it to be a single solid ramp to allow my Honda Civic, and a top-quality quad for hunting to drive in and park. The hydraulics for the ramp will be remote-controlled.

The forward half will be secure from the car compartment, but accessible. It will contain all items necessary to stay for up to a week, with sleeping quarters and a solar-powered refrigerator. I would include motion sensors, cameras, a state-of-the art security system, a police scanner, a television, solar power, computers, a remote monitoring system, and a super music system.

My college music professor believed, "Variety in music is the spice of life." I subscribe to that theory and have over 6000 songs that I never get tired of listening to, available on tape and CD's. Maybe I will ask Jason to help me update to a playlist.

Each security camera will look like an outside light and be set from 90 to 360 degrees and feed to its own twelve-inch square monitor.

It is actually quite easy to hide a big truck unless you are pursued. Then, it would be too late anyway. Busy truck stops, big box stores, and off the main road motels, all have parking. Big truck stops have so many rigs that look alike, it would require close scrutiny to find a certain one. I intend to paint my new toy a darker color.

Most truck stops have easy access to main highways. During my travels, I will identify many of the best locations to hide and log them by exit location or city. A big rig can stand out if parked in the wrong place, yet stay hidden for a long time when parked among other big rigs.

The sleeping quarters will have a narrow, concealed place under the bed to hide the guns. Enough space for one long-range rifle, one standard hunting rifle, and two pistols. Ammunition for all will be located in a tray under the pistols. I will make that part myself. Jack and his boys will do all the electronics and structure. When they are finished, I will complete all the cabinets.

♣ ♣ ♣

Picked up coffee to go from the Long Road Cafe, then I continued to Specialty Custom Trucks Inc. off Exit 284 in Manhattan. I wanted to see Jack.

"Morning, Jack," as I shook his hand. "How's my project coming?"

Jack Letcher, a barrel of muscle at five-eight, is as strong as any man I know. He has been a special and loyal friend for over fifty years. He sports an unruly mop of white hair. His blue eyes always hint at mischief.

Jack and his two sons can repair or modify parts on any big rig. Their location and reputation ensure they have all the work they want.

"Morning yourself, Del. Let's go look." A smiling Jack answered, knowing he showed me only half of his grip. We walked to the fifth bay where my Lilac Peter-Built was being modified. Holding the remote and pushing the top button, he lowered the back door ramp. "The ramp is done, and it works perfectly." With the ramp down, we entered the trailer and passed through a small door into the forward half.

"We have the structure ready, but Jason still has a lot of wiring to do before we can finish. I know you want to personalize the finish work, so we are hoping to have all the rest done in a week or so. Jacob will finish welding tomorrow and install the remote locking and starting systems."

Jack and I each climbed a ladder and watched Jacob preparing the top for the retractable remote-operated satellite dish and solar panels. "It's almost ready for Jason to install the equipment, Del."

Jason and Jacob are twins and bigger versions of their dad—same shape, same steely grip, same eyes, but with thick curly brown hair. Manhattan won two football championships when those two were juniors and seniors.

Jack and his sons have never asked about my motives for making the modifications. I have joked a little about going where I wished and being self-sufficient. Jack and the twins were hunters. We have hunted together, and they were aware of my quest to shoot a trophy mule deer and five-by five whitetail deer in as many states as I can. I have left them with the impression that when using this rig, I will hunt from comfort better than most hunting camps.

Jason looked up from his wiring to say, "I added two more storage batteries, Del. The specs for ten didn't have the forty-eight-hour storage that you asked for."

"Whatever you think, Jacob, you know best. I hope to be camping remotely often enough to need that extra storage. Cannot always count on enough sun."

Using libraries at many different sites, I researched electronics of every kind from every source. There are a lot to choose from, and so many levels of effectiveness. I selected the choices, picking some expensive gizmos, and gave the list to Jason. He added some things he knew about. I gave him cash, and he bought them online or at stores.

Spy gadgets were very sophisticated these days and becoming more effective all the time. He would set me up with remote monitoring, inside and out. Such a system would need a source of power, a device to turn things on, and a method of data transmission.

I know one person can cover only so much. I wanted to eliminate criminals who have dodged the law, even though everyone in the law enforcement world knew beyond a doubt that person had committed the crime. I intended to shoot from at least five hundred yards, as long as I can create an effective escape route. This would only work if I became a ghost, appearing and disappearing at will—untraceable.

If I landed on police radar at any level, local to federal, things could unravel quickly. If any of my alternate ID's become compromised, I would have to retire it. Del Sanderson did not ever want to be a fugitive from justice. I must perfect my escape routes from each safe house and test them. I believed Cliff would give me a chance to make myself scarce.

"This project is coming along great. It is way better than I hoped. Will it be okay for me to bring my tools and materials, and do my finish work here at your shop? I do not need to be in the bay, just park at the end of your lot?"

"Perfect." answered Jack. "Then you can buy lunch from time to time. We all like to eat. Just remember not to build anything under the retractable satellites."

"That works. Having it here will be better than parking on the street in front of my house."

It took me parts of seven days to do my woodwork and other finishing touches. I constructed most of the cabinets and cut all the other pieces at my garage. Only the assembly was completed at Jack's. I created a removable, storable four bunk arrangement in the car half of the trailer. No one saw my gun storage place. When I gave them the tour, the guns were in their place.

"Jack, we should get Del to remodel our office. He does nice work." A smiling Jason said. "What kind of wood is this finished with?"

"Maple framing and Mahogany veneer panels for the finishing stage. I will try to get a storage bay for the whole rig. Then make a trip to South Dakota for pheasant hunting. Thanks for fixing everything for me."

I left the rig at Jack's and checked on the storage options. I needed to call Molly and find a way to tell her about the money.

CHAPTER 13

"**M**orning Molly," I said when she answered my phone call.
"Morning, Dad, what's up?"
"I am hoping you can meet me in Boise this Saturday. There is something I need to visit with you about. It is very important to me."

"I can, Dad, but you have my worry feelings stirred up."

"Zero to worry about. I just feel it is important to visit with you face to face. I will have a room in the downtown Best Western in Boise. You can spend the night, and I know a great Italian restaurant. Come prepared to walk some Saturday after you arrive. Is there any chance Trevor could come with you? I do not see him enough these days."

"Okay, I'll leave early and should get there about three or three-thirty. I'll see if he can ride along."

"Drive safely, Molly, I'll see you Saturday."

I drove to Boise on Friday and checked into the double master suite I had reserved. I was enjoying spending Vinny's money. Through room service, I ordered a shrimp and scallop dinner, with a small carafe of chardonnay. I rarely drink wine, but I wished to make a toast to Amy. Eating alone was a mistake. I felt lonely. I should have gone somewhere and been around people. Loneliness overtook me, I was not prepared. I need to start coping better with losing Amy.

Breakfast was better down on the first floor in the coffee shop. Lots of people. People watching pushes loneliness aside.

The downtown street fair and farmer's market was in full swing—lots of tempting sweet things. After covering the fair from one end to the other, I stopped at a bookstore and sat in the corner, reading a book on how to become a published author. It seemed interesting enough that I chose to purchase it. Maybe I will start a book. Stirred my interest anyway.

I was sitting in the hotel lobby when Molly arrived.

"Hi, Dad. Trevor had A bunch of tests to grade, he couldn't afford the time to travel."

"Hi to you too, Molly." I looked into her smiling tapered face and noticed she wore her long brown hair straight today. She enjoys the natural look. We shared a special hug and walked together to the suite. I towed her small suitcase.

"Wow! This is some room." She danced from room to room, like she used to do as a little girl when we traveled. I chuckled. "What's the occasion?"

Ignoring her question, I said. "When you are ready, let's go for a walk downtown."

Twenty minutes later, we were on the street. I took her to a small bistro off the busy thoroughfare. I selected the same dark roast coffee I had tried earlier that morning, and Molly chose a spiced tea. We took our hot beverages to a two-person table by the front window. The fair was winding down, and the night crowd was at least two hours away. We had the place to ourselves.

"Okay, Dad, I don't want to wait any longer. Why the trip, why the fancy room and why the walk first?

I had my cheap bug detector in my pocket. While Molly chose her tea, I checked it. Clean, I knew it would be. But since stealing the money, my nerves were on edge. I was getting better, but was always looking over my shoulder. *Clean everywhere.* I thought to myself.

I told Molly about the money, leaving out details that could put her in danger.

Molly gasped, sat back in her chair, took a sip of tea, and for a moment, stared at me. "Heck of a story, Dad. Are you in any danger?" She asked, in a soft whisper.

"I am one hundred percent sure no one knows anything except you and me. No one saw me do anything. Just an old man in a canoe. I bought a cheap bug detector and have never had a hit. I will live in Bozeman for a while, take some art classes at the U of Montana, fly Dutch's plane, and hunt and fish. I found a nice boat and a super used truck. I also upgraded the camper. Maybe the Lincoln realtor I called will find me a cabin. Then I will be set."

"Dad, I have to wrap my head around all that. Three million. Wow! What are you going to do with the money?"

"Not much yet. I need to finish getting most of it laundered. Buying the Lincoln cabin is a priority. I have two corporations to help with properties and investments. I am going to travel a lot. I want to do some deep-sea fishing. There is a drug rehab facility near the U of M campus I will donate to. I am going to find a way to put some of this drug money into getting young people free of their addictions. Mostly, I will travel the west trying to be successful at hunting trophy big game."

"I am happy for you, Dad. You deserve softness in your life. Do you think the two young men made it safely out of the woods?"

"My guess is the injured man is dead, and his partner left him and is hiding somewhere, trying to stay away from his bosses. My intuition says he is okay. I worried for a while that I put those men in grave danger. What I have done is wrong, but I cannot go back. I justify it when I remember those drug dealers are out of business. That should be good. I plan to do positive things with the money. I feel very little remorse. The drug world is a violent place."

We talked of other things after the hostess seated us in the Italian restaurant. I enjoyed the Lasagna again, and Molly the meatless spaghetti. "One thing, Molly. I am never going to tell anyone else about the money, ever. You can tell Trevor if you choose after I am dead. I still hope the three of us can take the trip into the Bob next August.

We checked out late and walked to our vehicles together and shared a very long hug.

"Love you, Molly."

"Love you, Dad." We never said goodbye. It sounded wrong.

CHAPTER 14

Bringing the closeness back with four of my old friends was a priority in my new life. I have started with Dutch, Jack, and Dave. Now I need to do that with Cliff.

I called Cliff and left a message. Cliff and I have also been friends for over fifty years.

An hour later, my phone buzzed. "Hi, Del. You're living in Bozeman, now?"

"Yes. I live here now. How did you know that?"

"Dutch told me."

"Well, Cliff, I am alone, as you know, I wanted to start over. I could not stay in Great Falls."

After some catching-up talk, Cliff said. "First, I want to say how sorry I am about Amy. I know those feelings. Second, I want to thank you for your long personal letter after Mavis died. I still have it and read it every year on our anniversary. Now Del, why the call? What can I help with?"

"First, Cliff thank you for your long personal letter. It is one of my treasures. And thank you for visiting Amy. She told me during her last week about all the people that came to see her. She knew it was supposed to be a secret, but felt it was more important to tell me." I paused and sighed. I could hear the emotions in Cliff's voice. I am sure he heard them in mine.

"I have a favor to ask, Cliff, and want to ask you when I see you. I can be in Salt Lake City, Saturday and Sunday, if that fits your schedule. Nothing is wrong. I will stay at the Camelback and be in the lounge at about seven on both evenings. You come either day. It will be special to see you."

Like all close friends, we did many things together. Lots of basketball and family outings. He could, if he chose to, help me with some of the changes I plan for my 'new' life. I told him my arrival time, and I would have an Alamo rental car. Cliff was a high mid-level FBI agent. He ran operations, and will check my paper trail because that was how he operates. He did not like surprises.

The plane was on time. It always made me smile when I can say that. After picking up my bag at baggage claim, I started toward the Alamo car rental counter. A clean-cut young man folded up his newspaper and fell in behind me. I was not surprised.

I always paid for the option to have the car delivered to the baggage claim exit at the airport instead of riding the shuttle. When I slipped into my car, I saw the same guy enter a black suburban. "Company," I said aloud.

I talked to myself the whole way to the motel. Since stealing the money, I have been looking over my shoulder and watching for the out-of-the-ordinary. I knew I would have to become much more proficient at checking my surroundings, and yet look nonchalant. I have slept well since taking the money, but I was nervous about being found out. I do not think I am followed. I just feel the need to take care. I know so little about the criminal mind, but less about how law enforcement works.

I freshened up before going down to the lounge. I used my cheap bug detector. The indicator light flashed red, telling me a listening device was located in the phone and the bathroom light switch. "Hmm." I said aloud, then stopped talking. *What to do?* Just ignore it and make a note to get a much more sophisticated sweeper. I needed the practice. I am certain I am not being followed. I am practicing, because I have so much to learn. I do not want to be caught.

I put my cheap sweeper in the fake potted plant by the elevator. Judging by the dust, I knew it would be there when I returned. I wondered why I did not want Cliff to know, about the sweeper.

Walking into the lounge, I saw Cliff sitting in the same booth we had shared thirty-five-plus years ago. He got out of the booth and walked to meet me. "Long time no see!"

We held the handshake an extra second or two, then added a deep meaningful hug. "You have not changed a bit. You look like you could still play some basketball. How did so much time go by with so little contact?" I said, grinning.

After the waitress took our order, he smiled and looked at me for a second or two. "Knees are gone. Can't move well enough!"

"Yeah! We are getting old. How is the family?" I paid for the beer, and we talked of family and old times.

Suddenly, his smile faded and he asked, "Why are we here, and what kind of favor do you need?"

I took a sip of my beer, looked him in the eye, and tried to smile. "Are we not friends anymore?"

"Yes, Del, we are and always will be the best of friends. But we haven't been in touch much for a long time. Then you call my office and ask me to call you. So, I call. Then you ask for an in-person meeting and a favor. It made me suspicious and wary."

"I see."

He returned his business smile, so I surprised him by saying, "Is the help at the bar necessary, and are we being listened to?"

He stared at me for a long time. I did not react. I knew he was processing his options and trying to decide if I was guilty of something.

Looking at the young man at the bar, he said, "Carl, you can go home." Carl got up and left without a word. "Yes, we are taping this, as we tape everything these days. Finish your beer, and let's go for a walk." He offered a ride in a black SUV. I declined. "Just a walk in the courtyard will do."

"Fine. What do you need and why?"

"I will not tell you why to keep you insulated. I reached out and took his oversized pen from his shirt pocket, broke it and put the pieces in the trash. "When an agent needs to go under cover, you provide them all new identities, right?"

Cliff scowled, looked away a second then answered, "Yes."

"I need three new identities that would pass all inspections and inquires, including a concealed weapons permit."

"Criminal?" asked Cliff.

"Not from my point of view," I countered.

He stopped walking and stared off into space. "Would it be criminal in the FBI's point of view?"

"What I am planning would be frowned upon in your circles, but not cause a stir. I want to establish travel flexibility. I know you could point me to the people who can do this with the quality you would use yourself. The documents must be all-inclusive to make each new "person" complete and pass every test. Your people could and most likely will tell you about my new identities. That could make things difficult for both of us. You need to be immune."

Once again, Cliff scrutinized me. "I will have to think about this."

"You do *not*," I tried not to sound angry. "I know you have already checked on me. You know I am not a criminal and do not have a record and I have comfortable finances. I am alone, and live in a rental in Bozeman. You know I travel, mostly driving, and go fishing and hunting as often as I can. I fly Dutch's airplane. You will either help me or not. I do not want to, nor need to tell you why I want those identities." I stared at him. He waited for me to finish. "I will not be back for anything, ever. You have my word."

He walked away three steps and turned. "Okay. I will give you three names and the necessary contact info as well as a code word to identify you. I will ask them to give you their best work. You must pay in cash. The non-negotiable price is $12,000 for each set. You must be disguised and have passport quality ID pictures when you see them. These people are not criminals. They need to be immune, as you say, from you. All bets are off if you violate this agreement, and we will expose you. Understand?"

"Perfectly."

Back at his black SUV, Cliff removed a gadget from the center console, entered some codes, and printed three separate notes with names and the contact info. "Remember the falls we hiked to, once?"

"Talafufu."

"Yes. That's the code word. After that, your word will do. They will give you what you want. You do not have my or their permission to give this information to anyone. We will know if you do so. Don't copy the note, they will know if you do. Then you are done. Understood?"

"Yes. You have my word. Next beer you buy. Can you give me a contact number should I ever need to find you?"

He wrote two numbers on the back of his official business card. "Del, I sure hope you know what you are doing. These numbers are privy to only five people, now six. A message left on either number will get to me." He smiled, "Why did you destroy government property? Could be a felony."

"Destroy it? I just accidentally broke the pen. Pens break sometimes."

"Yeah, right." His smile remained. "I trust you. The people I can say that about I can count on one hand. I hope you're not in over your head. Godspeed."

"Always." We shook hands firmly, he hopped into his rig, and with a quick wave, he drove away.

I watched until the taillights disappeared. I looked down at my shoes, kicked two small stones into the street, and then looked at the night sky. I felt lonely tonight. I miss my lady.

Before flying back, I bought burner phones at eight locations, bringing my total to thirty. I FedExed all to my Bozeman address.

CHAPTER 15

On the flight back to Bozeman, I replayed my conversation with Cliff. Our friendship was still a deep bond—just two alpha males wanting to be top dog. I needed to obtain the three identities quickly. I did not want Cliff to change his mind.

I picked up the Ram, and on the way to the rental house, I also stopped at the post office, and gathered my mail, some stamps, and mailing envelopes. One of my corporation documents had arrived. JZII Inc. will own my hideaway in Cancun, if I decide to buy a condo there.

I stopped at Staples to buy supplies to set up my home office.

A fun stop at a Goodwill Store, netted pictures, books, kitchen stuff, and some used XL clothes, including an extra-large, decent Lennox coverall, Carhart bib overalls, and a matching coat. My purchases also included a battered maple bookcase and a medium-sized old oak roll-top desk—two garage projects. I could afford new stuff, but appearances, appearances. Right? I asked myself.

The garage at my rental house sported an old workbench attached to the back wall. The landlord had agreed to let me remove it and build a new one. He liked the year lease and a quiet tenant.

I made a quick stop at Home Depot to buy wood, tools and finishing materials for my new workbench.

Once back at the house, I tore out the old bench and loaded it for a trip to the landfill. On the way back, I stopped at Best Buy and bought a top-of-the line laptop, tablet, and all the software to set up the office. I added a printer, router, modem, shredder, and a quality carrying case for the laptop. As we walked past the security camera display, my sales clerk asked me if I thought a camera security system that I could monitor from my phone would fit into my home protection plans. I purchased the best system in the store.

I needed to be busy and wanted to know my way around the city and its suburbs, and how to access I-90. Knowing all the access routes to the old local highways could be necessary, if the authorities were becoming interested. The faster I could become an expert on traffic routes, the better. I tried out-of-the-way places for good breakfasts.

There were moments when I felt alone and lonely, but I enjoyed setting up my new life. Keeping busy was the key to avoiding loneliness for me.

They said the licenses for the truck and boat would take three weeks, so I would have time to refinish the bookcase and build the new workbench.

The incorporation papers for 'Speckled Prospector' were ready to mail to Phoenix, but I needed my new identities. I wanted Del to be somewhat hard to find. I wanted a remote property outside of Lincoln, Montana, and hired a local realtor to help find the right place.

I did not expect to find a place bordering the US Forest Service Land, nor did I know such properties existed.

Being wrong was wonderful news. If everything worked out, I would have access to the Bob from my cabin, and reach my Danaher hideaway in two days. No more parking at a trailhead. I would mark the trail, drop an old snag over the creek, and strategically create two or three observation lookouts in trees. My first night sleeping in the cabin I dreamt about being someone else hiking to Curtis Castle.

CHAPTER 16

Changing one's appearance can be easy if one had a lot of time. But I needed to learn the tricks to make quick changes in tight spaces, like a small restroom.

Yesterday, at my almost daily stop at the Bozeman library, I watched a clown tying balloons for preschool kids. Parents and librarians were enjoying ' Learning to Read Day'.

When the clown took a break, I asked him. "How long does it take you to make yourself into a clown?"

"About thirty minutes for the full face, but I can disguise myself in five or less."

"Why, are you interested in trying the clown business on for size.?"

"Looks like fun."

"Go to a clown convention. Ask Penny, she'll help you find one on line."

Penny worked as a librarian assistant. A petite young woman, with a ready smile and twinkling blue eyes, she helped everyone. She searched the internet for disguise items and clown conventions for me.

"This is fun. Something new." She found a convention in Denver. "Are you going to go to the convention?"

"I think I will. It should be exciting—a nice change of pace. Like you said, *something new.*"

"Tell me about it when you get back."

"Deal."

Denver turned out to be perfect. My first alternative identity contact was in a nearby suburb of Cherry Creek. I could learn quick make-up tricks and acquire my new identity in the same trip. I found a hotel near the convention site and booked a four day stay in Denver. This would be more than enough time to obtain the ID, spend as much time at the convention as I wished, and familiarize myself with downtown Denver.

Before going to the convention, I researched making changes, so I would know what to look for when I was at the convention. Changing one's appearance was not very difficult. But, creating an almost perfect or exact duplicate change was. My shooters will be chosen from two of my alternate ID's. They must look almost exactly the same every time.

I will need lots of practice and will listen for tricks of the trade. Facial hair and haircut changes work, but take a lot of time to grow back to normal. Removable scars and fake tattoos are easier for instant changes. I read once that when people were asked to describe a person, they focused on a birth mark or a scar. Birthmarks, scars, and moles are quick changes. Changing hair color will not be an option for me. Wigs can be discarded, but getting duplicate wigs that would fool a close friend would be harder. I felt I needed my alternate identities to be exactly the same every time I wished to use them.

I started a collection to put in a carry-on suitcase with many temporary quick-change items, bumper stickers, baseball caps, t-shirts, small magnetic door signs, a Black Lab bobble head, and trinkets to hang from the rearview mirror. Of course, a plastic Jesus for the dash. One of my favorite movies was *Cool Hand Luke*. Paul Neuman sang a song about a plastic Jesus. Easily one of his best scenes as an actor ever.

CHAPTER 17

fter a smooth flight to Denver on Southwest and a long ride in the shuttle to the Spritz Hotel, I asked for and was rewarded with a suite on the top floor. Beyond a doubt, it was the best room I have ever stayed in. It smelled rich, looked rich, and just smoothed my tension away.

The convention was to last three days. I hoped everything I might need to help me create my alternate identities would be available.

After a hotel buffet breakfast, including a super omelet, I walked the block to the convention center, paid the entry fee, and followed the crowd into the carnival atmosphere.

A young teen in front of me said it all. "Mom, this is awesome."

Curt would have loved this, I thought.

Hundreds of clowns in full costumes roamed every aisle. Numerous kiosks offered an endless variety of options, from uses of makeup to wigs. Taking the convention tote bag, a small note pad, and a pen, I started down aisle A. The center was full of kids, their parents and older kids like me—a different kind of noise. There was every kind of clown you could imagine—short ones, tall ones, young ones, old ones, lots of huge shoes, phony noses and colorful costumes. Even some young kids were dressed as clowns. No two were alike. Color everywhere was the way to describe the setting.

I stayed all day, writing notes, gathering catalogs, taking samples, and asking questions.

At a drug store near the hotel, I bought a quality spiral lined paper notebook, a highlighter pen, a stapler and staples.

Bag in hand, I went to the hotel dining room on the fourteenth floor. I asked for a window table so I could enjoy the mountain view. I chose a Chardonnay to go with a seafood platter dinner. Private reasons for the change. Amy loved a good Chardonnay. I occasionally shared a glass of wine with her; I wish she were here.

The half-page spiral notebook had eleven pages of to-dos when I returned to the convention's second day—one page each for a workable beginning for each new identity. I started a written description of my new identities, covering all phases of changes to create each new person.

On my first day, I witnessed a woman showing someone how makeup can drastically change a face, so I intended to spend some time with her today, before doing the other things on my multiple lists. I will try to master some of her techniques. She showed how to make hands look different. Not smaller, just different. How to make a face narrower and thinner, and how to change noses. So much to learn and practice.

After two hours of makeup training, I spent almost $800 to purchase make-up from her. Then went to each vendor on my list and purchased enough supplies to make ten changes for each of my new identities. One of those alternate identities would be my primary shooter. I needed enough quick-change supplies to make changes at a moment's notice. Most items I had mailed to my house in Bozeman. I purchased five sets of non-corrected contact lenses. Baby blue, steel gray, and teal green were the three choices of colors for each set. I saved one set for each new identity and for the required passport photo. I could change disguises in the hotel room, and obtain the passport photos while in Denver. That would save time.

I have an appointment at one p.m. tomorrow to see Cliff's contact in Cherry Creek.

CHAPTER 18

checked out of the hotel and waited at the curb for my rental car delivery. I decided not to change in the hotel. I may need to stay there again as myself. A Chevrolet Impala with a GPS arrived promptly at ten. I used three hours of idle time to find my way to Cherry Creek and to change to Spencer Morgan in a convenience store restroom. The disguise took about five minutes to complete. The beard, the small scar, and a wig were easy to change into. I added extra weight with snug body padding, that looked surprisingly real.

I took a short side trip to Walgreens to get my passport photo. I reached the address thirty minutes early. I did not feel comfortable waiting on the street. I located a small coffee shop three blocks away, and killed time there. I was nervous.

I called the number in Cherry Creek, Colorado as arranged yesterday.

"Hello, Spencer Morgan here."

"Tell me why you called." His answer was gruff.

"Talafufu Falls."

He gave me an address and directions again. "Have a passport-quality photo with you, and be here at one p.m."

I already had the picture and had disguised myself as Spencer Lyle Morgan. I wondered why he felt he needed to repeat those instructions.

The forger's location was a small yellow ranch-style house that sat near the back of a narrow lot in a part of the city with alleys. A tiny detached shed next to a single car garage, finished off a weedy backyard and a minimum of pride of ownership told the story. I surmised the guy did not live here, and someone only mowed the front. Most houses had at least one car parked on the street, making the street into one lane.

He did not offer his hand or his name after greeting me at his door.

"This way."

I followed him out his back door to the small single-stall garage. We entered through a side door, and I sat in a chair he offered. The space was cluttered and messy and smelled like old oil, and mice. It would then take some real detective work to find evidence of any use other than a storage, and a home for critters.

As he prepared his equipment, I studied his arrangement and noticed that he could take down everything in less than a minute.

"Six feet, 200?" was his first question.

"Very close, 215."

He worked for two hours. He offered no conversation and did not seem to mind that I watched. He had prepared some of the documents beforehand. Using a very bright head lamp and some special glasses, he never took a break. When finished, he handed me a birth certificate, social security card, driver's license, passport, Visa card and an American Express Platinum Card application, and a concealed carry permit.

When the forger was done, I wanted to leave immediately and drive to Cheyenne, Wyoming for the night. Spencer would be based out of Cheyenne.

Our arrangement was documents for cash. He gave me the documents. I gave him twelve thousand dollars in cash. We walked back through his house. It did not look lived in, I decided.

At the front door he said, "Don't come back. Only Cliff knows what I can do and my value. You cannot come twice. If you do, we will turn you in. You will go to jail. Capiche?"

"I fully understand." I stared until he broke eye contact and turned to leave.

Driving away, I did not see anything suspicious. *He protects his avocation very well.*

Hours later, I arrived in Cheyenne, Wyoming. The clerk at the Best Western suggested Buster's Brew Pub, so that is where I went. The back booth was unoccupied and offered a view of the front door. A young waitress dressed in a cowgirl outfit brought my Lagunitas IPA and a Reuben with sweet potato fries. I dug out my papers and read everything. Very good work.

The next day as Spencer, I rented a storage unit big enough to hold a full-sized truck. Then, I bought a five-year-old white Chevrolet Colorado crew-cab from the local Chevrolet dealer. "Three weeks for the plates, Mr. Morgan.

I put the truck and enough essentials in the storage unit to make it a short-term hideout. A port-a-potty, water, three changes of cowboy clothing, and a supply of nonperishable food would allow a two to four-day stay. I would be a cowboy in Cheyenne.

I arranged to obtain the other two identities before leaving Denver. I drove from Cheyenne to Apache Junction, Arizona to get Sven Hansen's identity. I carried Sven's passport photo. Sven and Spencer did not look anything alike. An attractive black lady over six feet tall with a shaved head, no makeup, and a beautiful smile greeted me.

"Cliff must think you're special. Got your picture?"

In under two hours, she handed me Sven's complete set of identity papers, exactly like the first guy produced. I handed her the twelve-thousand dollar fee. She held the money tightly to her chest and caressed it. "We don't know each other, sugar."

Using my Scandinavian accent, I nodded to her. "Ja, sure." Then turned to leave. The lady said, "Your wig is too noticeable. Let me show you." She retrieved and donned a huge Afro wig. I would only have noticed her height. She was that different.

"I can send you some very good wigs of the same quality that I'm wearing, as many as you want for $75 each. You call this number, ask for Vanessa, and say, 'Sven from Talafufu says yes'. I will give you a post office box to send me the money for as many as you want. If they aren't as good as I promised, I'll give you your money back. You'll have to trust me. I know what the wig should look like, and you will see how much better mine are. Remember, sugar, *secrecy* is my business.

"Ja. I order ten now. I vill call one month to send you da money."

It was time to fly to Mitchell, South Dakota to purchase Sven's residence. I must go to Great Falls in order to talk to Dutch about using the plane. I know there are items that will not match the new identity papers, but that will make me harder to find if the authorities are closing in. South Dakota is the pheasant capital of the world. Mitchell is the perfect location for Sven to pursue hunting those beautiful birds. Mitchell should be safe, yet close enough to most of the larger mid-western cities.

I flew Southwest to Seattle, passport picture in hand. I had an appointment for the next day. My flight to Seattle, on a beautiful cloudless day, passed close to Mount Rainier. I could see the column of a cloud that looked like steam rising near the top. If this mountain blows, the world will change.

I changed my disguise to James in an airport restroom, stall. The changes from Del to James were minimal. I have learned to make them using a small mirror. As James, I spent the entire afternoon and evening walking and studying the city, from the piers to the main high-rise district. I took time to enjoy a smoked salmon dinner on the waterfront.

When I arrived at the provided address, I almost stayed in the car. The place looked and felt abandoned. No one could live there. The place was in shambles, and that was a compliment. The forger met me at the door, as unkempt as the house. He accepted the code word, then led me around the house to a small garage at the rear of the lot.

There were four locks. The inside of the shed looked as messy as the yard. I shuddered to imagine what word described the inside of the house. Rats would not live here. He worked fast and acted like he wanted me gone.

The work was as good as the other two sets and just as complete. He took the money and did not say thanks or anything. His phone showed a call as soon as I left. Yes, I have a gadget that can check the numbers I had previously called. I needed to be within a quarter mile or so, and it only told me his phone was in use.

These people provided what I needed because Cliff asked them to. I played a high-risk game. Cliff could get the information if he wanted. These people needed Cliff's protection.

I would ask Cliff for a better phone tracer and a better sweeper. The criminal element might have better equipment than I had. I called Bisbane Industries to ask them to send a current catalog to me in Bozeman. I also wanted to see if they had a way to secure my 9mm pistol to my backpack. A standard shoulder holster would be in the way. I wanted to be able to use the pistol if a reason presented itself, whether wild animal, or human threat.

CHAPTER 19

Dutch called. The new-style canisters were ready. Good. I can go see him soon and test my new camo parachutes. I felt bad not telling him about the chutes, but I just want Curtis Castle to be mine. I called Great Falls Tent and Awning, and found my six chutes were ready. Not only can I visit Dutch, but I can put some things in my safe deposit box and then go flying.

My stops at the bank and to pick up the parachutes were completed before I opened the door to Dutch's shop. Kenny brought my six canisters out and loaded them for me.

"Thanks, Kenny."

"No problem."

"You going flying tomorrow?" Dutch asked.

"Yes. I am going to fly over Lincoln to look for cabin sites. I think I will fly along the Missouri River on my way. A clear day and little wind, it should be a soft ride. Hungry? We should go shoot some pool now and eat a burger." I enjoyed having Dutch as a close friend again.

The following morning, I parked my truck in the hangar after pushing the Cessna out. The chutes and containers were ready. I hoped the twenty-foot lanyard system would work as well as the first drop. I positioned the canister in the passenger's seat. I will fly as low and as slow as I dared over Curtis Castle to see if I can circle the valley quickly enough to watch the chute until the canister lands. I am licensed to fly helicopters as well, but am not current and using one of those would leave a paper trail, and everyone within a hundred miles would hear me and watch.

The drop looked perfect. It was much easier to push the canister out than my first drop. My homemade gizmo to hold the door open worked fine. I doubt anyone could have seen the chute open unless they were in my valley. The parachute floated down nicely as I turned back to Great Falls. I did not see anyone. Others could have seen me, but I cannot control that. I will do the second drop early tomorrow and then drive to Evergreen.

I needed to visit Dave Cummings, a longtime friend and mostly retired forester. He needed to know I plan to go solo into the Bob. If I do not come when I tell him to expect me, he will come looking for me. With a very small pack, I can make the trip in less than two days. I drove to Evergreen and stayed in the storage unit. I called Dave and asked for a ride.

We started our drive to the Meadow Creek Trailhead just before sunrise.

"Wish I could go with you," Dave said when he dropped me off.

"That would be a special time," I answered.

"I'll be back after six days like we planned, Del. Then I'll drive out here every day around four, until you are sitting here waiting for me. You be careful."

"I will, Dave. Thanks for the ride." After a firm handshake, I started walking down the trail. It was at least five minutes before I heard the truck drive off.

At the cabin, I put up a homemade sign over the door: *Curtis Castle*. He said he felt he belonged here. He does. The little creek that ran past the first mine Curt found, had a newly routed slab of Douglas Fir that said *Curtis Creek*. It was neatly tucked between two alder shoots.

Sitting on the stump chair before dinner, I softly sang my favorite song.

I found the first drop easily, just on the edge of the beaver pond. That canister contained two hard rubber wheels and an axle, which easily attached to the canisters. No carrying.

I climbed the escape trail and spotted the second chute caught high in a tree. It will be a tough retrieve. With the help of a two-finger hand saw, I climbed the tree where I reached the canister. I took off the chute, stuffed it in my backpack, then gently released the canister from the branches, and let it drop. There were eggs in that one, so we would see how good of a job Kenny did. In no time, all the gear was in the cabin.

Solar-powered items will greatly improve the quality of life here. Lamps, a clock, a heater, a five-gallon shower, and a charging system for GPS and cell phone, all solar powered, will each be tested today. Though I would take great care, so no gadgets would be visible from the air.

Tomorrow, I will climb the weeping wall, using the climbing gear I dropped in one of the canisters. The first canister included two dozen carabiners, a mountain ax, six pitons, a rappel kit, a dozen camalots, a climbing harness, a rope walker ascender and four ropes of various sizes and lengths.

I have never climbed and only have a demonstration of each piece of equipment to rely on. Very carefully, I set about going up the weeping wall on the west side of the wet rocks. It took a little over an hour following the instructions I had listened to carefully. Reaching the top, I felt a strong sense of accomplishment. I am never too old to learn and do. It took seventy-three feet of rope—higher than I estimated.

Standing on the four-to-five-foot ledge, I could only marvel at what I had discovered.

"Wow!" The valley was a panorama of beauty. I have heard an Irish song, Johnny Cash's *Forty Shades of Green*. A perfect description of my valley. Tears formed. I am not lonely in my mountain valley.

First, I secured a rope to be used for decent, and thus made other climbs much easier and safer.

The mountain side of the ledge revealed the source of the weeping wall water. It seeped from a pool mostly under the rock wall that continued twenty or more feet above the ledge. The pool was about twelve feet wide, with five feet exposed from the wall. I could not see any possible way to enter the water cave except to wade and swim in the cold water. Not a risk I needed to take.

The ledge was wide enough for an easy and safe walk to the east side of the pool. Dense alders choked the ledge on that side. I would bring the tree saw tomorrow and explore further.

The following morning, after an easier, fun climb, I used the tree saw to help me make a narrow, and yet concealed opening through the alders. Hard sweaty work paid off. When the bushes were finally thinned, a steep climbing ledge about three or four feet wide was exposed. After an hour of climbing, I found myself on top of a saddle between two higher steep rocky ridges. The view—spectacular! The Danaher was a thin ribbon of blue to the west, the magnificent mountains of the continental divide occupied the horizon to the east. I knew how far those mountains were from this saddle. I could easily see fifty miles in any direction—a special feeling few others experience.

I sat on a rock, overcome with emotion, thinking how lucky I was. Ever since losing Curt, I have become more easily moved to tears. I took in the wonder and counted my blessings. Curt was not here to share this scene, but I did not feel alone. Along the southeastern side of the rock face, someone had been prospecting. Two small shale slides and a gravel pile were visible.

As I carefully neared the closest slide, I found a small skeleton. *The prospector,* I presumed, had met his fate. One leg bone looked to be broken, but that was a guess. The skull lay only a few feet away and looked severely cracked. Again guessing, he must have been looking for his gold and had taken a bad fall. A very sad ending. I hope he is okay with my intrusion.

Moving the skull closer to the rest of the skeleton, I covered him as best I could. This was his final resting place, and I knew I should not change it.

Tomorrow, I would bring some climbing gear to see what the rocks would reveal.

Kenny made good canisters. Only one cracked egg. The canister drop system should keep me supplied with good rations each time I come here.

So, after eating the next morning, I returned to the new digs. Curt would want to name this spot, so I did it for him, *Prospector Saddle.* I climbed to the top of the first slide and saw nothing of interest. At the top of the second slide, however, I found a small ledge with five or six seams of quartz laced with gold. I worked the spot for an hour or so. I am no miner, but this was very good ore. I packed about forty pounds of the quartz I had loosened down to the ledge and lowered it to the meadow floor. Most of it would be stored in the cave. I felt an excitement I could not describe. Finally, some gold! Curt would have danced for joy. I intended to pack out just enough to have it assayed.

Dilemma. I did not need the money. I still had much to do to complete my 'adventures'.

I stayed two more days, fishing the Danaher and Young Rivers. Near where they join is a very large, downed, boney-looking, Douglas fir. It was gray; many of its branches were stripped away by heavy winter snows. I could create a concealed place on the topside of the trunk to hide a canister. Inside, I could keep a small one-person inflatable raft, a dry suit and accessories, a quality life jacket and three days of emergency rations. If I ever needed this equipment, I would risk drinking from the stream. I knew I could float all the way to Hungry Horse Reservoir from this river junction.

I hiked out in a day and a half with only a very light pack. Dave waited for me. He was a semiretired ranger, but married to his job. He was always there. A veteran of hundreds of trips into the Bob, Dave could find my cabin if he wanted to. We were on a fire crew in our early twenties and have kept in touch via a Christmas note every year. Over the years, we took five or six backpack trips together. Five of them into the Bob. Our favorite topic, when telling stories by a campfire, was backpacking.

Without my asking, he said, "Del, I was very happy to give you and Molly a ride to the Meadow Creek Trailhead a few weeks ago. I hadn't seen her in twenty years. She acts and sounds like her mother. I am sorry about Amy."

He changed the subject before I could respond. "You are going into the Bob a lot. Leaving your truck at the trail head for long periods is risky. Why don't you give me a heads up when you want to go in, and I will give you a ride? I would love to go in with you, but my back is shot, and I couldn't make a mile. Too many hours on the back of a horse. I love the Bob, and I will always find the time to bring you here."

"That is a kind offer, Dave, I will take you up on that. I am glad you could give me a ride last week. I am shopping for a cabin near Lincoln, so when I find one, I like, I plan to hike in from the Monture Creek Trailhead. It is an easier trail, shorter, and closer to Bozeman and Lincoln. But I will enjoy those rides with you until that happens. It gives us a chance to be together and tell stories. I practically live on fish and dry meals." I laughed, knowing I ate exceptionally well at my little hideaway.

"Never a grouse or two?" He smiled at me.

Grinning back, "Why that would be illegal, Dave."

We exchanged current cell phone numbers. He opened the door of my truck, offered his hand, and while closing the door for me, said in a serious tone, "You need anything I will do it, no questions."

Nodding, I thanked him. "You are a good friend, Dave. I know you came and visited Amy. I never thanked you for that. I will say thank you now. You know I will do the same for you. I would like you to plan on coming to Bozeman for Thanksgiving Day. I have a bed for you. Come a day or two early if you like."

"That would be wonderful. I'll be there."

I had much to think about on my drive back to Bozeman. Maybe I should detour to Helena to have the gold ore assessed.

CHAPTER 20

I made the U.S. Assay office on Broadway Street my first stop in Helena. It is a historical building now. The docent suggested I go to the Lewis and Clark County courthouse to have ore assayed.

At the courthouse, I was given a list of private assayers to choose from, as the state no longer does it. The docent should have known that. I called the first one on the list. Frederick Peterson and Associates were located practically next door to the county courthouse, in an older seedy strip mall that was home to five other small businesses.

Frederick greeted me when I walked in the door. The light reflecting off the clutter revealed a shabby, dull, mostly brown office with well-used furniture. The receptionist, an older, frail-woman did not look up when I entered.

"Good morning. I hear you have a task for me," Fred beamed, acting important.

"Yes, I do." I handed him my small five-pound bag of quartz. I thought the docent must have called him.

The shock on his face was very evident. He did a poor job of masking his delight.

"I don't suppose you will tell me where you found this ore."

I looked at him, paused, then said, "No, I do not think I will. I was trout fishing on a stream I often have fished, saw a fresh collapse of rock along a steep ledge. I found these few rocks and wondered if they contained gold. I acted puzzled. I studied mining with Curt and was pretty sure of what I had. "I gathered what I could find. I looked for more, but this was it. It does not look like I found the mother lode." I chuckled.

He picked up the sample and tapped it softly with a small rock hammer, and we watched it break apart, revealing gold flakes.

"Top quality!" His voice quivered with excitement.

Frederick is a smallish, thin man with a pinched narrow face. Close-set dark brown eyes under bushy brows framed a pointy upturned nose. His Adam's apple bobbed as he cleared his throat to speak. "If there are tons of this ore, you would become a very rich man. This is the best quality gold quartz I have seen in many years. Most gold I see is in the form of flakes offered by weekend panners who find some in streams on public lands. The origin of their gold would be impossible to find."

"Can I sell this as it is, or shall I try to do more separating?"

Too quickly, he answered. "Gold is about $1,200 per ounce now. I have a friend that buys gold, but he wouldn't pay full price. This ore needs to be processed and the gold extracted. Would you like me to call him?"

"Sure."

He did not try to mask his glee as he walked to his desk and made a call on his cell phone, from Favorites, I guessed. "Samuel, I have a gentleman here who has some raw unrefined gold he would like to sell." Listening to the response, he added. "About two ounces."

As my dad often said, "I was born in the morning, but not yesterday morning." My scam meter just buzzed.

Their eagerness and my senses prickled the hair on the back of my neck!

They offered to meet at Samuel's house, but I told Fred I preferred the lobby of the Best Western Hotel, not far from the Capitol building. Frederick agreed for both of them, but could not mask his disappointment. He had a twitch over his left eye now.

Samuel proved to be a look alike of Frederick, including the bobbing Adam's apple and the twitch. Frederick confirmed that they were brothers.

I felt like the last hen in the chicken coop with two foxes drooling at the door. We talked most of an hour without agreeing on anything.

They would keep the gold a secret to themselves. I was very sure they were not to be trusted.

Finally, Samuel said. "What room are you staying in? Frederick and I will discuss this and call you in the morning with an offer."

"Oh, I am not staying here. I just felt the lobby would be more private for our meeting."

A darkness settled over their faces. The twitches twitched and the apples bobbed. Frederick said. "How can we get a hold of you?"

"Give me your cell number, and I will call you. I have a trip to take. I may be back in Helena in a few days," I answered.

He gave me his number. We all stood, shook hands and left. I did not dare leave the sample with them. Both of their palms were damp. I was uncomfortable with that creepy feeling. I made a note of their vehicles, including license plate numbers. I wish I knew why I felt it was necessary.

Samuel drove a white crew cab Chevrolet Silverado three-quarter ton. Lots of those on the road. Fredrick's ride was an off-red Subaru Outback, an older model that showed much use. When I drove out of the parking lot, Samuel boldly pulled out behind me and followed. *Not good,* I thought. *Why?*

Helena main arterial system is confusing to non-city residents. The 'Noses', as I decided to call them, were going to be trouble. Butte was on my way, so I decided to go to Montana Tech and see if the Geology professor would see me and look at the ore. I was positive the Noses had written my license number down and knew it was a Bozeman number. Time to dig out the camera and the zoom lens. I have a standard Canon EOS Rebel T-6 EF-S 18-55mm coupled with an EF 400mm telephoto lens. I could take a picture of the whites of their eyes.

The professor at Montana Technical University in Butte agreed to see me after the receptionist told him of my request. After his class ended at three-thirty, we met in his small, cluttered office. Gary Lansing was a tall thin man with a runner's build and a grace to all his movements. He tied his long graying hair in a neat ponytail.

"You have some ore for me to look at?"

Handing him the sack, "Are you a runner?"

"All the time. I have thirteen marathons to my credit." Picking up the sack and examining the ore, while not showing emotion, he said, "This gold ore is exceptional quality. Old-time prospectors spent a lifetime looking for ore like this." I'd gathered that information from the behavior of the Noses. Little did he know.

"Often, when quartz like this is found, it's in small pockets, with others hidden nearby. It's very hard to find. Your sample is worth about $1,500. Take great care when you go back for more. This quality of ore will bring out the worst in people. Your find is safe with me. I am a semi-precious gem person. Those little gems are much easier to market."

I followed I-90 back to Butte, turning into a truck stop on Harrison Avenue. After topping off my gas tank, I continued south on Harrison and found a sports bar with a parking lot full of rigs with Montana plates. I figured it was a favorite place of the locals. I found an open seat at a tall table near the front window and ordered a barbequed pulled pork sandwich and local IPA. Samuel's truck passed slowly by, making sure my rig was in the parking lot.

How and why? I asked myself.

I took my time with my meal, reviewing all the options. I needed to stop this intrusion quickly. I followed I-90 to Bozeman, then proceeded directly to The University of Montana campus and waited in the administration parking lot. I saw Samuel go by twenty minutes after I arrived. I went back the way I came and parked in the Wal-Mart lot. Samuel was only two minutes behind me. He went into the store. I watched until he came out of the store, fifteen minutes later, and noticed he was talking on his phone. I picked one of my burner phones and dialed the number Frederick had given me. It was busy. I decided to say hello to Sam.

He did not see me until I was only three steps away. He almost fainted. *Sneaky, yes. Courageous, no.*

I almost said, 'Hi, nose two' but instead, "Hi, Sam." He set his jaw. He did not like being called Sam. "Fancy meeting you here. You following me?"

Stuttering badly and overworking the Adam's apple, he offered, "Uh, no! My daughter goes to school here, and I came down to visit."

"School is not in session now, Sam. Only a few athletes here. Tell me why you are here."

"Well, Frederick and I...." he started to say. But I stepped closer and interrupted.

"Look, Sam. I found some quartz above a stream. It is not much because I searched a couple of hours for more and did not find any. No other signs there could be more. No similar rocks. I have no plans to look any further.

Go home and tell Fred I do not like the sneaking around. I saw you in Butte. You need to mind your own affairs. I would not take it too kindly if I found you following me again. Get my drift, Sam?"

"Yes, I do. And don't call me Sam. It is Samuel." He was pissed.

"Respect Sam. It is called respect. Show me some, and then I will show you and your brother some."

Walking back to my truck, I muttered. "Not to be trusted. Maybe teach them a lesson. Careful, I mused, they could cause real problems." It struck me that just regular folks owning an assessing business would not act as these two are. They are up to something. I was also sure now they had called Lansing. He was just not surprised enough.

How did Sam know what exits to take, and where to find me when I parked without me seeing him? After watching him leave the lot, I put an old towel on the ground, got down on my back and looked under the truck. Easy. A small hide-a-key sized box with a short antenna was attached to the top side of the transmission housing.

Going back over the time-line in Helena, I figured it out. They came into the lobby separately. Fred was first by at least ten minutes. He must have been there before I arrived, so he called Sam to tell him which rig to place the tracker on. Sam then placed the device and showed up in the lobby. Sam was last to come in because I would not know which vehicle was his, and he would have access to the device, because Fred was at work.

I placed the tracker on the nearest motor home. Virginia plates.

At Marcy's Game Time Pub, I found a table near the window. I ordered a Reuben and tots, a glass of lager from the tap, and watched my truck. I killed two hours watching some college softball. Sam never came by.

Somehow, I knew I had not seen the last of the Noses. It would be foolish to believe they might forget. I am not a fool.

Now, I wondered about the professor. He seemed too casual and dismissive. Maybe call the school. I hoped he was not into something wrong because I liked him. I hoped he wasn't in cahoots with the Noses.

Back at my rental home, I put the truck in the garage. Then looked it over from top to bottom. Nothing. I needed a super bug detector.

CHAPTER 21

I was set in Bozeman, Montana. Alternate identity, Spencer Morgan was at home in Cheyenne, Wyoming. James Colbert owned a small condo in a Billings, Montana downtown high-rise. Now it was time to get Sven Hansen set up in Mitchell, South Dakota. There are pheasants to hunt, and Mitchell is the pheasant capital of the world.

When I picked up my first set of canisters from Dutch, I asked if I could use the plane for most of a week.

"No problem, Del. I think it's great that you are flying a lot. It's good for you, and I know by the look on your face every time you fly that it makes you happy. Just let me know when you are back."

Practicing my Scandinavian accent, I called a Mitchell realtor. The receptionist forwarded me to Sally Minor.

"Good morning. This is Sally. What can I do for you?"

"Ja, I am Sven Hansen, and I vant to buy a house in your town. I come tomorrow to see you." Sally listened while I described the type of house I wanted.

"What time is good for you, Mr. Hansen?"

"I am Sven. I vill be in Mitchell by nine o'clock. I vill be eating breakfast. Ve can meet there. Vat is a good place?"

"Denny's is close to my office. Would that be okay with you?

"Ja. Food good there. I meet you."

I gathered everything I needed for the trip, two sets of Sven's disguises, one Spencer Morgan's disguise, and the Browning 308. I drove to the Great Falls Airport and flew the Cessna to Mitchell. I had arranged for Rubin

Durgan to service the plane and provide a small SUV to use for two days. Rubin knew Dutch from somewhere.

"Dutch said you would be here one day. He speaks for you, and that's enough for me. The car's mine. It's the white CRV in the front lot. Here's the key. I've paid for it three times over by renting it to pilots. When'll you be leaving?"

"Tomorrow about noon to two o'clock."

"I'll have the plane ready for you. I'll be around."

"Great, Rubin. How do you know Dutch?"

"I got out of the service after my stint at Malmstrom AFB in Great Falls. I worked on airplanes at Gore Hill. I wanted to be closer to my family in Huron, so I found a job here, and my dad bought this company for me. It's been a great life. I worked on Dutch's plane a time or two, and we became friends."

"Neat for me to meet people that know my close friends. See you tomorrow."

I drove the entire town, noting all the houses I saw that seemed to fit my needs. Hunters Pub was Rubin's recommendation for a beer and a sandwich. The *Rooster Tail*, IPA was on tap—a perfect choice to go with the Reuben sandwich.

On my way to the Best Western, I stopped at a Safeway and gathered all the real estate pamphlets I could find, a poor choice of night-time reading. I did not see Sally's name anywhere.

Disguised as Sven, I arrived early for breakfast. As I sipped my coffee, I realized I needed to change some of my habits. An astute observer might see through my false persona. My breakfast order was in the works when I saw Sally come in and say to the Hostess, "I am meeting someone."

"He's in the back booth on the right," nodding at me.

"Mr. Hansen. I'm Sally Minor. Nice to meet you. I rarely eat a full breakfast, just coffee and toast." She seemed extra nervous. She was trying hard on her first impression. "I have five houses set up to see and may get a call on a sixth one."

Was she trying to take advantage of a bumpkin? *This should be fun.*

"Ja. Ven I am done with my breakfast, ve go see dem. I am Sven, not Mr. Hansen. Ja. I am trying to make my English better."

I ate, and Sally fidgeted with her papers, making notes on a small electronic device. She was over-working, trying to look important.

I paid for my breakfast and Sally's toast and coffee.

Sally drove a new Ford Focus. It had a rental sticker near a rear taillight. I sat quietly in the passenger seat and listened to a practiced running commentary about Mitchell, pointing out the famous Corn Palace as we drove past.

The fourth house, one on my list, was perfect. It was the first one not listed by Sally's firm.

"Ja. I buy dis one. Needs paint." The house, all white, with an unfinished basement, sat near the back of the lot. The one-lane driveway on the southside of the property led to a small one-stall garage with a newer ten-by-ten shed attached. All painted white.

"Ja. I buy dis one. I pay fifty-thousand dollars cash. You can git someone to paint? Ja. Someone to paint edges darker green and the whole house smaller green."

"You mean almost white but yet green. Right?"

"Ja. Not much green, but not white. Ja."

"We call that light green! Let me call someone. You know, I said the house is listed for sixty-two thousand, so I don't know if the seller will accept fifty."

"If he says no, den we look at some more houses."

Acting important, she dialed a number. "Joel, It's Sally. Can you come to a house I am showing now and give me a quote to paint it?"

She smiled, "You can! That's great. See you in twenty minutes."

Turning back to me, she beamed, "Joel will be here in twenty or thirty minutes."

"Ja. Ve wait, I look at house again."

I went back into the house, while Sally stayed outside. Every time I looked out a window, she was on the phone. I studied the shed carefully and decided I could make it reasonably burglar-proof. The basement was fixable but not worth the effort.

Soon an older white pickup with a ladder rack on the top stopped at the curb.

The *Joel's Painting* magnetic sign on the door looked new on the noticeably dirty truck. I smiled at that.

Sally introduced Joel, and he quickly spread his color chart on Sally's briefcase and turned to the green section. He tried hard not to let me see the Sherman Williams name on the front.

I pointed to a light green shade and said, "Dis one."

"Sally chimed in, "Pastel green, a good choice." Then pointing to a darker shade, added, "How about this one for the trim?"

"Vhat is the color again?"

Joel answered. "Pastel green is the light color, and forest green is the dark color."

"Ja. Good colors. You tell me how much for scraping, washing and painting soon, and we decide today."

Turning to Sally, I said, "Ven vill the papers be ready?

"I'll take the offer to the seller this afternoon."

"Mrs. Minor," I interrupted, "I no pay more. Da roof is old, and da carpet is bad. Also, da painting. Fifty thousand. I need to know real soon. Not dis afternoon. I have place to go."

Sally dismissed Joel. "Thank you for coming out right away, Joel." She turned to me. "I will do my best."

She gave me her card and wrote my number on the back of another.

I could say my conscience bothered me about playing the easy mark, but I would be lying. I stayed at the house, and Sally drove off to present the offer. I liked how both neighboring houses were neatly kept.

I was sitting on the front steps when the neighbor with all the flowers in his yard came out and walked over to say hello.

"Morning, I'm Oliver. Are you going to buy this place?"

"Ja. Maybe. I am Sven. Your place looks good."

"I like my flowers and bushes. They are peaceful."

My phone interrupted us. "Sven. Ja."

"No, Ms. Minor, I no pay more. We go look. I wait for you." I closed my phone, but before the phone was in my pocket, it rang again.

"Sven. Ja….OK. Ja good. He says ya. Den, you come get me, and I go get money." Turning, I walked over to Oliver's yard with him. "Ja, your flowers are good. I am trying to have better English. Looks like I buy da house."

"Sven, you may want to call another painter and ask him to talk to me. *Specialty Painters* did my house a year ago. I am very pleased with their work."

"Ja. I do that."

"I'll call them for you, Sven. What colors do you want? Are you going to be here a few days?"

"No. Oliver, I go back dis day. Colors are forest green and pas something green."

"Pastel green, correct?"

"Ja, pastel green. I give you phone number, you yust call. I pay you to help." They swapped numbers.

"No paying, Sven, you just buy the beer next time you're here. I'll take care of you. It'll give me something to do. I'll give you my phone number."

"Ja. Den, danka." I answered just as Sally returned.

Sally picked me up, and we went to her office. We then went to a branch of U.S. Bank and Liz Durgan agreed to take care of me. She arranged the wire transfer and called a friend at a title company across the street. She walked with me and Sally to the office.

"Hi, Jean. My friend here needs your help. It's a cash sale, and I already have the money."

"Wonderful Liz. I'll arrange my schedule to help him now." Two hours later, I owned the house.

I drove back to my new house and gave Oliver a key. "I go find carpet place, so I can get new for da whole house."

"Sven, my granddaughter works for Carpet City. I'll call her for you and have her give you a price and some selections. We can have it done and ready for you when you come back."

"Ja, good. I think some light brown is my color. You very good neighbor. I am lucky I pick dis house."

I wanted to make it back to Cheyenne, Wyoming, today. I went to the motel, changed back to Del, and checked out. I then staked out Sally at her office. Finally, at about one, she made her way across town to a small cafe, The Rump Roast. What a name. The only empty stool was three away from Sally. I enjoyed a super club sandwich. Sally had no clue who I was. Neat.

I would only go to the Mitchell house disguised as Sven. When in Mitchell, from now on, Sven would be the pheasant hunter. Del would be the pilot.

I flew out of Mitchell at 1:30. I made good time without a headwind. At the airport in Wall, South Dakota, Del became Spencer, the cowboy. I was alone at the airport. Perhaps someone saw a different looking guy get in the Cessna, but I would be gone.

Making Cheyenne by nightfall would be an easy flight. I enjoyed the sounds of silence as I cruised at one hundred sixty knots at 6,500 feet. I disabled Sven's phone and threw the pieces out of the window. Sven would use his new iPhone when he called Sally in a day or two to get the painting quote. Lucky me. I did make Cheyenne for a late dinner.

I parked on the apron next to a beautiful light blue Beach Craft Bonanza G-36, a new six-passenger twin-engine plane. I admired it from, what I thought, was a safe distance. I did not walk around it or look inside. While I finished getting my travel bag and flight bag out of the Cessna, a short Hispanic man came out of the General Aviation Office. As I placed the chocks under the wheels, he walked purposefully toward me. I locked my plane as he arrived.

"Señor, is it something about my plane you need?"

"Nope. Just admiring and wishing I could afford one like it."

"Sí. It is a nice plane. We have not seen you here before."

His stance looked martial arts to me, and I noticed he packed a gun.

"I am a Montana guy that likes to hunt, fish, and fly. This is a nice airport and a good place to rest. I do not live here."

Without smiling, "Sí. We will watch for you and your plane." He quickly turned and left.

My internal buzz meter hummed softly. I always trust that feeling. Now I had another reason to be extra vigilant. For some reason, the occupants of the G-36 felt they needed to keep tabs on who came and went at this airport, especially if someone parked next to their plane. They had not seen me before. Now they would just watch. I would as well.

I decided that a barbeque ribs dinner and a good night's sleep would complete a fruitful day. Back to Bozeman tomorrow.

If the Bonanza is gone when I get to the airport in the morning, I will discretely check my plane for bugs. I will not go directly to Bozeman, if the plane is still there. Instead, I will stop in Billings and check my plane for bugs there.

I left for Bozeman at six a.m. The Bonanza was gone, and my bug meter did not beep during my pre-flight check. I could not shake the feeling that I would see that man again, and he would not be smiling then either.

CHAPTER 22

returned to Bozeman late morning after my trip to Mitchell. I enjoyed a double egg sandwich at Betty's, picked up my mail, then went to the main library to read the papers. The quartz was in my office safe. I removed it and took it to my credit union and secured it in my safe deposit box.

I am not a television watcher. I skip almost all professional sports after a coach for an NBA team was allegedly assaulted by a player, and that player was allowed to play later. Privileged.

Most mornings, I read the national news at the Bozeman Public Library. I am known as a regular. I scan for crime stories to keep up to date and plan trips to places I may wish to visit. Too often, much of the news is negative, like the top story in the *Tucson Star*. The trial in Tucson of Lorenzo Depsoto, accused of killing two policeman and a deputy district attorney, starts this week. Ironically, Vinny works for him.

This could be my first 'adventure'—time to be part of the criminal justice system, my way.

I will drive straight through to Tucson, take the Browning 308 and test Spencer Morgan's identity. I stopped at a Love's truck stop near Las Vegas on I-15 and changed from Del to Spencer, everything but the face and hair. Those additional changes were done at a rest stop south of Searchlight, Nevada. I can change the body shape in less than a minute and the face and hair in just over a minute.

Del left Bozeman driving his Ram truck, on his way to Tucson. Spencer Morgan arrived at a 55+ rental resort village west of Tucson, just north of the Ajo highway.

I rented a neat park model very close to the front entrance and the office. The Ajo road was a very busy highway, yet an easy commute to downtown Tucson. I acted like a retired person and played golf each day somewhere, but not at the resort. My truck was in the long-term lot at the airport. I was currently driving a white Chevy Cruz rental with Arizona plates.

I scouted the city center for a building to use for my first crime. I could not decide if I was excited, nervous or just scared. The Lorenzo trial will take place in the county courthouse.

I had preset the Browning for a 450-yard shot. I located two buildings that provided a clear view of the front of the courthouse. Neither had a locked front entrance. The 'Mercer Mercantile' was the best choice as the top two floors were unoccupied. The first floor housed a fabric shop, the second and third a legal firm, and the fourth an office for the Winthrop Foundation, but I never saw anyone there.

I sat in a nearby park with a copy of the *Star* and a cup of Starbucks dark roast coffee and observed the action at the Mercer building. Building traffic was light, except at lunchtime. I carried a small salesman kit, looking like I searched for a base of operation for a mail-order company for corporate advertising giveaways.

As Spencer, I entered the corner door and climbed the stairs to the top floor without seeing anyone. The roof door was unlocked. The door needed a hefty jerk to get it open. I would get some oil spray so I could mask the noise. With gloved hands, I opened it and stepped onto the roof. I studied the layout. The roof did not present a place to hide or stand out of the wind. A prone position for the shot would not work either. The shooter would be very visible.

On the sixth floor, I found the ideal spot—a window with a perfect view of courthouse steps. I went in and out of the building seven times without talking to or seeing anyone. I felt unnoticed. I arranged to make the shot from the window. I would shoot with minimum disturbance.

Now, it's a waiting game until the trial is over.

A walk past the courthouse was in order. I do not want any collateral damage. Picketing the trial, the sidewalk-judges paced in front of the court-house, sun up to sun down. They predicted Lorenzo was cooked. The cops finally caught him, and he would pay. A group of twenty to thirty picketers paced there every day with signs calling him many things; none were nice. By the fourth day, the protestors' count swelled, and his chances to get off or fry were at fifty-fifty odds.

On day five, the defense caught a detective in a lie. His testimony differed drastically from the police reports. The *Star* headlined the story, hinting the detective was bribed or threatened.

Lorenzo did not testify, nor did he deny the killings.

The papers and the facts depicted him as 100% guilty. Local research of his past by one reporter showed him to be a leader of the criminal element in Tucson, and linked him to every type of crime. He always found a way to escape the long arm of the law. Arrested eleven times, he had yet to face a guilty verdict. Witnesses changed their stories or just disappeared. It was always something. He did what he wished and lived the charmed life of a rich man without rules.

The jury started their deliberations on the sixth day of the trial. They were sequestered in a room for sixteen hours over two days. They reported to the judge on the second day that they were deadlocked and could not render a verdict. The judge declared a mistrial, ordered Lorenzo held until 9 a.m. the following morning, and fitted with an ankle monitor, while the prosecution regrouped, but everyone knew Lorenzo would be gone.

I was ready, waiting in the Mercer building at 6 a.m. I was nervous, apprehensive and maybe a little scared. I rehearsed my escape many times; breaking the gun down took thirty-seven seconds. Hurrying quietly down the stairs took fifty-three seconds. I could be in the car and driving away in under three minutes. I tested the elevator one of my first days at the building, but it was too slow and confining.

If all went as planned, I would be at the park model in eighteen to twenty minutes. The suppressed shot would be three floors above the people working below in air-conditioned offices. The sonic boom of the bullet would be largely contained in the room.

Standing next to the tripod-mounted gun, I waited. The range finder showed five hundred sixty-two yards. A beautiful, calm, sunny day with no wind and almost no humidity, greatly reduced the effect of bullet flight factors. The gun was set to the correct range, and I was confident in my numbers.

Lorenzo came out of the courthouse followed by his attorneys. He stopped on the fourth step and said to everyone within hearing distance, "The cops messed up again. What can I say?"

I opened the window, stood behind the rifle, carefully aimed, and squeezed the trigger. I immediately closed the window and watched. Lorenzo dropped like a stone and slipped down two more steps. *Looked dead to me, Number one Curt.* Packing as I had rehearsed, I reached the car in under three minutes. I saw no one and felt sure no one saw me. I heard the approaching sirens. Seeing the chaos reported on the evening news would be enough for me.

Nineteen minutes later, I as Spencer, sat on the small patio at the resort rental in the shade sipping a Lagunitas IPA. The TV was on, and I waited for a news flash. I had just opened the second beer when the first story aired.

"Big story—Breaking news."
"Drug lord dead."
"Rival gang—New leadership."

I checked all the local channels. No one commented that he was assassinated by persons unknown. Police were checking all leads. Attorneys offered, "No comment."

I wore gloves in the Mercer building and the car. After wiping the few items, I had touched in the park model, I left a fresh set of sheets and towels, stolen from a hotel maid's cart when I was in Denver. I loaded my few possessions in the car, including the bag of linens and drove back toward Tucson.

On the way to the airport to collect my truck, I threw my garbage into a dumpster by a convenience store and leaned the bag of linens behind an old motel four blocks away. I hoped a homeless person would find them. Molly would approve.

Following I-10, I traveled to Chandler and rented a room in a Best Western. Applebee's was the choice for dinner. Their quesadilla burger and a Lagunitas IPA filled the bill. While waiting for the food, I put my head in my hands and muttered to myself, *"What **have** I done?"*

Normally a fast eater, I took a long time to finish my meal. The first IPA draft got warm. The waitress asked if things were okay. I said nothing, just ordered a second beer. By the time the food and second beer were gone, I had come to grips with my 'crime.'

A bad man was dead. I shot him. I did not feel remorse. I did not realize the feeling would be so cold inside. Maybe his loss would make a small dent in the criminal drug world. If Lorenzo was vulnerable, then maybe some others would quit being criminals. Slim chance, but maybe. Maybe!

Back at the motel, I changed back to Del, then started a list of all that happened, leaving enough room to edit comments. I knew it had been too easy, or I was lucky. Either way, unless I planned better to handle glitches, I might be easily caught. Maybe the authorities would secretly cheer that my targets were out of the picture. I knew they preferred not to look incompetent, and would try to arrest the shooter. Law enforcement does not like vigilantes.

I drove back to Bozeman via I-15 from Las Vegas through Western Utah and I-80 in Western Wyoming. Stopping in Jackson Hole, I wanted to look at things I could now afford, but probably would still not buy. I arrived home early the next afternoon, visited the library, and read the *Tucson Arizona Daily Star*.

Every police department has some smart, dedicated people. The press release revealed the police had found the shooter's position by the bullet's trajectory. None of the interviews of the people from the Mercer building yielded any leads. They had not seen anyone, heard anyone, or heard the shot. The police asked the public to come forward.

The police would withhold some facts, but did they really care? Lorenzo was gone.

Five days after the trial ended, the detective who changed his testimony, was found by some college students. He had been shot multiple times and left under an old bridge. Changing his story did not save Lorenzo, so the detective was expendable. The police used the shooting to clamp down on known drug traffickers.

CHAPTER 23

Captain Ryerson led the morning briefing at the Tucson Police Department the day after Lorenzo was killed. "Good morning, what happened yesterday?"

No one answered. A hush fell over the room. In the back, one patrol officer shrugged, another stifled a snicker, and then the room filled with whispers. Comments rose from around the room that ranged from; good riddance, drug fight coming, to sleazeball is a sleazeball no more.

Halting the murmuring, he added, "All right. Simmer down. No one expected something like that. Lots of good shooters out there."

They may have thought it, but no one said assassination. They searched national records all night to see if there were similar crimes, but did not find matches. Ryerson thought his people were inwardly happy to have a bad man out of their watch. They still had plenty on their plates to occupy their time.

Ryerson decided he could assign one man and only one to follow the few leads they had. The Feds may feel differently. They have the money, resources, and manpower. They may have been using Lorenzo to find others in the drug business.

"Keep working your cases. We will do the necessary investigation out of homicide. If we get some leads, we'll follow them," Captain Ryerson said, closing the meeting.

Captain Smyth, the assistant Chief of Police, led the meeting at the Marana Police Department Headquarters the morning after Lorenzo was shot.

"Big day in Tucson yesterday. Our cities overlap and share a similar drug culture, but there's nothing for us to do. We stay with our current cases. I'll let you know if I hear anything from Ryerson. So far, they don't have any leads."

A tall, thin, stooped black man was sweeping the hallway out of sight of the officers in the meeting room. He heard every word. He knew more of the workings of the Marana Police Department than anyone.

CHAPTER 24

T he Monday after Lorenzo was shot, Supervisory Special Agent Tino Barcello held a meeting at the Tucson FBI Field Office. His field agents had lots of questions about the shooting. Barcello gave back lots of *I don't knows*. In return, he received lots of guesses.

No one said the words assassination or vigilantes. But it was just that. Barcello knew it. By whom, was the operative question. They would start a file and work it, but they had bigger fish to fry. The file held a place in a cabinet. It would get dusty.

Tino said, "Stay with what you got, doesn't look like anything for us."

Cliff started a file of his own, as he did on all high-profile-cases he suspected could become a Bureau problem someday. He decided to review the file at home. The shooting didn't happen on his turf, but he could assign one of his new agents to research all the ex-military shooters, militia shooters, and competition shooters. The more he thought about it, the more he believed he was onto a big project and better get on top of it. Not everyone can hit a target at over five hundred yards. He would have the agent get everything he could from the Tucson Police.

"Charlene, please find Billy Crocker and have him come to the office on Friday."

"I will. He's on gang watch detail, but I'll have him here Friday at eight."

"Morning Billy, got a job for you. Here is a list of the information we need on long-distance shooters, but feel free to add anything remotely affiliated. You have two weeks or so, but this is your secondary assignment. Your gang surveillance in Salt Lake City is primary," Cliff explained.

"This about the shooting in Tucson?"

"Yes, Billy, it is. I realize the FBI doesn't have a complete database on long-distance shooting, and you need experience creating a database. Those databases are often the key to solving any type of crime. They apparently do not have any leads on the Tucson shooter."

"Sir, are there any special tricks or protocols to getting information from the military?"

"Generally, not basic stuff, but there is a written protocol they like you to use. You can find those forms in our databases. We will arrange a meeting date in a week and discuss any other ideas you come up with."

"Anything else?"

"Yes, Billy. This conversation is between you and me for now. When the database is complete, you'll get the credit."

Cliff's desk phone chimed. It was the regional director.

After nodding to Billy, and watching him leave, Cliff picked up the phone as soon as the door was closed.

"Hello Buck." He listened for a few seconds, then answered. "No sir, I don't have any reason to see us involved as of now, but I've assigned Billy Crocker, a new agent, a chance to research and build a database on long-distance shooting. It will be good for him and for us. This could lead to an undercover assignment at a shooting facility. I will keep you informed."

CHAPTER 25

My Lincoln realtor found a cabin with acreage twelve miles from town. I could make the drive by late afternoon. I met him in Lambkins, a long-time local restaurant, and rode with him to the site. I liked it immediately. I asked him to arrange for a survey and an assessment of the timber. The location was accessible year-round with four-wheel drive, and the thirty-acre plot was bordered by Forest Service land on two sides. Another two private parcels adjoined my property. I asked the realtor for addresses and a contact person for each.

A paper company owned property behind the cabin and an unimproved private parcel was just across the one-lane road. The realtor took me back to town. We wrote up the offer on the cabin, and I asked him to pursue a purchase of the two private properties and to light a fire under the survey company.

With the current owner's permission, I returned to the cabin and parked my truck and new camper in the small clearing. I decided I needed to become more of a cook and prepare my own meals. Amy always took care of me, so I had limited experience.

The next morning at sun up, I walked around, staying in sight of the cabin. The at-home feeling was there.

The cabin had been vacant for some time, and I did not see much evidence of use anywhere. The realtor and I had walked over most of the thirty acres. The Blackfoot River was visible from the top of the small mountain behind the cabin. A creek with brook trout and cutthroat trout, swimming lazily in the shadows, meandered behind the woodshed. The creek was fifty feet from the cabin, and its soft sounds could be easily heard. No neighbors now. Thirty acres was a lot of property, and I intended to learn every inch of it. The cabin would take some work, but it is the kind of work I like. The forest smell was intoxicating.

Renovating the interior of the usable cabin would be a pleasant task. I wanted it to appear vacant from about thirty feet. I would conceal the electronics, knowing a close inspection would reveal the other improvements.

I drove back to Lincoln and met the realtor at Lambkins. The seller agreed to my offered price, and the papers would be at the title company by fax before 2 p.m. today. I arranged for my bank in Bozeman to wire the money. The seller allowed me to take possession immediately. I could start on repairs whenever I wished. The plat map from the realtor showed roughly where the boundaries were, so I could walk over the entire property.

The plan was to keep the outward appearance of the old cabin looking, unused, almost abandoned.

During my exploratory hike of the property, I used compass headings to find the boundaries. Nearing the northern edge of the property, I came across a mostly collapsed clapboard cabin. The old weathered wood will make shutters and a cover for the woodshed behind the cabin. I planned to thoroughly search the old collapsed cabin site one day, and remove all evidence of its existence. Deciding to take two or three of the loose boards with me, I leaned over a break in the side of the collapsed cabin, through a gap for what could have been a window, and found myself looking into a hole in the dirt floor. My flashlight did not illuminate a bottom. No way to see how deep it was. Deciding it might not be the only hole, I probed with a long, pointed stick. I did not want to end up at the bottom of a hole.

One of the employees for a survey company volunteered to come this Saturday and complete the metes and bounds for the cabin property, so he could fish the Blackfoot River. The realtor called the private parcel owners and received permission to complete a survey of those two properties, if I paid for it. The surveyor agreed to perform his magic on the other two private parcels.

Lucky for me, he did.

CHAPTER 26

The cabin was mine. This property, 12 miles west of Lincoln, has a new owner, Del Sanderson. The day the realtor told me everything was in order for the cabin, I loaded my camper with enough supplies to camp at the cabin for three days, and drove north from Bozeman to Lincoln. I was excited. This undertaking would surely give me purpose for many days.

The local library in Lincoln did not have heavy traffic, and they rarely asked me to sign in to use a computer. Passing through town on my way to the cabin, I checked the stories I currently followed. Nothing urgent.

I repaired the bunk and made the place livable. Two bear-proof lockers under the counter would be full of everything I could stuff into them to keep the mice and pack rats at bay.

I made sure I had room for a top-of-the line backpack with all the gear for a two-week solo hike into the Bob, whenever I had the opportunity to go to my hideaway. After I became intimately familiar with the entire property, I would try to identify a connection from this property to the main trail in the Bob.

On my second exploration of the thirty acres, I placed six cameras with remote access as near as possible to some game trails. The cameras recorded the data, so I could see if hunting from the cabin would be possible without motorized transport. I would also be able to catch unwanted human company.

I walked every inch of my thirty acres. I was happy here. I could feel Amy at my side as I strolled along. The smell of the forest, it's sounds and colors filled me with an appreciation of a world so much larger than each individual.

Since my camper was off the truck, I could use the Ram to clean up the collapsed cabin site. I did not find a second hole. But did mark the one hole with a small tamarack tree and a couple of big rocks. I called Dutch to tell him about the new place, and asked him to scout around for a used pickup and a used quad, and the right mechanic to make both run like new. I wanted the outside of the truck to always look old, so I would fit in around Lincoln. Everything else would be in top condition. I needed the truck to be reliable. I drove the one hundred miles to Great Falls to visit him.

Greeting me with his customary bear hug, he smiled.

"Hello Del. You found your cabin, that's great. I can't wait to see it. After you called, I went looking and found a five-year-old dark maroon Chevy 4X4 with one bench seat. It would be an unnoticeable rig like you asked for. Just leave the spare tire and rusty chains and other sorts of usable junk in the back, and maybe an old used tarp and a couple of motor oil containers on the passenger seat, and you will look the part up there."

A Christmas tree air freshener hung from the mirror. I would carefully make the plates look old. I would drive over them first, then splash on some mud after attaching them to the truck. Dutch sold me his old quad, because he and his son had their eyes on a new one.

Again, three weeks for the titles.

In Great Falls and at Gore Hill airport, I used my real identity, Del Sanderson. The same was true for Lincoln. I would buy my hunting tags there, and make it a point to meet the local game warden.

It is a nice drive to Lincoln to eat and mingle. The Scenic 12-mile drive to Lincoln winds along the Blackfoot River. I imagined fishing every inch. Enjoying a Reuben sandwich with huckleberry pie and ice cream, made my day.

After my meal, I drove to the local airport. I wanted to see if it would work to land there on my trips to drop supplies at 'Curtis Castle' and put my drop canisters on the wheel struts instead of opening the door in flight and pushing them out as I have been.

There was a hangar for sale. *The Speckled Prospector would soon own it.* I would lease it from the corporation—a much better place for the plane and all my storage needs. The cabin had neither electricity nor running water. The hangar had both. I could relocate all of the stuff from the Evergreen storage unit to the hangar as soon as title was transferred.

The Monture Creek Trailhead provided easier access to the Danaher camp in the Bob and it was much closer to Lincoln and Bozeman.

I called the realtor and asked him to look into buying the hangar. He agreed to do that, then told me the private parcel owner was interested in selling his acreage next to my cabin and agreed to come up with a price. I told him to offer two hundred an acre less than the cabin parcel price. The paper company would entertain an offer, but wanted to keep the logging rights. I told the realtor to offer the same price as the other parcel, but get the logging rights worded to ensure that I had to give written approval to any action or trespass, and the logging rights were to expire after three years. I had no intention of logging any of the properties. This will get the paper company out of my hair.

Owning the hangar and how to personalize it spun around in my mind. Electrical power was available and a new ceiling heater would make the hangar comfortable. I would build a small room in one back corner with lights and baseboard heat, a half bath and shower, and set up remote control to operate all the gadgets and the security system. So much to do.

I am keeping my promise to Amy. I miss her every day. I know she would like this cabin.

I arranged for a Missoula contractor to make the hangar floor concrete instead of dirt, repair the doors and reset the rails. The new locks would be electronic and failsafe in the locked position, controlled remotely. The contractor would also add inside shutters and a burglar-proof steel grid for the only window. The twelve-by-twelve room would be insulated and sheeted with plywood, for extra security.

I always wore old jeans, a flannel shirt, a battered Dallas Cowboy cap, and white hair (long over the ears), when showing myself around Lincoln. My other three identities would never be seen here.

I never turned onto the cabin road if a vehicle followed behind me. Instead, I went past, U-turned, and came back. The truck was always parked up my road and behind the cabin. Then I would walk back and obscure the tracks, by dragging a fir branch over them. It probably would not fool anyone, but it made me feel better.

I am not trying to hide in Lincoln. I am going to be here often, so want to fit in. I will buy and eat locally whenever I can. I want to make it impossible for anyone to know about the other identities, and cover up my trips to the Bob and Curtis Castle. The locals will find out the Lincoln cabin had a new owner and was being used. Just a hunting cabin. My one-lane trail will be posted as a dead-end and private. Each year I will put up new no-hunting or trespassing signs.

I am quite sure the US Forest Service has ways to know who uses the Bob and a fairly good idea where users camped, fished and hunted. I was also sure they would learn that I was a new neighbor.

A truck parked too long or too often at a trail head into US Forest Service property, the same tent at the same location, and lots of other clues would stir their interest. License plates were easy to check.

Dutch and his mechanic moved the hood opener on the old truck to inside the cab. He and his son would drive it to Lincoln. The realtor would show Dutch where to park it behind the buildings. I wondered how much the realtor was telling the locals. I doubt there are any secrets around this little burg.

If someone did steal the truck or the battery while it was parked at the Monture Trailhead, it would be inconvenient for me. A twenty-mile hike to the highway on a good gravel road was doable, instead of sitting at the trail head waiting for someone to come along. In Montana, almost everyone stops to help.

I would risk leaving it at the Monture Creek Trailhead next time I went into the Bob. But I would need to tell Dave about my changes.

CHAPTER 27

The route from Great Falls to Helena along the Missouri River covered 90 miles of spectacular beauty. There were many geological changes, including an extinct caldera. Fishing can be the best in all of Montana. The *"Gates of the Mountains"* is a double turn of the Missouri River that looks like the mountains open for you to travel through, then close after you have passed. The guided tour boat, river trip, passing both ways, downstream and upstream, through those gates was something everyone should experience.

Arriving in Helena, I proceeded directly to Frederick's office.

He recognized me from fifteen feet away. He couldn't talk and stuttered a weak, "How can I help you?"

I let him fidget a short time.

"Two things. First, I had the gold checked by another source, but you know that, and while it is very good quality, it would not be worth the time or money to separate. Second, the find is small, and I searched everywhere within one hundred yards of the rocks I found and did not find any more quartz."

Angrily I added, "DO NOT FOLLOW ME ANYMORE, do you understand?"

He started to deny it, but nodded instead. I leaned on the dusty counter and whispered, "Say it. Nodding is not good enough."

"I will not follow you."

"Not good enough! I do not want you or anyone you could enlist to help following me! Clear?"

"Yes, sir. You have my word."

"You know, Fred, I hope you are truthful with me."

Leaving him standing and glaring at me was quite satisfying.

I walked across the street to a small pastry shop. I took my time selecting a cinnamon swirl and watched Fred's office. He emerged, hurriedly walking to his little red Subaru, and drove off.

"I must watch him and his brother. They are going to cause me trouble," I mumbled.

"What'd you say? I didn't catch your choice," the clerk asked.

"Sorry, Miss. I was thinking out loud. A bad habit I have. I will take two cinnamon swirls." At a Starbucks, I added a Pikes Grande coffee, sipped the coffee and ate my sugar bombs, then cruised I-90 to Bozeman.

The Noses are trouble, not to be trusted. I remembered something my dad told me after a kid I thought was a friend stole from me. "If you trust someone, tell them. Otherwise, do not trust them." I needed to tell Cliff, Dutch, Dave, and Jack that I trusted them. I am sure there will be others to say those words to.

I talked to myself the whole way. I needed to practice my disguises including voices, until I can make the transformation in a few minutes. It was time to find a top-of-the-line bug detector. It is also time to develop an escape plan from each hideaway and the Bozeman house. I need a small place in Arizona. A Palm Creek Resort rental in Casa Grande will work until I find a spot I like.

Maybe I should do a practice trip by having Colbert leave the country.

CHAPTER 28

C liff hit the intercom button on his phone. "Charlene, please see if you can locate Billy, and have him meet me for lunch at the Subway on 32nd street." He liked to meet there because of the layout and the windows—easy to watch vehicle and foot traffic.

Fifteen minutes later, Charlene buzzed back, "He's on his way."

"Thanks."

Billy had been to meets there before and knew which spot Cliff liked and why.

He tried to be extra early, so he could polish his information. Cliff liked to be able to read a paper version of documentation, not electronic versions. Cliff was a computer user but paper in his hand was his preferred way to deal with reports. Billy prepared three sections: shooters, guns, and shooting ranges. He planned to ask if he could learn to be a long-range shooter. He could see that if he were on top of things, he might have a niche that would allow him to be an expert in a specialized area.

"Morning, Cliff."

"Morning, Billy. Brought your work with you, I see."

"You bet! I came early to finish the narrative for closing each section. I wanted the data to match the separate topics.

"The long-range (LR) shooter report was organized by ex-military, militia members, civilians, and owners of ranges that specialized in long-range. I suspect each range will reveal a previously unknown shooter or two."

Cliff raised his right hand. Billy stopped talking. Everyone knew when Cliff raised his hand, he wanted the floor. "I'll read the report from cover to cover when it's finished."

"I made some small changes this morning and could adapt them this afternoon and give you the rough draft version by tomorrow at 0800."

"Perfect." After taking a bite of his meatball sub and taking a swig of Sprite, he continued.

"How is the gang surveillance going?"

"Good enough. We have noticed some newer members lately and are making profiles of each. Half of the newbies do not have ties to our area. It could mean they are having trouble getting recruits locally or something is brewing. Too soon to tell. Otherwise, just the same petty stuff. No arrests in over a month. My team thinks they may have spotted the surveillance, so we need to change some things. We have some ideas for the Monday team and staff meeting."

"Billy, I'll study your report and make my notations. We'll meet here Thursday at about 10 a.m. I have some options I am considering." Cliff stood, picked up his half-eaten sandwich and Sprite and left first. "See you Thursday."

Billy watched Cliff walk back the way he came. "Hmm. He didn't need to come here for this meeting. He could have just called and told me to have the report by tomorrow and inform him of Thursday's meet. Wonder why?" he mumbled to himself.

Billy used all his spare time to work on the long-range shooter database. Most days while on gang watch duty at one of the many rotated watching sites, he was on his laptop working the data. Watching was boring, working on his assignment was not. He effectively combined both jobs.

"There seems to be lots of ranges that accommodate long-range shooting," Billy said aloud to himself. So far, he had isolated six ranges, because they seemed too far off the grid and restricted who could shoot at their range. He kept them separate and decided he would get Cliff's permission to query the local FBI office nearest each range.

One fact really stood out to him. There were a lot of trained LR shooters. He was sure there were many unknown ones as well.

Salt Lake City had gangs like most larger U.S. cities. Generally, however, they stayed under the radar—so far, no gang war or turf dispute. *Boring assignment.* Billy thought often about finding a way to approach Cliff so he could learn LR shooting. He had a list of the six closest ranges to Salt Lake.

His research revealed a list of reported stolen long-range guns. There had to be others unreported. The local FBI knew of three such guns. One in

Spokane, Washington; one in Santa Fe, New Mexico; and one in Barstow, California. All involved multiple guns. All guns were high quality and expensive. So far, none had been used in criminal activity. Maybe there were enough bullet pieces from the Tucson shooting to work with, but they would need the gun to complete a match.

Billy started many lists in five separate three-ring note binders: things to ask; things to research; things to learn; people to learn from.

He didn't feel ready to make a presentation to Cliff, but he was close.

Cliff had Charlene call Billy to ask him to bring his report to the office Thursday morning and leave it with her. He also canceled the Thursday meeting.

Billy left his report with Charlene and returned to his shift watching the gangs. He knew something was up. Cliff liked talking directly to his agents.

Cliff copied Billy's report. He didn't want anyone else to know about it. He read it thoroughly and made numerous notes and two suggestions for more research. Then he copied it again. When in its final draft, this report was going to get Billy a gold star and Cliff a nice personnel file letter.

"Charlene, ask Billy to be at the Subway Monday at 9:30." The following Monday, Billy was at Subway working on his breakfast sandwich when Cliff arrived. Cliff ordered a similar meal and brought his coffee to the table. His meal was delivered.

"Good work, Billy. I can see you have been busy. This will be the beginning of a powerful database. I'll try to get you involved with the techies when they start building it."

"It has been a nice diversion from the gang stuff," Billy smiled.

"Do you like the gang duty?"

Billy just looked out the window.

"Shitty question. Would you like to try something else for a while?"

Billy shifted in his seat and tried not to look too eager or too reserved. The truth was he felt both. He knew some bureau assignments could be career killers, but he'd tired of the gang stuff.

"Sure," he said.

"There's a good reason why I was a little late this morning." He paused before continuing. "Getting your new assignment approved wasn't a slam dunk. Some higher-ups questioned whether you were ready or the right man for the job."

Cliff always put his left hand over his eyes and rubbed softly down to his chin when he was about to start the big story. He did that now.

"The big story is, we are thinking about some of the names on your shooter list. A bunch of them have criminal backgrounds. A range in Montana had hits on both criminal and militia names, some very bad people. You are very new, and these people know what law enforcement personnel look like, act like, and talk like. They have their own vocabulary. They are not easily fooled. We all started somewhere, and we all made mistakes.

"The perpetrators we've identified are capable of killing to protect their lifestyle.

"On your stolen gun list, three sets of good guns and equipment were stolen from bad people. Russians lost the Spokane guns, and some Ukrainians lost the Santa Fe guns. The other guns have Muslim ties. All groups will kill to get their stuff back.

"If you choose to do this undercover assignment as a new shooter, you will be relocated to Bozeman, Montana and will enroll in a shooting class at the Manhattan range. We know the owner. And, a good friend of mine shoots there, Del Sanderson. You'll like him.

"Here is a list of things you must do before the relocation date. Proof of their completion will be required. Come to my office at 8:30 tomorrow morning, and let us know. Bring your list of questions as we know you will have them. Saying *no* will not reflect negatively on you in any way. Most who are in on this don't believe you are ready."

Cliff stood. "See you in the morning." Then walked out the door.

Billy told Cliff the next morning that he wanted to do it.

"Okay, Billy. I'll get everything in motion. You start completing the items on your list, and we'll meet in a week to complete your transfer. You'll still be officially part of this office and report directly to me. The Montana agents will know you, but only function as an emergency backup."

CHAPTER 29

The next morning at 4 a.m., Billy called his dad in New Jersey. Ben Crocker, a retired Newark Homicide Detective, had more than thirty-five years in the trenches. He'd tried talking Billy out of applying at the FBI.

"Morning, Dad. Nothing is wrong, but I need your guidance."

"Okay, I'll listen." He was as abrupt as always.

Billy related most of the assignment on long-range shooting and every word of Cliff's comments.

"Tough task. Undercover assignments are dangerous work. You are among people who don't trust each other and are more than wary of strangers. Your New Jersey accent will stand out like a sore thumb. They'll know you ain't local." Pausing, Ben added, "Your mom will worry more."

"I need to make my own way. I trust Cliff." Realizing he had raised his voice, he calmed things down. "He knows I'm new, but he must believe it's workable, or he wouldn't risk it. To Cliff, the agent comes first."

"Keep me posted, Son," and Ben hung up.

"I will, Dad. Thanks," Billy said to the dial tone.

Billy walked down to Cliff's office and picked up a large folder from Charlene. A copy of his list was the top item. All of his questions had a brief answer. His undercover identity would be ready Friday. The Montana field office in Billings would provide his pickup and his rifle. He was to live in Bozeman, find a part time job and begin his training under Rick.

"Charlene, does Cliff know my dad is a retired cop?"

"Yes, he does."

"Do you think I need to tell him Dad doesn't approve?"

"Yes, Billy, I do think Cliff needs to know that."

"Thank you, Charlene."

"Anytime, Billy."

Charlene was almost sixty and had worked for the Bureau for thirty-one years, and with Cliff for sixteen of those. The empathy in her eyes told him, she knew heartache when she saw it. She motioned for Billy to wait for Cliff in one of the conference rooms to the left of her desk.

🌲🌲🌲

When Cliff came back to the office, she stopped him. "Billy's Dad doesn't approve of the undercover assignment. You might want to study options to answer him when he tells you," she whispered.

"What would I do without you?"

"You better start planning. I only have four years until retirement."

They both smiled. They had been down this road many times. "Let's send a letter to the personnel director, and notify him to ensure we will have your replacement at least a year before you leave."

"You mean that, Cliff? I can't believe it. Don't you think it's way too early?"

"I can't replace you, and you know it. If I don't get the Regional top position, I will retire only two years after you. If I do get it, I will need two people to do what you do. I would be authorized an assistant office person. I'll try to talk you into staying."

She just looked him in the eye. "Too far away to consider it."

Billy sat alone in one of the conference rooms, muttering to himself. "So much to learn. Just calm down, and let things work out. New Jersey to Montana, WOW!"

The conversation with his dad bothered him a lot. The abrupt hang-up meant he didn't approve.

Tony Marcello, his undercover name, would make Cliff feel like he picked the right man for this undercover assignment.

"Got a minute Billy?" asked Cliff pushing the door open wider?

"Yes, Sir, I'm just sitting here wondering if I'm doing the right thing, and finding I have more questions than answers."

"Exactly as you should be doing. Have you talked to your parents yet? Your dad is a retired policeman, right?"

"Yes, he is. He didn't want me joining the FBI and does not think I should do this.

"You can opt-out still. Everyone would understand."

"No, Cliff. I need to make own my way. I'm twenty-five years old. I'm going to do my best. All new and exciting, right?"

Cliff just looked at Billy, smiled, and said, "Do your best and keep the mistakes small. You leave a week from Tuesday."

CHAPTER 30

At the Manhattan long-range shooting club, I wanted to discuss the process I should use to calculate some longer shots. Rick was in his office. I knocked on his door.

"Rick, I have some questions. You have a minute?"

"Come in Del, what's up?"

"Well, first, you do not have to answer this one if you would rather not, but I was wondering how many regulars you have that come here to shoot?"

"I have eleven who hold the same status you worked under before you moved here that make three or four trips a year to my range. I have a militia that pays for six memberships, so I let them shoot if no more than six of their group come at any time. I have about forty in a pistol club, maybe fifteen singles, and a group of seven that look like ex-cons. I don't know what their status is—I don't know if any are on parole. I believe Jim seems to be part of the group, but separate. So far, no trouble, but they don't shoot much. I got a new guy today. He signed up for the whole school. He said he has never fired a rifle, just handguns. I have many hunters that come and sight in their guns before the big game season starts. Why do you want to know?"

"I am not here a lot, so I know I miss many of the shooters. I just noticed the militia group and the rough group are often here when I come. Just curious, I guess."

"I only worry about the rough group because their apparent leader, Bully, just makes my skin crawl. I have learned to trust that feeling," Rick said.

"Thanks. I have time to shoot for about an hour. I better get with it. I will review my process for making thousand-yard shots before I leave today."

"I'll be here," answered Rick.

I practiced with both of my guns. The risk is there, but thousands of rounds are imbedded in the embankment behind the targets.

The Browning 308 was effective to about five hundred yards. Six of seven shots were within five inches of the bullseye on a windy day. The Creedmore 243 scored five shots out of six at seven hundred fifty yards. The miss was nine inches. Unacceptable.

Rick, the owner and resident instructor, with a sniper background, offered little information about his past. He would change the subject if anyone asked. He shoots in competitions and has a championship or two. He was watching.

"Good scores today, Del. With this wind, it would be tough to do better. I went over your numbers and suggest you fine-tune your numbers when adjusting for wind."

"Okay thanks. Rick, I would buy another gun if it was tournament quality. Maybe a 300 Win-mag. If you hear of anything, let me know."

"I think Jim said last week he wanted to sell his. I'll ask for you without pointing you out."

I joined a late afternoon collection of shooters that were enjoying a break and telling tales of shooting and hunting. Some stories might even be true. I noticed everyone used first names only, and no one said where they were from. It was too big of a group to trust. I decided to keep my interactions on the casual side. More than one looked to be prison material, evidenced by the amateur looking tattoos. Some of them might be ex-cons, but they could be just regular people.

Rick walked over, stopped between the two groups of shooters, and spoke loud enough for all to hear, "Guys, if any of you want to buy or sell any long-range guns, let me know. I could have a lead for you."

A beefy guy, about five-ten with a thick full black beard to go with his shoulder-length unruly black hair, piped up. "Maybe, I would buy. I got a buddy who wants to shoot."

The new guy spoke next, "I might want a better one, so what kind and how much?"

I decided to check into this as well. "I am Del. I have a friend who saw me bring down a nice mule deer at five hundred yards, so he asked me to look for a long-range rifle like I have."

The new guy sounded a little like a New Jersey lad. He seemed friendly but did more listening than talking. He looked to be a fit young man about six foot one. Black curly hair framed a square face, with dark bushy eyebrows, and smiling blue eyes. His cheeks were a little rosy.

A small thin man, about forty or so, listened and said, "I'm Jim. I need to sell both my guns. I can't afford to keep them. I need the money. I got a sheet with the specs in the truck. If you're a serious buyer, we can talk." After a short version of the information, he added, "I live near Three Forks. We could arrange to meet to see if I can get a fair price."

"Call me Tony," the Jersey boy said. "I can do a meet."

I did not answer at first. Then I said, "I have two good ones, but I hope to find my friend his own gun. I do not wish to sell mine. We hunt together." I hoped my story sounded real enough.

Jim paused too long.

I bailed him out. "We could meet at IHOP Saturday in Bozeman for breakfast at say nine thirty, if that would fit your timeline."

Jim answered quickly, "I'll be there."

"I'll be there," Tony added.

I looked over at mister beard. "You coming Mr. aaaaahhhhh?" I waited for an answer.

"Dicky. I don't think so... I'll ask my buddy first, then see you here, Jim."

"Three of us, so Tony can buy breakfast."

"Why me?"

"You are cutest," Del said with a brief laugh.

Even Dicky laughed. At least one gold tooth showed.

Then, so all could hear, I said, "Guess I will put my guns away."

The Jersey guy asked us to call him Tony. He did not say his name was Tony. He seemed nervous, yet friendly. I did not think he worked at shooting, but he was new. There was something off about the kid. I viewed him with skepticism but gave him a pass—for now.

I returned to the range, gathered up about half of my gear, and made a trip to my white Ram. I noted who drove what, wrote down some plate numbers after each trip, and watched how they took care of their guns. I could not explain why, not even to myself. I did not dare to try taking pictures with my phone and be observed taking those pictures.

Tony's rig was a small white Nissan with Montana plates. He just put his gun in the passenger side and drove away.

Jim stood next to his ten-year-old, dented, hand-painted, dark blue, single-seat Toyota pickup watching Tony intently. Walking toward him, I spoke softly. "I do not know Dicky, but Tony is just too interested in you, it seems to me. How about we meet at the Love's truck stop at the Manhattan exit at 7:30 Friday?"

Jim offered a small wry smile. "Dicky is one of Bully's friends. I like the early meet. Do I have to worry about you?"

"Not in any way. Is Bully, the big beefy guy?"

"Yeah."

"See you Friday." I turned and walked away.

I sat waiting at the truck stop, sipping my coffee, until Jim came in at seven. He did not see me at first glance, but when he did, I noticed a small change in his posture and face—surprise and then a softness I would not have expected.

He took his time getting his coffee, then came to the booth and sat facing me.

"I should have guessed you would be here early to get the lay of the land. You were quick to lay the dodge on Tony." He paused to decide how much to say. Finally, "How long you been shooting LR?"

"I bought my first gun in 1995 and would come here and shoot four or five times a year. Even learned to hit some at 1000 yards," I answered.

"Why do you want my guns?"

"Your equipment is very good, especially the optics. You shoot some good scores and treat your guns with respect. I like the challenges this hobby affords, but I am not obsessed with shooting. I sense you would not sell to just anyone."

"You go by Del, right?"

I nodded, watching him.

"No, I don't want to sell, but I have no options. I'll bet everyone wonders how a poor man like me could afford to shoot here and where I got my guns."

"You are probably right about both, Jim. I have had those thoughts," I commented as I leaned back from the table. Jim needed a shower.

"I got them in Spokane from some Russian guys. I think they might've been criminals. Stealing from criminals ain't a crime." A smile spread slowly across his lips as if remembering.

I took a sip of my coffee and watched him over the rim of my mug. I carefully returned my cup to the table. "They are stolen?" I stated more as a fact than a question. Jim is not very bright. I knew I should not be part of this. "Are you even supposed to have guns?"

"I been in jail. Del, but I don't have a no gun clause in my release papers. No one saw me. It was a long way from here. No one knows where I live. I tried to pawn one in Butte, but they wouldn't take it. I need the money. I didn't bring the guns today, but could get them in an hour or so. I have pictures you can have now of all three. I know I said two, but you know hedging." Taking a folded paper from his shirt pocket and handing it to me, he continued, "Here is a list of all the specs so you can check what you want. Then we can meet and make a deal. I need the money by the Fourth of July, no later."

Picking up the pictures and the specs, I looked him in the eye. "I will have to think about if I should buy."

"Del, when you suggested this separate meet, I decided I would tell you about the guns, but not anyone else. I need the money."

Changing the subject, I said. "At the club the other day, I noticed some short conversations between shooters, but never with Tony or myself. You worried about me?"

Jim flustered, then caught himself. "Yeah, we talked. You and Tony are new shooters here and have no visible 'tats'! You both seem more educated than most here. Couple of the guys ain't perfect, you understand, and they don't like to be watched. You are tight with Rick. The new guy, Tony, doesn't look the part."

Pausing, he added, "We noticed you don't touch anything but your own stuff, and you pick up your brass. You and your truck are almost too plain."

"Jim, I came here alone. Just about the guns. I meant what I said at the club. You do not have to worry about me. Tony, I need to learn more about. He is new, not green. He just does not take great care of his guns, nor does he seem to fit the part of a shooter trying to get better, like you said."

"You are spot on about both Del, now what?"

"I think," pausing as two truckers walked by, "I will show up at IHOP Saturday, wait with Tony until ten thirty, and you skip the meeting. There is a convenience store across the street with parking on the side. You be there by nine and watch for Tony's truck. I do not think he suspects we have noticed his interest. You can leave any time you want using the alley and Cedar Street to avoid a visual from IHOP.

"I expect Tony to be there and on time.

"I will return to the truck stop Tuesday next week at ten a.m., and we will go from there."

Jim stood up, "I'll be around. If there are any problems or delays, I'll see you on Tuesday, same as today. See you at the range." He walked away, trying to hold his head up.

I arrived at IHOP early and parked by the door. Jim came out of the convenience store, nodded twice, and got in his truck. He saw Tony show up at nine fifteen, then drove away. Tony saw me, walked over, and said, "Where's the little guy?"

"Still waiting," I answered as I pointed to the other chair. "Want some coffee?"

"Sure. Are we having breakfast too? I'm hungry." He took the pot and poured a cup, and added some sugar. "I thought he wanted to sell some guns."

We ordered breakfast, talked about shooting and waited another thirty minutes. The waitress picked up the dishes, and Tony gave her his card.

He trudged over to the window. "Guess he isn't coming. Wonder why?"

I shrugged, "We will find out at the club. I have some errands to run. Time to hustle along. Coffee is on me next time."

"Coffee *and* breakfast. See you later." He waved as he walked out to his little pickup.

Three weeks ago, when Tony drove his five-year-old pickup from Billings to Bozeman, He thought about his journey from New Jersey to Montana.

He completed his FBI training in the top third of the class in everything except firearms. He qualified but most of the trainees were better. He was not a good shot.

He hoped joining the range at Manhattan would change that shortcoming. When Tony walked into Rick's office to sign up, he lied about shooting rifles. He was better with them than hand guns.

Tony was certain Rick saw through his attempt to be casual about joining. He worked harder trying to fit in than learning to shoot long-distance.

He knew he was not to talk to his dad about his work, but his dad was a thirty-five-year law enforcement veteran. That gruff man was a fountain of knowledge and wisdom. Cliff and Charlene knew and hadn't chastised him.

Nearing my truck my little bug sweeper showed a hit. Someone left me a present I wasn't supposed to find. I drove to Home Depot, parked between two dirty trucks and behind a motor home. Making a show of getting something out of the back seat, I caught Tony driving by. I found the bug under the rear bumper. I quickly removed the simple magnetic device and passed it to a new owner. I placed it on the motor home with the Alberta, Canada license plate.

Tony would find out soon enough that he goofed. I followed the motor home to see if Tony was the culprit. Sure, enough, he lagged two vehicles behind. Tony probably wondered where my truck was, but he followed the motorhome until he reached an exit.

When my exit came into view, I maneuvered alongside the motor home making certain Tony didn't see me. At the last second, I veered onto and sped up the ramp out of sight. I could hear the gravel pinging my truck's undercarriage as I slid to a stop on the overpass. From my vantage point, I watched them both emerge from under the freeway bridge. I counted ten seconds, re-entered the highway, and followed. Forty-five miles later, the motor home pulled into a rest stop. The woman exited the passenger side carrying a small dog. Attaching the leash, she started to the pet walking area.

Tony parked three spaces away from the motor home, searching all around for my white Ram. He picked up binoculars and seemed to watch the woman and her dog. I turned off my ignition and rolled silently into the parking space next to Tony.

I was both annoyed and amused when I climbed out of my rig, walked to his passenger-side window and rapped on the glass. He dropped the binoculars and scrambled. The look on his face was priceless. He lowered the window.

"Why?"

"I...I don't know what you mean."

I strolled to the motor home, retrieved his bug, and wiped it with a handkerchief. "Yours. Why?"

I dropped it into his hand through the open window. "No more bullshit. You are no shooter. You are not even a good sneak. You put the locator on my rig, and I need to know why."

"We are watching you."

I interrupted, "Who is we? And why me?"

"FBI."

"Show me."

Reluctantly, he took out his ID. I studied it carefully and noted it was from the same office as Cliff's and that his name was William Brent Crocker. I decided to act madder than I really was.

"Well, Tony, or William or whatever your name is, you answered the who, now why me?" I smirked and glared at him.

The kid took a deep breath. Clearly, he didn't want to tell, but his open expression convinced me it was not because I was suspected of a crime.

"Now why?"

"Cliff told me you were a shooter at the range. He assigned me to look after you.

He didn't say why, but told me to watch your back," he finally said.

"Try again. I do not believe Cliff would approve of you having your regular ID in your car while working undercover. You are working undercover, aren't you?" I sounded as angry as I knew how.

The kid was lost. His eyes shifted from side to side as if he searched for a reply.

"Look," I said. "You must be new and have a lot to learn. I am pissed that Cliff is still meddling. You get your stupid ass on the road and tell Cliff to call. Better yet, have him visit me at my house. He needs to come alone and sterile. Got that?"

"Cliff said I would need to be on my toes. He was right. He told me I could show you my creds with my real name. What are you going to tell him?" Billy swallowed hard. His life and career might be in my hands.

"Just the facts, Tony, just the facts." I watched as Billy called Cliff and left a message. After I turned and left, I called Cliff and left a message. Tony was sure he would be done and sent to Alaska.

Driving back to my house, I realized that Jim could have noticed Tony place the bug under my bumper. Not good for undercover Tony. It could help me, I think, as Jim might tell me stuff. Tony would need a friend. I intended to work at being that friend.

The coming conversation with Cliff will be interesting. Jim could become an ally if I do things right. But I knew I did not want any part of those stolen guns. I also knew I needed to tell Rick about those firearms.

CHAPTER 31

I wondered if, after Tony called and left a message for Cliff, he went to a small local bar, ordered a draft of beer, put his head in his hands, and shed a couple of tears. I felt a little sorry for him, but the young buck had to learn sometime.

Back at my rental house, I made sure everything was regular.

Somehow, I was positive Cliff would show up and not call first. I made some woodworking, hunting, and computer magazines visible. Those were all new as I bought them on the way back from the rest stop after my conversation with Tony. I made them look used, highlighting an item or two, and dog-earing a page in each. Also visible were a Sudoku book and a crossword book. I completed some in each and placed them next to the TV schedule on a small stand next to my favorite recliner.

Beside the crossword book, I added two John Sanford novels, and my favorite book, *One Man's Wilderness, by Sam Kieth.* It is the story of Richard Proeneke. He built his cabin from scratch and lived alone next to a lake in Alaska for more than a year. I fantasized that I could still do that too, somewhere.

My abode would appear sterile. Cliff would notice that. He would have to re-establish the level of trust we were used to. The ball was in his court.

Cliff rang the doorbell late afternoon Friday. A day and a half after Tony's call, giving me more time to do more puzzles and make my house look lived in.

I invited him in and offered him a beer.

He took the beer but did not smile as I checked him with my sweeper. Together we went out to the patio. Cliff took the back corner chair. My friend was very fit and does not look his age. At about five eleven, and 215 chiseled pounds, he had close-cropped brown hair with graying temples and piercing brown eyes. His walk was smooth, hinting at his martial arts training. He had a noticeable scar over his left eye and the broken nose look. He was always tanned. His two children were successfully on their own—his wife, like mine, a victim of cancer.

We have shared much. His prompt arrival at my house told me he was ready to explain.

"Del, we go way back. I need to fill you in on a few things. I placed my application for the Salt Lake City Field Office Director's position. I sense I am the frontrunner, but there are other qualified applications. If I am selected, I plan to work at least four more years at a bare minimum. I am one of the best at what I do.

"Your Tony, my Billy, is just out of the Academy. This was his first real assignment. Thank you for teaching him a lesson. Maybe he can see how easily and close he came to danger. I knew you practiced at Rick's range, and I told Billy to watch out for you. I was right to do so. There are real scumbags at your range. He's told me about them. Two of the shooters are on our radar. Jim Nelson is the little skinny guy trying to sell some guns. He is a person of interest, but is not currently on parole. Those guns are stolen property from a Russian residence in Spokane. Jim's friend is Selmer 'Bully' Varnell. There are few worse people in the USA than him. He will never trust you. Don't you trust him. He runs with a group of eight or nine-lifetime criminals.

"We don't have the manpower to keep track of every felon. We don't want to arrest Bully and his crew for a gun violation. We want to catch him actively working his drug business, and put him and his friends away for a long time.

"All have had jail time, including Jim and Bully. We're working to identify the rest. I was and still am trying to watch over you. You are a smart and intuitive man. And you care about things. The Bully boys do not. The Russians do not.

"I didn't ask for your identity info from my contacts, but they will tell me if I ask. I have too much on my plate to spend a lot of time wondering what a good man like you might be up to. Don't make me ask, Del.

"I must continue to monitor the group of ex-con shooters. Catching them and offering them some jail time would make my day. Bully's crowd has a loose network that is effective enough. I am guessing they know where you and Billy live. I am also betting the Russians want their guns back.

"Our man in Spokane says the Russians are looking for the thief, and he thinks they've sent their best two-person enforcer team. He believes they are traveling in Montana. You are not skilled in their ruthless way of life. Killing is fun for them." Cliff paused, so I interrupted.

"Tony had both his IDs," I said.

"Really? I'm surprised. I'll have to work around that. He's going to be a top agent. Only three of us know about his undercover. I have to decide how to handle his goof. I will talk to him. I bet he thinks he's on his way to Barrow, Alaska."

I ordered a large meat lovers pizza, retrieved us each a Lagunitas IPA, and we talked past sunset about old times, soft ones and dark ones. Some bakery apple pie left over from one of my, too-often stops at the Aroma Bakery near Home Depot, also bit the dust.

"Jim told me he stole the guns. I will meet him, just not agree to buy."

"Good plan." Getting ready to leave, he turned and whispered a phone number. "Memorize this number. Do not write it anywhere. It is your personal 911 number to me. Do not buy those guns, and always watch your back."

Sharing a hug, he said, "Godspeed." He walked out the back door and got in a parked car in the alley.

"Always."

CHAPTER 32

After he left, I stayed on the patio and studied my options. I will meet with Jim and not be able to agree on a price.

We met and haggled a little, but Jim sensed I did not want to buy stolen property or at least not pay much. He was quite nervous the whole time.

He remained friendly at the range. The Bully boys were around, but if Tony or I showed up, they made a hasty retreat. Tony asked about them. Jim dodged answering by saying he didn't know.

Tony acted like nothing had happened.

I told Jim some of my guesses about Tony because I was sure he knew or suspected some of those facts. But he accepted me as legit and not a threat to them for some reason. Jim paused next to me, watched me ready a shot, then whispered, "Bully and his close friends are watching you and Tony. They think Tony is a cop. You, they haven't decided. I saw Tony put something under your bumper when he came to IHOP. I told Bully about that."

Without moving or looking at Jim, I whispered. "Thanks for both tips."

Still not looking at Jim, I whispered as softly as I could. "Breakfast at IHOP Sunday at seven-thirty."

I squeezed off my shot, stood up, picked up the spotting scope, and looked at my target. I wrote the result in my log.

"Can I look?" asked Jim.

"Sure."

"Two inches. Damn good. I'll be there." Jim walked away.

I rode my bicycle to IHOP and sat in a back booth enjoying a hot cinnamon roll and coffee, when Jim arrived.

"Morning. Didn't see your truck." A smiling Jim took a seat facing me.

"I rode my bike today. I try to ride some miles every week. We should order breakfast. My treat as I invited you. Deal?"

"Can't turn that down."

"Order whatever you like."

The waitress saw Jim join me and came right over to get the order.

I spoke first. "Ham, two eggs over medium, hash browns, wheat toast, and a refill."

"I'll have the same," Jim said, smiling at the young woman.

Waiting for our breakfast, I told him why I offered him the meal. "Jim, you do not have to say anything unless you want to. Okay?"

"Okay." The smile was gone.

"You surprised me about Tony putting something under my bumper. So, I checked. It was a small bug of some kind. I do not know much about that kind of stuff. I left it on a few days to see what's what. He rarely followed that I could see, so I think he can keep track of me using his phone." I smoothly lied, as I was positive Jim did not know I had caught Tony.

"I lost it on purpose near Whitehall when I was there visiting a rancher about hunting antelope on his place."

"You got any idea why Tony put it on your truck?" Jim asked.

"No, not a clue. I am just a regular old guy who likes to hunt, fish, travel, and be outdoors. What do you think, Jim?"

Jim sat there, deciding what to say, if anything.

Our order arrived. Jim put his eggs on top of his hash browns just like I did. He took a bite of eggs and potatoes, chewed and swallowed, then said, "I'm just done with my parole time. I told you about me spending time in jail. Bully and Wolf protected me, so I owe them. I mostly did petty crimes, but I was dumb and got caught stealing a car. I wasn't in jail long. I live alone now, and Bully doesn't need me for his stuff. We just talk some. They know the local cops, and maybe the feds watch me some, so Bully and his friends stay away from me. Wolf told me Bully doesn't worry about you, but Tony is on their radar, big time.

"They think he is a cop, planted to watch them. They know most everything Tony does. They know where he lives, eats, and works. They know where he goes to watch movies most nights. I think they are going to be sneaky, but harass him. They'll do their best to get rid of him one way or another. Right now, they just keep track, but that won't last long. I think he's got a week, maybe ten days. Bully will not hesitate to have him killed to protect his business.

"Del, I don't ever want to be in jail again. I am trying to get a job, but it's hard, man. People don't want ex-cons much. I've been thinking, you seem to be a good guy, and are always straight with me, so if Bully decides you are a problem, I'll tell you."

"That's damn fine of you, Jim."

Switching our thoughts, I offered, "I know every place that has a good breakfast. Did you know the Long Road has been looking for a dishwasher for over a month? Just walk in and apply and ask them to give you a chance. Bet they do."

"I'll see. I ain't ever done that."

"If you can learn to shoot long range, you can learn to wash dishes."

"I ain't got any real friends, Del. Never really had any. So, thanks for looking out for me, and thanks for breakfast. Gotta go."

Watching him slide out the door, holding it for a young couple with two toddlers, I noticed a small spring in his step and eyes forward instead of looking at the ground. I think he will go see about that job.

"There goes a man with no friends," I said to myself. "I am so lucky. I do not ever want to be that lost."

After Jim left, I rode my bicycle to the University of Montana and enrolled as a student, pursuing an art minor. Photography and painting have always been a special interest of mine. I have my camera, so it is time to try my hand at painting and see if I have any artistic talent. I will do my best in that class, plus my student ID lets me use the computer room whenever I wish.

At the range, Jim, Tony, and I started betting a dollar on each shot, paying on the spot. No IOUs. Tony started to improve, but it was costly for him. He stopped acting like a Fed and began to fit in. Cliff did not want to start over and gave him another chance.

Jim must be clean in his circle and free to come and go and be visible. No parole allowed him to associate with anyone and pass information back and forth.

I always wondered about the Russians, but the topic of selling the guns never surfaced again.

Cliff told me Jim's prison time was in Arizona. I wondered if Jim knew Vinny. Bet he did. I would also bet the Marana drug community knew Jim was in the Manhattan area. I decided to continue cultivating this new friendship with Jim.

CHAPTER 33

I arranged to rent a park model residence in Show Low, Arizona, for a week. The Arizona summer temperatures were cooler at that altitude. But there was not as much to do there as around Casa Grande, so I rented a park model in Palm Creek just off Florence Boulevard for the following week. I only used four days exploring the Show Low area. My golf map showed many more opportunities near Casa Grande.

In many cities in Arizona, the libraries were part of the local High Schools. I have library cards in Mesa, Gilbert, and Casa Grande. I was researching newspapers in Casa Grande for stories of bad people to see if any should be on my radar and watching some students working on their lessons.

I noticed a young Hispanic boy, about twelve years old, working hard on math problems. The frustration showed, and he started to cry. Wiping his eyes with his fist, he leaned back in his chair, slumped, and threw his pencil on the table.

I went over to him and said, "Hello, I am Del. Do you need help?"

Looking surprised, he just dried his eyes and did not say a word. I picked up the book, chose the problem he pointed to, and copied it onto a separate sheet of paper.

While he watched intently, I completed the problem using progressive steps. He stopped crying. With another swipe at the tears, he copied the next problem and started solving it. One small prompt, and he got it right. He rewarded me with a small smile. He turned back to his task. I returned to my computer and searched for real estate, even though I had no intention of ever buying locally. I was sure my use of this library was temporarily compromised.

I saw him close his book and stand. He paused a few seconds while deciding what to do, then came over to me and said, "Gracias Señor, I am Emilio, would you see if the rest of the problems are correct?"

"Sure."

He easily fixed the one small error I found. He put his things in his backpack. Standing proud, he offered his hand. After a quick handshake and without another word, he left.

I stayed another fifteen minutes, then went to my Arizona car, a 2017 rented maroon Honda CRV. My truck was in Show Low.

Emilio stood by an older Toyota, talking to a woman in rapid Spanish. Seeing me, he came over and said, "My mother would like to thank you for helping me. Would you come meet her?"

I did not hesitate. Locking my papers in my car, I joined Emilio and walked to meet his mother. She stepped away from the car and waited.

"Gracias, Señor. Thank you for helping my son."

"Por nada," I answered. "I was happy to help."

She offered her hand, "I am Elena Sanchez,"

"Emilio did all the work. He understood easily."

She smiled, nodded, and looked at me for a long time. I was becoming uncomfortable. But before I could break the silence, she turned to Emilio and talked rapidly in Spanish.

My Spanish was not polished enough to follow her words. I heard something about father and family, as well as amigo and gringo.

Finally, Emilio turned to me and said, "We wish to invite you to dinner with our family tomorrow at four o'clock. I am to write our address for you, if you say *yes*."

With no hesitation and showing my pleasure, "Yes, I would be honored to come and meet your family." I was rewarded with a beautiful smile.

Emilio wrote the address for me, shook my hand, and got in the car with his mother, and she drove away.

Walking back to my car, I mumbled, "What just happened here?" I looked at the address and knew it was in the heart of the Mexican community in Casa Grande. I would be the only white person around.

At my rented park model, I reviewed my options as I had not planned to be here past Sunday. I can go to Marana, learn my way around, find potential shooting spots, and plan some escape routes. My next 'adventure' could be there if I can create a workable plan.

Chico Alvarez was a desperate criminal receiving his room and board in the Marana jail. I can use the scouting trip to locate a position for a long-distance shot if at all possible.

First, I located the Marana City Jail and checked for a suitable building within six hundred yards that I could use for a sniper position.

Second, I would visit the Marana airport to see if I could use it as an escape route if I did complete an adventure there.

Third, I would also check out an escape route from Williams Field, and the Mesa Airport.

I went to the Marana airport first. I was there at breakfast time and needed to try the 'chalkboard' omelet. It was easy to see that everyone knew everyone else, and I will not blend in. I will surely come back to eat again.

I have been to Mesa airport. It would suit me better. Williams Field used to be an Air Force Pilot training base, with a long beautiful runway, a golf course and an adjacent Casino. It would be a perfect place to blend in. And, if I departed flying south, I could easily fly under the radar and turn north on a direct route to Cheyenne, Wyoming. Spencer is a resident there.

CHAPTER 34

Salvadore 'Chico' Alvarez occupied a cell in the Marana Jail under special guard day and night. Alleged to be the American half of the largest human trafficking cartel in the Arizona-Sonora corridor, he was reportedly ruthless and unrelenting in bringing illegal Mexican nationals into the United States. He specialized in bringing young girls to America to become prostitutes, or so it is alleged. The Border Patrol captured him following an anonymous tip to the Marana Police Department. Someone had ratted him out.

The story was that his vehicle became mired in a desert wash while he attempted to escape a patrol helicopter. He and his two associates ran out of ammunition and surrendered. Two Border Patrol agents were shot, one killed and one wounded. He tried to bribe a prison guard and a food service worker into bargaining his extradition back to Mexico. He did not have friends in Marana. As a feared criminal, few people, if any, would care if he was gone.

His trial was currently on the docket for early November, no exact date. Witnesses were few, and the illegals were not likely to come forward, as they faced deportation. If this 'adventure' came to pass, it would be the second very scary criminal.

Stigman was a Native American, but I was not really actively responsible for his death. Criminals are from all nationalities and race, so I believed things would even out.

Vinny Gordon, one of Chico's associates, was sought by the Marana Police Department and the Feds. He must be the Vinny that Bo feared.

I used the better part of two days covering the city of Marana. I only found two possible shooting spots and one usable escape route. Golf at

Quarry Pines and a wonderful rack of ribs at the Texas Roadhouse near the course completed my second day in Marana.

I saw a thin black man leaving the building on my way past the Police Headquarters as I was leaving town. I took a phone picture of him and discretely followed him to know where he lives. I am not sure why I recorded him, but my intuition said he was a player somehow.

CHAPTER 35

arrived on time to the Sanchez residence and parked in front of the yard. The Sanchez home was a modest, neat, desert tan, stucco, low-roofed building that looked about 800 square feet. The entire family met me at the door. Emilio did the introductions, his father first. Ernesto nodded, completed a quick but firm handshake, but seemed reserved. He was uncomfortable having me in his home. Emilio had three younger sisters, Maria, Lupe and Ana. They just stared with those pretty brown eyes. Maria was the oldest and in third grade, and as I would learn, she preferred to use English. Lupe and Ana were pre-school aged.

Elena served a meal of enchiladas and refried beans. The family talked of school and work during dinner. They did not seem to mind my presence.

As if by some unseen signal, they all stopped talking and looked at me. Ernesto turned to me, "Why did you help a young Mexican boy you did not know?" Emilio translated for his father.

I did not hesitate. "He was trying so hard and became disappointed in himself. He was in a library, meaning he wanted to learn and do well." After pausing, I said, "Ernesto, I do not want to cause problems for you or your beautiful family. They obviously mean so much to you. To be invited into your home and share a meal with all of you is a special honor."

Emilio translated word for word for his father again. "Emilio likes you. He wishes to go to college. He tries hard." Ernesto, gathering his thoughts, continued. "I am a janitor at Cochise Elementary School. It is a good job for me. I am not an educated man. I cannot read English good yet. Emilio helps us all. Do you live here?"

"No, I do not live here. I live in Montana. I am renting here for a short time to find a location I like in Arizona. Then I can miss some of the cold Montana winter. I am retired and travel a lot. I hope to see all of America.

I am visiting the desert to learn more about the plants, the people, and the history. I wish to learn just like Emilio."

Emilio repeated my answer rapidly in Spanish to his father. Then he and his father went into a back room and talked quickly and quietly for nearly ten minutes. The rest of us waited in silence. I felt that silence was expected. They came back into the room, sat down, and a nervous Emilio spoke for both.

"My father wants to ask if you are trying to stay hidden from people because you have not said your full name, and you touch very little and try to clean what you touch. He wonders if you are a secret policeman. He wonders if you are rich and do not work. He wonders if you have a family. He wonders why you agreed to come to our home." He stopped abruptly.

I knew they expected answers to all the questions. I was a guest, not only in their home but in their neighborhood.

"I have a daughter and a grandson. I see them whenever I can. Otherwise, I am alone. I have enough money to travel when I wish. I do not work at a job anymore. I am not and have never been a policeman."

Turning to Emilio, "Comprendé?"

"Sí," both Emilio and Ernesto said in unison.

"My full name is Del Sanderson. I am not hiding from the police. I came to your home because I was invited."

Ernesto spoke, using Spanish. "How is it you speak Spanish?"

Before Emilio could translate, I answered using his language, "I like to learn. I plan to live much of my winter in Arizona, and many of the citizens are Spanish-speaking. I wish to learn more Spanish, just like you wish to learn more English."

Ernesto leaned back in his chair, closed his eyes, and slowly rubbed his hands together. He stood up and offered his hand. Holding my hand, he softly said in English, "You helped my son. Gracias! I will trust you. You can come here anytime for any reason. I will tell my neighbors that you and your car are welcome here."

I answered, "I cannot explain how pleased and honored I am to be a friend of the Sanchez family. Gracias. Maybe Emilio can help me with my Spanish."

Emilio said nothing, but he and his sister Maria smiled with their eyes.

Emilio and Maria walked with me to my car. The rest of the family watched from the doorway. Together they said, "Adios."

"Adios," I answered.

I could feel someone watching from each house as I slowly drove down the street toward Frances Boulevard on my way back to my rental. I was sure I may have made things a little difficult for the Sanchez family in some ways. I wondered how I could stay in contact and not cause further problems for them without disrupting my personal goals.

I hoped I was not taking risks. Keep things simple. Maybe set up something in the education field. I could help kids, and come and go easily within the Hispanic community. I could find people who would be interested in helping. I needed to have things to do, so I could keep loneliness at bay. There was a community college nearby and students who needed money.

As I traveled east on Francis Boulevard, a low rider black Honda Civic with tinted windows stayed a car length or two behind me. The car roared past me and noisily turned north on Treckle. Immediately, a big white Ford truck, riding high off the ground moved into my lane right behind me. I turned into an RV resort and made two quick turns. He did not follow. Out the back gate, I crossed Florence using Colorado, and turned into Lowes. I seemed to be alone.

Stopping at the Safeway, I stocked up for a longer stay. Watching every vehicle all the way back to my rental, I did not see anything suspicious.

At my humble abode, I turned on the baseball game, served myself a Longboard Lager, unwrapped a ham and cheese hoagie and replayed the entire evening over and over. I made some notes. I decided to do another rewind in the morning.

I wondered what Amy would advise me to do now. I miss her very much.

Morning promised a beautiful day, so I went to Robson Ranch 55 plus community to see if a single could get a tee time to play a round of golf. No one followed me. After golf with a score in the eighties and a Reuben for lunch, I used a different route home. Enjoying a Longboard at my rental I retrieved my notes, then did another rewind. I did not really see problems, except a more exposed profile than I wanted.

I am one hundred percent positive Ernesto was much more than he let on, and understood English better than he wanted people to know. He worked just as hard at learning as Emilio. If I asked at his school, I would hear that he was well liked and a hard worker. He may not be the top person in his community, but he was one of the respected leaders. He could ensure my safety there.

About nine o'clock the next morning, a middle-aged, very short man knocked on my door.

"Good morning, Señor, I am Jose. Ernesto told me you needed your car washed. If you park it on the street, I will get started."

I smiled.

When he was done, he put his supplies away, rolled up the hose, and got into his truck to leave.

Stopping him, I asked, "How much do I owe you?"

"Tutor fees paid." He nodded. Smiling, as he drove away.

On my way to Frisco Grande to hit some golf balls, I revisited the evening at the Sanchez home and Jose's visit to mine. I put my phone on the passenger seat and noticed a small brown envelope tucked next to the center console. I opened the envelope.

> *Señor Del, I think you have decided you are surprised and worried. Why would I welcome you. Let me say that your license plate and a computer made it simple to find out you were truthful with us. So, I am now truthful with you. Many of us are trying to get rid of gangs and drugs. The young men that follow you home are with us and on the inside. We want to get more of our children through school. We have an old church building that you can use to meet with our children when you can. My family and other families will be at the Golden Corral for breakfast about 9:30 on Sunday. You could join us, and we will talk of this. Please get rid of this paper. Ernesto.*

I shredded and flushed it.

CHAPTER 36

I have three more days to explore the area before the Golden Coral meeting. I decided to take an overnight trip to Yuma to fill in the time waiting for the Sunday brunch. Yuma gets lots of snow birds every winter. I would easily fit in.

On day one, I played golf at Desert Hills. I scored 88. Putts would not fall.

Next, I visited the historic Yuma Territorial Prison, lots of history there. Many writers of Western novels refer to the notorious prison. The prison was part of a museum. Very complete. The cells were quite small, with at least two small beds of wood construction. If a small SUV could get into the cell, you could not open the car door. I could not imagine being in that jail or cell. Winter days would dip below freezing and summer days could climb over one hundred twenty degrees. The chow hall would not have been first rate. The tour guide said escape attempts were common, but the desert and the Colorado River usually proved to be too much for the prisoners.

After touring the prison, I traveled the rest of the day visiting the city center and some of the age fifty-five plus communities.

Then I walked the entire downtown area and the farmer's market. I tried a Mexican pastry called a concha. Enjoyable, but I liked my pie and ice cream better. In a small art gallery where local artists displayed their work, two small paintings of Native culture that showcased an Apache warrior's skill and use of horses, caught my eye. I have a place in my office for them.

I sat in the shade nursing a Dos Equis Amber and read the local paper. Lots of petty criminal activity but no hint of a real desperado. Maybe that was because of the military presence and the Border Patrol Station.

I wanted to try a restaurant with traditional Mexican food. I knew I could find a Reuben, but not today.

While browsing in a book store, I asked an Hispanic lady where I should go. She said, "Just go to *Lupitas*. It is best. It is on 4th Street, south of Main Street." She was proud of her English.

"Gracias," I answered as I paid for a Spanish to English dictionary. The book just matched words without any frills.

At Lupitas, I enjoyed a beef taco, a chicken quesadilla, and a glass of very bitter beer. I never learned its name. While there, I used as much Spanish as I could.

I was the only white person eating there, but the people were friendly.

The next morning, I played golf at Barrancar golf club. Great breakfast, just so-so golf. Maybe just too hot. One needs a list of excuses if you play golf.

My second day included a trip across the border into the Mexican culture, The shuttle took me to the border, and I walked across. Bargaining with the vendors netted me a very nice shoulder holster for my nine-millimeter and a rifle stock band that held six rifle shells. I shipped them to Bozeman via Fed-Ex after returning to Yuma.

I left Yuma about 8 p.m., starting along I-8 after getting gas and a diet Coke. Setting the cruise control, I settled in for a soft drive to Casa Grande. I saw a sign for a rest stop. I decided to stop instead of being uncomfortable all the way back.

One other car parked in the first spot by the main door. I always park as far as I can from rest facilities, so I get to stretch my legs a bit before returning to driving.

Passing the little black Toyota, I noticed a young Hispanic woman in the passenger seat. She looked my way, showed her arm handcuffed to the door in some manner, and started crying franticly. I was positive she said "HELP ME" over and over. Her face looked the picture of horror.

I returned to my car, put on my dark blue windbreaker and dark blue baseball cap, adding my sunglasses. Retrieving my nine-millimeter from the glove box, I pulled the slide, loading a shell in the firing chamber, screwed on the suppressor and turned back. With the gun in my right-hand pocket, I walked past the car, nodding to the girl and entered the facility.

I stopped just inside the door. No one was in sight. The occupied sign showed on the second restroom door, so I waited. The place smelled of disinfectant and looked like it had just been cleaned. I heard the lock click, and a skinny, narrow-shouldered black kid came out and started toward me, doing the I-am-somebody strut.

I closed the gap between us to three feet. Just as the kid said, "Hey Man." I punched him square on the jaw. He folded up like a sack in the wind. Using my handkerchief, I removed the keys from his pocket, quickly used the facility and went outside and gave the keys to the girl, making sure she could not see my face.

"Can you drive?" I whispered'

"Yes," she answered.

Still whispering, I offered a little help. "The handcuff key is the small silver funny looking one. The other is for the car. Get going."

"Thank you, thank you." She had herself free and behind the wheel in ten seconds. I watched her speed eastward.

I walked back to my car, watching the facility door, holding my gun in my right hand, but I did not see the kid come out. I did not want to follow the girl. Making a Highway Patrol cross-the-median- maneuver, I drove west, retreating to Yuma.

Thirty minutes later, I sat in the restaurant at the end of the counter that wrapped around to the wall part of a truck stop on the eastern edge of town, eating a piece of strawberry-rhubarb pie and drinking a cup of old stale coffee. The jacket, ball cap, gun and sunglasses were back in the duffel in the car. My light blue polo shirt and snow-white hair looked nothing like the guy who threw the punch. After only two bites of pie, I saw the kid come in with a big burly trucker. They were right behind me, so I listened in.

"Thanks for the ride, man. You're cool. Let me buy you a burger or something."

"Thanks, but I ate at the last stop. Trying to lose weight. Take care."

The kid walked to the back booth near the front window, rubbing his jaw.

The trucker walked back past me, talking softly on his phone. "Dispatch?" Satisfied with the answer, he continued. "I just dropped a skinny black kid at the East Truck Stop off Exit 9. Something isn't right. He was alone on the road. Not a vehicle anywhere in sight. You should send a car or two." He hung up, went back to his rig and drove away. My seat allowed me to watch the kid. I felt I needed to until the police arrived.

The black kid did not look older than twenty-five, but tired and used. His gaze darted around and he looked at everyone. He passed over me like all the rest. Finally, he ordered a burger. He showed no interest in me and ate the burger like he had not eaten in days. His jaw bothered him while he chewed. Inside I chuckled. I finished my pie, left the rest of the coffee and a tip, and walked up to pay. "No charge for the coffee. It isn't any good," A smiling waitress said as she handed me my change. As I returned to my car, two Police SUVs entered the parking lot and stopped, one near each door. One officer from each car entered a separate door, while their partners stayed with the car.

I decided to watch.

Skinny was visibly shocked. He tried to walk by one of the officers near his closest exit and talk his way free. The officer talked into his mike briefly, then pulled his gun and appeared to shout instructions to Skinny.

I could not hear, but the second officer also pulled his gun.

Skinny quit, sat on the floor, and cried—a different person than the one that had a woman handcuffed to his car.

I guess I will read the Yuma paper to see what happened.

Just a simple golf and tourist trip. Good golf, food, bargain hunting in Mexico, and a visit to some of America's history. Then this. What a day.

Driving back to Casa Grande, I revisited what I had done. Mostly right, I told myself. Maybe another bad guy off the streets. Now to work on the Marana 'adventure'. Bobby Darin, The Beach Boys and other oldies artists shared the last hundred fifty miles with me. Who said I could not sing?

I felt anxious about the meeting at the Golden Coral. I should not be, but I was. I sensed it would become more than a meal with some Hispanic people.

The Friday edition of the *Yuma Sun* contained the following short article.

After receiving an anonymous tip, Yuma Police arrested Raymond Spelt without incident at a Yuma truck stop. Spelt is alleged to have abducted Angel Diaz, reported missing by her parents to the San Diego Police Department. SDPD issued an Amber Alert and, after establishing probable cause, obtained an arrest warrant. Spelt is being held without bail pending extradition to San Diego, California. Angel Diaz, after being stopped for speeding, told her story and returned to her family in San Diego.

CHAPTER 37

ive or six families were enjoying their food at the Golden Coral when I arrived. Ernesto introduced me to all of the adults, who, in turn, proudly related their children's names. I noticed lots of tattoos on the young men and one young girl.

A big, overweight man called "Macho" cleared his throat.

"Señor Del." A small wry grin appeared under his thick bushy mustache. "I have heard from Ernesto how you helped his son. I thank you. Ernesto believes you may wish to help more children." He paused, deciding what to say next. "We are a poor community, but we take care of our families. How is it you want to help?"

Only the small children were not watching and listening—lots of dark brown eyes staring at me. One well-built young man in his twenties, I guessed, sporting some elaborate tats, kept on eating. He did not miss a thing.

"I am sure there are many ways to help, but education is how I could best help. I would like to try. I will not be in Casa Grande all the time, and would need others to share and help. We would need a place to meet with the children."

Macho interrupted. "Education is good." Then switching to Spanish and spoke rapidly, conferred with the others. Some of the school-aged children smiled.

"We could clean up the old church Ernesto told you about and find some furniture."

"How about the money?" I asked.

"Up to you." They all smiled at me.

I was prepared. "Is it okay to go the Community College to find some students to be tutors?"

"Sí. We will trust you. Ernesto and Jose will help with what you need."

As I finished my breakfast, I listened to lots of laughing. Everyone made an extra trip to the buffet line, and all the adults, paid attention to their children.

"Thank you all for inviting me. I will see what I can do."

Ernesto stood, handed me a folded note card, and shook my hand, "Gracias, Señor!"

I felt especially good as all my new friends watched me move through the mass of eaters toward the exit. The aloof young man followed me, then whispered, "I am Miguel. Remember me." We studied each other for a second or two, and he turned away to add some food to his empty plate. I had the distinct feeling Miguel would watch my back if the wrong people ever confronted me.

I opened Ernesto's note on my way to my car. *Your meals are free at Cafe Taco.*

🌲🌲🌲

At the college on Monday, I received permission to post and interview students for tutoring jobs. Eleven showed up. Six decided to help. They liked the money.

I met the new tutors at the church late Wednesday afternoon. It was already clean, the restroom worked, and there were six tables and about twenty chairs. An Hispanic lady introduced herself.

"I am Selena. I am here to help the children behave and work. I am to tell Ernesto."

We set up the rules. Commit, be responsible, and tolerant. Melissa, a student at the college and one of the tutors, had her computer and entered all our email addresses and phone numbers. She worked the keyboard for a few minutes, and soon all our phones dinged, signaling the transfer of all the email addresses. We talked about goals. All math would be systematic, with all problems solved showing all the steps, not just answers. English was to be exact, not allowing the children to use slang or Spanglish words. Each tutor would keep track of their hours and the students they helped. The logs were to be sent to the other tutors and me. Total honesty and reliability in all their efforts would be expected. The Hispanic community would welcome them, but they needed to relate any problems to me immediately. Cell phone numbers from all were exchanged, including mine.

"Test time." I need to list my new friends' names correctly in my head. "Melissa, Jordan, Lindsey, Lucas, Wendy, and Sarah. I am excited to see the good we can do here.

Helping is always special. We have the emails established, thanks to Melissa. I will need a bank account number for each of you, as I will pay by wire transfer. Your salaries will be paid by a corporation I own to create a paper and an electronic trail to keep the accounting straight.

"Del," interrupted Jordan, "I have a Costco membership and could get the supplies. I can wait for reimbursement."

"I will set up a spread sheet to keep track of everyone's time and each student's contact information, including subject and lessons. I can transfer a copy to each of us and you, Del," offered Lucas. "I like making those."

"Are we good or what?" Wendy piped up. "I think we should have a lockable file cabinet and keep a file on each child and track their overall progress. I will manage that function."

"My friends. The six of you set everything up. I am already enjoying this. Jordan can get all the supplies after you finish brainstorming. I will ask Ernesto about the file cabinet. My main goal for the rest of my life is to have a purpose to every day. This fits the bill perfectly. I will not be here often in person. We will manage everything via phone."

While they were getting things going and making a list of needs, Ernesto arrived, and I introduced him to all.

In front of everyone, he said to me, "You have helped us more than anyone. I will make sure your new friends are welcome and safe. Ride safe, Mr. Sanderson, and come to my house whenever you return. I'll find Wendy one or two file cabinets, and Jose will find some more tables and chairs. Can I get more of anything?"

"Del. I think a white board or two would be helpful, especially for math and vocabulary," Sarah offered.

Ernesto smiled. "We like spending Del's money. I know a school that has some they don't need." He then shook each tutor's hand and called them by their name. "Thank You. I am pleased you are to help us." He turned and left the building.

We sat together around one of the tables. "I am paying you well. Our expectations are high. These people trust us. We must be at our best. Call me anytime. I have promised to help here and do expect to keep that promise. I expect all of you to keep that promise as well."

Six "Sí's" made me smile.

"I must be informed of any kind of trouble."

The tutors slapped high fives all around. We went our separate ways.

I did not look for followers in my rearview mirror. In Show Low, I returned the rental car and picked up my truck. I continued through Holbrook to Moab, Utah. I knew I did not have a locator on my truck. I also knew I had some new Hispanic friends around that I would never meet. My new tutor employees would help me have a purpose beyond the scope of my regular life. I felt extra good. Trust is amazing. No chance to be lonely when around Casa Grande.

I could trust Ernesto and his friends if I did not bring trouble. Next time Ernesto and I were together, I will tell him I trust him.

Driving from Show Low, Arizona to Bozeman, Montana, through Moab, Utah, is a mesmerizing journey. A lifetime's worth of things to see and do. One of my most beautiful trips ever. I plan to come back, do more, and see more things. Floating the Colorado is now on my bucket list.

In Moab, I opted for a room at the Best Western, then walked around the whole town. I was holding Amy's hand at every step, feeling her walking with me.

I found a local, not for tourists, brew-pub. They served the best local IPA I have found during my travels.

At the motel, I watched some of the Mariners' ball game and thought about the Sanchez family and what my small tutor program seemed to mean to them.

I called Palm Creek, spoke to the sales agent, and explained what I wanted. I next called a storage place that offered air-conditioned units. They added me to the waiting list. Casa Grande would become my Arizona winter home. I decided to keep an RV spot at Show Low for my 'Lilac Rig,' but I wanted to stay in Casa Grande to be closer to the little school and the nearby golf.

That little education experiment could be the beginning of something special. If my new friends believed me to be honest and trustworthy, I could have a safe haven from even the most prying eyes. Keeping my hands in the process would certainly be keeping my promise to Amy. A purpose for every day—helping kids that wanted to be helped! I felt extra special!

My new Hispanic friends would watch but not interfere with the new school and ensure the safety of everyone. I could call all the tutors and help them. I wanted them to earn their money and enjoy the experience.

Helping one-on-one is one thing, but creating a complete learning environment is another. I needed to go back often. There are other poor and needy children in this little city, and I wondered if Ernesto and his friends would welcome them?

At the library, I read all the stories in the Tucson Daily paper about Lorenzo. I especially liked a letter to the editor in today's *Star*.

I wish I could shake the hand of the shooter who disposed of Lorenzo Depsoto. That man was responsible for enticing so many young people to start using drugs. He was responsible for the overdose of our son. He met his real justice head on. Tucson is better off with him gone. Thank you to the person who was daring enough to shoot him.

I also checked the Spokane paper about the unsolved cases at Priest Lake and on Spokane's South Hill. Nothing new.

There are lots of bad guys in Arizona, but I have leads in Spokane, Minneapolis, and Marana. I already have pictures of the bad guys, and flight information to those locations. I have detailed maps of each city and the exact locations of the jails and courthouses. My research also includes precise escape routes to test.

CHAPTER 38

The day I moved to Bozeman, I started looking for the best places to eat, especially for my favorite meal, *breakfast.* There are lots of okay places, but I found two I really like: Betty's Breakfast Bar near Home Depot and the Broken EGGE on the southern edge of the city on Highway 84, just before it merges with 191 to West Yellowstone.

Number one is the Broken EGGE. They only serve breakfast Wednesday through Sunday from six a.m. to one p.m. Madeline and Cindy are the only employees, and because I have eaten there so often, they feel like old friends. I have learned a lot about the community from them. Madeline cooks, and Cindy does the rest. Lots of regulars love them.

I do not ever recall seeing Madeline without the net covering her light brown hair. She might be a few pounds overweight, but her full mouth, blue eyes, and a smile that covers her whole face conceal it. She handles any complaints with the same words: "If you don't like the food, eat somewhere else."

Cindy is a tall, slender young woman who makes her uniform look good. The short blonde hair roots often revealed a darker color. She is able to capture your attention with her soft smiling gray-green eyes. She has a narrow face with regular nose and chin, a long neck, a few freckles, and a manner that tells everyone that she is happy with herself.

She flirts with those she needs to flirt with, but doing her job comes first. A smile at the right time and a sashay when she feels like it. Tips are important, and she gets them for both.

I have eaten there often enough to know the slower parts of the day.

Cindy did not care who knew she attended the University of Montana to obtain her teaching certification. "Little Kids, I love 'em."

One day I overheard her telling a regular named Millie, "I have to scrape together money for next semester's tuition. I think I have enough, but it is going to be tight. I only have twenty-four credits and the student teaching left to do. I can't wait. No work when I get to the student teaching part, but I will cross that bridge when I get to it."

The next morning, I went to the Broken EGGE to enjoy the usual good food and all the coffee I could drink.

The cafe is an old-style diner with a counter, and eight red vinyl-covered stools with footrests bolted to the floor. Seven booths with the same red vinyl lined the street side next to the window, and six tables with four chairs each filled the rest of the space. The walls are painted bright yellow and adorned with kitchen stuff and flower pictures. A warm, friendly place with great food. The fresh baked cinnamon roll smell was there every day.

Sitting in the last booth, I lingered and waited for Cindy to bring one more cup of coffee.

"One more cup, Del?"

"Sure. May I ask you something?"

She looked at me sideways, put her hand on her hip, and with a half grin, said, "Go for it."

I lowered my voice and looked her in the eyes. "Would you be interested in joining me at Applebee's, say around three thirty this afternoon, for an early dinner? You may be interested in what I have to offer you."

She backed up a half step. Her expression changed to a serious look. She quietly replied, "I don't know about that, Del. I am not really in the market for dates."

"I am not in the market for dates, as you call it, either. I wish to propose something that will be of interest to you. You have nothing to lose except some of your time."

"I have a test to study for. I couldn't stay long."

"See you at three thirty then."

"Okay, I think. I may chicken out, though."

I sat at a table in Applebee's, nursing a so-so IPA. I arrived a little early and felt a bit nervous. Cindy arrived a little late, looking lovely in a light green dress with a soft yellow and orange pattern. People noticed her.

I stood when she got to my table.

Speaking quickly and softly. "Sorry I am late. I got here on time but sat in my car trying to find enough courage to come in."

She beat me to her chair and sat down. "I like my job, but can't wait to get the uniform off. I change into the quiet, shy person I really am. The work talk is for the customers and the tips."

"Cindy, thank you for coming, this is my plan for today. The dinner, wine, dessert or whatever you want is my treat. We will talk about the easy stuff, and when the meal is done, and the dishes are gone, I will explain why I asked you to come. Deal?"

"Sure…Deal?"

She did most of the talking. She talked about her family, especially her mother. She looked the part of a young girl, smiling, talking with her hands, and animating her story.

"My Dad was not a nice man. My Mom was my rock and best friend. My older sister left when she was eighteen. Kelly is married now and lives in Plano, Texas. We aren't close, but I will travel to see her when I am done with school 'cuz I want to get to know her better." Her face reflected deep sadness, "Our mom died three years ago. I miss her."

Putting the smile back on, she changed her direction, "I didn't work hard in school. Growing up was a tough story. I felt like I didn't fit in. We needed money, and I worked as a waitress at a local diner. I worked there for most of my High School years. I quit one day. I was trying to find my way, deciding where to go, and stopped at the EGGE to eat. The waitress pulled a no-show. Madeline covered everything. I was just killing time, so I jumped in to help. I started filling coffee cups and busing tables. Madeline carried some plates to a table. I grabbed a ticket pad and took orders. I've been there ever since—over six years."

I sensed she intentionally avoided some topics, so I asked, "Why do you want to be a teacher?"

"Kids, 'cuz I just love them. When I see them at the cafe and watch them in the park, you know. They make me feel good. I'll have a class of my own students one day—third grade or earlier, I think. When they still love school. Teachers work hard for not much pay, but have decent benefits and a lot of their own time." She looked to be enjoying herself, almost carefree, forgetting why she came.

She sat up straighter when the dishes were gone, fussed with her hair, and crossed her legs two or three times.

Time to get started. "Cindy! I am alone and starting a new life, staying as active as possible. I have never been a cook, and I eat out a lot, especially breakfast. The Broken EGGE is one of my two favorite places to go. I have more than enough money to do whatever I wish. You are a good person, and you should be a teacher. How many credits do you need to finish your degree?"

"I have been going to classes part-time for six years and still need 24 more credits and the student teaching, or whatever they call it now."

"How much will that cost?"

"About Fifteen thousand but I would have to quit work for the student teaching. Why?"

"I will give you twenty thousand, so you can finish. No strings attached, no interest, and no payments, at least until you find your position. The money will be in a joint account, but yours to use. If you quit school, I will spend the remainder on a fishing trip somewhere in Alaska."

She sat back in her chair, closed her eyes, and ran her fingers through her hair. She muttered to herself and breathed faster. It took all she could muster to recover her composure.

"Why, Del?"

"I do not doubt the Cindy I have come to know. You will be a great teacher. Listening to the things you said about your personal life and reading between the lines, I feel you deserve a break in life. I need purpose in mine. I cannot think of a better purpose now than helping you realize your dream." I wanted to tell her about my promise to Amy, but I just could not say the words.

"Gee, Del, I don't know."

"I will come by the EGGE tomorrow. When you are free, we can go to a bank where we are not known and set things up. Deal?"

She sat motionlessly. I thought she was going to leave. The gaiety of a moment ago had been replaced with a frown. Her eyes were downcast, and the fingers of her right hand softly tapped on the table. She looked fragile, scared, happy and worried all at once. I saw a picture of a girl with thoughts racing through her head. She toyed with her necklace.

"You've got my head in a tizzy. I was worried you wanted something that I don't. Now I'm mixed up. It sounds too good to be true, but how can I go wrong if it's real?"

"It is real. My sense of a person's worth and character have been very accurate all my life. I want to help you. Period. Before my wife Amy, died, she asked me to promise to have a purpose for every day. Helping you is my purpose for today. I only ask two things of you; never tell anyone where the money came from, say a rich uncle gave it to you, and sometime in the future, when you are able, you need to help someone in some way."

We sat for what seemed a long time. Cindy had tears in her eyes and a small soft smile on her face. She wiped away the tears and got up to leave, "I need to go home and think about it. I'll see you tomorrow."

The waitress came by and filled my coffee cup.

Am I out of line? I mused. Fussing over the check and deciding about the tip, I prepared to get up and leave. I did not see Cindy return to the table until she sat down.

"I don't need to think about it. Are you for real?"

"Yes, Cindy. Everything I have offered is for real. If you are comfortable, we could exchange phone numbers. You can call me when you are done with your shift at the Broken EGGE, and we can meet at the bank we choose. Will that work for you?"

"Okay. We can do the phone thing, and you pick the bank. I'll come and meet you." She stood and offered her hand. "Our secret!"

We looked each other in the eyes. I held her hand in both of mine. "Our secret."

We met the next afternoon at a small credit union not far from the college, deposited the cashers-check, and signed the required papers that included sending the monthly statements to both parties.

We walked out together. Nearing her car, she turned and smiled at me. Tears streamed down her cheeks and streaked her makeup, but her face glowed with the biggest smile ever.

"You are a beautiful man. Thank you is not enough. I will make you proud."

"No, Cindy, *YOU* are beautiful. I am just a nice old man. Your graduation will be special." Returning the smile, I said, "You are welcome."

Driving home, I had a few tears of my own, "Keeping my promise, Amy!" I said to an empty truck.

A few days after the Applebee's dinner with Cindy, I went to the EGGE. Cindy beamed a smile. "Good morning, Del."

"It is. I will have the ham and cheese omelet with hash browns today."

"Sure thing," she answered and handed me my coffee. I walked back to my favorite back booth.

Madeline noticed me, put three orders up for Cindy, and came and sat facing me with her back to the customers and to Cindy.

Wasting no words, she looked hard at me and said, "Cindy came to work the other day happier than I had ever seen her. I asked her about it." Looking back to see where Cindy was, she continued, 'Del and I had dinner. He is a nice man,' was her answer."

I held up my hand, signaling a halt to stop her from saying something she would regret.

Lowering my voice and looking her in the eye, I spoke very directly. "Yes, we did have dinner. Yes, she is happy. Yes, I am a nice man. No, we are not an item, just friends. She deserves to be happy. We do have a secret that will remain a secret. You are my friend, and so is Cindy. Friends are, and always will be important to me."

Madeline looked at me and sighed. "I am sorry, Del, but I just don't want her hurt. She has never said, but I am positive she has been hurt badly in her past. She is very dear to me."

"Madeline, Cindy told me how she came to work here and that you let her stay with you until she could make it on her own. She knows you are special. You and I need to be friends and let her be happy. She is going to be an excellent teacher. Are we good?"

She studied me, then answered. "Yes." She got up and went back to the kitchen to make my omelet.

Cindy came by. "More coffee, Del? What did Madeline want?"

"Yes, to the coffee. She just wanted to keep me up to date."

"She's buttin' in, right?

"Sort of. We will just let it ride. She is just showing that she loves you. That is great. We will let her be, right?"

A long pause, that brain turning everything over at a fast rate. "Okay, if you say so. I trust you."

Her smile was back. So was mine.

CHAPTER 39

I spent some of Vinny's money to become a season ticket holder, so I could attend Washington State University football and men's and women's basketball games where ever they might be playing. I bought the tickets to learn to get lost in a crowd, get a discount at away games, and be around the sporting college atmosphere. I wished I could go to them all. At every game, I attend, I practice fast changes. I change clothes, hats, facial hair, and wigs and practice different ways of walking. I am getting pretty good. Every change at a game fooled the security person I had talked to only moments before. Exciting and sneaky.

Most stadiums and gyms are very much the same. Building codes and access rules govern those layouts. When I was offered my choice between two seats, I took the mid-level one close to an exit. I enjoy the games and feel younger when around college-age adults.

Using more of Vinny's money, I bought a sweatshirt and a short-sleeved polo shirt for many of the Pac-12 schools. If someone asked to describe me, it would sound like, "He wore jeans and a such-and-such school polo shirt and had white hair." That would describe half of the men at the game. I would blend in—lots of older students these days.

My criminal mind was not very polished, and I do not know much about surveillance or the apprehension tactics of law enforcement. Thus, I must keep watching my surroundings and become good at evading and escaping, as well as changing my appearance.

CHAPTER 40

To his fellow Marana Police Department officers and friends, Bryan Kellerman is an interesting young man.

When I was following Lorenzo and reading the *Star* every day, I saw an article with pictures, which showed two Marana Officers received commendations for developing the evidence that solved an old Tucson murder case.

That same article outlined a Marana Department policy allowing their officers to enroll in up to two classes each semester at the University of Arizona.

The reporter interviewed both officers, Bryan answered all questions. The answer I remember most, "My main task is computer support, but during my down time I channel all my energy into solving cold cases."

Bryan was known to be a very social gym rat, with many friends, but did not let anyone into his personal space. He told those who asked, he didn't want to be in a close relationship, enjoyed his life, and hoped to be a front-line homicide detective. At age twenty-nine, he managed computer input for the department.

He picked the brains of the tenured detectives every chance he got and tagged along with them often. The police department used computer access to all related national databases except the deepest FBI encrypted sections. He enrolled at the University of Arizona as a student pursuing a Master of Forensic Science degree.

He regularly researched old newspapers for his cold cases online and left a contact phone number on the hits he created. He wanted people to call him. He printed a personal copy of many articles to include in his working file and was always looking for new leads to try.

Since finding the drug money, I have been checking newspapers at libraries about Bo, Zach and Vinny wherever I happened to be during my travels. They were Arizona criminals, so a Marana detective researching the same articles made the connection for me.

Modern improvements in forensics and the well-published results make many victims of unsolved crimes very willing to help.

This story was the common ground:

The Priest River, Idaho Police Department is asking anyone who may have been in the vicinity of Lions Head campground during the period of July 18th through July 22nd to call the Department if they remember any suspicious activity. The body of a young man was found on a little-used logging road. He was killed, execution style and there was evidence of torture. The victim's identity is not known.

The case was not cold, just not on the front burner. Bryan had started a file. He thought it was a drug crime.

Bryan could solve that case if he knew Bo and Zach met people from Arizona. I will bet he knew who Vinny was. I have to find a way to give him what I know.

🌲🌲🌲

Washington State is playing a men's basketball game at Arizona University next Saturday. I decided to go and see if there is a way to talk to Bryan.

Bryan rarely misses any basketball games.

I arrived in Tucson Thursday morning, went to the Registrar's office, and found where the law enforcement classes were held. On my way to the school, I stopped at a convenience store and added the phony extra weight. I wanted the old, fat guy look, to be ready for the game. They gave me a visitor's badge and let me tour the campus. Bryan's picture was in the records.

I sat on a bench under a tree near the main entrance, reading all the information given to me and watched the students move between classes. No sign of him.

After checking in at the hotel, I walked around town and passed the courthouse where Lorenzo met his demise. Just had to smile. Nearing the hotel, I stopped at a Mexican restaurant. Those were the best tacos I ever tasted.

Friday found me on my bench again, reading a book this time. No luck today, either.

I arrived early at the game and was rewarded with an aisle seat ten rows above the Washington State bench. As Bob Uecher, a major league catcher turned baseball announcer, would say, "Great seats."

Just before halftime, I saw Bryan right behind the cheerleaders on the Arizona side. He seemed to know everyone.

As the players hurried off at half-time toward the locker rooms, one of the cheerleaders came and sat with Bryan—good friends for sure.

I paid an usher twenty dollars to give a sealed note to him. *Call this number after the game, I have some information for you.*

As the usher handed him the note, Bryan tore open the envelope. He read it, quickly stood and searched the crowd, first on the Arizona side, then Washington's. He grabbed the usher's shoulder before he could leave and whispered a question. The usher pointed in my direction. I sank behind the spectators in front of me as Bryan studied the crowd.

I knew he would call the number.

After the game, Bryan and his girlfriend walked off together. She went into the restroom, and Bryan called. I was near the top of the ramp, mixed in with other Wazzu fans. His blond crew cut stood out. He was easy to follow.

"Hello. This is Bryan. How do you know who I am?"

"I do not know you," I answered, disguising my voice. "But I know about you. You work at the Marana Police Department and do mostly computer work. They allow you to work on unsolved cases when you have time. You made a computer inquiry recently to read and print a story about the execution north of Priest Lake, Idaho. Am I right so far?"

"How do you know about that?"

"Not important, Bryan. But I can help you if you wish. However, I hope we can help each other with those types of crimes. You help me, and I will help you."

Bryan paused before answering. His mind must have been spinning at a mile a minute. "Go on," he said in an encouraging tone. "Why should I risk helping you?"

Ignoring his comments, I countered. "I'll give you two leads. You follow them, and I will call you in a month or so."

"We will see if your leads are any good." The doubt and anger showed.

"Okay! Here are both leads. The dead man is Zach. He is from Marana and had a broken leg. He was killed by a man named Vinny or by someone working for Vinny.

Zach was transporting drugs to Canada and money back to the United States." I did not mention Bo. "Good luck." I hung up and watched him.

He put his head in his hands and leaned against the stadium wall next to the exit. After he had processed the information, he looked around. There was no way he could pick me out from the crowd. Especially since the usher probably described me as a white-haired old fat guy. I watched him greet his girlfriend as if nothing had happened. We went our separate ways.

The next morning, I called Bryan at the Police station, "Check the Spokane unsolved." Then I destroyed the phone and tossed it into a deep-water irrigation ditch.

I must try to keep up with things in Marana. That is what library searches are for. After a two-day stay, playing golf at Palm Creek and Robson, and visiting with Ernesto, I took I-17 to Flagstaff. I let Northern Arizona University honor my University of Montana student ID instead of relying on the premise that the public is allowed. I am not a resident, but I wanted to use their library.

Monday morning after the game, I saw a headline in the *Tucson Star*: *Marana detective identifies a local man slain in North Idaho. Zachary 'Zach' Erlington, a high school dropout and a recent release from the juvenile justice system was found slain on an unused logging road in North Idaho. An anonymous tip indicated he was involved in the drug trade. Other leads were being followed.*

I'll bet Bryan made the most of his new information. I hope he gets Vinny.

CHAPTER 41

I drove back to Tucson and stayed at the Best Western Motel. The following morning, I drove the sixty or so miles back to Casa Grande and arranged a Park model rental in Palm Creek for all of January, February and March.

After enjoying the Sunday buffet at Robson, I called Bryan about the Spokane unsolved, then found a tee time with three residents. Played well. Then I called Ernesto.

"Ernesto, this is Del. May I buy your dinner tomorrow evening?"

"Hello to my friend. I can enjoy a meal at Cafe Taco. I will be done with my work at six thirty and tell Elena I will be late, and why I am so."

"See you at seven then."

"Gracias. Del. It will be good to see you."

The Cafe Taco is in the center of the Hispanic community of Casa Grande. I found a parking spot across the street. Lots of smiles and nods as I walked in the door. They all seemed to know me, but I did not know them. I was the only white person in the restaurant, yet the smiles and nods continued.

A pretty young girl with a name tag that said Consuelo ushered me to a table, "Señor Del. A Dos Equis Amber?" She bustled away and returned with my beer and a Modelo for Ernesto.

Ernesto had called ahead. He arrived at seven and came directly to the table. I stood to greet him. He shook my hand and then waved for me to sit. Then he sat.

"Good you are here. We have done much at the school."

"I plan to visit there tomorrow."

"You will be surprised. You will be pleased. Many smiling children. All want to come. We have a long list of children wishing to come."

Leaning back, I smiled. "That is so great to hear."

Consuelo arrived with our meals, of seafood enchilada, refried beans and a ground beef soft taco. We had not ordered any. Ernesto just smiled.

I noticed almost everyone watched us.

"I remember you do not like the hot sauce."

"Not tough enough, my friend."

"Señor Del, we think you are tougher than you want us to know."

We talked of his family, the school and my traveling. I think he knew I was not telling all. He is a very respectful man and did not pry.

While enjoying a superb meal, Ernesto asked, "You have reason to stay here for so many months?"

I had not said a word about my rental. They seem to know everything that happens here. I must remember that. I told him I just preferred to be here instead of Show Low.

He lowered his voice to near a whisper. "There are people here we do not trust yet. You should know, Senor Del, my family is all American citizen. Elena and I passed the citizenship tests two years ago, and all our children are American. I tell you this. It is possible some of the children at our little school are not American, and their parents have not passed tests. I wish to know if that is a problem for you."

"No problem for me. I trust you, and only care about the school. Have others asked?"

"Not yet, but the news of the school is spreading. We worry someone could check."

"All the children that come to the school speak English, right?"

"Sí. They are all in school here. Some parents are worried about their families."

I sat back and thought about what he had told me.

"We will just keep going," I said, "We can put up a sign in the front of the building that says, Helping Hands, and tell anyone and everyone who asks that it is only a place to get help, not a school, for helping, not formal teaching. Also, we should start helping adults learn English so they can pass the citizenship tests. I will talk to the tutors."

Ernesto stood up and said, "I should go now. I will come to the school tomorrow when it is my lunch. Ten thirty."

"Good. I will see you there."

I asked Consuelo for the check.

"There is not a check. Señor Del."

I left a ten-dollar bill on the table and walked out with Ernesto. Lots of smiles from lots of nice people. Looking back, as I held the door, I noticed the money was gone.

The next morning, I was at "Helping Hands" by 9 a.m. The man who came and washed my car so many weeks ago was in the front yard working on the sign. Michelle, Lucas, and Jordan were there. I asked what they needed.

"A copier, a color printer for the computers, and a few reams of paper for each."

I explained about the citizen concern and that we would keep going and stressed we were just helping and not formally teaching. I wanted them all to join me at the Big House for breakfast the next morning to set up a way to help the adults.

🌲 🌲 🌲

"Michelle and Jordan, please tell the rest of the tutors about tomorrow. If you two come with me, we will get the printer and copier."

We were back in an hour. Michelle and one of the older kids set the equipment up.

I watched the process while I waited for Ernesto.

"Michelle, find a source and get name tags for all the tutors, that gives their first name and underneath, put tutor. Do you think we need any more tutor help here? How about when we start helping adults?"

Michelle and Jordan looked at each other, then both nodded, and Michelle said, "One of the TAs at our Community College is in danger of having to quit school. He is married, and they are about to start their family. He could use the money. He speaks Spanish better than anyone at the school. If it is okay, we could see if he could help here."

"You do that. Please tell him he can help but allowing him to stay can only happen after I meet him."

"Great," offered Jordan. "I know you will like him. His name is Peter Sullivan."

Ernesto called me and said he could not come. He would see me soon. I thanked Michelle, Lucas, and Jordan personally.

Time to golf. Frisco Grande beckoned. Dinner at the Duke would be a Lagunitas IPA and a very tasty Reuben. I like to allow extra time at Frisco because there is so much history. Old pictures decorate the walls from when the site was the spring training grounds for the San Francisco Giants. The outdoor pool is shaped like a bat, and the hot tub is shaped like a baseball. John Wayne often hung out there when he wasn't making movies.

Tomorrow, I go to Marana and see if the trial for Alverez will start soon.

CHAPTER 42

Bryan arrived at the station early Sunday morning. He was a bundle of emotions, hoping he hadn't been scammed, on the one hand, and hoping the data was true and he could make headway on a cold case involving local criminals on the other.

Leaning back in his rickety office chair, he mumbled, "Zach Erlington has to be the guy the informant alluded to." Zach had a long juvenile history, and Bryan knew he had been seen with other low-level drug users and pushers. Yet, he always seemed to have money. Another tell, Bryan could not find a record of Zach ever holding a job. Zach dropped out of high school after being dismissed from the football team. No record of a GED existed.

In vain, Bryan searched the newspapers he previously studied trying to find a record of another reader on the Idaho case. Closing down his computer, he muttered to himself. "Wonder if he will call again?"

The station phone rang as he was almost out the door. The station operator asked, "Bryan, this call is for you. Want to take it?"

"Sure, why not?" as he picked up the extension.

"Check the Spokane unsolved," was all he heard.

"Wow. My wish came true." He looked back at the operator and said, "I need to go finish something." Taking the stairs two at a time, he returned to his desk on the second-floor.

First, he dialed the Spokane Police Department, asking for the person in charge of their unsolved cases.

"Captain Blake is not in. May someone else help you?"

"I am Bryan Kellerman from the Marana, Arizona Police Department, and I just received an anonymous tip about an unsolved case in your area.

I would like to speak with a person who could get me a copy of the file to see if my tip is worth following."

"I'll transfer you to Sergeant Wilson."

"Thanks."

After two rings, Sergeant Wilson answered, "Yeah, Wilson."

Bryan explained the whole story and Wilson didn't interrupt. "Your tip could be real good. I'll fax you what we've got, which ain't much. Want the pictures too?"

"Yes please. Info and pictures. I'll call you back if we know the people and can help."

"Ten minutes. Good luck."

"Thanks," Bryan said to a dead phone. He went to the break room, got a cup of warm coffee and started writing a press release on Zach. He liked writing his own, and Captain Johnson liked to see what was given to the press. He started working on a draft for the *Star*, and his activity report to the chief. His preliminary draft about Zach was done, so he walked down the hall to the com room. His fax waited for him.

Back at his desk, he read the three pages of the police report and studied the pictures. Jesus Zapata was the dead Hispanic man found in a South Hill residence with multiple gunshot wounds. He had been dead five to seven days when he was found. A neighbor reported the same black Buick came once a month and always with the same two short fat guys. A neighbor kid mowed the lawn and his fifty dollars was always under the rock by the back door.

The picture and the prints matched 'little Zap' perfectly.

He called Wilson back. "It looks like a one hundred percent match to one of our fine citizens. I'll talk to my chief on Monday and get his okay to close your file."

"Great. One less we have to worry about. Nice when some cases get solved."

Bryan called the Priest River Police department and explained what he knew and asked for a fax of their file.

"I'm Beth Booth. I'll send you a copy right now and give Chief Booth a note. Please call him Monday after talking to your chief."

"Thank you, Beth, and I will."

He pinned a note on Chief Johnson's order board in the number one spot. *Five minutes. Something good.*

Time to go to the gym.

Monday at six thirty, Bryan sat at his desk at the Marana Police Department Headquarters. After he typed a summary of his findings on the two tips his new informant gave him over the weekend lay on his desk, he checked to see if his sticky note was still first in line on the Chief's door. While studying his file on a Salt Lake City unsolved Chief Johnson called him to his office.

"You have five minutes," the chief said.

Taking one of the chief's 'too soft' chairs, Bryan started talking. "I attended the U's verses Wazzu basketball game Saturday night and an usher gave me a note to call a number. The usher's description of the man who gave him the note covered half of the men in the arena. No help.

"So, while my girlfriend stopped at the restroom on the way out, the game, I called the number on the note.

"The man on the other end of the line mentioned a crime that happened near a Priest Lake, Idaho. I looked it up. The lake is almost to the Canadian border. We know there's a drug pipeline from Canada. Sunday morning, I came in and checked it out. The unsolved from Priest River is 99% Zach Erlinger from Marana. And, Vinny is one of Marana's unsavory drug dealers on our radar. Priest River forwarded all they have, including pictures. I was on my way out when I got another call through the department switchboard. "Check the Spokane unsolved." So, I did. The Spokane detective sent me all he had, including pictures." He handed the Chief the pictures of Zach and 'Little Zap' Jesus Zapata. He added, "These are two of ours. Zap was Vinny's number-one bodyguard and enforcer. With your permission, I would like to give this to my reporter friend at the *Star*."

"Do you think this is the same source we often get tips from?"

"No, Sir, I don't. Those tips are mostly vague clues that, when followed, they sometimes open things up for us. This one used names and places and seemed to know the facts. I am sure the voice was disguised enough to eliminate recognition. I never saw anyone. I would not have a clue about his identity."

The chief studied the pictures. "I agree with you. This is Zap and the other is Zach Erlinger. What's next?"

"I'll expand things, but this may be all we are going to get."

Chief Johnson tipped forward in his chair, stood up, and walked around the front of his desk. He met a standing Bryan with a hearty handshake. "I'll be back around ten. Write a release for the paper to give to your friend, but let me see it first. Three things. One, talk to the usher again, two, do you think he will call again, and three, do you know how he knew to call you?"

"I'll talk to the usher, but he described an old fat guy with white hair. There must have been hundreds that fit that description at the game. Yes, I believe he will call again. He hinted that he would help me if I helped him. I don't have a clue what he wants. I think he saw my contact info in the Spokane paper. He reads but doesn't leave any record. I'll have the release ready in an hour. Do you want a department slant, an inroad on drugs slant, or a you and I slant?"

"Your choice. You did everything. You'll figure it out." Waving his hand, he picked up the phone and started punching numbers.

Bryan returned to his desk, saying to himself, "That means the Chief and me. Great."

CHAPTER 43

o found a new job at Captain Dan's open-air restaurant on the beach. Ft. Lauderdale felt like home. Steph felt extra close, and they were often together. Deeply tanned with shorter hair, a neatly trimmed mustache and a chin-nubbin beard, Bo looked like a new man, and felt comfortable. Always wearing sunglasses and a Rays baseball cap, he looked totally different than the Bo who lost the money. No more slouching, especially when standing still, to look his full six-two. He watched people, cars, and his back. Vinny and friends would never forget about him.

He hung out with new people. His one-room bachelor pad was just off Lemon Pine Street, about two blocks from the beach. His routine changed in some way every day, but he did spend extra time at the Sea Gull Marina, admiring the boats and fishing from the Pelican Pier.

Bo's new friend, Dillon Buckingham, worked at the marina on a fishing charter as either a deckhand or acting Captain, hoping he could have his own boat one day, by saving every nickel. He also liked to fish, and knew the best ways to catch his quarry.

On a Tuesday in early October, Bo fished off the pier when he saw Jose Zapata at the Pelican Pier. Jose rented a fast boat. Bo knew he was a bigger and meaner version of Vinny's bodyguard, Jesus. Bo's heart raced. He knew Vinny and the Big Boss he had never met, used the Florida drug pipeline and the Nogales route. *They are not here to find me,* he said to himself. But it was his day off, so decided to watch the boat leave. Jose and a skinny little white guy roared away.

Bo went home and wrote down everything he had done since making his getaway from Priest Lake. The only possible link was the stolen truck. Mr. Nice Guy had given a typed note to the Alamogordo Police while he had waited for his money.

He was sure the Big Boss could find out about the truck he left in Alamogordo if he knew where to look. Did they know about his hidden money in Mesa? He doubted that anyone knew about his stashes. If they knew and checked, they would know he was alive. It was necessary to use his real name to get his money transferred.

"But the chances they know I'm in Ft. Lauderdale are so small," he mumbled aloud. "Just be your new self. Just be yourself." That fast boat used the same mooring slip always. Bo would check every day until it returned and be extra vigilant.

Saturday morning, while sitting on a bench with a book and a latte, Zapata and the skinny white guy returned with the boat. Zapata was talking on the phone. A white van arrived in a matter of minutes. Three men exited the van and went aboard the boat. Zapata and the three men came ashore in less than a minute with two duffel bags each. They climbed into the van and were gone.

Less than five minutes, thought Bo, *and they never looked at me.*

Bo became a regular at the Surfer's Bottom, a small brewpub on the beach with a view of the pier. He ate small meals, enjoyed a beer or two and wrote in a journal. Rarely noticed, he watched the pier. His shift started late afternoons into the evening at Captain Dan's, usually getting home about eleven. Tuesday and Wednesday were his days off.

Three weeks later, Zapata returned, rented the same boat, and returned the following Saturday. The same white van. The same three men. The same black duffel bags.

"Bingo a pattern," Bo said, grinning from ear to ear.

"What did you say Bo?" asked another of the fishing regulars.

"Nothing, Bobby. I just figured out the way to start a chapter of my book."

Bobby turned back to his fishing, and Bo took pictures—Zapata with the boat, all four with the duffel bags, the white suburban, and the license plate. Bo would give the pictures and a note describing the process to the cops. He felt he had at least two weeks before Zapata would return. Give the cops a week to prepare.

He put the pictures on a disc and copied a computer letter typed at the main library to the same disc. After reviewing his handiwork, he placed it in a padded envelope with a small sterile note and mailed it to Lieutenant Brayden Davidson. This man was publicly heading a task force to "Put an end to drugs." Bo made sure all his items were clean. No fingerprints or DNA.

Shelly Ward worked as Davidson's secretary. She always opened his mail and gave him the important stuff first. When he came to his office after meeting with his task force, she gave him the disc first.

"Brayden, this is strange. I dumped the contents onto my desk as always. I haven't touched the disc or the note. All it says is 'important.'"

"Call Ed and ask him to come ASAP and dust for prints. When he is done, put it in the player. I'll be right back."

"No prints, Shelly. Whoever put this together knew how to avoid DNA and prints." said Ed.

Shelly relayed Ed's findings to Brayden.

"Put it in the DVD player, and let's look."

Together they watched the pictures and read the computer note two times. Bo's note read:

> *The Mexican renting the boat is Jose Zapata from Mesa, Arizona. He transports drugs and money. A very dangerous man. About every three weeks on a Tuesday, he rents the same boat. He returns the following Saturday. Check out the pictures. The white van picks him up. It has been two weeks since the last one. Might want to check this Tuesday. Also check Spokane homicides. I am gone.*

"Get everyone on the task force back in the conference room, Shelly and set up the player there. I will see if the chief is available."

Shelly took the disc and the note, set up the room, and made new coffee. The chief was coming.

"Watch this," Brayden said to all as soon as the chief arrived.

After watching it twice, the chief stood and said to the Lieutenant, "Your baby. I'll call the judge, and you'll have the warrants. If you want extra people, stop by."

Davidson assigned his people and turned to one of his senior squad members. "Sammy, you're a fisherman, so you fish on the Pelican Pier on Tuesday and see if this dude rents the boat. We'll meet here Tuesday at 4:30 p.m. If it's real, we'll set up for the bust on Saturday. Not a word to anyone. Not anyone. Are we clear?

Ronnie, you check the Spokane homicides." Someone in the back teased Sammy. "You always get the good jobs."

All laughed and mumbled the usual doubts and hopes as they left.

Bo saw the new fisherman. *Cop,* he said to himself. *Good. Maybe, just maybe, we get some of the bad guys.* Bo decided to fish today and Wednesday. The cop had to think Bo was one of the regulars. The cops would guess that the tip came from the pier, but it would take a lot of leg work to check everyone that spent a lot of time on the beach.

The Big Boss in charge of drug distribution in Mesa could send someone for a while. Bo would watch for new people.

The next Saturday, Bo watched from Pelican Pier as Jose and the other three bag men were arrested along with the van's driver and the boat driver. The boat was impounded, and the rental clerk was detained. All without incident. Bo wished he could say there was a wild and noisy gun battle, but no shots were fired and no fanfare.

Monday morning Lt Davidson called the local television stations. He gave a press briefing in front of police headquarters. Mr. 'spit and polish' strode to the microphone and outlined his findings.

"Good afternoon. This Saturday, we arrested five members of a drug cartel. The five people are major players, Jose Zapata of Mesa, Arizona, Jorland Drumba, Jo Jo Petty, Felton Blue, and Ben Sarvino of Miami. We are following leads to attempt to apprehend Billy Turrot of Miami and Rocco Weltey of Mesa. We confiscated more than 150 kilos of cocaine and more than six million dollars. We are pleased to announce this success in the War on Drugs. We will continue to make more arrests in the future."

Bo enjoyed a beer at the Surfer's Bottom and wondered if Davidson's teeth were real. The smile was. Lt. Davidson's star is on the way up.

The cop fisherman was gone—no other new people.

Bo often thought about the money he lost, but he liked his new life. He felt safe. The bad guys had more to worry about than little old Bo. He called Steph, "Let's go celebrate something."

"Sure. Sounds super. Would this be a good time to drive down to Key West? I can get the week off. Things are slow at the paint shop."

"I will talk to the manager and see if I can get some time off. See you in an hour at Captain Dan's."

When Steph arrived at Captain Dan's, Bo greeted her with a kiss and the good news. "I have the week off as well. Key West here we come. I already have a room set up. Let's go in your car and hit the road."

CHAPTER 44

ort Lauderdale welcomed me with beautiful weather, blue sky, some puffy clouds, little wind and the weather lady's promise that it would be like that the whole week. I hoped to use this city as my base for fishing. The adventure in St. Petersburg targeting a Jamaican criminal, would also be thoroughly researched.

I might also use it to travel to Cancun as my alternate identity, James Colbert. My three-day fishing trip would allow me the time to check out all three.

I booked three days on the boat. Just me, the captain and his deckhand. My quarters were a neat one-room cabin near the ocean with access to the beach and the commercial strip. After an interesting cab ride with a local who talked for the whole twenty minutes, I checked in. I changed into shorts, a polo shirt, and sandals then headed for the beach.

I saw my boat, the Billfisher Two. Someone was loading items, so I stopped and introduced myself. He held out his hand. "Wade Shaffer, I am the deckhand and the most important person. Captain Eddie and I have been together for eleven years. Word around says the fishing has been good."

"Nice to meet you, Wade. I am excited. See you tomorrow at 6 a.m."

"Just your clothes, Sir. We have all the rest of the equipment. I suggest a real light wind suit with long pants and a full-sized sun hat." With a quick wave, and a smile, he took his load onto the boat.

"Say, Wade," I called out. "Where would I get the best seafood dinner within walking distance?"

Without hesitation he answered, "Captain Dan's." He disappeared below deck.

On the way back to the cabin, I found a shop and bought the suggested light wind suit. After a nap and shower, I headed for Captain Dan's, seven blocks away. I was trying to decide between the shrimp and blackened swordfish when I heard a familiar voice behind me.

Bo, how do you do? I thought. He was not my waiter, but he passed by my table. I would never have recognized him. The voice was Bo, one hundred percent. I was glad he was alive. I would have to think about Bo.

The blackened swordfish was superb. I will skip the Reubens and sample other fish entrees here. My first day of fishing was fun enough to make the entire vacation worth the trip. Chasing and catching bonefish is a fisherman's dream. They are easily spooked because they are most often in shallow water, and shy away from boats, so finding them and catching them is extra exciting.

The next morning, I drove the Everglades Parkway and I-75 to St. Petersburg in about four hours. I located the courthouse, three possible buildings to shoot from, and a hotel less than three blocks from those buildings. My long-range shot would be near seven hundred yards from either site. A large construction project, across the street from the office building I planned to use, would again cover some of the noise from the shot. The building would be a shooting option if I could get a high enough rental office, and I could open the window. I would need two or three days to ensure the shot was doable.

After day two of fishing, I drove all of Ft. Lauderdale, including the best-recommended route to the Miami Airport. Returning to my cabin, I stopped at a convenience store to get a city map and a six-pack of IPA. I noticed a small strip mall advertising lockers for fishing gear, saying they provided twenty-four-hour access. I rented one for a year. A rifle and some gear designed for fishing off the pier could be hidden there. In a sell it yourself-weekly paper, I found lots of fishing gear for sale. One ad caught my eye. *Lost my husband. Will be glad to get rid of all the fishing gear.* A pleasant-sounding lady answered. "Are you calling about the fishing gear?"

"Yes," I answered. "How did you guess?"

"My husband's phone. I have a special price if you take everything, otherwise I want market price, as he had pretty good stuff. Where are you calling from?"

I told her my location was near Captain Dan's.

She gave me directions. "About fifteen minutes."

I took it all at the special price—with four of Vinny's one-hundred-dollar bills. My new purchases made the locker look full. I took one medium-sized

Penn casting reel and a full tackle box to Wade the next day and asked what I should use off the pier, as it was too windy to go out on the ocean. The TV weather lady missed today's wind in her forecast.

He gave me some hints. "This is a good setup, Del, and the tackle box is loaded. Nice find. The fishing may be okay near sunset, but otherwise, you might as well watch TV at Captain Dan's."

So, I did. Bo was not there. He was off on a week's vacation, they said.

It was damn cold in Bozeman when I returned. People noticed the tan—time to start packing to go to Arizona, as I would not have time after I return from Hawaii in early January. I will drive to Casa Grande. I have some little friends to surprise.

CHAPTER 45

C liff knew all. I guess I expected that. He would cover himself. I suspected it when I noticed a tag team following me in unmarked cars. I am trying to improve my awareness of things around me. The old Del would never have noticed.

Did he get the information about my alternate IDs from his contacts? He said he had not asked, so I hoped he was still in the dark and could not be implicated. No, I decided, he would find out only if he felt he must. He would stay away as far as he dared.

I also decided he would call me first and ask me to 'retire'.

I have some prep work to do for the possible St. Paul 'adventure', which has been moved from Minneapolis. I do not have a selected building to shoot from and need to drive my potential escape route. The Spokane adventure still needs more research.

I am going to see just how good Cliff's tag team is.

I had completed most of the banking and money laundering before I first called Cliff to ask for the favor. So, they did not know where the money was. They may not know about the long-distance shooting club.

They know the Ram and where I live in Bozeman. They must know about the boat.

I am going to take my new boat to Glasgow, Montana. The fishing in Fort Peck reservoir can be fantastic, walleyes, Northern pike and trout. Paddlefish in season and the ever-present perch are catchable.

I had a list of places to go to stock up for the trip. At Home Depot, I parked in a "Reserved for Veterans" slot, pretending to get something out of the back. I made a mental note of the cars and trucks. I took my time in the store, selected some paint, and a new screen door for my house. I paid and walked to the Ram fussing with my billfold. Only two vehicles remained that I knew were there when I parked. The white compact sedan was empty. There was a fiftyish man in the light gray SUV. He had short gray hair, a thin mustache, yellow shooter's sunglasses, and a mostly gray baseball cap. He was talking on the phone.

A young man from the store, loaded the screen door for me, while I put my package in the back. A woman about fifty, trim with a purposeful stride, but no Home-Depot bag, slipped into the white sedan sporting a Montana license plate. I could only see a five and a 'W' on the plate before she drove away.

Sorting through the CDs in the visor holder, I watched the SUV. When I left the lot, he followed me until I parked at Safeway. The SUV passed the turn, but before I entered the grocery store, the white sedan parked in the same row, five spaces from me.

The woman made a show of fixing her makeup in the rear-view mirror.

The produce is at the front of the store. I slowly tied a bag of oranges, watching the main door when the woman came in, picked up a plastic carry basket, strode to the Starbucks coffee kiosk, and ordered a latte. She took a cell phone out of her purse and seemed to visit with a granddaughter. With a nice laugh and a loud voice, she said. "Since you are busy now, I'll call you tonight. Love you." Leaving her basket, she walked out.

Cliff, you have poor help. I have much to learn about the clandestine world, but these two must think I am a bozo.

I have a choice to make. Lose them on my way to Glasgow, call Cliff, or let them put me to bed. I decided that testing them would be fun, and then I would call Cliff.

After moving to Bozeman, one of my first purchases was a quality bicycle. I like to ride and keep in shape. Hiking, coupled with riding, would improve my cardio and my stamina. I decided to find out where they were staying. I was sure their motel would be near the Lincoln arterial, as that was the route I usually used to get to the house.

I pulled into my garage, closed the garage door, walked through the kitchen, turned on the living room lights, powered up the TV, and showed myself in the window.

I ran out the back as fast as I could, grabbed the bike, rode quickly to the alley entrance and turned to watch the street that passed my house. The sedan was parked near the corner allowing for a direct view of my front door. The woman watched for half an hour, then left. I followed. The stop signs and stoplights made it easy. Both cars were at the Comfort Inn. Perkins Restaurant was across the street.

I was the first patron at Perkins when they opened at 6 a.m.

The "tag team' came in together at seven-thirty. Laughing about something, they ordered breakfast, never suspecting I was there.

The look on their faces was priceless when I joined them at their table. "They serve excellent omelettes here. Hi, I am Del Sanderson. But you know that, I am sure."

Recovering quickly, the woman calmly answered. "What do you mean?"

I offered my cell phone and scrolled through the list of eighteen pictures I had of them. Good ones. Both cars, and both faces.

I looked at each of them and said softly, "Cliff is my friend. You two are not. You can call him and stop wasting his money. I will ask some friends to watch you leave town. You will not know they are around. I am not aware of everything, but I am pretty savvy and certainly not stupid. You two did a very poor job. On your way out of town, ask Cliff to call. He has my number."

They would not know I do not have any one to call to watch them leave.

CHAPTER 46

C liff called Billy. "Take everything that is yours and move out of your apartment. Everything. Leave the place sterile. Drive to Wendy's in Laurel, just west of Billings. I'll meet you there at seven-thirty. Do your best to make sure you are not followed."

"Yes, Sir," he answered. "That dial tone and I are having too many conversations. Wonder what is up now."

Billy found Wendy's at seven. He hadn't eaten since breakfast, so he decided on a single with cheese, no onion, and a frosty. He was almost finished with his meal when Cliff walked in.

Cliff nodded and motioned for Billy to stay seated. He ordered a chicken sandwich and coffee, then joined Billy.

"Were you followed?"

"No, I was extra careful," Billy answered.

"Good, because the Bully Boys have targeted you. They have been following you for weeks. They have you pegged as a cop. You will be relocated to Minneapolis via Ohio as of this instant."

"WOW!" Uttered Billy as he sat back and ran his fingers through his hair.

"Any chance we could let this play out a little longer?"

"No, Billy. Your cover is blown. Your life is more important than this undercover assignment. I talked to Rick. He has a friend in Litchfield, west of the Twin Cities. You are to join his friend's shooting club and work hard to be a good shooter. When we are done here, you are to drive to the Billings field office, turn in the truck and the gun, but keep the Tony cover materials. They will have your ticket ready. Ohio and Minneapolis are expecting you, and an agent will meet you. I believe you are going to be a top agent. I suggest you study all the undercover material you can get your hands on. Learn disguises and practice using them. Learn to speak without the New Jersey accent. I would be very disappointed if you and I lost contact."

"May I ask how you learned I was in danger?"

Cliff sat back, relaxed, and rubbed his hand down his face, brow to chin.

"Del. He gave me the heads up. I called Rick, and he agreed. Del rented a vehicle and followed you for two days. He saw all of the Bully Boys following you at one time or another. Del told me Jim informed him that Bully had you pegged as a cop. Those boys know everything about you. You should realize they know about cops. They don't trust each other and surely don't trust anyone they believe to be law enforcement. I am proud of you. You have learned from your mistakes and will learn more every day. I'll miss having you around."

"Cliff, I feel like I let you down."

"Not a chance. We never leave agents when we learn they are in danger. Your accent hurt your credibility, but we knew that going in. We knew you were inexperienced at undercover. All in all, it played out about how we expected. Your time in Bozeman was a positive learning experience. Now it's time to move on.

After Cliff left, Billy sat alone awhile. "So, Del saved my life. Yet I didn't get to thank him or say goodbye," he whispered.

He reported to the Minneapolis field office the next afternoon. He knew he liked Del. He felt he owed him big time.

CHAPTER 47

The following morning, I was home, drinking coffee on the patio and doing the crossword when Cliff called.

"I will be on your patio in twenty minutes."

"Super."

I poured his coffee and walked out to the patio, as he pushed open the back gate and strolled to his favorite chair.

"Does it bother you to need to come here today?"

"Yes, Del, it does. I could say I was worried about you, but you wouldn't believe that. I could say I was covering myself, but you wouldn't believe that. Right?"

"No. We both know better. You want to know what I plan regarding the extra ID's and have been digging around. I do not like, nor do I deserve any scrutiny. I have done nothing wrong." I hated lying to Cliff, but if he knew what I had planned, would he let me continue or would he stop me and send me to jail? I couldn't take the risk. "You had those three forgers give you everything, right?"

"Do you trust me?" Cliff asked after a long pause.

"I will always trust you, Cliff. I gave you my word, and we shook hands, but then you dig and followed me. Am I missing something here. Am I a problem to you?"

I waited for Cliff to answer. Finally, he answered. "I did not get the names for your identities, but I could. They would tell me. That's not why I'm here, and that's not why I'm having you followed. A couple of things you should know. Because of your tip about the Bully Boys, Tony has been transferred. Thank you for saving his life. We have identified all but one of the gang. We are also close to the last one—quite a group in one place. We want to find where they hang out. The agents following you were for your protection, not to pry."

"I just want to live softly, hunt, fish, travel, and spend more time with my friends. I wish I had a really good bug detector and a device that can tell if a phone number is in use and where the phone is. That could give me the edge if the Bully Boys start causing me concern."

"I have one that can detect anything. I have a phone monitor as well," Answered Cliff.

"Even old stuff. Even burner phones?"

"Yes, even the top foreign stuff."

"May I have one of each?"

"Look, Del," he said, looking down at his hands and then directly at me. "We owe you for saving an agent's life. We owe you for the tip about the Petersons—the Noses, you called them. We are close to them now." Pausing, he added. "I'll get you those devices. We will do anything in our power to ensure your safety, but we can't be everywhere all the time. You ask, and the posse will arrive asap. Fair enough?"

"Yes."

Out of the blue, I changed the subject.

"You want to know why I wanted the three new identities?"

"Only if you want to tell."

"You know I am trying to shoot a record mule deer, a five-by-five white-tail and a trophy elk. Those species are in the Western USA. So, I want to apply for hunting permits four different times in lots of states. Then I will have four chances instead of just one. If life allows, I may expand to other species, but who knows?

"I have registered at the University of Montana to take an art class. Just something I have always wanted to try." I smiled at Cliff, not sure if he bought my hunting story. It was a good one, but was it good enough?

Cliff sat back and relaxed, took a sip of his coffee, and smiled from ear to ear. "I am not a game warden. I don't have the time. Send me pictures, but don't tell which one of you shot the animal, and don't get caught."

Cliff stood up and walked to the back gate, looking at his watch.

"My ride is here. Godspeed."

"Always." Our closing words for over fifty years.

CHAPTER 48

T he following morning, a package arrived overnight by FedEx to my Bozeman house. Two small gadgets, each the size of a small cell phone, and a note from Cliff. "Two presents with instructions. Go to the federal building in Helena Monday by nine a.m. Burn the note. "Godspeed"

I served myself a fresh cup of coffee, picked up my paper and went out to the patio. I burned the note in the gas patio grill and said, "Always."

I went to the library at the University of Montana campus and looked through some newspapers for updates on all of the possible 'adventures' I have been watching. Nothing new. Then searched for new 'adventures', and the list was long. Lots of scumbags looking for ways to get off and not pay for their crimes. Now that my big rig is almost done, I should plan an extended trip through the Southern states and do some serious recon.

Just keeping my promise.

I packed up my fishing gear on Monday and arrived in Helena before nine a.m. I chose a seat in a bakery facing the Federal Building and Peterson's place of business. A dark roast coffee and a cinnamon swirl will make the wait extra fine. They sold a lot of pastries in the hour while I waited.

At exactly ten-thirty, three black SUVs arrived, and two agents got out of each one. In twenty or thirty minutes, all came back out of Peterson's office, escorting Frederick, sporting a set of handcuffs. He got to ride in the center vehicle.

"Wow!" I said too loudly. Five or six customers looked my way.

I know I was smiling.

I downloaded a trial subscription to the *Helena Independent Record*. I wanted to keep track of *the Noses*.

I went back to Bozeman via highway 69 through Boulder, often stopping to fish the Boulder River and enjoy a beautiful *Big Sky*-day. No wind and not a cloud in the sky. After releasing two nice rainbow trout, I sat on a rock and thought about Amy. Wiping away the tears, I yelled to the sky. "I miss you, Amy."

Tuesday's *Helena Independent Record* headlined the arrest of Frederick and Samuel Peterson. The story alluded to another person of interest but offered few details. Citing an ongoing investigation and hinting at a fraudulent scheme regarding mining claims, more arrests were expected.

In Thursday's paper an article described a suicide in Butte. Professor Greg Lansing, a geology instructor at Montana Technical Institute, had been found in his home with an apparent self-inflicted gunshot to his head. The FBI airlifted him to a hospital in Salt Lake City. His actions could be related to the arrest of Frederick and Samuel Peterson in Helena recently. The FBI was involved, and the investigation has revealed information that could be far-reaching, involving arrests in other states and Canada.

Samuel and Frederick were in trouble. Maybe they will leave me alone for a while. They will figure out that their problems began after I brought that gold sample to them.

CHAPTER 49

I decided to go to the range the next day after breakfast. If he was not too busy, maybe Rick would have time to work with me using the Win-Mag. Maybe we could plan a competition inviting outside long range shooters.

While I was eating at Betty's, one of the regulars in a coffee group came up to me and introduced himself.

"Morning, I'm Bill Davis. Our little group has seen you here a number of times and would like you to join us on the weekdays whenever you can. We are not real nosy, but we solve the world's problems every day and complain about the weather."

"Sounds fine to me." I picked up my coffee cup and joined six other elderly guys at a long table in the back of the cafe. I had noticed that a group of regulars sat at the back most mornings. They laughed a lot and were obviously good friends.

"Morning, everyone. I am Del Sanderson. Thanks for the invite."

Introducing themselves, I heard, Butch, Desmond, Zig, Hank, Joe and Frank. Frank was last, so he must have been the designated questioner.

"New in town?"

"Yup, I am. Moved from Great Falls a few months back. Needed a new place without so many memories. You guys all old timers here?"

"He's calling us old, and he just sat down!" Zig chimed in, laughing.

Surprisingly they did not pry much.

Butch offered the most information. "I still own a small ranch east of town. My boys do all the work now. Desmond is a retired deputy sheriff, and Zig had a paper route."

"Rural mail route," interrupted Zig.

Butch continued, "Hank worked as an investigator for the IRS. If he doesn't know you, then you're on the up-and-up. Last and least is Joe, a long-term elementary school principal. Now you get to tell us how you made your millions."

"I did financial consultations for small businesses and some personal financial planning, so I traveled a lot. Most new businesses that are not successful have poor financial acumen. I still have nineteen clients. But I will not tell you how I got my millions because I am still working on one million. I plan to hunt, fish, travel, and spend my winters in Arizona."

An hour later, I thanked them again for the invitation to join their group. While paying for my breakfast, I watched them in the small mirror over the busy entrance to the kitchen. They were all listening to Hank. Comparing notes. Frank and Bill never said what they had done to earn their millions. I will ask next time I join them. I will bet this association can lead to deer and antelope hunting opportunities.

CHAPTER 50

inally, at the range, I went directly to the office, noticed the five shooters at the far side—Bully and four of his friends. Only Bully faced me, but as he talked, the others listened with serious expressions.

Rick met me at the door. "So glad to see you, Del. I can take care of myself, but those are five not-so-fine fellows. I wish they would go somewhere else to shoot."

His nine-millimeter Smith and Wesson lay on his desk. He picked it up and put it in the holster he always wore. I had never seen the gun out of the holster before. He opened his bottom drawer and handed me a look-a-like gun and holster. "It's loaded. Thirteen shots, with a spare clip in the holster pocket."

While I put the holster on my belt, Rick said. "Let's shoot the Win-Mag at 550, 650, and 850 yards today. You make all the calls and adjustments. I'll record the settings and results."

After two shots, the Bully Boys left. They had three pickups.

"They only waited for us to shoot twice. They seldom stay if others come. They pay, but they only have one gun, and all use it. They ask questions once in a blue moon, but I never see their targets. They never buy anything here," Rick paused and watched the three white trucks exit the gate.

"There is a rumor that the Feds are going to make all range operators register all long shooters. The word is they will be using ex-military cops and shooters as enforcement. I doubt it will ever happen."

"Maybe that will get rid of them, Rick. I doubt they would pass the background check."

We finished our shooting. All shots at the first two distances were in the six-inch circle. The first shot at 550 yards was high and left. We talked about why, and I made some small changes. The last four were in a six-inch circle.

Hauling all the gear back to the office, we continued our conversation about the Bully Boys. "Del, I used my spotting scope to read all the license plates and attached my camera with a new card. I took a picture of each person. Over the past three weeks, I have eight different faces, including Jim.

"What are you going to do with them?"

"Lock them in my safe."

"Will you make me a copy of the pictures and the plate numbers?"

"I could. Why?"

"I know someone who can check all this information for us."

Rick just looked at me for a long minute. "And bring us trouble!"

"The info will not, but if those are bad guys, and we both believe they are, they will be smart enough to know how they were made. My contact knows how to be discrete. Your decision."

A somber Rick put the rifle in the gun safe and stowed the rest of the gear. When he finished, he turned to me and said, "I'll give you the stuff. Two things: I need a heads-up before anything is done, and two, every precaution must be taken to keep us clear."

"I totally agree with both statements. I will send in the info today. I will tell him of our agreement."

We were talking and planning a competition to set up before the end of the year when I had an idea. "Why not set up a competition here? Just long targets. You must know a way to make that work. Then we can ask the Bully Boys to help and see what happens. I think they have a safe place near Bozeman where they go to as a group. Most are travelers, but they must feel somewhat safe around the Bozeman area."

"Good idea. Actually, most range guys will close their ranges and bring their best to the shoot. Let me make some calls."

I walked to my truck, stepped in, and called Cliff. One ring, and he answered. "Yes?"

"I am sending you some critical info on the Bully Boys. Rick and I need a heads up if you act in any way."

"You have my word, Del."

As I drove home, I noticed all three white pickup trucks were at the truck stop diner, and the Bully Boys sat by a window. They wanted me to see them. Why?

I crossed I-90 and entered the McDonalds' parking lot, choosing a spot in the back near a lilac hedge. Shielded by the hedge, I saw all three rigs turn onto the eastbound interstate ramp with only four people. Someone was following either Rick or me.

On my way back to the range, I purposely drove past the truck stop. One guy still sat by the window. Watching for Rick was my guess.

I told Rick all I had seen.

"They are going to be trouble to both of us, Del. I can feel it."

"I know you live just up the road past the range and do not have any close neighbors."

"Yes, Del, but my security is beyond tops. If I am there, I win. I'm going to upgrade my security here at the range. It's good now, but not foolproof. When it's upgraded, I'll win here as well."

I lifted myself back into my truck, rolled my window down, and said, "I will call you if he is still there."

"If you call, I'll come by the truck stop and go to the hardware store in Manhattan. If you don't, I'll just go home."

No one sat by the window, but the small dark-green older Subaru outback was gone.

Bet a breakfast that was his ride. I bet I would eat for free.

I decided to call Rick anyway. "The guy is gone, and so is a green Subaru."

"Yup, Del, that car has been here a time or two. That is the ride for the smallest Bully Boy."

"I called my security contact, and he is in Spokane. He will be here Friday. You know where my place is. Bring two pizzas around five or six, and we will discuss things."

"Okay, Rick. I'll do that!"

"Not just any old contact," I mumbled to myself.

Driving for twenty-five minutes with the aroma of warm pizza circling through the truck is torture. A new navy-blue F-350 Super Duty STX almost filled Rick's driveway, dwarfing his little red Mazda. Rick's security contact traveled in style.

Rick met me at the door, took the pizzas and shouldered his way into his small kitchen, letting me follow.

Opening the two boxes, he said, "Lagunitas IPA okay with you?" I knew Rick was a strong man, but he wore a t-shirt with a graphic design of a shattered window with a bullet hole in the center. It fit him and showed a sculptured body not usually noticeable when he was at the range.

"Perfect!"

Rick handed me the beer, put two slices each on three plates, gave me one, and carried the other two plates into his small living room.

"Del, meet Art Archer."

Art stood, walked to meet me and extended his hand. "Any friend of Rick's is a friend of mine."

I am quite fit and would not be considered weak, but Art could have crushed my hand and bested me in any manner he wished.

"Rick and I have known each other a long time and are very close friends. He speaks highly of you."

"Are you a long-range shooter, Art?" I asked, sitting down on a nearby chair.

"I know how," was his short, terse answer. Art stood about six foot, two hundred twenty pounds and solid as granite. His head seemed too small for his neck and body. He sported a military haircut masking a square hairline and exposing small ears. Bright blue eyes, a small mouth and nose completed the look he wanted you to see. I thought to myself. *"He can disguise that head in record time."*

He knew I sized him up just as he did me. A knowing smile creased one side of his mouth. Rick just watched.

"Let's eat. I'm starved," Rick said.

"Del, Rick said you have thoughts about improving your home and vehicle security." He took a bite of pizza.

"I had not thought much about it, but after Rick and I talked the other day, I am sure I need to protect myself better.

Art interrupted, "Rick told me about the Bully Boys. I agree you have at least concerns. They will be after your guns if nothing else. You can be sure they know where you live. Give me your address and leave your back door open, and I will be by at 3 a.m."

"Coffee?" I asked.

A small smile. "Dark roast. Zero frills."

Rick and Art discussed the improvements needed to upgrade the security at the range. Money was never mentioned. They had a bond and I shared the room but not their inner dynamics. They were close. They knew I was there, but not included. Rick was a friend. Art was to become one.

CHAPTER 51

I was awake, and the coffee was brewing when Art arrived. I never heard him, just noticed the candle flame flicker.

"Morning, Del. Nice with the candle."

"Morning to you, I learned that from a police friend. I am not sure what to expect tonight."

Art said. "Security is my business. My firm stays committed to being on the cutting edge of technology and laws. My company consists of six people and myself. All others have a real job that allows them to be flexible. Security is my passion and their hobby. We trust each other. Rick's house and property is a fortress, and his range building will be one in a week. He asks, and he gets.

"Del, Rick is my best friend and the only person I would trust with my life. He is not as big as I am, but I would not want him for an enemy.

"Rick told me a lot more about the Bully Boys, and you two have a right to be concerned. They are a threat to you both. We do not know how many of them there are. We don't know how they get money to live, without working, and buy long-range shooting equipment. Rick and I believe that local law enforcement watches them loosely. The authorities may know how many are fixtures in the Bozeman area, but they would not tell us. Let's look your place over." I handed him his coffee.

An hour later, he had a plan. "Fortress or just really good?"

"What is the difference in cost?"

"Thirty-seven hundred verses Sixty-two hundred."

"Fortress. I plan to be hunting and in the woods a lot. Also, I have a cabin near Lincoln, Montana, that I would like to protect as well."

"Fortress it is. When will you be in Lincoln?"

"I can be there within a week after the house is done, whenever it fits your schedule.

It's a small, 800 square-foot older cabin on thirty acres. I am working to acquire the abutting parcels. That would make the total two hundred ten acres. I think fortress for that would be different than this house."

"A fortress means no one can come or go without you knowing. You will have a dedicated phone, one hundred percent surveillance, one button defaulted to 911, and a connection to local law enforcement. Also, my company has a group we call the posse that is closer than you think. Some could be minutes away. How good is your sweeper?"

"The best I could find." I did not tell him about Cliff's.

"I'll get you one that can detect everything."

"How much?"

"You pay for all gadgets. You pay for all apps. You pay for all upgrades. That will be about six thousand for your house. The cabin should be under eight thousand. Only Rick gets a better deal. It will be about two weeks out to do your cabin. I'll call you."

Art turned and studied me. It made me uncomfortable. "Rick said he would trust you with his life. That says everything to me. Until now, Rick and I have only had each other. I am happy that Rick has another friend."

"What's next?"

"A woman will be here in three days. She will have a long ponytail and be wearing a yellow vest with a small black fly-fisherman logo on the left upper chest area. She will ask you to name your favorite movie. Your answer will be?"

"A River Runs Through It."

"I know that one. Norman Maclean wrote that and Robert Redford made the movie. The young woman's name is *Mandi*. She will do everything and brief you on operations. You prepare your entry codes and passwords."

He gave me a 6x6 inch piece of maple wood one half inch thick. There were ten routed numbers on each side and all rows in between; one hundred in all. The numbers were painted three different colors; red, green, and yellow. He showed me how to read it.

"If we need to contact you in a coded manner, we will use the board, otherwise we will just call."

"Do you know how many solutions there are on this board?" Asked Art.

"Depends upon the number used. I would have to check myself, but I think I would start with ten-factorial and then go to one hundred-factorial. Then a factorial system based upon the numbers of each color. The formula is based upon the number of characters in the code being used," answered Del.

"Good answer. You're the first person that has been even close to the correct process. The results are yours and only yours. They'll not work for anyone else. Rick might figure it out. But he wouldn't waste the time." He handed me a business card containing only a phone number and a picture of galloping horsemen.

"This phone number is one of mine and exclusive. If that number ever gets compromised you will get a new piece of wood and a new phone number by FEDEX the next day. Everything is dual recorded. You will have access instantly to all applications."

"Art, I am not a stupid man, I am not questioning, just wondering, why the coded secrecy?"

"Del there is no such thing as too much vigilance. The Bully Boys, for some reason, do not trust either you or Rick. Rick knows how to hide. You must learn. And you must trust Rick."

Only Cliff knows I have alternate ID's. My secret would stay my secret. I knew I could trust Rick.

"I plan to become an expert with my new toys, Art, because I have so much, I want to do yet. Hunting is a priority, and there are many places I have yet to visit. I will be at the cabin often during hunting season. Should I pursue martial arts?"

"A little can be dangerous," answered Art. "If you do start then finish. I suggest getting a black belt. You will enjoy the process and learn life-saving skills. Nice to meet you, Del. Thanks for the good coffee."

We shook hands. Then a slight pause, a dip of his chin, and he was gone. Another small flicker of the candle flame. I did not tell him I had been working towards a belt for years, I just had not been diligent about finishing. If I started back aggressively, I could finish in about two years.

Three days later a small young woman rang my door bell. She was wearing a yellow vest with little black fly-fisherman on the front, and sporting a very long blonde ponytail.

"Hello, Del. My name is Mandi. Your favorite movie is…"

"Nice to meet you, Mandi. *A River Runs Through It.*" Somehow that did not seem very clandestine, but simple as I only told Art the movie name, and she had a business card that said Mandi. Nothing else.

"Nice to meet you, Del. You have two nosy neighbors."

"Really?" As I pushed the door wider to invite her into my house.

"Yes. The lady across the street and your neighbor next door. Let's tour the house, garage, basement, and backyard first. Then we will sit in front of the window and visit about what I will do and why. Will your neighbors ask about me?'

"I do not know the lady across the street, but the next-door neighbor most likely will."

"Okay! My regular job is a personal financial planner. I have all the certificates and licenses. I have four hundred clients in Montana. Thirty in and around Bozeman. I live in Billings and will leave enough stuff to make this appointment legit. Serves two purposes as I can cover why I am here, and the briefcase gives me a space to carry the gadgets."

"I didn't find any bugs anywhere," she said as she opened her briefcase. "The folder is yours and the phone is yours." She waited for me to pick them up. "The folder and the phone are sterile to you. I'll be here at one a.m. and enter through your back door. I'll be here a little over two hours. Read and study all I have provided in the folder, believing that you need a perfect score or you are dead."

"Wow!" was all I could say.

She was on time. Worked silently for a little over two hours, then explained everything and asked a dozen questions. Shaking my hand and adding a small smile, she disappeared out the back door as quietly as she came.

Her parting words were, "Act regular and notice everything without letting others realize you are noticing." I must have passed. But I knew I needed to become as close as I could to one hundred percent proficient with my new toys. I must never go places using a regular routine.

CHAPTER 52

Rick and I sat in his office at the shooting range discussing Bully and his pals.

"Del, Cliff said he wanted to arrest those guys on something bigger than a weapons charge. You and I need to brainstorm and find a way to make that happen."

"I have been thinking along those lines. Do we dare to try to find where they hang out?"

"Risky, Del. Maybe we can work some kind of tail. I just don't trust any of them. I am positive they carry a pistol or two in every truck. They don't worry about a weapons charge."

"Maybe we could disguise ourselves, rent an old truck and follow one of them," I offered.

"If we got caught, they would kill us," answered Rick. We talked another hour about our options without deciding what do.

I stood up. "I have some errands to run. We can talk again in a couple days."

"I agree, Del." See you.

We both worried about what Bully and friends were up to.

Bully loved being a career criminal. His little group didn't have to work, except to do what they were told. He controlled everything. "Jim told me he saw the new guy, Tony, put something under Del's truck. Cops do that. That means they ain't friends. I think Del's an old guy that moves around a lot. We don't have to worry about him.

"I think Tony is a cop, planted to catch us. We are going to start hassling him and get him gone one way or another. Dicky will make out a tail schedule. We give it two weeks."

Wolf asked if anyone wanted a beer. Hearing three yeses, he went to the kitchen, retrieved the beers, opened them and returned to the meeting. He then offered a comment. "Dicky's our best shooter. Maybe we should ask Rick to help all of us get better at shooting."

"I like that," grunted Bully. "We'll do that. Now we need to get rid of Tony and figure out a way to steal all those fancy rifles Rick has stored in the vault."

Dicky said. "We could break into his house, I bet he has an alarm so he will go check. Then we break into the vault."

"Okay," said Bully. "Bellamy and Buff will do the house. Wolf, Spike, and I will do the vault. We will do that tomorrow." Bully continued, and when his plan was clear, he left the room.

CHAPTER 53

While I went to set up at my usual station, Rick worked on the competition we planned to hold at his range. He made a lot of calls. Most contacts thought they could send a team. Rick wanted to, but couldn't ask the Bully Boys to help—they had not been around in a while.

Later that morning, Bully and two friends arrived and approached Rick, asking him to help them with their rifle skills.

"That's why I'm here. I'll need to see your equipment and do a test at three different ranges. Then I can help with the settings and ammo choices."

I couldn't believe our luck. Rick and I had discussed finding a way to keep an eye on these guys, and the opportunity had strolled right up to Rick.

"We didn't bring our gun. So, how about we come Friday, bring the gun, and get started."

"Fine. I'll be here," answered Rick.

Bully and friends drove away in one of their white pickup trucks.

Rick walked over to my shooting station, where I was setting up to do some six-hundred-yard targets. I wanted to make sure I could always set up my own shots so they would be in the six-inch circle every time.

"Did you hear Bully?'

"Yes."

Sitting on the bench, Rick put his hands together, "Why now?"

"I think they are watching us while we watch them. Mutual distrust. They believe we will be easier to keep track of. And, I suspect they are planning something," I answered.

Rick watched me set up and sat on his hands. "You're spot on. Bully wasn't really smiling. He doesn't know how. But he is the leader. No doubt about that! We watch our asses. No one behind us."

Rick's phone vibrated. He looked at it quickly and said, "Someone's at my house. Put your gear in the vault, and we'll lock up and go together to check." I recoiled, and he noticed my reaction.

"I can't leave you alone here. When you go into the office, take everything out of the lower left-side drawer of the desk—minimum of two clips each. Close the vault and spin the handle. I'll get my truck. When you're done, get in the truck and lock the door." I followed orders to a tee.

We drove to the house a mile up the dirt road as quickly as Rick dared.

There were two bodies on the ground. "The tasers got them. Stay in the truck and have your gun ready."

Rick jumped out of the truck and ran around his house using a military-style crouch, gun in hand. Then he pulled both bodies at the same time to the side of his detached single garage. He made five quick punches on the keypad, followed by a quick ten-second trip in and out to get the duct tape and zip ties. He immobilized the perpetrators with zip ties to secure their hands and feet, and taped over their eyes and mouth. Then chained and padlocked each to a wooden post in the ground.

I was impressed by his efficiency. I had exited the truck and came to help, but Rick would not let me. "Those two are Buff and Bellamy," I told him.

"Get in. You drive. Back to the range as fast as you can."

We had been gone less than ten minutes. Rick was out of the truck before I had come to a stop. He had his gun in his hand.

Bully and his two buddies were trying to break into the office and the vault.

"Stop!" Rick yelled.

Bully raised his hands and said, "We ain't armed. We give up. We'll leave."

"Bullshit boys. On the ground, hands on your heads."

Wolf, the biggest, fattest, and obviously dumbest, drew a short-barrel revolver from a rear holster, and raised it to shoot.

Rick shot him through the heart. Bully lay on the ground, his eyes wide with fear. He lay face-down and stretched his hands above his head. Spike started to run. Rick shot him. He crumpled to the ground and lay still.

"Take your two dead friends and leave. If you ever come back, or I see you anywhere around Bozeman, you're dead."

Bully never said a word. Red-faced and fuming, he loaded the two bodies in the back of his truck. Fatso was a lot of work, and we did not help. He just drove slowly away.

"Can you follow him, Del? We want to know where he goes. He can't stop anywhere with the bodies in the truck. Don't take any chances."

"I will try." I was equally scared and excited.

Rick put his hand on my shoulder, "This didn't happen, right?"

"Oh. I understand better than you think. I never saw a thing. Doubt I will ever be asked."

I followed Bully until he turned north off the interstate toward Whitehall. If I went any farther, I would be seen. So, I went back to the range. Rick was cleaning up.

I did not ask about the two he tied up at his house. I figured he would tell me if he wanted me to know. My guess—he would never say. I was sure Bully's boys had been reduced by four.

Rick was strangely quiet.

"Rick, are you okay? Want me to stay awhile."

"How about you come by the range in a couple of days."

"Sure thing, Rick. Call me if you need to. See you in a couple of days."

Rick looked at me for a long time. His eyes were glistening. "Thank you, my friend."

"You are welcome, my friend," I answered.

Driving back to my house, I decided to go to Home Depot to replenish my supply of sandpaper. That roll-top desk was a lot of extra sanding. *I am almost innocent,* I mused. *Just another secret.*

Four of the thugs were out of the picture. That left Bully, Jim and two others that we knew about. Those were all that we had ever seen at the range.

Four is still a lot to watch. Maybe Cliff can help. I need to talk to him.

I went to see Rick the next morning, driving slowly and carefully. He had not answered his phone as I tried to reach him five times. Something was wrong. I knew I needed to go see if he was okay, but my worry meter was maxed out.

I stopped my truck in full view of his house. Then waited with my hands visible on the steering wheel. I did not see or hear him, until suddenly he looked in my passenger window. He was armed. After a few seconds, he tried to smile.

I lowered the passenger window.

"Morning, Rick. I thought we should go eat a good breakfast."

He just stared at me until I was uncomfortable. Then stepped back, lowered his head and shook it side to side. Finally, he looked at me.

"Good idea. I'll go get cleaned up. You wait here."

We ate breakfast at the Long Road Truck Stop. Jim caught a glimpse of us while he washed dishes. He nodded at us, trying not to smile. Not a word was said about yesterday. I watched Rick go through a release process from a tight steel-coiled weapon to the usual Rick I had come to know.

"Thank you, Del. I owe you. I'll never forget this." His face said everything.

CHAPTER 54

Bully drove the truck back to the farmhouse. He knew he couldn't stop anywhere else. He would bury his two convict friends. He was betting Buff and Belamy were dead. He decided to get the last two guys still available, take all remaining cash and go to Wyoming somewhere. He needed to go to Salt Lake first and get his drugs to deliver to Billings, then find a new hideout place near Sheridan, Wyoming.

Dicky and Jeff were at the ranch house when Bully drove into the yard.

"Git out here and help me. Now!" Yelled Bully. "Dicky, get the shovel and the potato fork from the shed."

Dicky ran to the shed and got the tools, never asking why or looking in the truck bed.

"Jeff, you drive. Dicky, in the back with me. Take the truck down to the creek near the three big cottonwoods."

Dicky gasped when he saw the bodies of Wolf and Spike as he put the tools in the truck bed but didn't say a word. Jeff stiffened and whipped back around, hands on the steering wheel, after he glanced through the back window to make sure the others were safely on board. But he didn't say a word either. *They didn't dare.* Bully thought clenching his teeth tight together.

Jeff parked in the shade of the big trees. And all three gathered at the tailgate to handle the bodies.

"We got caught trying to break into the range office. Rick shot Wolf cuz the dipshit tried to pull a gun. He shot Spike cuz he tried to run. I don't know what happened to Buff and Bellamy, but I believe they are dead, too. Rick told me he would shoot me if he ever saw me again. I knew he was a handful, but didn't expect him to just shoot. We bury these two, clean out the stash of cash and drugs, and our stuff, then take the Suburban and go to Salt Lake, get the drugs to take to Billings, and go to Wyoming. When we get stuff set up in Wyoming, we come back and make that Rick bastard pay."

"Was that Del fella there?" asked Dicky.

"Ya. But he was in the truck the whole time. He didn't do nothing. I think he was scared. We were right. He's just an old man. Nothing to us," answered Bully.

The makeshift graves were not deep. Digging holes like that wasn't fun. No one said anything, but they all knew the critters would find the bodies one day soon. The remaining Bully Boys didn't care much. They would be gone.

They cleaned out their stuff. Jeff was elected to go down into the cistern and get the money and drug buckets. They were sealed to keep the money and drugs dry. Then they drove down to Willy's house, left two months' rent and a note that they would be gone for a couple of weeks, maybe more. "That will buy us some extra time, and we can come back here when we are ready to take care of Rick," said Bully. "Let's go gas up and get on the road. Jeff, you drive. We'll stop at the Long Road, fill up, and get a sandwich to-go. We got no extra time."

At the truck stop, Jeff pumped the gas and Bully and Dicky went inside the convenience store and selected premade sandwiches and other snacks for the whole trip. They only stopped for ten minutes.

I was at the Long Road truck stop dinner, on I-90 near Exit 284 in Manhattan, drinking coffee, when Bully and his two remaining Bully boys pulled up to the gas pump. But I was intently reading my paper, so did not notice them.

I was on my way to see how far along Jack and his sons were on my big rig modifications.

I also wanted to talk with the management at the truck stop about renting an indoor truck parking garage. They had two old converted service buildings with five bays each. I wanted to be on the list, if one was not available now. I already owned my storage unit for my other toys, and I hoped to get a safe place for the lilac ride.

Gazing out the side window of the café, I saw Bully and, two Bully look-alikes come out of the truckers' lounge at the back of the lot. They did not look my way. I was sure I had not been seen. They all piled into a forest-service green Suburban with tinted dark windows and Nevada license plates. I had not seen any of the Bully bunch drive that vehicle before. I decided—if they believed Rick's ultimatum, they were leaving. Cliff needed to know this.

Bully let Jeff drive.

Earlier, Cliff mentioned Bully was a person of interest. I went out the front door, got a burner phone from my truck, hid behind a fully loaded woodchip-hauling eighteen-wheeler, and dialed Cliff.

"Now," I said and hung up.

The Suburban had barely entered the interstate when Cliff called me back. I told him what I had seen. He listened and said, "Thanks, Godspeed."

"Always," I answered, and he was gone.

Cliff immediately called the Butte, Bozeman, and Pocatello offices and sent agents in motion. All had the description of the Suburban, and good enough descriptions of the three Bully boys.

The next morning, I sat in my recliner, sipped coffee, and read the headline on page three of the Bozeman Chronicle. *FBI apprehends one of its ten most wanted. Selmer "Bully" Varnell and two associates, Richard "Dicky" Sheffler, and Oland "Jeff" Shortway were taken into custody at the rest area off I-15 near Dell, Montana.* The brief article added little. Varnell had been a fugitive from justice for three years. Sheffler and Shortway had extensive criminal records. I wondered if Bully was smart enough to figure out what went wrong, I would need to be more vigilant.

"At last. One of our worst fugitives behind bars," said a beaming Agent, Joe Seeman. "The other two were on the fugitive list at the Bureau. Yes, a good day for law enforcement."

I was positive Bully and friends knew where I lived, what my truck, camper and boat looked like. They always used those three white pickups, so I could never be sure of a tail. I had watched and practiced evasion, and

Cliff had given me other ideas after his two-person tag team had failed. We laughed about that now.

I needed Cliff or Charlene to tell me if and when Bully or his friends are ever released from jail.

CHAPTER 55

Jim lived in a single wide, faded, robin's-egg-blue mobile home. It's location in a small clearing surrounded by a juniper and pine thicket at the end of a two-track road about four miles south of Manhattan allowed Jim privacy. Utilities came with the rent. He stole things whenever he could find an opportunity with limited or no risk. He looked for a part-time job but did not interview well and had no luck until he risked trying the lead, Del gave him. He used a Coleman lantern to save money. He ate mostly microwave meals or pizza. The dishwasher job had to be his first in years—the life of a solitary and lonely man and ex-con.

Messy would be a kind word to describe his place inside and out.

No one knew where he lived, not even his parole officer or Bully. He always parked his ten-year-old, dented, rusty, hand-painted blue Toyota pickup in the trees just off the paved road that served as access to a run-down development of eight or nine ranch-style houses on three-acre plots.

He had never met any of his neighbors. He worked hard to keep his place a secret from everyone.

Jim stowed the stolen Russian guns behind his refrigerator in the trailer.

He left the Shanty Seven Bar just before eleven on Saturday night. A dark, partly cloudy, night with no moon, and the air smelled of rain. He parked his truck in the usual spot, stepped out of his truck and took a deep breath of Montana air.

He was almost to his trailer when he felt the shock of the taser. He fell face first, unable to prevent the fall. He broke his nose, and blood oozed from a gash on his forehead.

The next thing he knew, he could smell the unwashed floor of his trailer, his hands and feet were secured with zip-ties and one of his own dirty socks in his mouth.

The light of his Coleman lantern revealed the silhouette of his captors. *The Russians found me. How?* He wondered.

Using poor English in a heavy accent, the smaller man said. "Ver are da guns?"

Jim didn't move or answer.

The bigger man kicked him savagely. Three more kicks, and he was lifted onto one of his two chairs and tied in place with an electrical cord.

"Ver are da guns?" Repeated the smaller man. "We watch you shoot from hill and see you with guns. We know you have dem."

Jim just shrugged.

"Now, Ivan?" asked the designated hitter.

"Ya, Sergo."

Sergo produced a very large knife and proceeded to cut off all of Jim's clothes. Jim watched wide-eyed, his scream muffled by the sock, as Sergo cut off his left nipple.

Jim nodded furiously, so Sergo took the sock out of Jim's mouth.

A whispered whimper of sound passed through Jim's lips, "Be-hind... the...fridge," he panted against the pain.

Sergo easily pulled out the fridge and removed the guns. He left the trailer and took the guns to the Russians' car. When he returned, Ivan nodded, "Put the fridge back" then got up and left.

Sergo beat Jim unconscious, slit his throat enough to get a slow blood flow, then taped Jim's nose and mouth shut. Jim was supposed to die before he regained consciousness. Not bothering to pull the door shut, he also departed, after pushing the fridge back against the wall.

CHAPTER 56

The next day, two small boys from the housing development went through the clearing that hid the trailer. They were using their favorite shortcut on their way home from school to explore, as they had often done. The usually locked trailer door was ajar, so the boys dared to peek in. They saw Jim looking right at them. Falling over each other to get back down the two-step riser, they took off running, as fast as little kids can, to tell their mother. She called the sheriff.

Protecting the boys, and assuring them they did the right thing, she said to the sheriff office dispatcher, "I want to report a body my boy and his friend found." A pause as she listened to the dispatcher. "Yes. It is in a rundown trailer near Ponderosa Acres. You know where that is? Good, the boys and I will wait on the road and show you where it is. We thought the place was vacant."

"The Sheriff, himself, is coming? Good, I voted for him."

Sheriff Colton Shaver was a small man who wanted everyone to know he was a one-time welterweight boxer. He prided himself on being in top physical condition. He told anyone who would listen, "I could still get in the ring and take care of myself."

He sported a Clark Gable mustache. His brown hair was cut short, and he walked with a small, but noticeable, spring to each step. The deputies avoided Colton's piercing beady dark eyes. The broken nose gave his narrow face a mean look. Colton was a serious man, who only smiled when he needed to. He rode to the crime scene with two of his deputies. "Hope the kids are wrong," he muttered to himself.

Colton knew who the victim was as soon as he saw the body. An ex-con, James Brent Nelson, who came to Bozeman as a parolee from Arizona. He was known as a model parolee and had never missed anything required of him. The overworked parole officer had not taken the time to learn where Jim lived. Jim was not quite done with his parole when he moved to Manhattan. He reported to his parole officer in Bozeman and gave her a phony address. She had too many parolees to watch, and Jim was a short-timer who followed all the rules. So, she told Colton about him, but left Jim alone.

The Sheriff knew Jim had a federal rap sheet, so he called the local FBI office. An agent arrived within an hour.

Colton talked to Jim once, telling him not to get into trouble in his county. He looked up the facts and knew Jim had a few minor federal convictions.

A deputy checked Jim's neck first as a matter of procedure. "I've got a weak pulse here." An ambulance arrived, loaded Jim in the back and sped away.

The FBI agent called his office and asked another agent to cover the hospital. No one knew why Jim had been left for dead, nor if anything had been taken by the ruthless killers.

Sheriff Colton liked his job and felt he needed a clean record in his town to keep being elected. So, he let the FBI do everything. They had the resources and the money—no costs to his county. He loved 'washing his hands' as he would often say.

I was in Bozeman, enjoying one of my favorite home-cooked breakfasts with coffee. Reading the morning paper, I came across an article on page three that piqued my interest. The article offered few details, only that an alleged homicide had been committed and was related to organized crime and drug trafficking in the Western USA. The victim's name was being withheld until the authorities notified the next of kin.

The *Chronicle* interview I read, confirmed the victim was not a local person and the FBI might have more information. Agent Bleeden thanked Sheriff Shaver and his staff for their cooperation and promised to relate any further developments.

I wondered how many others said, "Bullshit" after reading the article. I did.

Closing the paper, I wondered if Cliff knew who the victim was and if he would tell me.

The only thing I noticed was that Jim did not come to the range anymore. I figured he left when Bully left. I knew he was not working at the Long Road any more, because I asked.

CHAPTER 57

eing early for my morning coffee and breakfast sandwich at Starbucks on the University campus allowed me to be first in line to secure a computer at the library before the rush. I wanted to look for bad guys. Lorenzo needs company. Searching headlines in many major city newspapers, I scored a promising option in the tenth one, the *Spokesman Review.* The Spokane, Washington, case had been on my radar for some time, but the legal posturing was extensive. It looked like things had changed quickly.

Five papers later, another possibility surfaced in St. Paul, Minnesota, for the same name as the Minneapolis case. I would later learn it was a change in venue.

The stories led me to expect the Spokane opportunity to be more pressing than the St. Paul one. Keeping track of both would be my new daily routine.

The Spokane police had arrested Vladimir Grolov, reputed to be the head of the Russian Mafia in the Pacific Northwest. Lots of posturing about a trial or deportation. A trial would be on the docket for early February, but if he was going to be deported, that would happen in a matter of days. I will go to Spokane now and watch the developments in St. Paul by reading the newspapers at the Spokane library. Vladimir no doubt did everything bad the police alluded to, but they caught him kidnapping young girls to sell and ship out of country. The girls were transported to Seattle and put aboard Liberian ships—the destination, Russia. He was caught at the scene when his helpers put some of the girls into a van. He was trying desperately to get deported in lieu of a trial.

A trip to Spokane was in order. I wanted to see if things will work out, go to REI, a sporting goods retailer in Spokane, and Cabelas Outfitters in neighboring North Idaho. I would keep my information current.

It took two days to drive from Bozeman to Spokane. Only about 400 miles between the two, but there were numerous fishing opportunities along the way. Fall fishing can be some of the best as the rivers and streams are low, and the fish are hungry. The Blackfoot, the Clark Fork and Henry's Fork are all blue-ribbon trout waters. No way I could pass them all by. I wanted to get better at fly fishing.

I stopped first at Cabela's to select some camping gadgets, fishing lures, and a packable fly rod.

I treated myself to a stay at the Davenport Hotel in downtown Spokane. It is billed as the Grandest Hotel in Washington State. The restaurant was old style elegant. Plush and warm, they made me feel special. A menu item caught my eye. Amy's favorite was a lobster tail and an accompanying filet mignon. I allowed a tear or two to trickle down my cheek. My waiter stopped by and asked, "Is everything alright, sir?"

"Things are okay. I am just missing someone that cannot share this dinner with me."

The next morning, I walked the entire downtown. I located the Courthouse across the Spokane River and three possible buildings I could use to complete my Spokane 'Adventure'.

My first choice was impossible as I could not get to the roof. Both of the others were possibilities, but my second choice did not offer a reasonably safe escape. The Russian was not worth the risk of getting caught and going to jail. Time to stake them out to watch the auto and foot traffic. The old Metro Furniture Building's front door was always unlocked during business hours, but a security camera covered the approach from the sidewalk. It was effectively pointed at whoever used the push bar. The people going in and out paid no attention, but I must assume it was operating.

The rear entrance did not show evidence of a camera. The entry to the vestibule, where the fire escape was located, was also unlocked. A ten key entry keypad protected the door to the main building that had no window and lots of dust. I could park in the side lot twenty steps from the rear door. I needed a disguise to risk checking the roof.

In my car's trunk, I located my baggy Lennox coverall that I found at the Goodwill thrift store in Bozeman. Well-worn work boots, a semi-dirty baseball cap, and a scruffy reddish beard completed the look of the man who tested the stairs. The small toolbox had a black 'Lennox' stenciled on both sides. Kind of dumb, but like they say, *it's not rocket science*. It took me eleven minutes to walk up to the roof door with my bag of tools. The door was locked, but thanks to a YouTube demonstration I had studied, it opened on the first try.

The roof was rimmed by a three-foot high wall thick enough to support a bi-pod for the gun, at four stories up and about four hundred fifty yards away from the target. The top floor seemed vacant and showed no signs of use for many years. I could risk camping there the night before the shot, if I knew when to expect a chance.

I watched from a bus stop across the street for parts of two days. I saw just one vehicle enter the alley behind the building. That person went up the street and not into the building. Free parking was my guess. The parking lot on the south side filled up by seven forty-five, but the rear lot remained vacant.

Traffic was light until lunch breaks started. The suppresser would make my shot virtually soundless. After the shot, I could lower all the gear in a duffel down to the alley and drop the rope. It took twenty seconds to hurry down the stairs. My test showed it took about a total of fifty seconds to make it to the parked car. I would be driving on Monroe Street in about one minute. Small risk.

I practiced an escape route to the interstate and the route to Felts Field. The interstate was considerably shorter, but the traffic lights on the way to I-90 could make those seven blocks a nightmare. Felt's Field was just too far and risked too much exposure. The third route via Washington to Mission to Sullivan and then to I-90 East would be the easiest and safest route. That would be my choice. I could stay at a motel in Post Falls, Idaho, a mere twenty miles away, before the day of the shooting, and no one would ever see the shooter. I would rent the motel, and Spencer Morgan would be the shooter.

My visit to REI netted me two lightweight nylon 100ft ropes—enough to get the gear down to the alley in a hurry. Leather gloves completed my purchase.

I found an obscure older, off-the-beaten-path, but clean motel near Post Falls. I rented a kitchenette for a week. The young receptionist seemed more interested in her phone than me. "Hang a note on the door when you want clean sheets or towels." Were her parting words. Poor help. Fits my needs, though.

I had my Browning 308, my golf clubs, and two sets of my disguises for Spencer in the trunk of the car. I set the measured shooting distance in my optics.

At a remote pullout on the Spokane River, I rechecked the optics. The weather forecast did not hint at major problems for at least a week.

The paper had an article with a breaking news story about Vladimir every morning. Still no decision. I played Circling Raven Golf Resort south of town twice. I used the driving range at The Highlands in Post Falls on other days. Four days into my week at the motel, the headline in The *Spokesman: Russian makes a deal.* He was scheduled to meet before the Judge the following Tuesday at 9 a.m. and receive his deportation papers, then spend a night in jail before being transported to the Russian Consulate in Seattle. Wow! There is much to do to make sure I was ready.

This 'adventure' was going to happen on this trip—no coming back. I rechecked the shot's logistics and escape route, then decided it was a 'GO'. Good! I can check out Monday as late as possible for an early Tuesday morning departure. Before leaving, I wiped everything clean, removed the sheets and pillow cases and piled them on the bed. The evidence of my stay would soon be washed away.

Allowing half an hour to get to the Old Metro Building, I could be on the roof by 4 a.m. The weather was to be mostly calm, with a temperature near 52 degrees and partly cloudy. The range finder fixed the shot at four hundred ninety-seven yards. My gun was set.

Disguised as Spencer, I was on the roof at four a.m. and ready. I would recheck all the optics for the rifle before the activity started. Waiting and watching was tough when a person was on edge.

They brought Vladimir to the courthouse by car. I did not have an opportunity to shoot when they went in. The police left four well-armed guards on the courthouse steps.

A crowd had formed when they all came out thirty-five minutes later. They were not pleased that Vladimir was going free. I watched through the scope. Someone in the crowd threw a rock or tomato at Vladimir. That action caused the group surrounding the Russian to pause, leaving Vladimir momentarily uncovered. I pulled the trigger.

Dead Russian. Number two Curt.

I raced to the alley side of the roof, loaded all the gear into the duffel, lowered it to the ground behind the lilac bushes, dropped the rope, and ran to the stairs in a crouch. Less than one minute to the car, I never saw a soul and drove away on Washington Avenue in under two minutes. Following all laws, I turned on Sullivan and headed to I-90. I exited at the Huetter rest stop in Idaho and changed back to Del. I have practiced those changes so often. I can make the change in less than a minute.

Fifty minutes later, I parked at Stoneridge Golf Course in North Idaho and played eighteen holes. Cool, but perfect! My score of eighty-seven proved I had already destressed to my regular self.

In Coeur d'Alene, I stayed the night in the Best Western. All three local TV channels reported their version of the breaking news. Vladimir was dead. The police had suspected the shot came from the crowd but did not find anyone with a gun, though they admitted that most protesters ran when Vladimir fell to the sidewalk. I will follow the story for a while but felt safe.

I enjoyed the motel breakfast buffet, then drove directly to Bozeman. I think I will do a fishing trip. Maybe to Fort Peck, in Northeastern Montana. I was still trying to get that trip on my schedule.

While driving back home I was feeling stressed. My hands started shaking. I exited the freeway and sat with my head in my hands for most of an hour. Losing Curt and Amy, laundering the money, living in a new location, planning the hunting trips, and definitely, the 'adventures', were causing extra stress.

I needed to stay at my Lincoln cabin, work on the repairs, and explore the dim trail through the Forest Service property. I needed to know if it joined the trail into the Bob. I needed relaxing time badly, so I will take care of myself, starting now.

CHAPTER 58

Captain Bill Bower held a press conference at 9 a.m. the following morning.

"Vladimir Grolov was killed on the Spokane County Courthouse steps yesterday at approximately 9:45 a.m. An angry mob of more than one hundred had gathered to protest Grolov's deportation. They wanted him tried and convicted instead. We are continuing to follow all leads. A member of the crowd could have made the shot, but as soon as Vladimir fell to the sidewalk, the crowd dispersed in all directions and none were detained. Some other bystanders, not part of the crowd, said they thought they heard a shot, but no one really knew where the shot originated. We will do our best to locate the person or persons responsible for this crime. Thank you all for coming."

Back at headquarters, Captain Bower went to his office and called the mayor.

"Sir, we don't have any leads. We went into protection mode when Grolov went down, the protestors panicked and disbursed. We haven't determined if the shot came from the crowd. If it was a sniper, we will find the shooter's location, but I'm afraid he's long gone. That person could have been out of Spokane in less than a half an hour, and unless we get a solid lead, we may never find him." Bower paused to listen. "Yes, Sir, we will keep you up to date."

He called a staff meeting for 11 a.m. and had all patrol officers return for the meeting.

"A high-profile foreign national was killed on our watch. I'm not sure what will happen, and we aren't to speculate. I'm sure we will be visited by the FBI. Don't theorize with them. Refer any and all inquiries to me." He wiped his brow and continued. "The Russian community will start posturing as we speak. They aren't a large group, but they have some bad guys that like to be rough. If any of you are confronted or threatened, come see me A-SAP. No delays!" Putting his pen in his pocket, he added. "Division leaders, in my office. The rest of you be careful. Watch your back a little extra."

In his office, he told his four division lieutenants, "Absolutely no leaks about this. You know I like to let you do your job, so cover all the bases, and keep good, clean, records. This is going to go political at some point. We need to prove we have done, and are doing, all we can. Thanks."

After he dismissed his officers, when he was sure no one watched or listened, he smiled and said, "Damn, the shit hit the fan. Lots of political bullshit coming, but it will be worth it. Damn. One real sleeze down, a million to go."

The smile lasted most of the day. He expected the FBI to show up and do their own thing. They had more resources and they had more powerful people to answer to. He said to himself, "No chance of finding this shooter." If he were being honest, he really didn't care. Grolov got what he deserved.

The FBI did come calling. They agreed to be the national cover and have their people watch the Russian Mafia. The Russians never made a public comment. Maybe they too, were happy Vladimir was gone.

CHAPTER 59

Time to talk to Cliff. I used a prepaid throw-away phone to call the FBI office in Salt Lake City. I said, "For Cliff," and hung up. I took the phone out to the garage and destroyed it. The Waste Management truck would haul it away in the morning.

Always an early riser, I retrieved my paper, poured a steaming cup of black coffee, located my reading glasses and stepped out to my back covered patio.

Cliff sat in his favorite place in the darkest corner. When I realized he was there and turned to greet him, he put one finger under his nose and grinned. That meant he didn't want any reference to his being at my house.

Silently rising, I returned to the house, picked up my portable tape player, selected an hour-long oldies tape, poured Cliff a mug of black coffee, and returned to the patio.

"My Favorites," I uttered as I checked to see if my neighbor was outside. "Gone to his McDonald's coffee klatch. Good."

We listened to music in silence as I solved part of the crossword.

Finally, Cliff asked, "You called?

"I did. I want you to visit me in Hawaii in December and fish with me."

"I would love that. When I get back to Salt Lake, I'll study my schedule to see if I can work it in."

I went to get us more coffee. I needed to remain calm. Seeing Cliff on my patio scared me. It had better not show when I returned with fresh cups for both of us. I resumed doing my crossword. In time, I interrupted the silence.

"Cliff, I just called you late yesterday. Then here you are on my patio first thing this morning. I know you would tell me if anything would affect me. Neither of us has ever liked surprises. I read about the Russian who was killed in Spokane and wanted to know if that was part of the same group Jim stole the guns from."

"Yes, it is the same group. Del, I have some undercover stuff in Great Falls and Billings that isn't going smoothly, but I decided to come by and see you first. I'm working on something that involves you." Noticing the change on my face, he quickly added, "But in a good way, no need for you to worry. I'm involved in a program that pays civilians to inform the FBI about criminal activities they witness. I would like to involve you.

"What I'm going to share with you is a departure from bureau policy, but I trust you completely. When I finish, I will have a proposal for you. I want you to know about Billy. You saved his life. First a couple of other things. Bully and two of his crew are in jail for a long stint. They had money and drugs when we arrested them. I am glad we held off on the gun violation. They're in bigger trouble."

After a long silence, Cliff started talking. "I need to bring you up to date. I should've told you sooner. I told you Tony was relocated to Ohio. He is now in Minneapolis. He asked for another undercover assignment, and the Minneapolis Office needed someone unknown to the locals, so they invited him. Tony will join a shooting range near Litchfield east of the Twin Cities. He is undercover from day one. Rick has a friend who owns the Litchfield range. Tony is to work hard to become a decent shooter, and we can look after him.

"The Noses, or Gold Dust twins, are in jail. But as you found out, the business is still operating with two new brothers. We should have dug deeper before arresting Sam and Fred. We are digging deeper now. Many new leads have surfaced. It appears a very big operation is happening right under our noses.

"Gary Lansing, the Butte college professor, is still alive. He was taken to the Butte hospital, then airlifted, while on life support, to Salt Lake City. The FBI took over then, and he is still improving slowly. He is awake, but still seems distant. We hope he recovers enough to be helpful, so we can cut a deal to put him under witness protection.

"The Noses believe him to be dead. His only living relative is his mother, and she is in a home in Indiana. Gary, for whatever reason, has not talked to her or visited the home in fifteen years. She has the beginnings of dementia. Bully, Dicky and Jeff are in the federal penitentiary in Utah. A trusted snitch there told his attorney he heard Bully say, 'It's the kid shooter cop from the range who turned us in.' The snitch also revealed Bully plans to send some of his friends to get even with Rick for some apparent transgression. I am asking you to tell Rick.

"We haven't seen the remaining four of Bully's group for a while. Maybe you could ask Rick if he has seen them since Bully was arrested. The two Russians who attempted to kill Jim are in the Federal penitentiary in Washington, serving life sentences.

"Jim had a weak pulse when the Deputy checked. Cutting to the chase, Jim is at the same Salt Lake City hospital. Evidently, the Russian who tried to cut Jim's throat didn't cut quite deep enough. It clotted enough to stop the flow. The sweat and body oils were enough to loosen the tape over his nose so he could get enough air. He still needs more reconstructive surgery to fix his face. He has already agreed to become a paid informant for the FBI. You won't recognize him. He asked about you. He knows you are still alive.

"Rick called me a week ago. I will try to use his exact words. 'Cliff, you need to find a spot for Del. He could be an ace-in-the-hole for you. Trust me, he was at least as much on the ball about the Bully Boys as me. Maybe more so. He helped me more that I could ever explain.'"

I sighed deeply, "I had no idea so much has happened. I prefer a quieter life. More coffee? You have known Rick forever, right?"

Handing him his refill, I said. "I will be glad to talk to Rick. I need to tell him enough about what I will do for the winter and when I will return."

Cliff changed the subject. "Your neighbor is now under full surveillance. We believe he uses his big rig to haul drugs. On every trip, he drives I-90 to Sioux Falls, South Dakota, then goes to different cities in different directions. We will keep watching.

Changing direction again, Cliff started a whole new subject. "The DEA has asked for FBI help to stop or to at least slow drug traffic across the Canadian border into Montana. Our problems are different than the southern border. Border Patrol has a much wider space to watch up north, and carriers can walk across most anywhere. The walkers just boldly cross almost every night somewhere. The winter gear they use is top of the line. Most of the ranchers on the border on both sides are afraid to confront or turn them in. Yes, I have known Rick for many years."

"We have trouble finding undercover people to fit in and work there that can blend in. City people are easy to notice in and around the rural communities in Northern Montana.

"I know you're going to be in Arizona and enjoy an easy winter. We will visit at length when you return. You know Great Falls, so we hope to find a way to use you safely, but I don't have agency permission to tell you what we have in mind."

"Wow. Lots to digest." I wished I could tell him what I knew about the Priest Lake murder and the missing Bully Boys. But secrets and promises must be kept. Maybe I will figure out a way to bring those tips into play.

"So, the FBI thinks I am ninety percent safe from the Bully Boys, the Noses and the Russians? Great."

"Yes, but don't stop watching. Keep getting better at watching. They all have ways of being nasty. I'll need a ride to the Cabela's parking lot. Your truck in the garage? Del, we have lots going on in Montana. More than one deep undercover operation, but none involve you or the range. Good enough?"

"Yes, thanks."

"I will hide in the back. Wear a coat."

On the way, he said, "There will be an older white Suburban in a cluster of other rigs. Try to park as close as you can. My friends own the rigs. After you park, get out and open the back door. Take off your coat and toss it in on the back seat."

I did as he suggested. Cliff slithered out. "Don't look down. Thank you for saving my agent. Godspeed."

"Always."

My mind was spinning in circles. Cliff filled my head to overload. Reading between the lines of our conversation, I decided I needed to get rid of everything that could tie me to the 'adventures'. He knew I would figure out the reason he came to my house. Cliff's long discussion adequately covered my reason for calling him. He trusted me. He would tell me if I needed to know that someone saw any of the shooters related to my 'adventures'. Comforting.

CHAPTER 60

I wanted to go to South Dakota pheasant hunting on opening day, the twenty-first of October. To do that I must let my college art professor know about my plans. I would also make a day trip to St. Paul to see if the 'adventure' I planned against the serial kidnapper was possible. I might need to get everything ready, as the killer was running out of options.

My Art professor, Dr. Margo Thorn, agreed to listen to my request to submit assignments early and miss some class time.

Entering her office and taking the offered chair, I spoke first. "Thank you for seeing me today. I will not take up much of your time. We have three projects due between now and November third. I plan to travel to South Dakota and do some pheasant hunting. If I have those assignments completed before I leave, and take the test I will miss as soon as I return, would that meet with your approval?"

"Depends upon the quality of your work," She answered. "Just any drawing to complete an assignment doesn't reflect that you've learned anything I've taught you."

"Agree. I have all three assignments with me. If any or all are unsatisfactory, I have time to recreate them."

She studied all three, scrutinizing every detail. Ignoring me, she turned each drawing to every angle, looking, scowling, smiling, touching, and finally said, "Your talent is evident, though unpolished! The landscape drawing is quite good—a unique setting of mountains and pine trees from stream level. Interesting. It has some depth problems, but you will learn that. I think it is a special place you are portraying? The detail is quite good. The street scene drawing is somewhat plain, but I would accept that as it is. The angle of perspective is what I wished to see. Your active campus scene has only one student. That is not what the assignment asks for. The landscape is quite good, but the people part is lacking."

"Okay!" I said, "I'll leave the first two as my submissions for the class and do the other one again. Will it be satisfactory to add to this drawing, or should it be totally redone?"

A wry smile and a sigh. "Adding may be difficult. You can try that, but don't settle for a poor effort. I suspect that would be a shortcut, Mr. Sanderson. You do not strike me as a person who takes shortcuts."

Her comments made me smile. I knew she was being coy, or even shifty because she obviously wanted me to do it over. "I see your point. If I finish by October tenth, will that be soon enough?"

"Yes." Standing, she added, "You are the oldest student I've ever had in any of my classes. I wish all my students were as interested in learning as you. Enjoy your trip."

I handed over the two drawings and put the rest of my things in my backpack. "Thank you for your time. Back for the test in November."

I stopped at the campus coffee shop and said yes to a cinnamon roll to go with a large cup of good dark roast coffee. Then I made my way with my calories to a bench on the southern perimeter of the quad. I ate my treat and finished the coffee, while choosing a place to set up for my active campus scene.

I decided I should be closer to the middle of the action and draw a panorama centered around a lone girl sitting on a bench, ignoring everyone. She had her legs pulled under her so she looked to be sitting on her feet. She slumped over a thick textbook, held in place by her legs. She wore holey jeans, sandals, and a too large long-sleeved t-shirt. Her long brown hair was pulled on top of her head and held in place with a large pink butterfly clip. Stray hairs danced about her face, reading glasses perched at the tip of her nose, and pink earbuds attached to a cell phone completed her student look.

A perfect pose. I took a picture using my cell phone. If she stayed long enough so I could at least get a rough draft completed. I could remember the rest. The girl made the scene. I would add four or five distant walkers, including a couple holding hands and looking starry-eyed at each other. I knew Dr. Thorn would approve.

A beautiful day, with perfect, mostly white, cumulus clouds for the backdrop, made it hard to stay on task. I slaved over my drawing for over an hour. The girl never moved and never turned a page. She was studying the back of her eyelids.

Enough for today. I started packing up when a familiar voice interrupted me. I did not need to turn and look.

"Hey, Del. Like, what are you doing here?"

I wish I could say I jumped up, but I do not jump up anymore. I turned quickly and smiled, "Cindy! What a pleasant surprise. I am a student just like you. I am in art 101 and have a drawing to complete, so I can take a trip and miss a few classes. I am done for today, so we should go eat some calories, and you can tell me how things are going."

"Dang! I have class now until four. Bummer. I so want to tell you everything. Are you going to be around?"

I smiled at her. "Are you looking for a date?"

Blushing, she quickly answered, "No. You're funning with me. God, I am so slow. It never would have happened at the EGGE. Gotta go." She laughed.

"Cindy, I will be in the cafeteria on the window side at four-thirty. Date?"

A sideways glance, batting eyelashes and a soft pout, the little girl in Cindy answered, "Yes, Mr. Sanderson. Date."

Humm, I have been called Mr. Sanderson twice in the same day. Respect for their elders. Good.

The student-to-woman change was evident when Cindy joined me at four-thirty. No books, just holey jeans, a hair band, and some make-up. Same smile. She sashayed the whole way, and people noticed. She sat with a flourish after patting me on the shoulder.

Naw! I do not blush. I am too old for that.

"On time today, Del. I'm so happy to see you. I have about an hour, 'cuz I still have things to do to get ready for my night class. I have so much to tell you."

"Tell me everything."

"My grades have been tops since I started eons ago, and they let me take fifteen credits this term. I can take fifteen next spring, two classes over the summer, and then student teaching next fall. Those extra credits allow me to add a math minor. I'll be done next December, almost three years faster than my old plan. Can you believe that?" She was talking fast, her whole face smiling, hands talking just as fast. "Wow! Who woulda thunk it? I'm almost there." She paused. "That's the good news. But my car quit, so I have to walk eight blocks. I usually have two friends to walk with, but we almost run when it's dark."

"What is wrong with the car?"

"I don't know. It just won't start, and I don't have time to get it checked. I wouldn't know if they were cheating me or being true."

"Will you let me take care of the car for you?"

She gave me a serious look. "I...gosh, Del, you have done so much for me."

"Tell, you what, Cindy, you give me your key, the address where it is parked, the make and color, and my friend and I will see what it needs. If it is more than the car is worth, I will not waste the money."

A hint of tears. She crossed her legs, and a worried frown framed her attempt at a smile. She took a deep breath and let it out as a long sigh, then a real smile appeared. "Okay! Okay! 'Cuz, it would be nice to have the jalopy. I want to say don't do too much to it because it isn't much of a car, but who am I to tell you anything."

She retrieved her keys from her purse and took the car key off the chain. I noticed the pink rabbit's foot. "Okay. Gosh. What can I say?"

"Tell me more about school."

She switched back to the carefree student in the blink of an eye. "Super. I'm on top of it. I love it. The methods class is so much work. I'm so busy, I hardly have time to eat. Study, study, study. Oh, more good news. The Education Department is going to see if I can do my student teaching at the elementary school four blocks from the Broken EGGE. Some of the teachers eat at the EGGE. Whew, I talk too fast when I'm excited and happy."

She put her hands in her hair, sat up straight and looked me in the eye. "I'm extra happy, thanks to you."

"You are welcome, Cindy, I am doing quite well. I have so much on my list, and one of those items is to find out if I can put what I see on a canvas. That is why I am taking the art class. I hope I have enough time to do everything I want. Seeing you today and watching you talk about school brightens my day more than you can imagine. You make me feel younger."

We walked out together. She was sashaying again and looking proud.

"Everybody is watching us, Del."

"That is neat, Cindy, Thanks for the date."

"It's my second one in five or six years. See ya soon."

"See ya."

A brief touch of hands, and she was off.

Three days later, I called her to see about delivering the car. I drove it Saturday morning to the EGGE. Madeline treated us to breakfast, and Cindy gave me a ride to my house.

"Not a rich man's house."

"No, Cindy, it is not, and that is how I want it. I do not want people to think I have money. Thanks for the date."

Playfully, she teased, "That's three now! We better slow this thing down. I gotta go study now."

Acting like she forgot something, "Are you going to tell me what you did to the car?"

"Sure. Cindy. My friend Jack tuned it up and replaced the battery."

"How much do I owe you?"

"Well, I asked Jack that same question. 'The I am going to have some fun with Del look' showed on his face, so he teased me a bit. 'Del,' he said, 'This, smells like a woman's car, so it depends upon how good-looking she is.' I answered, 'Looks like you worked for free.' 'Okay, you got me Del. When do I get to meet this looker of yours?' I said, 'Never Jack. I do not trust you.'"

She laughed with tears in her eyes. "That's so special. You have nice friends."

"I do," I answered, looking her in the eye.

She knew what I meant. "You go study now, and maybe at Thanksgiving break, we can play a trick on him."

"I will be at the EGGE over most of the Thanksgiving and Christmas breaks 'cuz the new gal wants to visit her family in Wyoming for both holidays and asked if I could cover."

"Beautiful. I will be by one day, and we will set it up. We will get a smile out of old Jack and have some fun."

We shared a soft touch and she drove away.

CHAPTER 61

ennis Dolder was arrested in early July. For over four years, some of St. Paul, Minnesota's street population of young women would simply disappear. His victims were usually described as nineteen to twenty-five, young, female, petite, and at least a part-time drug user with a petty crime rap sheet.

When officers conducted their interviews after a missing person's report was filed, a small blue pickup was often mentioned.

Barnaby Webster joined the St. Paul Police force after graduating from the academy. A patrolman in his third year, he covered the general area where the missing girls were frequently seen before disappearing. As officer in charge of three of the missing person reports, the blue truck was mentioned in two of them. He knew street people would move on and not tell anyone they were leaving. Often, they would suddenly show up again. Most knew a friend or two, but operated alone in their own world.

Witnesses guessed the blue pickup was a Toyota, Nissan, Mazda, or a Ford.

He and his partner, Jane Larsen, patrolled in South St. Paul when they were asked to go to the Maplewood area and check a report of a man walking down the street, brandishing a firearm, and yelling at everyone. The gun turned out to be a plastic nine-millimeter look-alike. The middle-aged, shabby-looking man was obviously under the influence of whatever the paper sack he carried contained. He was subdued, cuffed, and placed in the patrol car. Barney noticed a small blue Mazda pickup parked near the corner, one block away. It was unoccupied, with Minnesota license plates. He wrote the plate number, date and time on a blank sheet in his notebook, deciding to complete the check at the station house.

After booking the toy gunman, Barney checked the plates from the Mazda and found out the truck was registered to Genevieve Dolder, an eighty-seven-year-old woman who lived seven blocks from the location Barnaby had noted.

Four days later on a Friday, he and Jane were in the same area, having lunch at a corner deli, when a very nervous young woman approached them.

She just started talking, speaking rapidly, almost in a whisper.

"Betty is gone. She has been gone since Tuesday. We were going to go to the park, and she didn't show. We share a room, and she's not been back. You've got to find her!"

Jane interrupted, "Slow down, please. What's your name?"

"Sonje. You gotta help."

Jane completed the interview and read everything back to Barney as they were driving back to the precinct. "The same day we booked the toy gunman, the blue truck was a block away. Let's follow that up when we get back."

"I agree."

When they arrived back at the Police station, the number one detective from the Minneapolis Police Department was in the lobby chatting up with, the receptionist.

During his rookie year, Barney had been a small part of a high-speed interstate chase using both Minneapolis and St Paul police forces.

"Hello, Detective, I am Barney Webster, and this is my partner, Jane Larsen. I was in on the high-speed chase on the freeways two years ago, and met you briefly then. What brings you to our humble abode?"

"We got that bastard. Nice to meet you, Jane. Just here for a meeting. My favorite way to waste my time."

Barney turned to Wanda and asked. "Is Inspector Colston in the building? I want to see if he will let us follow up on the blue pickup lead."

"Yes, he's on his way down now and is going to the same meeting."

When Colston arrived, Wanda stopped him. "Jimmy, Barney has a question before you go into the conference room." Colston was a twenty-five-year veteran who never applied for upward promotion. He liked being chief of detectives and didn't want the stress of a higher-up job.

"What do you need, Barney?"

"Jane and I made an arrest last Tuesday in the Maplewood community where a lot of homeless people hang out. We noticed a blue pickup matching the description of some of the witnesses when some of the homeless girls went missing. Today, at lunch, we were approached in the same area by a woman who reported her roommate has been missing since Tuesday. That was the day of our arrest. We ran the plates, and the pickup is registered to an eighty-seven-year-old woman, who lives seven blocks away. We think we should follow that lead more and see if the lady drives it."

"I agree," answered Colston. "But don't let on you're checking. If the lead pans out, you must keep the info close to the vest. May I suggest something?"

"You bet."

"Barney, talk to Randy Johanson. He has done undercover work a lot, looking like a homeless person. I'll set it up. He knows how to look homeless. He always looks that way. He can give you some hints that he would use to watch that truck. He has tricks that really work."

"Thanks. I'll get right on it. What about Jane?"

"Lots of ifs now," Colston answered. "If the truck is in the mix. If it is used to pick up the girls. If Jane were to try to be a new homeless girl, she'd be noticed and checked. If the perp keeps his girls awhile. If he kills them and disposes of the bodies. See what I mean? Jane would be at too great of a risk. No way to watch her every second. If you prove the truck to be a lead, you can work on a stakeout system," Colston called Johanson and set things in motion.

"Good points, sir," answered Barney. "I'll talk to Randy and get myself geared up. Then I'll come see you to work out the details."

With the handshakes and see ya's over, Barney said to Jane, "I'll call Randy as soon as we finish our reports. We will find Sonje and talk to her again Monday."

Barney called Randy. They met at a Minneapolis thrift store, and Barney became homeless. He was allowed to be unshaven, get a tinge of the dirty look, and shadow Randy for three days. Then he returned and started watching the truck. Jane talked to Sonje a second time and confirmed that Betty was still missing.

It only took two days of watching the pickup to learn the usual driver was Dennis Dolder, Genevieve's son.

Barney and Jane caught Dennis two weeks later, trying to kidnap another homeless girl. After the arrest and obtaining the necessary warrants, they searched the entire property. Genevieve Dolder was confined to a wheelchair and suffered from dementia. The basement turned out to be where Dennis held his girls in captivity.

Using a FINDAR, a ground penetrating radar, a forensic team searched the entire property. They uncovered twenty-seven bodies of young women buried in the backyard. All were hidden under flower beds and crushed rock paths; the yard was grass free. One very new disturbance proved to be Betty.

After the search and arrest, Dennis lawyered-up. The lawyer hinted Dolder was not fit to testify. They worked on a plea arrangement or insanity defense. Letters to the editor wanted him dead.

The postponements were over, and the trial was scheduled for mid-October.

Since I had already arranged to be in Mitchell, South Dakota for pheasant hunting season, I would watch the developments closely. My lilac ride would take me there. I can have all the disguise items with me and bring my best rifle. I reserved a spot at a RV park in Zumbrota, a small town south of St. Paul. Disguised as Sven, I would drive a rental from Zumbrota to St. Paul and stay at the Hyatt Hotel, a block or so from the courthouse.

CHAPTER 62

n my Sven disguise, I would fit in around St Paul, as lots of folks still used a Scandinavian accent. My room at the Hyatt was on the 19th floor, facing northeast.

The room was at the end of the hallway, next to the stairway. Better for the Escape Plan B. I asked for a room with no one above me and facing the morning sun. The clerk said they aren't using the top three floors, and no one would be above me.

The view of the Courthouse, where the trial was to be held, seemed just okay, but would work.

Enjoying my dark roast coffee, I studied about the noise of the shot and the time it would take to shut the window, close the drapes, break down the gun and case it, and hurry with the gun to my car. I ate slowly and processed the information over and over. Plan B was to cut a hole in the window. If I had to go to plan B, I would abandon the shot. I would eventually be caught if I cut that hole. It would be the end of Sven. Dolder was not worth the risk.

Back in my room, I opened the big window without a screen. It only opened about nine inches, but the rifle would have enough space to project far enough to make the most of the noise outside. Eleven seconds to close and lock the big heavy window and four seconds to close the drapes. Not good but, okay. I opened the window as far as possible and the drapes just enough to allow me to see my target.

Then practicing Sven's small limp and using my cane, I walked to the courthouse. I stopped at the door that was used to bring inmates to court. Pretending to be a lost tourist, I looked back at the Hyatt and my room. I could see the drapes were open slightly, but not that the window was open. I decided even if a guard or two happened to look directly at the window, they would not see it close or notice the small change in the drapes.

While standing by the courthouse door, I heard five airplanes from the Minneapolis-St Paul Airport depart and fly almost overhead. The noise was enough to cover most of the shot.

I limped to a small park, picking up a cup of dark roast coffee from a stand. They tempted me with a fresh apple strudel dessert. "It sure was good," I mused, throwing a few crumbs to the pigeons.

If it is taken, this shot will be my most risky one to date. I could change my mind at the last second.

From my room window the next two mornings, I watched the routine of bringing Dolder to the Courthouse. I watched the news. Dolder pleaded not guilty by reason of insanity. The public outcry was substantial. A reasonably large group of protesters formed on the second day, but the authorities had anticipated that, and kept the protesters behind a barrier, allowing the escort party entry to the building.

When Dolder arrived with his three-car Police escort, he was surrounded by six armed and vested officers, while he shuffled along to go inside. Those chains made walking slow at best, and Dolder made it look even slower than necessary. He made the short walk take a minute at least. Protesters threw things at him, but he pretended not to notice. He got hit often.

When he stepped up the first step, I would take my shot. It was the only option. At that moment, four of the police escort were still one step below. The trajectory would then hit Dolder and none of the escort personnel. The bullet could ricochet but should fragment if it hit the stone wall. Little if anything would be found.

The trial was in slow mode and would last a week or more. I decided to shoot on the third morning. The weather would be the same as the first two mornings, and the planes would be overhead. If the shot was not available on day three, then day four would be an option.

As Sven, I dressed like a conservative tourist daily during my hotel stay. Jeans, sneakers, and a Viking or Twins sweatshirt. I also carried a medium-sized backpack.

On the first day at the hotel, the doorman asked, "What is in the backpack, sir?" as I neared the door.

"Yust da camera stuff, da lunch and da book. "You need to see?"

"If you don't mind."

"Ja sure."

"Camera, lunch, and books, like you said. Thank you."

"I am Sven, and you are welcome. I go now?"

"Yes, you can go. Enjoy your day. I am John."

The second morning, carrying my backpack, I stopped at John's station.

"Morning, John. You need to see da backpack again?"

"Not today, Sven."

John's television was tuned to the morning news. The woman anchor discussed the trial with a guest.

"Dolder's attorney filed a motion to dismiss, and Judge Bittern denied it. He was instructed to begin his defense," The guest said, answering the woman's question.

"John, vhat did this Nobler do?"

"Dolder?, Sven, he killed a bunch of homeless girls, they say."

"Vell den put him in jail, ja."

"Most people say to give him the chair."

"Vhat is da chair?"

"Electrocution."

"Ja dat would be goot. I go now."

I decided that John might still check my bag again, so after the shot, I would get the rifle to the car by taking the elevator to the parking garage. Then I would come to check out, carrying the backpack for John.

Day three, I ate breakfast in the hotel restaurant at six thirty as I had the first two days. I returned to my room and readied the backpack in case John wanted to check again. Then I opened the window and the drapes and settled in for the shot. As always, I had reviewed my numbers a dozen times. Yes, I felt ready. Yes, I was nervous. Yes, I hated the waiting. At eight-fifty-three, I went to the elevator and pushed the up button, hoping it would arrive at my floor just when I needed it. The three practice tries had shown it would arrive close to when I needed to use it to go down to the parking level.

At eight-fifty-five the three-car procession arrived. The airplanes were going overhead. The crowd was at least twice as large as the first two days. When the escort was ready, Dolder eased out. An airplane was overhead, at full power, roaring as it climbed away.

Dolder stepped up on the first step, and I squeezed the trigger. I immediately closed the drapes. Then standing by the wall next to the window, I closed it as fast as the big window would let me. I peeked just enough to see Dolder prone on the steps.

Dolder died instantly *"Dead serial killer, Number three Curt."* I whispered.

The suppressed shot was muffled by the plane, but I knew, if anyone else had their window open near me, they would have surely heard it—not likely but maybe.

I took care of my rifle, packed my travel bag, and hurried while carrying both to the elevator. It had just arrived. "Lucky me," I said aloud.

I exited on the parking garage floor, stowed the two items in the trunk of my rental, and limped back to my room. "Be glad when I don't have to limp anymore," I said to myself.

Back in the lobby with my backpack, dressed as Sven, I checked out.

"Morning, John. I go today to canoe part by Ely."

"The Boundary Waters?"

"Ja. I get more pictures. You check bag today?"

"Please."

"Da Camera, lunch, and books. Ja." I pasted a big smile on my face. Have a goot day, John."

"Ja, you too. Sven. Nice to have you as a guest," John answered, trying to copy the accent.

I followed North Roberts to arterial Five, then to I-94 south. I left the freeway as soon as I was out of the city and wound my way to Zumbrota, driving through all the little towns. I stopped at an antique store in Zumbrota and found a beautiful Terry Redlin painting of three pheasants at near sunset, flying toward a set of abandoned farm buildings. I had a place on my wall in Bozeman for that. More of Vinny's money gone.

Before returning the rental, I wiped it down completely, hiding my vinyl gloves before handing over the keys. I picked up my Honda Civic, returned to the RV campground, stowed my Honda, and then drove to Mitchell. I parked my lilac ride in the Cabela's lot, backed out my car, and went to my house. I hunted for three days, sharing breakfast with Oliver and friends each morning.

I left the Cabela's lot at sun up on the fourth day and headed to Bozeman.

Talking to myself, I reflected on my 'adventures'. "So far, the surprise has worked, but I know they will learn to protect the defendants better. Bad crooks gone is one thing; looking poorly is another. I have to start believing someone somewhere was working to connect the dots. I still have the edge as of now. I have been around Cliff enough lately to realize he has to be tracking these killings."

Time to turn on some oldies and practice my vocals. I decided to detour near Custer to watch a buffalo roundup. Those animals are big. Watching something new eased the tension.

I arrived in Bozeman and parked the lilac ride at Jack's just before dark. Picking up my Ram, I drove home. My house was as I left it. After processing the pheasants, I sat in my recliner and slept through the Discovery channel programing.

Being a crime fighter was hard work.

CHAPTER 63

At 11a.m. the morning after Dobler was shot, the St. Paul Police Department confirmed what social media had already told the whole country.

"Dennis Dolder was shot and killed by person or persons unknown. Leads, as of now, are few. If anyone has information that would interest the police, please come forward. We will let you know if there are further developments.

A reporter asked, "Captain Nelson, do you know where the shot came from?"

"No, Sandra, we do not. We have all the resources we can muster, canvassing the area we believe the shot had to come from. We know where not to look, but that still leaves a huge area that could have been used. We do not believe it came from a protester, but most of them have not been identified. If it was a long-distance shot, that could make the shooter's location a mile away. We plan to do everything we can to locate and arrest the shooter.

Thank you for coming." Captain Nelson made a hasty retreat back to his office to get ready for his department briefing. He did not like news conferences.

"Morning to all." Captain Nelson's opening words for the eleven years he has been leading the morning meeting each day. "I have changes for some of you because of the Dolder shooting. The drawing on the TV screen shows the scope of the area from which the shot could have been made. We don't believe it came from the crowd. Three of the protesters stayed and, in separate interviews, said they did not hear a shot. All said they would talk to others there and call us if anyone heard differently.

"Our own escort team did not hear a shot.

"We need to look for positions that would afford a shooter an opportunity." He clicked the TV remote.

"Your assignments are posted on the TV screen. Get back to me ASAP with anything that may be useful. Enjoy a safe day." His closing words for those same eleven years.

Captain Nelson walked slowly down the hall to the chief's office. The chief never attended any of his morning meetings. He always briefed this chief of three years, alone in his office.

"Dolder is dead," Offered Captain Nelson. "We don't have a thing. We are 99.9% positive the shot did not come from the protesters. So far, we haven't found enough pieces of the bullet to be useful. If we did find enough to know the caliber, we would learn that it is sold everywhere. Odd, in a good way, there was not a scratch on anyone else. I feel we have a capable long-distance shooter who knows his stuff. And, he works alone. He can hide in plain sight. I am sure he was out of the state within a few hours, maybe less if he is also a pilot. He could be in Texas by now."

Pausing he added, "We need to manage our press releases, but the general public is glad Dolder is dead."

"Stay on top of all your regular assignments, captain. Dot the I's and cross the T's, on this case. But, don't waste any extra time. Dolder is gone. Let him stay gone," grunted the chief.

Captain Nelson walked back to his office, sat down and started talking to himself, as was his custom. "Somebody saw Dolder's shooter. He or she is someone that would never be suspected. Just a regular person. Well educated and a shooter at a range close enough to the Cities to pull this off.

"I need to review everything that Barney and Jane did on this case. They may have earned a commendation at the very least."

He left his office and decided to walk the downtown area himself. He was going to see if he could act like the shooter and locate where the shot came from. He didn't know much about long-distance shooting.

He could talk to himself all day. That is how he found his answers.

He was positive he would not find any answers this time.

CHAPTER 64

Back in Bozeman, I found a letter from Garage Safes in Manhattan, 20 miles west of Bozeman, when I picked up my mail. My personal storage unit was finally completed and I could come by, pay for it, and finish the paperwork, then put my toys away. Stopping at my house, I hooked up my boat, after loading my camper on the truck, drove to Manhattan, then completed the paperwork. The boat and camper hardly made a dent. I had lots of room left. My unit was the center one in a row of five. Utilities were metered, including water and electricity. I needed to submit any interior construction plans. They assured me they wanted the unit to suit my needs. Allowing Garage Safes access to my unit was optional. I chose not to okay that. This unit is for my toys and will become my workshop instead of my garage. The hanger in Lincoln is for the plane.

I may fish Pend Oreille Lake in Northern Idaho for Kokanee salmon if all goes as scheduled. That will be my first time back on that lake since I put Bo and Zach's packs on the bottom. Kokanee can be very active in the fall. I would fish right over the spot where those packs are.

I walked out to my covered patio at about 6 p.m. with my beer in one hand and a paperback in the other. I selected a tape from the waterproof container and played some Chad Mitchell Trio folk music. A light mist sifted through the sky. No stars tonight.

Cliff startled me. He sat in his usual corner, a mischievous smile on his face. We listened to three songs before he spoke. "I was hoping you would show soon. Little busy today? I came by this morning, but you were elsewhere. You have been gone from home awhile."

"How do you know that?"

"I gave a new agent a surveillance job."

"Why?"

"I wanted to talk to you. I have a proposition for you."

I sat back in the lounge chair, took a sip of beer, and went over my last week or so, trying to figure out who the agent was. Since I had not suspected I was being followed, two things occurred to me. One: I was taking my everyday life for granted, and two: I must have more of a routine in Bozeman than I thought. I will fix both.

"Why follow me? We agreed you would not do that."

Cliff leaned forward, took off his glasses and asked, "Do you have a beer for me?

I returned with a beer for him and a refill for me. I sat down and did not say a word. We sat in silence for over fifteen minutes, enjoying the beer, the music, and the rain. I had no idea what was on his mind, but I rummaged through everything I had been up to and everywhere I had gone. I berated myself silently. It is stupid not to watch better.

"The slim short woman with the blonde ponytail. She wore a security uniform and was at Home Depot every time I went there. She ate breakfast at Betty's at least twice at the same time I did."

Cliff smiled. "She was pretty good for her first try at surveillance. Her reports were detailed, but she added you lead a dull life. 'Boring' is the word she used."

I smiled to myself and thought, *Little does she know.*

Cliff took a sip of beer, sat back and got that, I'm serious now facial expression. "Look, Del. You travel the Western states often. You have three alternate identities. I want you to work with me."

"NO. Not interested."

"Hear me out," he countered.

With a short push toward him, I held up my hand and said," I do not want to work. I do not need to work. I do not want any restrictions in my life. I do not want people to know what I am doing. I do not want anyone following me. I just want to travel, fish and hunt. How did you capture or even know about the Russian thugs?"

"Remember when I told you not to buy the guns, that they were stolen from the Russians?"

I nodded.

Cliff paused, deciding what to tell me. "We have a man in Spokane whose only job is to know what the Russians are up to. Only three FBI people know he is there. The Spokane office does not even know. So, we always know when a Russian leaves town. Ivan and Sergo are the thugs we apprehended, and they are expendables. We had a loose tail on Jim. Those two thugs tried to kill Jim. The guns and a pretty good surveillance picture of Jim were in their car when we arrested them. They also had a picture of you, Tony, and Rick at the range taken from a remote hillside somewhere around the range in Manhattan."

"If you followed them loosely, how did they get to Jim?"

"Our agent saw them park their car near the housing development and start walking. We weren't tailing Jim 24/7, so we didn't know about his trailer. Our tail copied the car info and saw Sergo return to the car with the guns. It was late, around midnight, when they both came back. Our man did not know where they went on foot. He just assumed they knew where the guns were, went to get them, and took them back. As soon as we heard about the possible homicide and got the call from the sheriff, we gave the Montana Highway Patrol the car information and asked for assistance until our Missoula office could muster the troops. We arrested them near Frenchtown."

"Are they in jail?"

"Yes, charged with murder one. They believe Jim is dead. The attempt was very over the top. Jim didn't give up the guns easily. My guess is they would make Bully look like a choir boy. They haven't talked yet, and their Spokane family hasn't offered any help."

"Another beer, Cliff?"

"Sure," he continued. "I brought pictures of all the Russian Mafia people we know about. They will find replacements for Ivan and Sergo. These pictures are yours to study. Don't keep them around. Get rid of them when you feel you would recognize the people behind the pictures. You seem to sense things around you, and you will notice them. You must call me if you suspect you have seen any of them. You are on your own as of now, but if you call us, we will be there as quickly as possible."

While changing the music tape, I asked him, "Do you think the Russians know who I am?"

"No, we don't. Ninety-five percent, we don't. I brought the pictures to give you an edge. Spokane is their safest place, and they feel they can hide there. Their number one man was being processed to be deported but was shot and killed. The word on the street is the Russians believed Jim was the shooter, so they went all out, found him and brutally tried to kill him. Jim stole the guns from a residence belonging to Russian citizens. They got Jim's picture from the security camera tape. They found him and attempted to kill him and retrieved their guns. Ivan and Sergo are killers, not thinkers.

"If you work with me, there will be ways to communicate you can't imagine. Very sophisticated. You will not be an employee. You will be paid if, and only if, you have been useful. We would just wire you some money to a safe banking location you specify." Finally, he paused.

I got up and walked to the back fence. Lots to think about. Turning, I went back into the house, picking up Cliff's empty bottle as I passed by the table.

I knew I did not want any more beer and neither did Cliff, so I made a fresh pot of coffee, and while it brewed, I stewed. "Wow!" I said aloud. I knew not all criminals are stupid. I knew there were a lot of risks involving myself in the 'cops and robbers' world. There are no secrets; someone always knows.

I decided Cliff knew or suspected more than he let on. I think he suspects things about me that he cannot prove. He is reaching out to keep me safe. Back outside with fresh coffee, I said. "I am listening."

The Mitchell, South Dakota, bank could be used. Liz Durgan could take care of things. When Cliff said I would be paid based on the value of the information I supplied and I would need a secure account to receive the money, I thought Liz might be my best option. "How safe?"

"Accept a wire transfer and be clean of computer access for anything," he answered

"I can make a change and supply one. Cliff, I got lucky with the Petersons and Bully, I may never have another lead." I will never tell him about Stigman and the black skinny kid arrested in Yuma, or the four Bully boys.

"I know that, but you are a natural at seeing what is out of place—people, cars, and things that shouldn't be where they are. You know to look over your shoulder without looking over your shoulder. You know how to plan.

You know how to make changes. You don't take chances. Some agents never get as good as you are. After today, if we arrange for you to join us, I know you'll become much better.

"Look, Del. You have a lot to run through your head. I'll be in Salt Lake City waiting to hear from you."

"I cannot do anything until the semester is over. I need to finish my class, so I can take the next one. It would be early December, if I chose to come. I will call you after I decide. Is the private call number still good?"

"Yes, the number is good. I will need at least a week to set things up."

"Okay. Will there be others at this meeting?"

"Yes."

"I doubt I would come if others are involved. Just you and no recordings or surveillance."

"That could be tough. Others know I have a source."

"Is our friendship, okay?"

"Never better." His, I-am-having-fun-face and a softness that he only showed around family and good friends made me smile.

"I'll need a ride," he said.

In the Walmart parking lot, he directed me to a row of motor homes near the back of the store on the north side. Cliff was on the floor of the crew cab part of my pickup. He slithered out and under the nearest motor home.

"Godspeed," I heard him whisper.

"Always."

On my way back to my house, I asked myself many questions. How did he get from the motor home at Walmart to my house? It is over four miles. I pondered the options, cab, walk, bum a ride, local agent, or pose as a jogger?

It was misting—he did not walk or jog. He was not wet. No bus comes close enough, and I would have heard a car. He was testing me.

CHAPTER 65

T ime to run the errands to gather all I need for the Kokanee fishing trip. Purposely, I went to Home Depot. No blonde pony-tailed security guard. I ate at Betty's without the follower. Super.

What to do? There is no class for me Friday through Monday. I will go fishing for Kokanee. I decided to sweep everything with my bug detector like I always do every day. All was clear until I checked the boat. The left taillight showed a hit. I looked it over and the entire light fixture looked like it had been replaced. How did I miss it before? I did not, I decided. It was new.

On my way home, I stopped at Beltman Marina. I asked the serviceman to replace it as fast as he could—less than a minute.

Now what?

I called Cliff, without using the NOW phone number. He called back in about an hour.

I asked, "All is well?"

"No." That meant he did not have a secure phone or location or both. Our rules for such a situation were for me to go to a pay phone and call the main office number. He would record my number and call me back from a secure phone.

When he called, I asked him if the device in my boat's taillight was his. "No."

I described it. Cliff thought it was a GPS locator and described how to disable it.

Then suggested I bring it to Salt Lake, since I had replaced the light,

Back at the house, I opened a Longboard Lager, started some notes, and reviewed the pros and cons of Cliff's proposal. Both lists were long, covering everything I could think of.

Cliff expects me to come to Salt Lake. I knew I would not go and expose myself. The Russians could be a real problem.

I read my lists two or three times, expanding each option. Having Cliff and friends looking out for me could be a lifesaver. The Russians and Bully's friends would react violently if they found out I was the one who helped the authorities.

I will lay low for a time and do my art class assignments to complete the requirements to be eligible for the next art class. Then, if the weather is okay, I'll go pheasant hunting. The professor expects me to go. Kokanee fishing will have to wait. I put the disassembled tail light in the dumpster at Home Depot.

CHAPTER 66

will to go into the Bob one more time. The quiet time and the deeply relaxing feeling I have at my little cabin and the meadow beckoned me. It could be cold and maybe even snow there. Mother Nature was my planner this time. Big game hunting season is open. I rarely see deer or elk in the valley, but both often left their evidence by the creek where I usually cross. A couple of times when up on prospector ridge, however, I saw two very nice whitetail deer and a small herd of elk in the valley north of mine. I intended to drop most of the gear and food and carry a rifle. I would pack my Winchester 30-06 with six power Leopold optics in a hard case and carry it in. A very small pack with three days of meals and a spare set of clothes was all I would take. If I could harvest a suitable animal, I wanted to process the hide, store it in the cave and see how my handiwork survived the winter.

Dutch and his son hunted antelope near the small town of Winnett, Montana and were not due back for three days, so I drove directly to the hangar. I pushed the plane out and did the pre-flight. The supply canisters were ready and in the plane. I looked in the toolbox under the tray. Dutch's note read.

Friends say two guys with heavy accents have been asking. Sparky saw them try the hangar door.

I took Dutch's note, tore off a small blank part, wrote thanks, and put it under the tray.

I drove the truck into the hangar, closed and locked the door. I did not see anyone.

After completing the two-canister drop, I returned to the hangar. I could easily tell the lock was broken.

How many were there, and where were they? It had to be two, like Dutch's note. I took my Smith &Wesson nine-millimeter out of my duffel, attached the suppressor, stuffed it in the waistband of my jeans, covered it with the left side of my open coat, opened the hangar door six or seven feet, and stepped in. Three quick steps forward and two to the left put me behind a solid wood workbench. I caught a whiff of body odor over the regular hangar smells. I had company.

I moved the suppressed nine-millimeter to my right hand and hung it next to my leg. If I had to use it, I knew it would make some noise, but most of the sound would stay inside the hangar.

A whisper filtered from my right and was answered from the back of the hangar. Somehow, I was sure they would not shoot now because if that were the intent, I would already be dead. I first saw the man on the right but did not see a gun. Maybe he had one, but I could not take that chance. The man in the back said something in a foreign language to his partner, and both chuckled. Together they started walking toward me.

"What do you want?" I asked softly.

"To hurt you."

"Why?"

"You a friend of Jim. We watch him. We see you shoot guns by at range. We see you bote laugh. We kill all Jim friends. We have two in jail, so we hurt you bad, then kill you. We, how you say, get even."

"How did you find me?"

"We follow from where you shoot."

"Why!" No answer. "STOP!"

They kept coming—both grinning a sinister snarl. I knew I could not win a fight. The man on the right was closest, ten or twelve feet away. He swaggered slowly toward me. "I am first," he growled.

"Stop!" I demanded, a second time.

"No Stop."

I lifted the gun and shot him. Before he hit the ground, I aimed at enemy number two. He raised his hands but kept walking and said, "We can talk."

"Stop!" he kept coming. So, I shot him, too.

My knees went weak. My heart pounded. I could smell the gun powder over the usual gasoline odor. I gripped the bench, or surely, I would fall. I took a deep breath, then a second and a third. Finally, I felt recovered enough to carefully check each body for a pulse, but neither man was alive. Both shot through the heart. I practice with the nine-millimeter more often than I shoot long-distance. Those practice sessions paid off and will continue.

I remembered a part in a Clint Eastwood Western movie. "If you want to shoot, shoot. Don't talk." Something like that.

Now, what am I to do? I needed to get rid of them. Many times, I had flown in and out the same day, so I pushed the plane into the hangar, loaded one of the men into the passenger seat, and gave him a ride over the 'Bob.' Like with the canisters, I banked right as steep as I dared and dropped him into a valley devoid of foot or pack trails. There are many such valleys in the 'Bob.'

I returned, and following the same process, gave the second man the same ride. If anyone saw me, I would just tell them it was easier to roll the plane into the hangar and load stuff than haul it out to the plane.

I needed clean-up supplies and a new padlock. I took a quick trip to Home Depot, located at the first exit below the airport. They had what I needed. I only cleaned up the small spots of blood. I knew driving the truck and moving the plane in and out would remove almost everything else. I dragged some cardboard next to the workbench. Russian number two had died a foot from the bench. The cardboard looked like it belonged there.

After the plane and the hangar were cleaned to my satisfaction, I pushed the plane inside, locked up, and drove to the Frontier Inn to drink a beer and be by myself. On the way, I threw all the cleaning debris into a full dumpster by an auto body shop. On the northwest edge of town, the Frontier Inn has been around forever. There were only two other customers and a pool league setup with eight guys, so I enjoyed an IPA in solitude. *Damn, Dumb, and Dangerous.* But I had no choice.

I mentally matched both men's pictures to those Cliff had given me of known Russian mafia from Spokane. They were both in the set.

I called Dutch and told him I got a new lock for the hangar and gave him the combination.

I called Cliff using a burner. He was in Helena. We arranged to meet at the Hare and Hound Lounge. Two hours later, I found him in the back booth nursing a beer. Passing the bar, I ordered a draft of a local IPA.

"Hello, Del. Busy day?"

"Yes. I am a bit shook up."

"Why?"

"Are we off the record and secure?"

"Yes."

I told him a good version of the story, starting with noticing the broken lock. But I did not tell him of Dutch's note. I did not want his name in any way connected.

"Wow!" Issuing an audible gasp, he leaned back and wiped his face with both hands. "I will not remember a word you said."

We each silently sipped our beer. Then he beckoned the waitress, and we ordered a sandwich and a second beer. We sat in silence, ate our food and sipped the beer. Finally, he asked, "Russians?"

I showed him the pictures of the two men I had on my phone and told him I thought they matched the pictures he had given me.

"This match looks 99.9% to me. They had heavy accents, and they said I was a friend of Jim. Do you think they will continue to come after me?"

"No idea. But my guess would be no. They have only so many people here. They need to keep their operations going. They are a loyal group, though. Study the other pictures I gave you until you positively know them instantly. I will see you get a picture of any new faces we uncover. I'll also find a way to have our Spokane man keep you in the loop. Get a book of Russian phrases and learn them. It could give you an edge."

"Since you will not remember my story, I am the only one who knows what happened and where the bodies are. Only bones will remain come spring. I will be right back."

I retrieved the two sterile baggies containing the personal items from each Russian. "Do you want these bags of their personal items?"

"Yes. The FBI needs to keep track of foreign nationals, especially criminals. I will have to think of a good story, as I shouldn't say I just found them."

"Maybe something undercover, and you were called. The bodies were already disposed of to keep the locals out of the picture."

Cliff sat, looked off toward the mountains, took a sip of his beer, and then softly said, "You are more capable in a tense situation than many of our agents. You must be careful not to cross the line and become a criminal." After a long pause and a sip of beer, he continued. "Provable self-defense, is one thing. Murder is another."

Too late, I thought. "Cliff, you are correct. But I can assure you that I would be dead if I had not acted. Talking to Jim was not enough of a reason to become targeted. I need to study and figure out how they knew to be in Great Falls and come to the hangar. Does the FBI know of Russians in Great Falls?"

"I will check for you and get an update."

"Cliff, I plan to hunt when I can. The applications in other states' big game pursuits will begin next fall.

I will be in Hawaii for all of December. Then Arizona for January, February, and March. Hopefully that long absence should allow me to separate myself from the Russians. I will tell you and Molly the what, where, why, and how about my travels as best as I can. Dutch will have access to my house and know most of my intentions. Rick will also know most of what I will do over the winter."

"Good enough, my friend. I have an idea for the story of the Russians. Those baggies will be delivered to the Salt Lake FBI Office in a clean Post Office soft envelope with a clean note that says, *I hunt Russians.*"

"That works, Cliff." We walked out together with that good feeling only special friends shared.

Our customary hug.

"Godspeed."

"Always."

I decided Cliff would have shot them as well, and I am positive we have not seen the last of the Russians.

I drove back to Great Falls. Then to my cabin near Lincoln, staying the night so I could hike into the Bob at sunup the next day. I planned to winterize my hide-away cabin, hunt some and bring out two canisters. I drove to the Monture Trailhead and hiked to Curtis Castle. I hunted for two days but only saw two small bucks, so I winterized Curtis Castle, leaving the rifle in the cave. Then hiked out carrying two canisters with all the spare chutes inside. I left the two canisters and chutes at my Lincoln cabin, and drove to Bozeman.

I feel less stress when I am in the Bob.

CHAPTER 67

I hosted a catered Thanksgiving dinner in Bozeman for my family and friends. My daughter Molly, grandson Trevor, and Cliff flew in Wednesday. Dutch and Dave arrived late that same afternoon and settled into their bedrooms. My three-bedroom rancher had a full basement, which now included three more bedrooms and a Tv room. Jack, Jason and Jacob, came for a couple of hours. They returned for dinner the next day and Madeline and Cindy joined us as well.

Jack and Madeline seemed to share a private conversation most of the time they were at my house. Trevor and Cindy sat together. Molly talked to everyone.

When we started dessert, Cindy went over to Jack and said, "Del told me you said my car smelled."

A flustered Jack answered, "I said it smelled like a woman's car, help me out here Del."

I just smiled.

Jack continued, "I said the cost depended upon how good looking the woman was. You are a nice-looking lady, Cindy, so your cost is zero." He looked around at everyone, saw the grins and added, "Ah, you got me. I love you all."

CHAPTER 68

To make sure the caterers had enough room in the garage for their equipment, I had taken my plastic rolling garbage receptacle out to the street. Friday was the usual pickup day. Around 1 a.m. I took the last of the trash out to the curb. The street light was on my corner and my driveway is mostly shaded by a dense mature ash tree, now with most of its leaves gone. When I was almost back to my garage door, standing in the shadows, two dark-colored F-250 Ford crew cab pickups drove into the Russian neighbor's driveway across the street on the opposite corner. Six Bully look-alikes emerged from the two trucks and went into the house using the small front garage door. There were no visible lights in the house.

Entering Cliff's bedroom, I shook him awake and whispered, "Something odd is going on across the street."

Cliff sat up and listened to me relate what I had seen. "Is that the guy you told me about?"

"Yes."

He picked up his phone and called the local field office. He told the duty team about what we had seen, and he gave them instructions.

"Cliff, did you identify the guy in the house after I alerted you to the new neighbor?"

"We are about 90% sure he is Boris Spovok, a Russian that came to the US nine years ago and became a US citizen. He has no record here in the USA, but failed an international inquiry miserably. There is a small locator in the grill of his rig. If he is anything bad, we haven't seen it yet.

The phone vibrated. Cliff let me watch the screen and the worded message as he listened to the agent. "Both plates are registered to a Boris Spovok. He uses a P.O. box at the main U.S. Post Office in Bozeman."

"We will watch and call you when they leave."

"Use two cars and use the hope-you-are-right type of tail. Do *not* risk being seen," added Cliff.

CHAPTER 69

veryone except Jack and sons and Cindy and Madeline, were up by 8:30, so we made scrambled eggs to go with some of the Thanksgiving leftovers, hot coffee and tea, and lots of laughter. Some commented on the nice layout of my remodeled basement. I added three bedrooms and a sofa-bed in the TV room. Those rooms are the result of an agreement between myself and my landlord. I did the work and he supplied the materials. He cannot sell without offering me first option.

Cliff needed a ride to Home Depot. He had set up a retrieve there. He had things to do.

After letting him out, I drove to the Exxon to fill up with gas. It was across the street from Boris's rig parking location. The Russian neighbor's rig was there, as I suspected. I discretely took a picture. No sign of the two big pickups. I stopped at the Safeway and picked up some dark roast coffee and enough cinnamon rolls for two each.

The rolls were a big hit, especially with Dutch.

"Better than eggs," he mumbled with a mouthful of pastry.

Dave and Dutch left together. Dave was going to spend a night with Dutch in Great Falls.

I took Molly out to the back fence, saying I wanted to tell her where the other keys to the safety deposit box were.

"Molly, just listen and then give me a hug. If anyone asks about us being out here, say we were visiting about your mom." Then I told her where the other safety deposit box keys were and the air drops in the Bob, and the Lincoln cabin. I also told her about the type of security I had here and at the cabin. I told her about the gold, saying we would climb and I would show her how to find the ore.

She gave me a hug and said in my ear, "Wow. Does anyone else know?"

"No, Molly. Only you, ever. I debated for a long time about telling you, but you needed to know about the gold and where it is. Thanksgiving again next year?"

"Yes Dad. You have nice friends. I like them all. Cindy seems to think you are extra special."

"She does. She has had a tough life, is my guess. I learned she was going to the University to get her teaching degree, so I am helping her finance that goal. I thought that would be good use for some of the drug money.

" I try not be lonely. I work hard at that every day. It is not easy to avoid feeling lonely some days. This gathering has been good for me. I have a bucket list a mile long. I will attempt to complete it on my own. I do not have time to waste being lonely."

We walked back to the house acting like a father and daughter should act.

CHAPTER 70

O ver tea and coffee Saturday morning, Molly asked out of the blue, "What did Jack mean, your semi is unique? You have an eighteen-wheeler?"

"Yes, I do. We will go touring in the lilac rig tomorrow to Great Falls and see Dutch."

"I haven't been back since Mom was in the hospital."

"Neither have I, and I didn't go anywhere else when I did visit," added Trevor.

"That was a tough time. You two should know that Dutch went to visit Amy often, just never when I was around. He also arranged for Dave, Cliff, and Jack to be around without telling me. They have never said why they sort of hid this from me, and I will never ask. Dutch's way, I'm guessing.

"Cliff's wife died from cancer many years ago. Jack's wife got tired of Jack and the twins always fishing or hunting or fixing trucks. After a quick divorce, she left and is in California somewhere. Dutch's wife left him thirty years ago, and he never talked about why. Dave married the U.S. Forest Service and has always lived alone.

"The five of us have been close friends for fifty years. Each of us has a story that includes all of the others coming to help when life threw a rock at one of us. Any of them would help either of you, no questions asked. Enough said.

"Bring your travel bag, and we will go have some fun. We have until Tuesday."

Molly gave me the I-remember-when-look, "You went to truck driver school when I was in college. Right? You drove some actual trips, and Mom went along on one or two."

"Yup, I drove over thirty, all west of the Mississippi. Amy did not like the long-haul boredom. She enjoyed the short ones to Seattle, but only went on one long one to New Mexico. She liked Taos. She even commented that it would be a possible retirement choice. We will leave right after breakfast at the EGGE. Lunch will be with Dutch."

Madeline cooked and Cindy served our breakfast. "Our treat today, Del." Cindy gifted us with a smile meant for all. "More coffee, Trevor?"

"Yes," he blushed. "Thanks, Cindy."

Next stop was Jack's to pick up the truck. All five of his bays were filled with a truck, so we just waved as I parked next to my Lilac ride.

"A lavender truck, Dad?"

"*Lilac*, and it is beautiful, and it was the best deal." I did not tell them the truck would be another color when they next see it.

We followed I-90 then I-15 to Great Falls. A beautiful winter drive along the Missouri River. I never tire of mountain scenery. The Missouri River canyon road describes mountain beauty. Mountains like themselves. Touching the Montana Big Sky makes a person feel like they are part of those mountains.

We used the off-ramp to the airport, left the Lilac Beauty at the truck stop and took the Honda Civic to meet Dutch at Classic Fifties just at the bottom of Gore Hill, where the airport is located.

We shared four hours with Dutch, then drove back to the lilac ride. Molly road with Dutch and Trevor rode with me.

"You need to see his pink truck, Dutch." Laughed Trevor.

"It is lilac, most drivers call it a semi or a rig. Be happy to show you, Dutch. It is parked up at the Pilot truck stop off the airport exit."

Those two talked about me, I am sure. That is okay, because they are special people in my life. Trevor and I talked about the 'maybe' trip into the Bob.

Arriving at the truck stop, I parked next to the lilac ride. I opened the trailer and the living quarters.

"Hunting in style, it looks to me," Dutch said, looking the rig over thoroughly. "Why pink?"

"It is lilac and it was the best deal by far," I answered.

"This trip has been super. I met all Grampa's friends, overate, played cards, ate breakfast at the EGGE, and traveled in a pink rig." It was Trevor's turn to smile.

We said our goodbyes, then off to Glacier Park and a stop in Evergreen to see Dave.

CHAPTER 71

Taking her time getting strapped in, Molly looked at Dutch as he said, "Molly is your dad saying much about what he does and where he goes? You don't have to give up any secrets. He is flying my plane quite often and never tells me where he goes. Most of his flights in the log just list the hours and VFR. That's okay, because it's none of my business. It's just, he's my best friend, and I care."

"Dutch, he doesn't talk to me about stuff like that. Mostly, I think he is trying to adjust and make his way doing things he wants to do. He likes to hunt, fish, and travel, so he is doing that. I can tell he's hurting."

"You are probably right, Molly, but he seems more private about where he goes and his trips. Did you know he bought a cabin near Lincoln?"

"Yes, I did. He always hunted and fished around Lincoln, and he wanted a place there. He says it needs a lot of work. His hunting place, he says. I'm sure I couldn't find it."

"I know where it is and so does my son Eddie. I should give you his phone number."

Dutch became silent, with that squinty-eyed look. He paused for a moment, shifted in his seat, and turned to Molly. "Do you think he's doing okay? He just seems a little close to the vest since Amy died. He went to Priest Lake to pick huckleberries, but came back early, and started living in Bozeman. He never talked about any of it."

"Like I said Dutch, he is hurting big time. He tries not to show it, but the hurt is there. He came to visit me about a month after she died. He didn't call. Just showed up. We spent four nice days on the coast. He seemed okay, but didn't want to talk about Mom. He never talks about Curt either. He keeps it all inside.

"I know he sold almost everything they owned to have money to fight cancer. I don't know how much is left. Semis can't be cheap, so I just don't know. I believe he will tell me when he's ready."

Dutch nodded. "He's a strong man, mentally and physically. He can handle more than most. But he has a lot on his plate. Retirement, house sold, Amy's death, and the old hurt for Curtis. I promise I'll call if I see changes."

"Dad has nice friends."

"Yes, he does. I am lucky to be one of them. Let's keep in touch," answered Dutch, then continued. "Cliff said Del has been in contact with him a few times. Cliff talks funny sometimes, his FBI lingo."

Dutch handed Molly his phone, and she set up the numbers, including Eddies.

"Thanks for the talk and for caring about Dad."

"I owe him a lot. We all do. Cliff is very good at what he does, but Del is the strongest of all of us."

Dutch saw me and parked by the semi, as I opened the ramp to put the Honda away. I also opened the living quarters.

"Sleeps one," I said.

"Hunting in style, it looks to me. Why pink?"

"It is lilac," I answered acting hurt.

"When do I get to ride in the pink truck?"

"It is lilac and maybe I will let you ride along when we go hunting antelope next fall. I have a storable, removable bunk system for up to four guests. Lots of room."

"Deal. You guys enjoy the rest of your trip, and say hi to Dave." Dutch gave Molly an extra-long hug and whispered. "I loved your mom. If you ever need anything, just call."

Dutch surprised Trevor with a bear hug.

After a four-hour leisurely drive from Great Falls to Evergreen, my US Forest Service friend, Dave met us at Charlie's. We completed a short sight seeing tour before settling in for the night. We chose to stay at some cabins instead of unpacking my bunk system in the semi.

Dave took us to a small five table café called Sally's for breakfast. Great food. It was obvious Dave was in love with Sally. I bet he finally gets married.

Mother Nature graced us with another big sky day for our trip through Missoula and down to Bozeman.

"We must play cards again when we get back, I need to win a game," said Trevor.

🌲 🌲 🌲

While we were playing cards, I replenished the chip bowl, then reached in and took out one chip and ate it.

"Why do you do that, Dad?"

"What did I do?"

"Took one extra chip from the bag."

"Habit, I guess. Curtis asked me about that on our last trip into the Bob. I do not know why I started doing that, I just do it."

"Why did you buy the Semi, Dad?"

"Lots of reasons. Mostly, though, I am in quest of a trophy elk, and mule deer in as many states as I can. I hope to include moose and bear as well. I justify this rig for the comfort of having my sleeping quarters and hunting gear with me. I enjoyed those over-the-road hauls I did very much. Plus, I have the money."

I returned from my office with an envelope for each of them. "These casher-checks are for you to use anyway you wish. If anyone asks, it is part of your inheritance. Someday I will tell you how I came to have extra money." I know they had a hundred questions. Molly acted like she did not know about the drug money.

"Hopefully, we get to hike into the Bob, Trevor. Molly and I are going in early August."

"Wow, Dad. This is a lot of money." Molly had to check, as I knew she would.

Trevor opened his and just stared. Finally, he mumbled. "Grampa, I can't take this. You may need it later. I'm doing fine."

"You know we sold almost everything, hoping to win the cancer battle. I have more than enough money left. I could keep all of it and give it to you in a will, but I want you to have some now. I will never need it. I do not do things I do not want to do. I do not say things I do not mean. Those are motto's I live by. Please enjoy the money. A nest egg, a better car, a trip, or some classes you want to finish. It is yours."

Dropping them off at the airport was especially hard for me. "Thanksgiving next year?"

After we shared long hugs, they walked away arm-in-arm.

"Beautiful," I uttered aloud. "I hope life allows them to come back next year."

I noticed three or four people looking at me. I just smiled. I knew it was okay to talk to myself. Glistening eyes is not crying, right?

CHAPTER 72

The Wednesday after Thanksgiving I was enjoying my coffee and cinnamon roll, reading the newspaper on my patio, and listening to an oldies tape, when my neighbor, Ben Delger, called to me from his side of the fence. "Did you see the trucks across the street Thursday night?"

I was positive Ben had seen me make my trip out to the garbage bin. "Yes, but after such a long day of company, I was too tired to pay much attention. I saw the trucks come when I hauled the last of the dinner cleanup out to my can. I have some cinnamon rolls. You want one?"

"Twist my arm, Del. I have my coffee so will be right there."

"Warmed up?"

"Yes thanks."

Pushing his plate away and sipping his coffee, he started telling me what he saw.

"Two trucks, both crew cabs, one maroon Ram and the other dark gray Ford 250, pulled into the driveway, and three guys got out of each truck. It was close to midnight, maybe a little later. Totally, quiet 'till 4:10. Then all six came out carrying a black duffel about four feet long and sixteen inches or so deep. The rigs were quiet, and they sneaked away."

"Did you sleep at all?"

"I was at my sons for Thanksgiving and ate too much. Two pieces of pie. I got home about eleven, but the stomach was acting up, so I was pacing. I do that a lot."

"What do you make of those two rigs coming so late? They both looked like Fords to me."

"Positive, Del, one Ram and one Ford 250. Those guys all carried a big bag coming out and took nothing in. They are up to no good, Del. I know it."

"What do you think we should do, Ben?"

"Nothing, I don't want trouble, and those guys are trouble with a capital 'T.'"

"I agree. Since you saw it all, maybe you should start a log of what you see there, with dates and all. We might need it if we see something we are not supposed to see," I added.

"Damn, good idea. I'll get a spiral notebook and start today. Did you know Mrs. Sutherland watches everything you do?"

"Really! I would never have suspected."

"Yeah. She watches both of us but can see you better. She's been by herself since before Bertha and I moved into this house. Got to be lonely. Well, thanks for the roll, Del. I gotta run. See ya."

I will start keeping records myself. Ben will have more complete ones; like he said, they are trouble. I know I can get the facts for Cliff. Just offer Ben some sweets and some coffee. I will let him think he is watching for both of us.

CHAPTER 73

fter talking to Ben yesterday, I decided it was time for a neighborhood get-together. So, I made up an invitation and taped one to each door on our block on both sides of the street.

Thursday
Del Sanderson Residence
3467 Bellows
9:30 – 10:30
Coffee, Tea, Cinnamon rolls
Back Yard Patio
(use the side gate, please)

If only a few came, I would have a lot of excess calories to eat. I know Ben will come. I wondered if the new, never seen neighbor would come.

At seven thirty, the next morning, I traveled to Aroma's bakery to pick up the cinnamon rolls. The smell filled my truck. I decided I would learn how to make cinnamon rolls.

Ben arrived first. He poured his own coffee, put the biggest roll he could find on a paper plate and sat in the corner—Cliff's chair.

Lester and Linda Wilson, Ben's other close neighbor, came next. This was a first meeting for me. Senior citizens, not overweight with white hair, and in a nutshell, retired folks who enjoy talking about their grandchildren.

From the end house, Bonnie Stevens pushed her walker through the gate and into the backyard. She greeted the Wilsons warmly and Ben curtly.

She shuffled right up to me and said, "You must be Del. I am ninety-one. Call me Bonnie."

"Nice to meet you, Bonnie. I hope I look as good as you do when I am ninety-one."

"You're a dear. But I'm not available."

Mrs. Sutherland came next. Offering her hand and a coy grin, "I am Martha. You have the place looking better than it has for years."

Boris came. He introduced himself to all saying, "I am Boris. I come from Russia many years ago. I am American citizen. Thank you for inviting me. I can't stay long. I will enjoy coffee with you."

All greeted him, and Ben poured him some coffee.

The accent was there, but he has been working to perfect his English.

I introduced myself, telling them only enough to hopefully prevent a bunch of questions I did not wish to answer. "Good morning. I am Del Sanderson. Nice, you all could come."

Bonnie answered first. "Thank you, Del. A person should know their neighbors. The Rockers are gone to Billings to visit their daughter. They won't be here, so I put your note through the slot in their door."

I used Styrofoam cups for the coffee. Boris thanked me with a nod and left after only ten minutes. He did not eat a roll and only touched the cup he took with him.

Martha asked, "Are you rich?"

"No, Martha, I am not. I am retired, and comfortable is the word that applies to me."

"You had a pretty lady friend a couple of weeks ago," she commented.

"She is my financial planner. Would you like some more coffee?"

"Yes, thank you." She knew I was stopping her questions.

The gathering was a success. Bonnie agreed to do one next month, and we settled on the third Thursday.

Martha was the last to leave. "I have a confession. I am a busybody. But I like you. A man came to my door some time ago and asked me if I wanted to earn some money. I do not have much money, so I said I would listen. All he asked was for me to call when I saw you leave. He said he would give me twenty dollars a week. So, I did. I called him this morning and told him I would not spy anymore."

"Did he answer the phone?"

"Oh yes. I would recognize his voice anywhere. See you next month."

After she left, I decided to see what Cliff knew or could find out.

"Charlene. How is every little thing?"

"Del, all is well. When are you coming to my office so I can meet you? Telephone dating is not my style."

"One day soon," I smiled. "Where do we go on our first date?"

"I will have it all arranged if you ever ask, and it will be expensive. What must I convey to Cliff?"

"Three things. Are Samuel and Frederick still in jail, and is their Helena business still operating and if so, by whom."

"Is tomorrow soon enough?"

"Perfect. Whatever would Cliff do without you?"

"Why, he would be lost."

"See you one day."

"I'll believe that when you walk in the door."

An amazing woman. She never asked who I was. Somehow, she knew. I do not think burner phones have caller ID. I will ask her when I finally meet her."

After hanging up I called my landlord. After a short discussion, we agreed on a price and I purchased my rental. The papers would be prepared tomorrow. I then called a painter Jack recommended and arranged to have the lilac ride painted a dark gray.

CHAPTER 74

called Kellerman from Denver on a burner while waiting for a connecting flight to Ft. Lauderdale.

"Kellerman," he answered.

"Check Ft. Lauderdale recent arrests. Who's Rocco?"

"Is this the same informant with the Priest Lake and Spokane tips?"

"You have thirty seconds to answer my question, or the source dries up."

"Rocco is a high-position drug dealer in Tucson. No record. Keeps his hands clean. Word is he's a mean bastard."

"Seen Vinny lately?"

"Not in a while."

"If you ever try to trace my calls, I will know, and we are done." I hung up.

Bryan called the Ft. Lauderdale police and asked about Rocco. He was transferred to Sergeant Shank. After listening to Bryan's question, he answered. "We arrested a Marana citizen, Jose Zapata, about a month ago along with four locals and confiscated a lot of drugs and money. Why do you ask?"

"I have been getting tips from an unknown. He has been very right every time. Jose's brother was killed in Spokane, Washington. Another tip. Can you send me a copy of your file?"

"Give me your fax and I'll send it now."

"Great, and thanks."

Bryan talked to the chief. "I have no idea who he is, but the info meshes with our stuff."

CHAPTER 75

Bryan was coming around. Doing my next 'adventure' in his backyard could be extra risky. I needed to update my info on Salvador "Chico" Alvarez as the trial in Marana could be soon. There were often articles about his alleged drug trafficking in the *Star,* but today I got lucky. Chico granted a *Star* reporter an interview. Chico just wanted to complain about everything, especially only being allowed one thirty-minute daily outing at one p.m. in the maximum-security exercise yard. "Only time I get to see the sun."

That interview gave me a valuable clue for an opportunity to have a thirty-minute window for a shot instead of a short opening during his walk to the next-door courthouse.

My chosen shooting spot was the roof on a building only four stories high. But one that afforded a satisfactory look at the entire south wall of the jail courtyard. I climbed the outdoor fire escape in total darkness to look. Lights in the yard proved the southern exposure was enough if he stood by the wall. He wanted to see the sun and feel the ninety-degree heat. He would stand facing the sun to get the maximum beams.

The Marana Adventure was a go. Spencer would love to be the shooter this time, and the distance would be about eight hundred yards. I needed to be on the rooftop and ready to shoot before sunrise. It was impossible to make those preparations and climb the fire escape in the daylight. I would be seen as there was no cover anywhere on the rooftop. The shooting spot I selected started in the sun, but as the earth rotated, it became semi-shaded after about eight thirty a.m. Most of the east side, where the fire escape was, is shaded by then. I should be safe to use it for the escape. Going down that fire escape in a hurry would be a great risk.

I practiced on a similar fire escape in Chandler five times during a fake run, going up and down. I dressed the part and worked up a good sweat. I told a handful of watchers this workout would help me climb a mountain. The descent took thirty-one seconds on the fastest trip. I would allow for forty. The gun would be dismantled on the top landing after the seven seconds it took to get there from the shooting position. It took eight seconds, my best time after many tries, to break down the gun and case it. A scraggly oleander hedge bordered the entire parking lot at the back of the building. I would be hidden except for the step out to get into the car. It is to be unlocked to save precious seconds. I will be in the car in one minute or less, if all goes well. Once in the car, access to I-10 via Tangerine Road should be easy.

I decided the shot was doable. The Win-Mag 300 was in Casa Grande, stored in a small climate-controlled storage unit. I picked it up the night before the planned shooting day, made sure the gun was ready and preset the optics. I would check the settings after I was on the roof.

I was in position at five fifteen a.m., disguised as Spencer. I parked my white Ford Focus rental in the closest spot next to the building, the fire escape, and the hedge. According to the TV weather woman on a local Phoenix station, the temperature will reach about ninety degrees by noon. They are never wrong. I attached a small hydration pack with a tube feed and using Velcro, I attached a thin body-sized desert tan blanket to my shoes, belt, and collar. That blanket would help me blend in. It was almost the exact color of the roof. Waiting when nervous was not easy.

Salvadore 'Chico' Alvarez stepped into the exercise yard at eleven a.m. He strolled directly to the southeast corner as soon as the entry door clanged shut. He leaned back against the wall and tipped his head to the sun. I squeezed the trigger. *Number four Curt.* Chico slumped to the ground in a sitting position, back to both sides of the corner. He looked like he just sat down. I was sure the suppressed shot had been heard, but nearby road construction had a jack hammer pounding somewhere, and each thud was louder than my bullet.

As soon as I saw him slip down, I slithered on hands and knees to the fire escape, still using the cover blanket. I broke down the gun and cased it. Rolling up the blanket, I peered over the edge. No one saw me descend the fire escape and walk to the car. The parking lot was empty of humans. A group of four or five women dressed neatly in work clothes stood by the main entry to the building, but they did not appear to look at my car.

Driving on I-10 west, I decided I did not want the rental car seen in Palm Creek. I returned the gun to the Casa Grande storage unit, then drove to the Mesa Airport to return the car. I wiped it clean at the storage unit and wore cheap vinyl gloves to drive to the rental car return lot at the Mesa Airport. I picked up my Honda CRV, followed Williams Road to Gilbert, and went to Whiskey Row for the rib basket and sweet potato fries. A Lagunitas IPA made the meal perfect.

A TV tuned to a Tucson station reported, *"A breaking news story: the Marana police department confirmed the rumor that Salvadore Alvarez had been assassinated while under maximum guard. The assassination took place between eleven and eleven-thirty. The shooter is suspected to be a long-range sniper. The department was still processing the crime scene, and will release any further developments."*

No leads yet.

I will watch this investigation more closely than the Depsoto Adventure, as I was much more exposed this time.

'Adventure' number four, and I know I still need to improve the recon, the planning, the escape route selection, and become more observant. They will, sooner or later, compare this one to the Depsoto shooting. Different gun, but the rest is quite similar.

CHAPTER 76

Marana Police Chief Ed Johnson addressed a room full of police personnel.

"Wow. Twelve-foot walls! All alone! Not the regular exercise time quoted in the *Star*. Someone is a quality planner and a daring risk taker. Our initial scan suggests a signature similar to the Tucson shooting. We need to work that lead. We also need to find all the locations within a thousand yards that could have been used. We canvas those neighborhoods. The shooter couldn't walk into a building or down the street with a long gun, and not be seen by somebody."

"Chief," interrupted a voice from the back of the room.

"Yes?"

"Sir. I am quite certain there are long-range guns that can be broken down and cased. They would look like a backpack."

"How small?"

"The length of the barrel, sir. The rest of the pieces will be smaller. 80/20 it's a breakdown gun. Lots of different makes. The shooter won't wear a trench coat or anything like that, he would stand out way more than carrying a case looking like a backpack."

"Thanks. Good point. We must look for any surveillance cameras once we find the sniper's position. We have a lot of stuff on the docket, so we need to stay focused on those. If anyone finds they have free time, you can help with this one. The media will not be real kind to us. It would be nice to catch the shooter, but he is probably in another state by now, and we will be lucky to find a witness."

"The shooter might be a woman," the same voice interjected.

"Yes, it might, but we need to find some clue to lead us somewhere. The bullet is worthless. I am certain the shooter expected that would happen.

Jennings and Sproul will look for shooting locations. Smith and Seville will make a file folder and coordinate the information. All four of you will canvas the possible locations. Kellerman, you interview the jail staff, locate all long-range facilities in our area and visit them. The rest of you listen to the rumors on the streets. Tell me everything. Maybe we will get a lead from our regular tipster. He always seems to know something about our cases. The FBI will undoubtedly contact us, but usually don't meddle in local cases, unless invited. If they or a reporter tries to get info from anyone of us, you let me know. Watch yourselves."

CHAPTER 77

laid low at my Palm Creek rental in Casa Grande. A diluted glass of lemonade, rested on my reading stand next to my recliner. With communications as advanced as they are now, somebody somewhere will decide to give criminals better protection and maybe even have undercover people around the jail perimeter just in case. I thought about everything over and over but kept coming back to the older thin black man that was always around the Marana police station. I had his picture and knew where he lived. But my sixth sense would not let him go. Why? Somehow, he was a player. I felt I needed to know more about him. He has not been listed in any of the searches I made on the internet. I would need to be really lucky to find anything.

Mostly shooting criminals is kind of fun.

Jefferson Carter Washington is a janitor at the Marana Police Department Headquarters. He has never been suspected of being extra nosy. No one knows what he does with his free time. Everyone in the Marana Police Department likes him and believes him to be a slow old man, mentally and physically. J.C. is what they know him by and how they address him. He has mastered his subtle deceit. He has fooled them all for forty-four years. His favorite comment is "I have cleaned up after nine chiefs." Always with a soft grin on his face.

When asked about his name, he always says, "My mama named me after three presidents, but I wonder how she knew Carter would win." The same small grin.

He liked his janitorial job. He worked steadily and made it look easy, usually taking four to five hours to finish each day's work. He has never missed a day. He takes his two-week vacation in December every year and goes to Hawaii to fish. One of his good friends is his substitute when he is gone. He has friends at the Kona Harbor Marina. He never keeps any fish, just the pictures. He has lots of pictures. When asked why, he always says, "I put them back and make another fisherman happy."

When the new police building was erected twenty years ago, he asked for a small office in the basement behind the locked evidence vault. The vault is the only room he has never been in alone. His small office was adorned with fishing pictures. He made sure it was just an old man's work cave. A small desk, a TV, and an old radio with a tape player are his companions. He leaves the copies of his favorite jazz music cds neatly lined up in a separate rack by the desk. His real collection is in his small paid-for house, four blocks away.

If he stood up straight, he would be nearly six-two. The stoop is part of the impression he wishes to make. A rail-thin black man with mostly gray curly hair, gray curly eyebrows, black eyes, a broad, mostly flat nose, and a full straight mouth describe him.

He likes Bryan and always asks, "How are the cold ones going Mr. Bryan?"

"Still cold," was always Bryan's answer.

Bryan had received tips from J.C.'s group—he just didn't know it.

J.C. worked a second job at the Safeway store in Oracle one day a week. He says this is his fun money job. The department knew about the job, but didn't care. "I get good deals on food," he said, showing his soft grin.

In reality, he and two other custodians from Safeway and two from IGA grocery meet every Tuesday at a small coffee house in Oro Valley and talk about investments. Two were black, two were white, and one was Hispanic. All spoke some Spanish. All knew people who knew people who knew other people.

Calling themselves the 'Sweepers,' they have been meeting for thirty years. Absences were rare. All were well-to-do, but no one would ever suspect. They found deals on cars, trucks, boats, houses, rentals, and stocks and bonds. They bought and sold and divided the money six ways. J.C. got two shares because he did all the work. They had only two rules. One: never a word to anyone outside the group. Two: J.C. handled every deal.

The Sweepers knew J.C. invested on the side, but they did not care as he had helped all of them to a net worth in excess of five hundred thousand dollars.

Each time they meet, they put their hands together and say, "Two more years." It started at thirty. They were at year twenty-eight and positively stopping in twenty-three more months. They all could retire then if they wished, and it was time.

J.C. had a net worth of over one million. He could quit but, "The fun is in the doing." He was going to retire and fish every place he could. He didn't own any fishing gear, only an old gray fishing hat.

He overheard Bryan tell a fellow detective about the phone tip after the basketball game.

He knew the tip hadn't come from his group.

"Kinda odd about that tip, Mr. Bryan!"

"Yes, it is J.C. I talked to the chief, and I will continue working on both tips. The chief asked me if those tips were from the same people from whom we often get tips. I told him it was a different source."

J.C. just smiled his usual soft grin and shuffled away. "See you, Mr. Bryan. Hope you get some leads about Alvarez." He would ask the sweepers if they knew anything about the new tip source. At their coffee meetings, they always discussed things they learned and decided together what to pass on to the police. They each had private sources, but all were considered a grampa figure in their neighborhood. Kids know more than adults believe.

CHAPTER 78

The office was quiet. Charlene was preparing to go home, she stopped to give Cliff a couple of papers that needed his attention. "You look tired."

"I am. Would you have dinner with me tonight? I have something I would like to get your opinion about that I only want your ears to hear."

Charlene did not immediately answer, "Yes, Cliff, I would like to have dinner with you. Where should we go?"

"How about Maridux?"

"Perfect. I haven't been there in a long time." She smiled.

When they were seated at their table, Charlene started the conversation, "You have been distant. I know something is troubling you."

The waiter brought the wine Cliff asked for when he made the reservation, then took their order.

Charlene, I am worried about Del. He told me why he wanted three alternate identities, and I believe he actually does use them to apply for big game tags. He has always kept things to himself. Rick told me he is the best, non-special ops, shooter he has seen."

Charlene interrupted, "Does Del know Rick is working closely with you?"

"Yes, I told him a few days ago. He already assumed I did."

"You knew he would figure that out."

"Yes, Charlene, but he hasn't agreed to my offer yet so I didn't say much. Del was in Arizona when both of those desperados were shot from long distance. He was pheasant hunting in South Dakota when the serial killer bit the dust in St. Paul. Spokane is a one-day drive from Bozeman, and he was not at home. It took him longer than I expected to catch my tag team. He is my special friend. I will do anything legit to help him. He has suffered much. But I know he is more than capable."

Charlene stopped him. "Look at me please." Cliff looked up from a downcast posture. He had tears in his eyes. Charlene continued. "I have only talked to him on the phone and I have never felt bad vibes. We kid about meeting and going on a date, but he rings true to me. Are you going to do anything about your suspicions?"

"I have racked my brain, trying to think of a way. When I told him I didn't obtain the info about his ID's. I told him not to make me ask. He didn't flinch. I trust him but these coincidences scare me."

Their food arrived. "Let me think about what you have said. We should visit this topic again, Cliff."

"I agree. Let's eat and talk of other things. He is a good guy under a lot of stress."

CHAPTER 79

I procrastinated calling Cliff about his offer to become a paid asset to the FBI in Cliff's region. I know it is because I am sure they are, at some level, trying to catch the long-distance shooter. I do not want to be caught. Sure, some bad guys are gone, but crimes have been committed. BY ME! There must be dedicated agents trying to move up, and solving one of those shootings would be a big score. I have to assume someone is looking and trying. Also, if I am caught, Cliff would suffer greatly.

On the other hand, being sort of on the inside at the FBI should give me enough warning and a chance to flee if someone is getting too close.

Sitting on my back patio, trying to get a few answers to the New York Times crossword, I decided to get off my butt and get the call out of the way. It was time to get the discussion out of my worry zone.

The phone switched to his voicemail, so I left a short message. "Cliff, I would like you to stop at my home and discuss your offer before I think about going to Salt Lake City."

After making the call, I finally felt a little relieved. I decided to reduce the tension further by working on the old oak roll-top desk. I moved it to the workspace in the front of the garage. I had the sides off, the top separated, and the drawers that needed repair reglued and clamped before the phone rang.

My caller ID said it was Charlene. "Morning Charlene, you have our date arranged yet? You know I will be around one day soon."

"I have had that date in mind forever! I will believe it when it happens. Cliff asked me to see if tomorrow afternoon would be suitable. He is tied up with the deputy director today."

"Perfect! Your day is coming."

She chuckled, "Del, I hope to live that long! Bye."

"Bye, and thanks."

CHAPTER 80

Cliff called around five p.m. "Where is the best place to get a fried chicken dinner with all the fixings to go? My turn to feed us."

"Martha's Country Kitchen, next to Lowes. Dark meat for me."

"See you about six. You have the beer."

About six fifteen, a white F-150 Ford crew cab parked in my driveway with all four doors painted dark red, framing some black lettering that read 'Gallatin Land Management and Surveying Inc'. A heavy guy in lineman tan bibs, a red flannel shirt, and a red baseball cap, stepped out and came to the door carrying a large cardboard box. He rang the bell.

I opened the door halfway, and heard a familiar voice. "Your dinner delivery, sir."

Cliff hid for a reason. I nodded and finished opening the door. Cliff walked in and went straight to the kitchen. Without a word, he put the chicken on the table, removed his plastic-wrapped clothes from the box, and went into the bedroom he used when he stayed here over Thanksgiving.

He emerged wearing jeans and a Hawaiian shirt.

"Now I feel better. That outfit is very hot." Joining me in the kitchen and making himself a plateful, he said. "Let's eat first, then hash things over."

While we were eating, Cliff asked. "Del, how come you hike into the wilderness alone? Dave says you stay a week or more most of your trips."

"It is a deep special part of who I am. Are you checking up on me again? I have minimal stress there. I am not lonely there. I feel a different kind of friendship with myself. I plan to visit the Bob as often as possible, for as long as possible. Both Molly and Trevor are planning a trip with me. Would you ever do a trip with me?"

"My left knee won't allow that. I need a replacement, but right now my life and job won't allow time. Maybe after the knee is fixed, we will see. No, I am not checking. Dave commented about your trips at Thanksgiving time."

We cleaned up the mess together, opened a second beer, and moved to the patio. I lit the propane heater.

"I came with the disguise, so no one would see me come to your home to tell you about Gallatin Land Management. You can tell anyone who asks that you might do some logging on your land near Lincoln and want professional help. That should cover the truck showing up at your door.

The guy who owns the company is a one-time FBI informant who worked exclusively with me. He is under a protection protocol. We can act as employees and use the trucks because we provided them. He operates a legitimate business and does quite well. We have watched over him 24/7 for five years."

I interrupted and asked. "Do they know about me?"

"No, Del. I am the only one who knows anything about you. Charlene knows, but has yet to see you in person or a picture, for that matter."

"Cliff! I am reluctant to become known to a lot of FBI people. I wish to remain as just a source of information. You can arrange the payment process if you feel that is still what you want to do. The envelope I have prepared for you is on the table by my recliner. It includes the account info you requested. If I get paid for anything, I want to give the money to Molly. But I do not want to be a face to anyone but you."

"Del, I respect your answer. It is what I expected you to do. You would have been exposed if you had come to Salt Lake City. My counterpart at the office there is pushing to have you come, but he is against my proposal to allow you to know more of the workings of the Bureau. His name is Will Biggert. He and I are the two finalists for the Salt Lake office Regional Director position.

"If I get the position, I plan to work for at least four more years and see how the job goes. Whichever one of us is passed over is to retire, as we both have the requirements and then some. No more promotions for whoever is passed over."

When he paused, I asked, "Before we go any further, do we have anything on the boat trailer light or my Russian neighbor?"

"We have nothing on the taillight. Our tech man said he was positive it is old."

"How old?" I asked.

"More than three years. It is not government issue, and can be purchased at a hundred different locations. The Billings office is working the research on the new Russian neighbor. We don't want the local agents in Bozeman exposed. We decided not to tip him off if he's a bad guy. We have a locator on his over-the-road truck and a loose tail when he comes to Bozeman, but don't follow him on the highway. You'll know what we know when we know it."

"Thanks. That is good enough. I still cannot figure out when and how the light was changed on my boat trailer. I have gone over the whole process since I bought the boat. I guess I will put it way back in my mind. But since it is that old, it must come from the new "Noses' in Helena. My neighbor, Martha, who was spying for them, told them about my boat. I will not forget them, just not worry. What can you tell me about the new 'Noses' keeping Fred and Sam's office open?"

"We are watching, but the new group is proving hard to catch. They learned after Fred and Sam were arrested. Also, we have Lansing, the professor, hidden away while he recovers. It looks like a deal for him if he helps us. We let the world think he died. He was inches away. He is trying to recover most of his mental facilities."

"I liked him. Glad he is not dead. Cliff, I like the cloak-and-dagger feeling. I find it fun and fascinating. I now look at my surroundings and people to see what is amiss. It will be neat to get paid if I help you. Did you get the credit for the arrests of the bad guys I tipped you about?"

"Yes! All of them. My team has had a very good year. We had the usual small successes and three other bigger ones. The best I can tell, the three you helped with were all extra promotion makers."

"Do I get paid for those?" I smiled and held my hands open, mostly playing with him.

"I am working on that because you deserve it, not because you are begging. The answer has to come from the deputy director. Will doesn't want you to be paid. He says you were just lucky."

"You want some pie and coffee?"

"Good idea. Let's go inside. Got any ice cream?"

"A fully stocked hotel, Mr. Rawlins."

"I need to get rid of the truck." He made a quick call.

The sun set, and the hazy overcast hid the crescent moon. Cliff dialed the heater off, killed my patio light, went into the bedroom, retrieved his disguise, and placed it by the back door. Ten minutes later, a young man entered, put on the disguise and asked me to walk him to the front door. There, carrying the box, he shook my hand. Said, "Thanks for the business," strolled to the truck and drove away.

We finished the pie and ice cream, and he told me about the scope of the Salt Lake City Director's job. He told me he likes to be where the action is, and a lot of that is in Montana. His undercover agents are stressed to the max: too many bad guys and so much remote country. Out of the blue, he asked, "I know you like to go into the Bob. Do you ever see teams of backpackers there?"

"I rarely see anyone at all. I do not camp by the main trail ever. I have a couple of well-hidden spots I use. I never see evidence of others using my spots. Why do you ask?"

"We heard a new drug pipeline has been using the main trail from Meadow something to some outlet near Ovando. Just a rumor so far. This is a heads-up for you. I doubt any of the 'mules' are nice people."

"I will watch for them, but hiking that far must be for something extra special. The highway between Browning and West Glacier is so accessible. I doubt the extra miles are worth it, but I will watch my back. You stay the night. It is very late. We can finish talking in the morning."

"Good idea. A shower and a break from the phone will be so nice. See you in the morning."

"Night." I watched a tired man type a short text, shut off his phone, and enter his room.

🌲 🌲 🌲

"Morning, Cliff. I have your breakfast ready."

"Morning, Del. Perfect."

After eating, I continued our conversation from last night about the 'Bob.' "Back a few months ago, you gave me a phone number and said you trust me, and the people you can say that about, you can count on one hand. If I am one of them, and I think Charlene is one, that leaves three. Billy is out, he is too new. Out of the remaining three, could you introduce me to one of them. I might need to get a hold of you when you aren't available."

"Fair Question. First, I think you are right about the bugged taillight. I think it's the new Noses. Excuse me." He stood, picked up the trash bag and bottles from last night, went into my garage and closed the door. I heard the bottles settle in the recycle bin and the trash bag plop. Then silence. I finished cleaning up the kitchen and the patio as well. The fried chicken and the breakfast smells are a great way to start a day. I was sitting in my recliner working the crossword when he returned.

"I just talked to one of the others. He agrees with you, and we will work to set something up—safe and secure. There is only one other, and you will never know anything about him. The best way to explain this is, he is to me what Dutch is to you. Dutch will do anything for you. He told me so when we were all together at Thanksgiving. That kind of friend is critical in this business. "We wouldn't want each other as enemies, Del. It is damn nice to have a few really good friends. I will call for help if I need it. I know you will have my back."

"What if something happens to you? I would need a contact for at least a short time?" I asked.

"I will give you Billy's contact number. Remember, he will be under-cover and could ignore you or delay calling back. I will give you Charlene's as well. Just say, Charlene or Billy, asked you to call. One of them will take care of you. Billy believes with all his being, that you saved his life. Charlene will also help you anyway she can. That is the best I can do now. When you meet the other person I trust, you and he can decide on any arrangement that works for you two."

"Do you have a picture of Charlene?"

"Yes."

"May I see it?"

Cliff took his phone out of his pocket, scrolled the screen and stopped and handed me the phone.

After a brief study, "Thanks. I will recognize her. She and I will set something up when I pass through Salt Lake City on my way to Arizona for the winter."

Cliff covered all of the details of my new arrangement with the FBI, especially communications. "Charlene will be the detail person as she will be the only other FBI person who will know what you look like. I have never told Billy about the tips you gave me. He is close to becoming another person I can trust, but those tips are between you, Charlene, and me."

"Cliff when I get to Arizona, I plan to disappear for a while. I want to test one of my ID's. And, I have been on the go since the day Amy died. I need the time to de-stress and come to grips with her loss and my new life. Molly will know where I am hiding. Deep sea fishing is going to be my main pursuit. Cancun, or Hawaii."

Cliff stayed all day. He was on the phone most of the time but he just eased the stress. I noticed he only told Charlene where he was. We decided on Chinese take-out, made our selections, and I went to pick it up.

"Just the kind of day I needed. Thank you, my friend."

"I am glad you had a relaxing day. Refurbishing that old roll-top desk is my soft time."

"You have a note pad I can borrow?"

"Sure." At my desk, I selected a yellow four by six-inch sticky note pad and handed it to him.

"Write 'Always' on the bottom half."

Cliff stayed the second night, but was silently gone when I started my day. I heard him moving around, but did not suspect he would be gone when I got up. The envelope was gone. So was the bottom half of the note. Godspeed was written on the top half, and the indentation of always was lightly shaded and visible on the page below.

CHAPTER 81

was all set for the test of James Colbert's ID papers, and his disguise. Only the closer at the title company in Billings (when James bought the condo), and the building manager Johnathon, have seen him.

A wire transfer completed the cash purchase of the one-bedroom condo in downtown Billings, Montana. The manager accepted the expected deliveries and all were neatly stacked just inside the door. The sale was mostly turn-key and little was needed. Johnathon, *the Supe*, as he liked to be called, instead of the manager, had supervised the installation of the new king-sized bed. A new lockable desk, a smart TV, and a remote monitor system that controlled an interior security system made the place comfortable for a gentleman who would rarely live there.

As James Colbert, I would reside there for three or four days. His disguise was the simplest. Special shoes and sandals made me look taller, and my makeup was designed to make my face look thin. Full but neatly trimmed white hair and noticeable white but narrow eyebrows helped make my nose look much narrower. Clear wire-rimmed, glasses revealed gray eyes, and a small dark spot on my left cheek added details that a person might remember when first meeting James.

I created a noticeable purplish, irregularly shaped birthmark about the size of a fifty-cent piece on the back of my left hand. I made James left-handed, and the birthmark set that disguise apart. The narrow white mustache, small goatee, and expensive tailored clothes gave the impression that I expected things to be exactly as I wanted them to be. As James, his manner of talking, using a radio baritone voice, and manner of walking were brisk. He looked people in the eye when addressing them.

I wanted people to think James Colbert liked himself and wanted you to know it.

The supe recognized James immediately when he came in the front door.

"Morning Mr. Colbert. Nice to have you visit us."

"Morning, Johnathon. My deliveries are in the unit, yes?"

"There are four that I know of, plus the bed."

"Then they are all there. Thank you. I would enjoy dinner within walking distance. Do you have a recommendation?"

"Fine dining, or a sports bar, James?"

"One or two of each. Then I can look up their menus and decide."

"The Yellow Jacket is a sports bar about eight blocks west on 4th Avenue North. Bud's Suds is a sports bar three blocks west on First Avenue North. Fine dining is either at The Orange Room next door to our building, or Bronte's across the street from Bud's. Lots of people ask. I have eaten at least once at every place within twelve blocks of our building. You should find one of those to your liking."

"Thank you. How far is it to Bozeman from Billings?"

"About one hundred fifty miles, following I-90 which is about a mile south from our building on 27th Street South to I-90."

"I have a friend there I wish to visit. Thank you again, you have been very helpful."

"I love my job, James, and I like my tenants. Helping is what I do. I believe in protecting their privacy."

"I'll be in Hawaii all of December, and in Arizona all of January, February, and March. I'm sure I'll be stopping here a time or two. After this winter, I'll be staying here more. I'll drive to Bozeman early tomorrow. Then I'm not sure. Thank you again Johnathon."

"My pleasure, sir. Have a safe trip."

🌲🌲🌲

Disguised as James, I left early. My garaged Honda CRV was as I left it months ago. It started easily. While driving to Bozeman, I decided two things: to visit Molly, and to eat breakfast at my neighbor Ben's McDonald's coffee klatch spot, to see if the disguise worked.

Ben's McDonald's was super busy. As James, I ordered the Big Breakfast, then walked past Ben and his group. Ben looked at me and turned back to his group and continued talking. Good. I sat so I could watch Ben. He never looked at James again, even when I walked out. The food was not as good as the EGGE, but I was sure the James' disguise would not fool Cindy or my close friends.

Definitely not a risk I needed to take.

CHAPTER 82

I left my car in the covered garage at the Bozeman airport, so I could use the heated elevated walkway to check in. I went to the airport restroom before boarding and changed back to Del, except for the white whiskers. Then enjoyed a beautiful flight over the Rockies—nothing like snowcapped mountains peeking at the sun. I am on my way to see Molly. I will arrive just at dinner time.

"Hi, Dad."

"Hi yourself Molly. I have missed you."

"Same here, Dad. My roommate is at her parent's farm near Bend. Her father had a small stroke. She won't be back for two weeks, so you can bunk with me and the cat. Trevor is coming for the weekend."

"Great. My flight back departs early Monday."

"I have today off so we can do whatever we want. I told my boss, Nadine, I would be late Monday. What's with the whiskers?"

"Just trying something new. Not sure I like them."

"They're okay, but I like your clean-shaven look better. What do you want to do?"

"Just some quiet time. We have things to talk about. We can find a nice place for dinner. I would enjoy some seafood."

"The Crab Shack it is, then. I'll be ready in ten minutes. I'll drive."

We arrived twenty minutes later and ordered our meal. Then I said, "I am going to Kona next week. I hope you and Trevor can come for a few days." I handed her an envelope with four thousand dollars. "Your ticket money. Fly first class."

"We are working on some dates during Trevor's Christmas break. So far, it's a go. We can't finalize until Monday, when I find out if I can use that time as part of next year's vacation."

"I will want to talk about your mother then. Painful, for sure, but I know I need to."

"Me too, Dad, good idea. How are you going to fill in your time?"

"Getting a tan, deep sea fishing, snorkeling, touring the island on every road, golfing, and taking surfing lessons. I hope I am not too old to learn how to ride a wave or two. My health insurance is top of the line, but hope I will not need it.

"I am a little tired, so will call it a day. Tomorrow you are in charge. I know there are things I should experience here. Maybe a walk around downtown Portland."

Trevor couldn't make the trip. Molly and I just let two soft days relax our part of the world. I am happy that we are getting together more often. Sorely needed and long overdue. I can tell she likes it as well.

Monday morning at the airport, she asked, "Is the backpack trip in August still on?"

"Oh yes. I wouldn't miss it for the world. Trevor coming?"

"He says he has it worked out, and will help us set the dates when we go to Hawaii."

"We three will have a great time in the Bob." A long hug and I turned to enter the security line.

CHAPTER 83

After the Portland trip, I spent a night at my house in Bozeman, setting it up for a long absence. I wanted to see Dutch after returning to Billings for two days. I would travel back to Great Falls through Roundup and Lewistown. That drive is through superb hunting country.

Arriving in Billings, I booked a room at the Best Western on the west side of town near Cabela's. I did not want Johnathon to know I returned to Billings.

♣ ♣ ♣

While driving the two hundred fifty miles to Great Falls, I cheated the speed limit as much as I dared. Still, two young men driving a big black Ford 350 passed me easily.

I decided I must make coded checklists for each disguise change because I could easily make simple mistakes with the switches to James Colbert to Del Sanderson and back changes. I especially wanted to keep Colbert isolated.

Dutch greeted me with a smile and the customary bear hug.

"What's up, I didn't know you were coming."

"I have been to Roundup and Judith Gap to see about hunting next year, so wanted to come here and tell you about my winter intentions. You know about Hawaii. But I am going to Arizona for the winter. I want to give you a key to my house and the two codes to work the alarm system. I made a deal with my landlord to purchase my rental house. When you go down to check things, you are welcome to stay. The extra bedroom will be ready for you. I cannot stay now as I need to get to Lincoln yet today. And, Bozeman tomorrow or the next day and get ready for Hawaii. Are you going to make it to the islands?

"Not this year. Maybe next time. Eddie and I have late season mule deer doe tags and he has his Christmas vacation time scheduled up."

"I am going to the Lincoln cabin for a day or two. I am having a security system installed using the same codes as the Bozeman house.

"I'll see you after Hawaii and before going to Arizona. Good luck hunting."

Hugs and I left for Lincoln.

I met Art at Lambkins. Over breakfast we discussed our options. We settled on almost fortress, emphasizing the remote surveillance. We could not use tasers or a couple of similar devices. We knew a hunter may disregard the signs. We did not want to alert the world of the extra coverage. Art completed the work himself, and was finished just after 3 p.m.

"Your package includes the same coding system as your house. Two subtle changes to set them apart, but they are not complicated. My company's response team is over an hour away from here. I like your location very much."

I locked everything and set the alarms. We left at the same time. He turned toward Great Falls, and I toward Missoula. I will use the Helmville route through Helena.

I arrived at my house at sundown. I stopped in my driveway to watch the spectacular sunset for a few minutes. While watching the orange and yellow color changes, Boris arrived at his house. Just as Ben said. Garage door went up, Boris drove in and the garage door went down. I continued to watch from my garage shadows. The TV came on and three minutes later a pizza was delivered.

I was sure Ben just wrote an entry in his log.

CHAPTER 84

The four-bedroom condo rental on the Big Island of Hawaii is in downtown Kona and on the beach. I did not care about the size, as much as the location. Inviting everyone at Thanksgiving time I mentioned the condo had four bedrooms, and they were invited to come share the space. I called and informed the condo association of my arrival date in Kona. Maybe someone will join me after I arrive in downtown Kona on December third.

Other islands have more accessible beaches but there are more golf courses on the Big Island. The public can play in the rotating skins games, even though they are donating to the local pros. But the greens fees are often one fourth of the regular prices. I will play these nice courses as often as I can.

Kona Harbor is fifteen minutes away from my condo, and home to a lot of fishing boats. The ocean south of the island is reputed to be some of the best deep-sea fishing in the world, especially for Marlin. Who knows, maybe I will get to catch one.

I called and informed the condo association of my arrival date in Kona, and they agreed to accept a departure date of January second. A full-sized SUV would be my rental car.

After two days of walking, relaxing and learning my way around, I went to the harbor to see about fishing. I arranged a separate day with three different boats. The Harbor House was recommended for dinner by the receptionist at my condo, so I decided to give it a try. It was maybe the best cheeseburger I have ever had, served with a shrimp side noodle dish and a Kona Brewery Fire Rock IPA.

The next morning, I enjoyed an all-day bus tour of the whole island. The black sand beach and the orchid nursery were highlights. If I get any company, I will treat them to that excursion.

My first fishing charter consisted of eight people, each assigned to a numbered rod and reel. We caught one fish in four hours, not what I had in mind. I went to see the captain of the second-day trip and asked for the rate for one or two people instead of eight. He did not want to change things, so I canceled. He had a waiting list and said he could fill my spot.

The third day boat captain said. "Call me Captain Noah. I can arrange anything. Let's look at the log and see what we can find. We will move you. I can get someone to fill your slot. Wednesday, I have an opening with a long time regular, who is just like you. No more, than two people fishing. Will that work?"

"Perfect."

"Done. Pick a box lunch from the list posted on the back wall. See you Wednesday."

"The number two. Ham, provolone and slaw is perfect. I am excited."

I was due at the harbor by seven, so decided to go early and have breakfast. I tried the seafood omelet, but while it was very good, I do not think I will mix fish with my eggs again.

I carried my day pack with all the essentials the captain suggested to be comfortable out on the water most of the day. I ambled toward my boat's location in the row of fishing boat look-alikes. In front of me was a tall, skinny, stoop-shouldered black man that boarded Captain Noah's boat. From the back he looked exactly like the man I took pictures of in Marana. "Not possible," I said to myself.

Captain Noah greeted me like a long-lost friend. I liked him. "Good morning, Del. The weather is perfect. Good fishing today."

Introducing his deck hand, he smiled. "This is Deke. Anything you need, just ask him. He'll do it. I just sit in the chair."

Then he turned to the black man, who faced the other way stowing his gear. "J.C. meet Del, he's is your fishing partner today."

J.C. turned around, smiled, and offered his hand. "Nice to meet you. Del."

"Nice to meet you as well, J.C." I hoped I hid any hint of my surprise. Unbelievable. I am fishing in Hawaii with the mystery man from Marana. The odds of that happening have to be greater than the lottery.

The aft of Captain Noah's boat was set up with two identical fishing chairs and rod holding straps. "I only use a one chair setup when I have a full boat. You guys can decide who sits where. Deke will watch the lines and lures."

"I have fished with Captain Noah for many years, Del, so you can pick the one you prefer."

"I'll take the right one then."

"Glad you did, as the left one is my lucky chair! You a sporting man, Del?"

"What do you have in mind?"

"Twenty-five dollars for the first fish, and seafood dinner at the Harbor House for the biggest."

"Deal. I will be happy to let you buy my dinner." I liked my mystery man.

Twenty minutes after the lines were in the water, J.C. caught a fourteen-pound Dorado, Mahi-Mahi to islanders.

After Deke boated the fish, J.C. grinned and held out his hand. "Yes sir, my lucky chair."

"Guess it is at that," I said as I handed him the twenty-five dollars. We settled in and waited for the next strike.

"Where are you from, Del?"

"I live in Montana, am finally retired, and plan to hunt and fish whenever I can. I will mix in some traveling. How about you J.C.?"

"Marana, Arizona. I am the custodian for the Marana Police Department H.Q. I plan to work a little less than two years and then retire. I have a good job. I come fish with Captain Noah every year on my vacation. Always in December. I keep track of the fish I catch. No Black Marlin yet. A three hundred fifty-pound blue Marlin is my biggest fish."

"That must have been fun. I once went deep sea fishing in Florida, but the only decent fish was a twenty-four-pound barracuda. We got some smaller redfish but no Tarpon. Plan to go back there this winter."

Finally, I caught a twenty-two-pound Ono, often called a Wahoo.

J.C. had a marlin follow his lure for a long while, but it turned away without a strike. He also had a big Mahi Mahi on the end of his line for a while, but it spit the hook.

After we entered the slip in the harbor, Captain Noah said. "You two want to go on a *most of the day trip* on Friday? I usually take my deck hands on the third Friday every month, but only Deke can go this time, so he said he would work if he could have a line in the water."

We both said yes at the same time.

J.C. bought the seafood dinner at the Harbor House. Never a better meal anywhere. It will take some walking to use up those calories.

"Captain Noah is a very nice man. He has always been good to me. What and where do you hunt, Del?"

"Well, J.C. mostly I love to be in the woods. I like getting as close to game as I can without them suspecting I am around. But I hope to harvest a trophy bull elk, a five-by-five whitetail deer and a trophy mule deer, then we will see if anything else is an option. I apply in eleven Western states each year now, so should get drawn for a tag somewhere. I can always hunt in Montana. Some nice trophy's there."

"Cost a lot of money?

"Not really. Small fees to apply, if any. Out of state fees and tags are high, but you only pay those if you buy the tag and go hunt there."

We walked to our cars, shook hands, and J.C. said, "See you Friday."

"Looking forward to it. Bring your money."

"Oh, I'll have it. Just won't need it."

I was one half mile behind him when he reached the Queen's highway. He turned left. My condo was a right turn. I could not shake the feelings, wondering how and why fate brought us together.

🌲🌲🌲

When my phone rang, I was sitting on the balcony, hoping for the Green Flash at sunset. My caller ID said it was Jack.

"Hello Jack!"

"Del, me and the boys are coming to Hawaii to stay with you from December eleventh through the sixteenth. How about them apples?"

"I like them apples. Anything special you guys want to do?"

"We all want to fish at least once. The boys want to learn to surf and do a lot of snorkeling. We also want to see the volcano and the lava. The rest we will leave up to you."

"I will have it all set up for you. How about a Range Rover for your rental?"

"Works. See ya," and he was gone.

By noon the next day I had it all set up. Damn, some of them are coming. I could feel the little bouts of loneliness drift away. I had made a new friend, and old friends were coming to spend some time with me. Life does not get any better than that.

♣ ♣ ♣

I wanted to get J.C. talking about the police department and his job. Maybe he would mention Kellerman.

Captain Noah took us nearly to the southernmost point of the island.

"There are very strong currents around here, but we will stay far enough away to be safe. No extra risks, and we'll wear our life jackets for a while. I'll let you know when we are far enough away from the most dangerous places, so we can take the life jackets off."

I caught a thirty-two-pound barracuda, for the first fish. After weighing it we returned it to the ocean. It was out of sight in a flash.

"Here's your money back. Del." His smile said it all.

Deke shifted to a deep running lure and was rewarded with a solid hit. We brought in the other lines and gave Deke the lucky chair. Forty minutes later we all helped land a 245-pound tiger shark.

"My biggest fish ever! WOW! I'm excited. He danced around the deck smiling from ear to ear.

"Told, you it's a lucky chair. J.C. knows."

What does J.C. stand for?" asked Del.

"Jefferson Carter Washington at your service," he answered as he slipped back into his lucky chair.

"J.C., you were born before Jimmy Carter became president?" I countered.

"I always wondered how my Mama knew about that." He turned to look at the ocean. We drifted an hour trying to entice another shark, but were unsuccessful.

Noah came down to the deck. "We're going to try a new place. What do you two want to try for?"

"I would like to get lucky and catch a Marlin or maybe a big tuna," I answered.

"Fine by me," echoed J.C.

Noah let Deke pilot the boat, gave him a list of instructions, and watched until he was sure Deke had everything under control, and then he efficiently set out three lines.

"I get the lucky chair if I get a big fish on my line. I am the captain. We can take off the life vests now." We caught six Mahi-Mahi and kept three for table fare. We also kept all four Ono. I had company coming, and they were big eaters.

Deke was much further out than the first day, as we could barely see the Island. Without Mauna Kea showing us where the island was, it would not be on our horizon. He turned toward the harbor.

Checking my orientation, I asked if I was right. "Yes, you are. Good for you. All deckhands are taught how to navigate out here. Every captain needs a backup. The hands need to know how all equipment works."

I turned to J.C. "How long have you been with police department?"

"Thirty-eight years, Del. I am retiring at forty. Haven't told them yet. Me and four of my custodian friends are all quitting at the same time. We have been friends since school days. A tight group. We have coffee twice a week, regular like. We call ourselves the Sweepers. We all know how to work a broom. People never pay any attention to an old man with a mop or a broom."

Changing the subject, I asked, "Have you ever hunted, J.C?"

"No Sir. I've never fired a gun. Don't want to. I see and hear too much bad stuff about guns. No Sir, no guns for me."

He turned, looked out over the ocean, and halfway hung his head. He was silent for a time, then added something not looking at anyone. "I see too much. I see lots of bad people with drugs and guns. It doesn't look to me that jail helps much. They get out and go back to being bad. I often wish they would disappear. We need more places to help addicts kick their habit. My heart and soul hurts for them. Better to spend the money on helping than on jails. Lots of addicts are good people. Bad people cause them trouble. Yes sir, I will be ready to retire. I can fish in Cabo, Belize, Costa Rico, and Florida. I hope to die with a fish on the end of my line."

"I agree about the really bad people. I often wonder how we can get rid of them," I said hoping he would keep talking.

"Del one of the worst ever to be in our jail was shot while he was outside in the security yard. A real big surprise. Some people at HQ are easier to talk to than most, so I hear most of what is being planned. I got a couple who always talk to me. Sometimes we sweepers hear things working in the jail or at the grocery store. We call in those tips. They don't know it is us. Never will."

"Another inmate kill him?" asked Del.

"No, Sir. My friend, Mr. Bryan, said they think it was a long-distance shot, but they don't have any leads. They think the shooter was long gone in less than ten minutes. They looked at every building and talked to hundreds of people. No one saw or heard a thing. Lots of road construction noise. Good riddance we all say."

Deke asked, "I thought those guns made a lot of noise, supersonic or something like that."

"Mr. Bryan looked that stuff all up. He says suppressors are getting better, but the shot still makes enough noise. Though, unless you are close, it is hard to tell where the shot came from. Mr. Bryan was checking gun ranges for a while, but decided that was a waste of time. He likes working old cold cases. He's a smart thinker."

Deke yelled, "You got a big one, Del."

We used most of an hour getting a nice Blue Marlin next to the boat. Captain Noah and Deke both guessed it was over four hundred pounds. Close enough for me. We let it go, after taking lots of pictures. Several as it lay on its side resting before swimming away.

J.C. bought the seafood dinner again.

"Glad to Del. That was a fine fish. Best day fishing ever for me. Six Mahi-Mahi, four Ono, a barracuda, a shark, and a Marlin. Yes sir, a real fine day."

We gave some of the fish away as Deke knew some people that need the help. I like to do that.

"When you prepare the fish, just cook the fish meat enough to see a soft white change. After you taste all the species, you will be sad you didn't keep more," Deke explained.

I am leaving Sunday, Del. If you ever get to Marana, you stop by."

"I will for sure. I have a lease in Casa Grande for three months. I do not want to be in Montana for the whole winter. I will be by. You have a number that I should use?"

"Yes, sir."

We exchanged cell numbers. Maybe we could work together on a rehab center in Marana.

🌲🌲🌲

Back at the condo, listening to my kind of music, I mumbled aloud. "I cannot believe it. Meeting J.C. and fishing with him. We are going to be friends. My Marana mystery man is more than a player. His group is the other tipster, Kellerman alluded to."

Captain Noah and Deke were taking Jack and sons fishing twice. They will be excited after they see the pictures of my big fish.

Sitting on the balcony with a Kona Fire Rock IPA, again hoping for the Green Flash, I received a text from Molly. She and Trevor are coming over to stay for a week during Christmas break. They will fly first class whatever dates they are able to arrange. I have lots to set up.

Yes, I am very lucky.

Could use a special lady's hand to hold tonight. You cannot hug a memory, but one's heart can feel those memories. I miss my dates. Sometimes being alone is worse than awful. I know a special companion is precious.

CHAPTER 85

I picked up Molly and Trevor close to three in the afternoon and took them to the Harbor House.

"I have a few places planned for you two to see, otherwise we are just relaxing. Trevor, your first surfing lesson is tomorrow. Downtown is only three blocks away. I have a key to the condo for each of you. I made a small list of the three places you must visit in downtown, but the rest is your time. When you go to the market, I would like to join you, then we can choose some local things to try."

"Neither of us have been in Hawaii. This will be a special time," said Trevor. "Grampa Del, I have the dates for you when I can go into the Bob." He handed me a short note with two possible time periods.

"We will do the second window, as that is two extra days and we will need them as it is a day and a half hike in and out. I will take care of things. You need to bring your personal stuff, with extra socks, and lots of mosquito repellent. Thirty-five to forty pounds in your backpack should be enough, even including two quarts of water each. You will need your trail lunches for two days." The five days passed by too quickly, as special times often do. Trevor will be back as the surfing lessons turned into daily rides on the waves. I went with him one time.

"Thanks, Dad. You enjoy your last week. I hope you get to see the Green Flash."

"Thanks, Grampa Del. Surfing is totally awesome. See you soon. Love you."

"Love you, Dad," Molly whispered as we shared a long hug.

"Love you both." They walked away. Yes, all my special people are closer.

When Molly was in Hawaii staying at the condo in Kona. I told her of my, intention to disappear for a while. We talked about her mother, and felt better, coming to grips with her being gone. Molly said she couldn't take the time to come to Cancun this year. That would make things easier for James Colbert and or Del Sanderson. I know I want to continue looking for bad guys. I am positive I can only hide in Cancun for a short time. I needed to be visible in Casa Grande, so I must come back a time or two.

Thinking about what Art said about martial arts, it would be a good plan for James to join a class while in Cancun. That class and running on the beach would help reduce the tension building up in Del. Maybe I can make ninety days there, but I really doubt it.

The St. Petersburg Adventure flashed back on my radar earlier than I expected. While waiting my turn to talk about tickets and hotel reservations, I read the *Miami Herald*. An article on the front page said the Jamaican's attorneys received another extension. So instead of tickets to Miami I arranged to fly from Hawaii to Bozeman instead.

CHAPTER 86

fter a smooth red-eye flight back from Kona, arriving at 7 a.m., I went to Betty's for breakfast. The coffee boys were all there, so I joined them.

"Morning everyone, sorry I have not been here much, but am still trying to finish getting settled. Lots of trips planned. Working on my hunting for next season starting with turkeys in the spring. I hope all of you have been well."

After lots of good mornings and some friendly ribbing, I decided since I had disclosed my line of work, Frank and Bill should as well. So, I asked.

"Last time I was here, I revealed how I made my living, but Frank and Bill did not have time to let me know how they made their millions."

Frank answered after a short pause, looking at each of his friends around the table.

"That was a test Del. We voted unanimously to ask you to join us. One no-vote, and we would not have asked. Desmond did some legal checking, and his findings placed you in the best of people category.

"Bill and I didn't say anything on purpose. We appreciated your courtesy. Bill can add things if he wishes, but I will say he was a State of Montana Senator for over twenty-five years. He still plays at politics, but his rental properties in Helena provide him with a quite satisfactory retirement. This group you are now part of all work to make Montana a better place.

"I have a large cattle and hay operation near Harlowton. I would hope you have the opportunity to visit my little community and hunt with me. You've heard of the Boone and Crocket Organization, I am sure. They keep track of rifle-hunting trophy animals. Anyway, a Boone and Crockett trophy five-year-old mule deer stag was shot on my property last season. There are others like him," Frank explained with pride.

I sat back a little in my chair. "Frank, thank you. I sensed when I walked out last time there was more to this group than just a bunch of friends drinking coffee, but I would not have guessed the scope you just described. I am struggling to see how I could possibly fit in with this group."

"Del, one of your financial planning clients, Sylvia Delany Daniels, is a member of our group. She recommended you. You know she has sufficient wealth to live quite comfortably. Our group is based in Bozeman because this is where it started. We have members in every county. You have lived in Great Falls for many years. We know about your wife and please accept each of our good thoughts on your behalf. We don't ask anything special of our members, just to do what they can, when they can."

"Gentlemen. This is, I am quite certain, a special privilege for me. I am going to Arizona for the winter. When I return next spring, I promise to learn what it is I can contribute."

An hour passed quickly and the group started to make their way to the door. "Zig, it's your turn today," said Desmond referring to a small notebook. "Butch you're next."

CHAPTER 87

Leaving Betty's, I drove out to the range. The gate was locked. I had not paid attention. It was one of Rick's days off. He was usually closed on Monday and Tuesday. I decided to risk calling him.

He answered on the second ring. "Del, what do you need?"

"I wanted to stop by and let you know my winter plans and share a couple of Aroma's Cinnamon rolls and coffee with you."

"I'll be right there. I don't often go get cinnamon rolls."

Rick drove up from the range office on his quad. He unlocked the gate, waited until I passed through, then locked the gate and followed me to his office.

Four young men were at stations in some phase of getting ready to shoot long-range.

Rick noticed my interest.

"I do military training for promising shooters. These are teams of two, one spotter and one shooter. The kid with the red hair is going to be extra good. Let's go to the office."

We spread the rolls on his neat desk, each poured himself a cup of coffee, then devoured half of our roll before Rick broke the silence.

"Del, when you came out and made me go to breakfast after the Bully Boy incident, you saved me in more ways than I could explain. If you ever need, anything, you call me," Rick said his eyes sparkling with gratitude.

"That's what friends are for. I just felt you should not be alone. You would have done the same for me."

"I do have a question," he said studying me.

He took a bite, and washed it down with a swig of coffee. "How did you know to park away from the buildings and stay in the truck with your hands on the wheel?"

"I read somewhere once about keeping your hands visible. When you showed me your camouflaged rifle, I guessed you had some experience and had been part of some special unit or something like that. I also watched you with the four Bully Boys. Not just anyone would have been so decisive. I could tell you were wound a little tight, but I felt you expect things to be a certain way, and if they do not pan out as you expect, you act."

"I was more than a little tight. I've been trained to intensify if I feel threatened, I was threatened. I was taught to protect myself at all costs."

"Rick, we are more than just friends. You need me, just call. Maybe you should come visit me in Arizona."

"I think I will." Changing the subject, he added, "The training I do is part of the financial arrangement that bought this range for me. Everything here is mine, but they send me recruits that they believe have what it takes to be special ops. These teams have to pass here or they are out of the program, and they're aware of that. I earned all of this and then some. People can only do special ops for a time. Then they need to 'retire'. Retired ops are well taken care of. Let's go watch."

We watched for an hour.

"You are right, Rick. The redhead is a good shooter."

"Yes, he is, but the other shooter is more like me. Much tougher inside. Both teams will pass, but the shaved-head shooter will get better marks in more areas. His spotter is of the same mold. I wouldn't want them for enemies."

I told him of my winter plans, and what Cliff had told me about the comments made by the Bully boys that Cliff had learned from the prison snitch.

"Thanks for the heads up about Bully. Are you aware Cliff and I know each other?"

"Yes, too many things did not fit. I decided you two knew each other."

"I will let you know if I can make it to Arizona, and I will take you to a range there. The owner is a friend. Enjoy your winter in sunny Arizona."

I saw a rare small smile. My friend was back in control.

CHAPTER 88

I returned to my house. Dutch was parked at the curb sitting in his truck, drinking coffee, and playing solitaire on his phone.

"I needed to see you before you left, Del. One, I want to sell my plane and you said you were interested."

"Yes, I am."

"Okay, we do the deal when you get back. Two, I wanted to actually do the security stuff. I learn by seeing how things are done."

"Great idea."

We practiced the on and off procedures three times.

"I got it. No worries now. Glad I came."

"Are you staying here tonight?" I asked after explaining the small code differences at the Lincoln Cabin.

"No, you told me you had to leave today to get to Salt Lake City. I've used up a lot of your driving time as it is. Drive safely and keep in touch. Stay out of the sun."

"I have plenty of time as my meeting has been changed, we have all day. I would like you to share a lunch with me. I have some things to tell you and you alone. Cliff knows some and Molly knows some, but neither knows much of what I intend to do this winter."

"Sure Del, it doesn't take long to drive back to Great Falls. Lunch it is. Let's go to Denny's."

I went to my office, took an envelope from the top drawer of my desk, then returned to the living room. "I am going on a trip to do some deep-sea fishing, sometime after mid-January. I will be staying at my rental in Casa Grande, but have arranged a trip to Cancun. Not sure how long I will be gone, at least ten days, but less than fifty. The money in the envelope is for you to use to fly the plane and pay the next hundred-hour inspection. When I call you on the burner phone that is in the envelope with the money, I will be on my way back and will hope to go flying. I will ask for the navigator. Your answer is, 'He's in washing his fingers.' I will come back with 'Because pilots don't pee on theirs.' Then I will be in Great Falls within a week."

"Why the codes stuff?" A frowning Dutch wanted to know.

"Some criminals may know it was me who tipped off the Feds and got them arrested. Not likely, but I have been advised to be extra careful. Some of those criminals may be Russians. I think those guys you heard about and warned me to watch for, that were seen around the hangar in Great Falls, were Russian. So, I am going deep-sea fishing in Florida and Cancun and other places. I am not sure where yet, but Belize, Costa Rica, Cabo, are all possibilities. I want to try for tarpon, redfish, and bonefish in Florida, and some of the large-mouth bass there. I get to skip much of the winter weather of good old Montana."

"Is there anything else I can do?"

"Do not think so Dutch. You are my closest friend. I trust you."

"You just ask, anytime. He opened the envelope, took out the money and the phone. "Way too much money here, Del."

"No, Dutch it may not be enough. You go fly. If I do need help, and I call—you may need some of that money."

He drove to Denny's. We talked about hunting antelope next year. After our meal was finished and the dishes bussed, we lingered over coffee refills.

"Years ago, my wife came to the shop one day and said, "I don't love you anymore. I don't want anything. Please sign these papers. Well, I read them and signed them. I remember it like it was yesterday. My heart has never healed. When you heard, you came and sat with me, talked to me, and didn't meddle. You were the only one who understood and let me be. You came when I needed someone. That's how special of a friend you are to me. You need, you get. Enough said. Good luck fishing, Del. Let's talk about those fishing places when you get back. I think it's time I did one of those. You drive safely. Stay in touch."

"I will, and you take care," I answered as we walked to his truck. I could feel what Cliff meant about someone to trust. He dropped me off at my house and left for Great Falls.

After Dutch left, I finished some laundry, and made sure everything on my checklist was done, before I left for Arizona. The afternoon passed quickly.

I took my dinner sandwich and coffee out to the garage and worked on the roll-top desk for a while. The part that rolls is a lot of work. I hoped to have that sanded before I left.

The sandwich and the coffee were gone, and the sanding job was three-fourths done—time to quit for the day. Almost bedtime.

CHAPTER 89

The next morning, I was in the garage sanding the last three slats in the roll-top part of the desk, when the phone rang.

"Morning, Del, you have a burner handy?"

"Morning, Cliff, yes, in my office desk, why?"

"Please get it, give me the number, then take the first call."

"Here is the number. I-509-337-3379."

"Be seeing you, have a safe trip. Godspeed."

"Always."

Waiting for the call proved that time slows down when a person is trying unsuccessfully to be patient. Exactly eleven minutes passed before the phone rang.

"Del Sanderson."

"It is."

"What was Cliff's wife's name?"

"Mavis."

"What river did you and Cliff fish the most often?"

"The Big Blackfoot."

"Morning, Del. I am Wendell A. Norton. Cliff asked me to call. We are to arrange a session for our mutual benefit. Cliff has told me much about you and how you two are working toward your future involvement. He said you plan to be in Arizona for most of the winter. I own a home in Scottsdale, if that location would be satisfactory to you. Cliff and I trust each other completely. We believe we should include you. Rick and Art once worked for me," he paused. I was sure he expected me to comment.

"Very satisfactory! I do plan to winter in Arizona. I could stay longer if it was necessary. Rick and Art, I should have guessed. You have known about me for some time. Am I correct?"

"Cliff said you would say something like that. He said also, that you are an intuitive man, that is hard to fool. I plan to be in Scottsdale in March from the thirteenth through the twenty seventh. I suggest you keep this phone and use it for one more call. You call me during that two-week period and we will make arrangements to start our discussion. I will answer one call from that number, no subsequent ones."

"Wendell, I look forward to meeting another of Cliff's close friends."

"As am I! Take care. Be seeing you."

Now that meeting is something to look forward to. I cleaned up the garage and moved the desk and tools. The truck would fit easily. Everything I could think of I completed. I was ready. I had time to watch a little college basketball before bedtime.

I was on the road to Provo early. I have a date.

CHAPTER 90

I left the motel in Provo an hour before my scheduled meeting with Charlene to be sure the heavy traffic around Salt Lake City did not make me late for my date. I was early enough to pick up a small vase of flowers. We were meeting at the Purple Iris, so I sneaked the flowers in and put them on the table for two near the rear window.

When I returned, Charlene sat admiring the flowers at our table. She looked just like her picture. I would recognize her anywhere. A scent of perfume hinted she had slicked up for me.

She noticed me when I was six feet away. We smiled at each other and she offered her hand.

"The famous Del Sanderson. I must now believe you are real—our date at last. I see you arranged for flowers. How did you know what kind, and that we would be at this table?"

"I arrived a little early, asked a couple of questions and chose this table. Taking her hand in mine, "Yes, our date at last. You are taller than I imagined, and your hair is darker, but otherwise my picture of you is pretty accurate. This is special for me."

"Thank you for the flowers. I don't get them often. You and Cliff are not to be trusted."

Two hours passed quickly.

"I must attend to some errands, Del. But first, some business. Cliff talked to me about your new role and your wish to remain hidden and anonymous. Cliff and I do trust each other. He trusts you and that is good is enough for me.

"I lost my husband the same year Cliff lost Mavis. Cliff and I are very close, but never intimate. An arrangement we made when we first became a team!" She paused, and looked out the window before continuing.

"Cliff and I have talked about you often. I know about your special friends. Cliff worries about you. If you ever call me and mention the name of this place, I will go to the ends of the earth to help you. Cliff expects that as well. He told me Billy is also a deep confidant for both of us." She reached for her small purse, put her other hand over mine, and added, "I have enjoyed our date. You are better looking than Cliff's description!"

"Charlene, now that we have had our first date, what will we talk about on the next one?"

"Mostly business, but we could plan an anniversary date each year."

We walked out to her car. She carried herself nicely. A pleasure to enjoy. "Nice wheels."

"Yes. I do like to drive a special car and a Lexus IS with all the bells and whistles fits me."

"We will plan each anniversary. I enjoy being with beautiful women."

"Flattery, Del. You are a charmer, and thank you. It's a date. Right here next year."

I received a surprise peck on the cheek. She got in her car, and with a flutter of her fingers, she drove away.

I thought about her all the way to Casa Grande. Another deep and personal close friend. I am so lucky.

CHAPTER 91

I went to *Helping Hands* the morning after arriving at Palm Creek and settled into my park model rental on the twelfth green. I watched Peter Sullivan working with the adults trying to learn English and the criteria necessary to become a US citizen. Beautiful. I walked over to him and said, "You are hired permanently."

"Who are you?" He asked.

"Del Sanderson."

"Sir, you have a beautiful thing going here. I am very happy to be a part of it."

"Interesting Peter, because "beautiful" is how I described your work to myself a moment ago. It is super that you can help us. Are you a student still?"

"No, Mr. Sanderson. I can't afford that right now. We are expecting our first child, and I don't have the time. So, I will go back when the money straightens out."

"You are welcome here, and do come back when you can, after your child is born."

I will study Peter's situation. Helping him might be a good use of Vinny's money.

Sarah, one of the six original tutors, told me she was going to enroll in ASU in a month and would not able to continue at Helping Hands. "Del, this short time here has been eye-opening for me. I had not decided what to study, and felt I was wasting my parent's money. I just love helping these kids. I'm going to get my teaching credential. I know that is where I want to start. Then who knows? Thank you for asking me to join you here."

"Good for you. Come see us if you wish, you will always be welcome." Watching her leave, I said to myself. "Another good thing."

CHAPTER 92

My trip through all of New Mexico in the lilac ride (now painted gray) for ten days was therapeutic. I am so glad I hired Jason and Jacob to drive it down to Show Low for me. I saw so much—some very poor communities and some real money around Santa Fe and Taos. I ate at the Spider Web Bistro in Taos, where Amy and I stopped so long ago. I miss everything about her.

I called Molly the evening of January fourteenth.

"Are you having a good day?" I asked.

"Yes, Dad. One of my always-homeless guys got a job today. He hasn't held a job in five or six years. He decided to try life again. He's fifty-three.

"Hope he makes it."

"So do I, Dad."

"You do good work."

"Are you on your way out of the country?"

"I should have known, you would guess. I have replayed and rewound our Hawaii conversation. I think you are right. I need to go someplace and begin the healing process. I have talked to Dutch. He is going to watch over things. He has your number, and said he will be in touch. Remember the ninety-day rule I mentioned when I gave you the safety box key?"

"Won't need it, Dad. You are a strong man. You'll find your way. I, too, have replayed our conversation, and am much better as well. And remember, I have my work and Trevor is close. A tad easier for me, but not much. I work at something to smile about."

"I have tickets for my flights for tomorrow. I will be in touch often. I love you, Molly."

"I love you too, Dad. Be good to yourself."

Long distance hugs do not amount to much, but do feel good.

CHAPTER 93

isguised as James Colbert, I easily traveled to Cancun, settled into the condo and visited the bank that took care of one and a half million of Vinny's money. They were happy to see me. James was now on all the security systems. That was okay because James was the only one of my identities who would ever travel to Cancun.

After three days of sitting in the sun and doing little except my martial arts class twice each day, I went to the newsstand across the street and bought the daily *Miami Herald*.

It looked like the St. Petersburg Adventure would happen before I was scheduled to leave my rental in Cancun or Palm Creek. The Browning 308 and optics were in a locker in Ft. Lauderdale, sharing space with a complete set of ID items to bring Spencer Morgan to life. I now owned four long distance rifles. Rick found them for me. I arranged to have a copy of the *Herald* delivered each morning.

Checking departures assured me a flight to Ft. Lauderdale was available most days. I could arrange things if I gave myself five or six days in Florida. If I were ninety percent or better positive my shot was safe, I would risk it. Otherwise not. I called the leasing agent for the office building I planned to use for this 'adventure', selected the office option we had earlier agreed upon, and wired the required six-month's rent.

I knew there would always be other opportunities,

I would not stay ninety days in Cancun, but would return to Arizona.

I knew I would be an informant for the FBI. They were a part of the criminal justice system.

None of my special people would approve of my 'adventures'. But I did. Satisfied, would be a good word; I did not see myself as a criminal.

I could only guess at my involvement with the FBI, but I thought it might be exciting. I knew I would not need ninety days. I would go back to Billings at least once.

As I contemplated my James Colbert disguise, I realized I needed to find a better way to make the spot on my face. It did not last long enough. I created a small blemish and said the mole had been bothering me, so I had it removed. I was so happy to have it gone. I doubted anyone would ever ask. It would make the change to James Colbert much easier.

I ran every morning on the sand. When it came time to return to the U.S., I would be in my best condition in the last twenty years. Amy never ran with me but she does now. I feel better on every time I run. I am coming along. Amy is always with me and I like that. My next trip into the Bob would be easier. As James, I became a regular at two different eating places, and The Beach Hut, and an open-air restaurant and bar on the beach.

I enrolled in a karate dojo the first day in Cancun and worked hard to progress through the many layers of levels and belts, still remaining in my quest to receive a black belt. But I specialized in the defensive aspect of the school more than other specialties. Art said to be good or do not waste the time or money, so I was going to be good.

In the James disguise, I went fishing a dozen times. I caught fish every time out on the ocean, but nothing spectacular. I did get a decent thirty-pound tarpon. I traveled to Belize, but did not stay long enough to learn my way—another time. I enjoyed the sun and the sand, but I was restless. I was not living up to my promise to Amy. I was too alone here.

CHAPTER 94

The *Miami Herald* reported Mr. Diaz's attorneys arranged to have him deported and allowed to return to Jamaica. His court date would happen within the next ten days. I needed to fly to Ft. Lauderdale tomorrow and speed up my plan. I had a rough idea, but would need to hurry, setting everything safely in motion. I was nervous and excited. Casa Grande would have to wait. I had an 'adventure' to complete.

Dressed in my James disguise, I landed in Ft. Lauderdale and changed to Spencer. I rented a small pickup. Spencer would be the shooter. The office lease I arranged while in Cancun was ready. I could meet the leasing agent in the lobby, take care of the paperwork, receive the keys and start to make it my own.

That done, I stopped at two thrift stores and selected the furniture I would use. I took my treasures to the building. While I was hauling them into the lobby, two young call center workers offered to help. I would be ready in two days and hoped the court date would not happen before I was ready.

The St. Petersburg Adventure was going to be higher stress than all the rest. When I canvased the city during my first visit, the office building I had chosen covered two corner lots and was eighteen stories high. I rented an office on the twelfth floor facing the courthouse steps. A law firm occupied the first floor, and listed eight partners. A call center used the entire fourth floor, and a non-profit business most of floor eight. Most other floors were home to a multitude of offices.

I paid my two young volunteers from the call center to carry my small collection of office furniture up to my location. They took my one-hundred dollars without asking any questions. The thrift store furnishings will be left on site when Spencer's job was done. I would be prepared to camp there, using a blow-up mattress and a small refrigerator. Traffic in the building was almost nonexistent on weekends, which allowed me to get my shooting equipment on site the second day. My target's hearing was scheduled for Monday morning at 10 a.m. at the courthouse.

I needed to plan my escape. The entry lobby to the building consisted of a two-story atrium, with a balcony on three sides and full two-story glass on the street side. The left balcony led to a long staircase, with the last three steps turning toward the main entry. Fake leather chairs and fake potted plants adorned the edges, of the dark maroon carpet.

Two elevators, next to each other, faced the front entry. They were old and slow. I tested and timed both, while my helpers were busy hauling my office items. The call center employees used the stairs often, but should be working during the shot. I rode the elevator down to the second floor to study my options, then used the stairs to the lobby. That would allow me to walk to my rental truck safely, because I expected lots of foot traffic to this building Monday morning. I felt extra tension, but I did not know why. If necessary, I could retreat to my office and discreetly watch the street. I was prepared to stay a second night only if unsure about making a safe escape.

When I moved into the office, a cleaning service I hired removed all evidence of the previous renter. Neat and clean, I only had to wipe down anything I touched. No leads for the authorities. Two long narrow throw rugs would cover the floor from the door to the desk and the window. The desk would be the location for the bipod and rifle. The rugs would be given to the homeless camp.

That same Sunday I stowed my rifle and bipod with the carrying case in the coat closet. I installed a deadbolt keypad lock on my hallway door. The latex gloves left no fingerprints—my gift to the landlord.

A Ft. Lauderdale pawn shop supplied the tools, a local hardware store, the door lock and silicone spray for the window lock, and a beauty supply shop for the latex gloves and two scented candles. All paid with cash, and purchased more than twenty miles from my building by Spencer. There would be no paper trail.

During my reconnaissance, I noticed some street people near a seedy city park along my planned escape route. They would get the duffle with the extra food, the air mattress, the rugs and the tools. Most items would be carried to the truck early the next morning before the shot. Only the untouched furniture would remain in the office. Time to walk to the courthouse, look back at my window with the small piece of white paper in the corner, and determine the bullet's path of travel. I sat on a nearby bench and compared the distance to my office calculation. Great, both at 776 yards.

The *Tampa Bay Times* headlined the settlement for Aduke Diaz. The unofficial comments heard on the street, believed he would be back smuggling drugs as soon as his plane touched down in his homeland. He would be deported to Jamacia, after a hearing before a judge at 10 a.m., Wednesday morning. A crowd of protesters was expected.

As Spencer, I went out to eat near 1 p.m. on Tuesday, walked around until nearly 5:30 when most of the employees in my building would be gone, then returned to my office.

Aduke would be vulnerable for the first ten steps after getting out of the police car. I was concerned about the crowd and hoped they would be kept out of the way. I wanted the crowd to make Aduke stop.

I settled in for the night. A Subway sandwich served with unsweetened ice-tea, was satisfactory. I read a crime novel until 10 p.m., noting how the author described his characters. Maybe I would try to write a book.

The numbers were done and rechecked twice. For a 776-yard shot, with the humidity and downward trajectory accounted for, I expected the bullet to pass through, fragment on the steps, and be worthless as evidence. I hoped the crowd would be out of harm's way. The last thing to do is to open the window.

I awoke to a beautiful sunny day. I checked my numbers one more time. The Browning 308 with elite tactile optics was ready, the suppressor clad muzzle three inches from the window glass, bipod resting on the desk. The duffle and all the items, except the rugs, for the homeless drop were in the car. Waiting until ten a.m. was going to be torture.

I was ready at eight a.m., with everything packed and, in the car, the room sterile. The police convoy arrived at 9:45. Aduke stepped out after three blue-clad police personnel.

I opened the window, readied myself behind the rifle, and waited for my opportunity. Aduke was shackled and moved slowly. The crowd was small yet very vocal, but I would have to rely on most of the sound of the shot staying in the room. When Aduke reached the third step, I pulled the trigger. Aduke collapsed like a popped balloon to the steps and didn't move.

"Dead Jamaican. Number five Curt." I said aloud as I quickly closed the window. I watched the police escort assume crouched defensive positions, but they did not look toward the window. The crowd ran.

I broke down the gun, placed the pieces carefully in the special backpack, picked up the duffel, and the rugs, exited and locked the door, then slowly walked to the elevator.

While waiting for the slow elevator, I began to pace nervously. Stepping out of the elevator on the second floor, I walked to the railing and started for the stairs. Two policemen stood by the main entrance. They seemed to be just loitering. I was scared, wondering why they chose to be by my building. Afraid of being caught, I almost retreated to the office to regroup.

While I decided what to do, one of the police officers keyed his shoulder mike, listened, then he and his partner sprinted to their car, flipped on the lights, and sped away toward the courthouse. My heart was pounding, I watched them leave from the shadows of a large fake potted plant.

"Whew," I said aloud as I hurried to the stairs. "Slow down, Del," I chastised myself. Using a purposeful stride, I reached my truck and drove off in the opposite direction from the squad car. Dropping off the goods with the homeless group I proceeded to a convenience store I had visited on a previous stop. I went into the store, served myself a cup of dark roast coffee, selected a fresh Danish, and looked at the TV.

A reporter on the shooting scene offered, "Aduke Diaz, allegedly the number one smuggler of drugs into Florida, was shot and killed on the courthouse steps at nine forty-seven this morning. Officer Davis, can you elaborate for the viewer?

"Samantha, we are not sure of anything yet, but we will follow all leads and tell the public what we learn."

I asked the clerk about the news bulletin.

"Some Jamaican bad guy got shot and killed. They say he was a drug dude. Coffee and Danish are free today. You have a nice day."

"You are a good man. Thank you."

As Spencer, I sat in first class on the flight to Phoenix, from Fort Lauderdale. I changed to Del in an airport restroom. Flying back to Phoenix followed by a fast turn around and then back to Ft. Lauderdale would help cover some of my actions in St. Petersburg. I worried about the small hang-up, and why the police officers were by the office building's front door. I doubted I would ever learn why they were there.

I would read the local news to see if it was part of a plan, but could not rule out coincidence. I needed to plan my future escapes more carefully and always have a workable backup option.

CHAPTER 95

utch flew to Fort Lauderdale. I wanted him to experience ocean fishing. We would stay at some cabins near the ocean. Our plan was for him to stop at Pelican Pier, see Dillon about fishing. He had some openings. Dillon and Dutch set things up. Del had a ticket to fly from Phoenix back to Ft Lauderdale. I arrived three hours after Dutch. I needed to be able to prove my presence was timely.

I placed a call to Dutch as soon as I had my items from baggage claim. I needed to de-stress after the close call yesterday.

"When are you coming to fish?" He asked.

"Today, late. I will rent an SUV and see you at about ten. See what you can set up for fishing."

"Already set up, Del. Dillon is taking us fishing Wednesday, Thursday, and Friday. I Must take care of my friends. I have an interview tomorrow at a trade school for an experienced metal worker. Some kind of assistant position. When I told them about my business in Great Falls, they asked me to come and talk to them."

"Super but you still have your business in Great Falls," I countered.

"The position is for the fall semester. I have been thinking of selling out for a long time. I am ready to call it quits. See you in a few."

I went to my rented locker and retrieved some fishing gear. I needed to keep the locker a secret from Dutch. He must remain immune from my 'adventures'. He would be tied up all day at the job interview. I was on my own tomorrow.

I called the Florida Fish and Wildlife Office to get a recommendation to ride an airboat and fish off the beaten path for big largemouth bass. Buggies and Bogs was my choice from the three selections.

The owner, Bill Bayes, looked the part. Bib overalls and a faded flannel shirt framed a large-bodied man with long unruly red-hair. He greeted me warmly.

"What's your pleasure, man?"

"What are my options?"

"All day, seven to seven is $125, half day is $75.

"I would like the full day and hope to get remote enough to catch a big largemouth bass. If it is legal, I would like to drive the airboat. What days do you have open?"

"Me and a buddy were going after some big snakes tomorrow, but we can go anytime. Be here at six-forty-five, and we'll go tomorrow. You'll need a hat with a chin strap and neck flap. A lightweight full-body silk-like cover will keep you from a bad sunburn and mosquito bites. Bring your sunscreen and repellant. We could get a little wet, so you may need to reapply the stuff. Bring your lunch and water. We'll have some fun."

"See you tomorrow."

I drove back to our cabin, stopping at a Safeway to get my lunch for tomorrow and other necessities for the week. I already owned the items he told me to bring. I stuffed my items in a small backpack, sorted a dozen bass lures, selected a rod, and loaded all in the SUV. Dutch could see about the job, and I would drive a swamp buggy and fish for big bass. Just what I needed to relieve the stress.

Bill let me drive his swamp machine as soon as we were out of sight of anyone else. I was like a kid with a new toy. We fished many likely places, but a six-pound largemouth was as big of a monster as I could attract. I wished all day for Amy to be with me. She would not enjoy this kind of activity. She never hiked or fished. I talk to her every-day. I sing songs to her like I used to. Sometimes I believe I can feel her hand in mine. I sense I am slow to move on. I must fix that. A part of martial arts is mental preparedness. I need to start applying that mental toughness in my regular life.

The Seattle serial killer was next on my list of possible targets. I started to plan for it, in my mind. That mind was overflowing. Can I or should I continue shooting bad guys? I know I am risking my friendship with Cliff. Is the shooting risk worth the potential loss of that friendship? Is Cliff offering the FBI informant possibility to keep tabs on me? The unanswered questions were getting to me, I could feel it. I lay awake some nights going over the details of past adventures, and the details of each new possible one. Others may soon start to notice changes in my demeanor. The only thing I knew for sure was, I must revisit these thoughts. I might have been caught if those police officers had stayed by the door and questioned me. Jail is terrifying, I had best get better or back off.

CHAPTER 96

After fishing with Dutch, I changed back to James and returned to Cancun. I lasted ten more days there, then decided to return to Casa Grande early. I would receive at least a partial refund. When I told the manager of the condo-complex I was leaving early, she said she would call to find a replacement. Two days later, I found a note under my door informing me early departure was approved, and I would receive a full refund of days not used.

I called Molly, Cliff, and Dutch. All three calls reaffirmed my feelings. No more long stays in Cancun. I would find a different place for my hide-away money.

I think Amy is glad I am back.

CHAPTER 97

I felt I should call Wendell, Cliff's extra special friend, and arrange to discuss whatever he had in mind, as soon as I arrived in Casa Grande on March Fifteenth.

"Morning, Del. Nice that you are back. May I treat you to a round of golf at Hillcrest on the sixteenth? I hear you enjoy the game."

"I cannot turn that offer down. Of course, I would love to play. How did you know I was gone?"

"Cliff told me. I have been in Scottsdale since the first of the month and thought we could meet earlier. Since I did not have your number, I called Cliff. He said you were out of the country and planned to be back, so we could meet at the regular time I proposed to you. The tee time will be at 10 a.m. See you there."

I noticed Wendell does not take shortcuts with his words, and I responded without shortcuts.

I arrived at Hillcrest at nine, hoping to use the driving range and warm up and spend some time on the putting green. I left my clubs at the Drop Zone, parked my car under a shade tree, and went into the pro shop.

"Morning, sir. What is your tee time?"

"Ten," I started to say more, but was immediately interrupted.

"Mr. Sanderson, we are very pleased you could join us today. Mr. Norton is at the range. Sean will take you and your clubs to join him there."

Sean was very polite and stopped behind an all-black new Club Car golf cart. He took my clubs to a station next to Wendell.

"Good morning, Del," he said, extending his hand. "It is my pleasure to know you."

"Good morning, Wendell. It is my pleasure as well."

"Two other good friends will join us today. We have a friendly wager based on handicap. You are welcome to join."

I must have hesitated just a bit too long.

"If you lose in every way, you will donate fifty dollars."

Wendell would measure a little under six feet and might weigh one hundred eighty pounds. He did not impress me as special operations person. Instead, a Wall Street exec came to mind. His face was as average as average could be. Dark brown hair, dark brown eye brows and eyes, and a dark complexion, defined a serious face. His mouth was not quite a thin line. He, like Art, worked to present a certain public image. Both could change their look easily, so even close friends would not recognize them.

Sean carried both bags back to the cart, secured them, then asked. "Do you need anything else, Mr. Norton?"

"You have done well as always, Sean. Thank you. Hop on, and we will give you a ride to the first tee."

After dropping Sean, Wendell continued, "Del, I have been a member here for over thirty-five years. They take good care of me, and I like that. The two gentlemen we play with will not learn your purpose with me. They do not know Cliff, or my relationship with him."

We arrived at the first tee and joined a cart with two polished and sophisticated-looking gentlemen.

"Del, meet Jerry Whistler and Dom Silverton. Both are long-term members here. They will try to take all your money."

I shook each gentleman's hand, and after all the pleasantries, Joel smiled at everyone.

"Don't let him kid you," offered Dom. "He has a low handicap and won't want us duffers getting his money. Oops, Del, I should have asked if you're a scratch golfer before I opened my mouth."

"I can usually break one hundred. My current handicap is seventeen. I have been away from the game for a while."

We started at exactly ten. No one had started in the thirty minutes before us, and we never saw anyone behind us. Yes, they take good care of Wendell.

Jerry explained the money game. They let me tee off first. A little too much draw, but useable.

Wendell was the better player, but the three of us were not making it easy for him to take our money. Dom would end up losing seven dollars, myself four and Wendell one. Jerry would get to buy the first refreshment after we finished. We talked golf and listened to Dom's jokes. Wendell had the only birdie by the time we reached hole ten.

After teeing off, we returned to the cart and Wendell started what he had often referred to as a discussion. "Art and Rick, whom you know, were part of my special ops team. Both were elite members. Rick was as good as it gets and saved Art's life once. We, three and one other person, are interwoven completely."

We parked next to the green. Wendell made his birdie putt. The three of us had our pars.

"That birdie putt saved me a lot of money," said Wendell "You guys are tough today."

I did not tell him I had seen Rick in action. Our secret forever.

"Rick made an arrangement that got him his range free and clear. He trains special ops from an evaluation perspective. Lots of young men and women go through his process. You shoot there. You may have seen them."

He hit his drive down the middle on hole eleven after watching mine go into the left rough, then continued. I noticed his left little finger was not straight, and the second knuckle above the fingernail had a scar.

"Cliff and I became friends early in his FBI career. My special ops team, Cliff, and two other FBI agents worked together on a domestic terrorist threat. That was the first either of us knew of each other. Cliff was undercover and had an agent within the terrorist cell. When things got dicey, Cliff felt he needed to come to the aid of his agent."

Walking to the green, he said. "Hope you make your bird. No pressure."

When it went in, I looked at him, smiled, and shrugged. "Lady Luck shows up once in a while."

Jerry added, "Saved you some money. Our cart needs a bird or two."

Back in the cart, Wendell continued. "The details are not important. After the operation concluded, we met with our wives for dinner in Washington, DC. We were at the restaurant for over five hours. We were based out of Arlington, Virginia, for about three years before he relocated to Salt Lake City. The following year my family moved to Scottsdale to be closer to my work. I was shot during one of our operations against a militia in Southeastern Utah. I was in a Salt Lake City hospital for some time. Cliff was a constant visitor. During those forty days, we developed our lifetime bond. Blood Brothers. Each of us has another such person, but we have chosen not to share those names. You and Cliff are my only two I will watch out for. My other person has his own similar arrangements. You call Cliff first if you can. If not, call me. We will set all the procedures over dinner at my club."

Dropping the serious tone, he smiled a little. "Let us go take some of Dom and Jerry's money."

After Jerry paid for our nineteenth-hole beverages, we said our goodbyes, and Dom and Jerry left. Wendell gave me the address of his club and the best route to use. He was in the lobby waiting. Members only.

His procedures were so simple: one burner with one number to call. His people would track the phone and send the rescue team.

"My private company is completely organized, staffed, and equipped with the best of everything." He paused, nodded when asked if he wished to be billed, and walked me to the door.

"I noticed a person sitting by himself in the club. I have business with him, so I will bid you goodnight." Wendell paused then continued. "Del, we shared a good day. You are exactly as Cliff said you would be. We will become friends. You now know as much about me as I know about you. That is enough for me."

"Thank you, Wendell, for the golf, and the dinner. We will do something like this again someday soon. I agree we will become friends, and I can see that you and Cliff are on the same page."

We shook hands—a firm handshake, and he turned and entered the club. The man at the door watched intently. Not just any doorman, I was sure.

Driving back to Casa Grande, I realized the only other thing I learned— he was alone like Cliff and me. He said I knew him, but I felt I had not learned anything about him at all.

That was his intent. I would get him to my nine-hole course and say that to him. I did not know him well enough yet. I was pretty sure that either Rick or Art was his other go to person.

Am I getting too deep in this group of special ops? I think I will watch and make sure I take care of myself. Cliff had alluded to some involvement in Great Falls. I decided to stay on the fringes where I belonged. True, the shooter was back, but he needed to be free to stay in his own world.

Doing what a person wishes can be tough sometimes.

I have a possible 'adventure' in Seattle. There is a cop killer in California that needs my attention.

I must go to Saco, Montana and let Jody teach me how to ride a horse. I needed to buy Dutch's airplane. I wanted to talk to J.C. about a drug rehab center in Marana.

Bill Davis's group was often deep in my thoughts. Peter Sullivan needs to finish school, and I can help him. And there is my new role with the FBI.

I must complete my exploration to see if I can get from my Lincoln cabin to the Danaher River in the 'Bob.'

I need to fish Fort Peck Reservoir. I still have so many items on my bucket list to do.

And, I get to be a small-time player with the FBI, so I can watch what they are doing about the shooter.

I need to stay lucky. I have so much to do.

I have decided I like the feeling when I shoot and hit a target almost a mile away. It is the same kind of rush I felt flying over a thousand miles an hour. You feel in a different place. Exciting is an understatement. My path, for now, is chosen.

DYNAMIC OPTICS
A DEL SANDERSON NOVEL

Today's shot, if I risk it, will be 836 yards. The wind factor effect is great. The weather report for tomorrow is only marginally better. I feel my numbers are precise, but I do not want to miss the target. This woman is a killer.

I ride the bus a lot.

My bus today makes six stops before I reach my destination of the main library.

I was about ten minutes early, so I picked up any litter in my area, as I often do. I noticed a folded paper tucked next to one of the spiraea. I retrieved it and boarded my bus.

I took my usual seat three behind the driver, opened the paper, and unclipped a hundred-dollar bill and read the note.

It was addressed to a person named Michelle. I guessed it was a coded message.

Yours: Numbers ok (47-94)	*Slice the watermelon*	*88*	
Spin the red bottle, (13-26)	*Meet Jordan*	*15*	*225*

"Gibberish," I mumbled, then stuffed the note and money into my shirt pocket. I put the note out of my mind deciding to study it further after returning to my Bozeman home.

Solving this cryptic message would take Del Sanderson on a dangerous and risky journey throughout much of Montana.

Coupled with four special 'adventures' that place him in harm's way. He becomes deeply involved in the actions of an FBI office. He must alter his life more than he intends.

Del Sanderson

Don Jaspers lives in Idaho. He is a certified commercial pilot, experienced woodsman, and veteran of numerous trips into wilderness areas. His flying experiences include jet, propeller, and rotary planes. He is a certified financial planner, but lists his role as a math teacher as his most rewarding endeavor. Don lives in Twin Lakes Village with his wife Patsy. He gets to golf with her any time they wish to play.

Printed in the USA
CPSIA information can be obtained
at www.ICGtesting.com
JSHW011540030824
67392JS00004B/15